I dedicate *Tennison* to the wonderful
Dame Helen Mirren, who gave the character
DCI Jane Tennison in *Prime Suspect*
worldwide recognition.

Acknowledgements

I am very fortunate to have Suzanne Baboneau and Ian Chapman of Simon & Schuster, who are always encouraging and a delight to work with, as my publishers. I am very grateful for the tremendous support from all the team there. They have so much talent and enthusiasm, and in particular I'd like to thank Matthew Johnson, who designed the jacket and endpapers. He is very creative and I was thrilled when I received the first copy as the jacket was exactly as I saw it in my mind. Working hard behind the scenes are Emma Capron and Jane Pizzey and I give huge thanks to them both. Also to Louise Davies for her editorial advice and guidance, and Toby Slade-Baker at Studio 32 for his help with the music.

Music has played a big part in the writing of *Tennison*, not only transporting me back to the 1970s, but being able to include one of my favourite songs, 'Nights in White Satin', written by Justin Hayward. Thank you, Justin, for your generosity in allowing me to use the lyrics.

I have also been fortunate to have a great team around me at my new production company, La Plante Global. Running the company is Nigel Stoneman, and I have found working alongside him a joyful and productive experience. My Personal Assistant, Tory Macdonald, has taken so much stress out of my life; her organisational skills are quite extraordinary.

Two other people have been a constant support in writing *Tennison*. I have been fortunate to work alongside Callum Sutherland (Cass) for many years on numerous television series and novels. His wife Anne also helped greatly with the research of this book. Both were stationed in the East End during the '70s, Callum at Hackney itself, so their input has been invaluable. My thanks, too, go to the Metropolitan Women Police Association and I am grateful for the assistance of Beverley Edwards, Eileen Turnbull, Siobhan Elam, Gina Negus, Janice Gammon, Wendy Rowe, Monica Tett, Valerie Lowe and Kathi Broad. Also, my thanks go to Dr Ann Priston and Brian Rankin of the Chartered Society of Forensic Sciences for their advice.

I'd like to thank Stephen Ross and Dan Ross at Ross Bennett Smith for their continuing support. Robin Hilton and James Sully at Sheridans for their outstanding legal and professional advice. Camilla Campbell and Robert Wulff-Cochrane who have proved to be an exciting and enjoyable partnership for La Plante Global. Kevin Lygo for his enthusiasm and belief in *Tennison*. Thanks also to Peter Fincham, Steve November and Victoria Fea at ITV for all their encouragement and support.

TENNISON

CHAPTER ONE

It was Monday afternoon and Jane was sitting in her usual seat at the rear of the top deck of the 253 bus, as it travelled up Mare Street in Hackney. Popping the single plastic earphone into her ear, she turned on her prized Zephyr pocket radio, which she had treated herself to after her first month's wages in the training college. She tuned into Radio Caroline on Medium Wave, and although she knew it was a pirate radio station, it didn't bother her as she was a huge fan of the rock music they played. The DJ, Spangles Muldoon, announced that the next song was the Janis Joplin hit 'Piece Of My Heart'. Jane was a big Joplin fan, and often reminisced about how lucky she had been to see her in concert at the Royal Albert Hall for her eighteenth birthday. Although she had been sitting in the gods it had been an electrifying and unforgettable experience, watching Joplin strutting and dancing, all the time holding the audience spellbound through the power and emotion of her amazingly soulful voice. As the song began Jane turned up the volume.

And each time I tell myself that I, well I think I've
*   had enough,*
But I'm gonna, gonna show you, baby, that a
*   woman can be tough.*

1

I want you to come on, come on, come on,
  come on and take it,
Take it!
Take another little piece of my heart now, baby!
Oh, oh, break it!
Break another little bit of my heart now, darling,
  yeah, yeah, yeah yeah.
Oh, oh, have a
Have another little piece of my heart now, baby ...
You know you got it, if it makes you feel good ...

Jane was singing along to herself when the bus suddenly jerked to a halt, causing her to lurch forward and nearly drop her radio. She peered from the window and sighed – it was still raining. The light drizzle when she got on the bus had now turned to a dark-skied downpour. She wished she'd worn her uniform cape, but she always kept it at the station in her locker. When Jane had first arrived at Hackney Police Station as a probationer her reporting sergeant had advised her not to stand out on public transport wearing 'half-blues'. You didn't want to be recognized as a copper, he'd said, and have an egg chucked at you, or be forced by a bus conductor to step into a trivial situation that might escalate because you were 'Old Bill'. Instead she wore a buttoned-up black trench coat to hide her police uniform, and was carrying her police hat in a plastic carrier bag. Jane looked at her watch and saw that it was twenty to two. She was due on parade at two o'clock for a late shift until 10 p.m. She glanced at the mirror by the stairs and saw an elderly man being helped on board by the conductor. She had three more stops before she had to get off at the station in Lower Clapton Road.

It often amused her to think of the time years ago when she had been driven to Hackney by her father, who had some business to attend to. He had gestured to the run-down housing estates and shaken his head in disgust, saying it was a part of London he detested. Jane, aged fourteen, couldn't help but agree with him. Compared to Maida Vale, where they lived, it looked like a dump and seemed a very grey and unfriendly part of London. She recalled being horrified reading newspaper articles about the trial of the notorious East End brothers, Ronnie and Reggie Kray, and how they had lured Jack 'the Hat' McVitie to a party in Hackney where Reggie stabbed him repeatedly in the neck and body with a carving knife.

Jane smiled to herself at the irony. Little could she have imagined back then that her first posting as a probationary WPC, aged twenty-two, after sixteen weeks at the Metropolitan Police Force's training college in Hendon, would be in the very area she considered a dump!

She suddenly sprang up, realizing that in her day-dreaming she had missed her stop. Clattering down the stairs, she shouted to the conductor.

'I've gone too far – I need to get off.'

'Not a lot I can do about it, love – you should pay more attention. I'm not allowed to ring the bell in between stops, so you'll have to—'

Jane couldn't wait and as soon as the bus slowed down at the traffic lights she swung her job-issue black-leather handbag over her shoulder and jumped off. The grinning conductor wagged his finger disapprovingly. Jane had no option but to run the quarter of a mile back down the road to the station; she knew she would be drenched by the time she got there. Pulling up the collar of her trench coat she put her head down and set off. Seconds later, she bumped straight into a woman, which sent her reeling backwards and knocking the woman's umbrella into the road. Her brown paper carrier bag of groceries split open, spilling tins of soup, apples, bananas, potatoes and a loaf of bread onto the wet pavement.

'Oh no! I am so sorry,' Jane said.

The woman shook her head as she looked down at her groceries and the ruined carrier bag.

'Oh my God, you bleedin' well ran into me – now what am I gonna do?' she exclaimed in a strong Cockney accent.

Apologizing profusely, and feeling somewhat embarrassed, Jane surreptitiously took her police hat out of the plastic bag and stuffed it in her handbag. She bent down and started picking up the groceries, placing them inside the empty bag.

'I'll get me brolly.' The woman stepped off the pavement without looking.

'Mind the traffic!' Jane called out anxiously and stood up.

She gently grabbed the woman by the arm before instinctively holding her hand up to stop the traffic and retrieving the umbrella herself.

'Is it still working?' the woman demanded.

'There's no damage,' Jane said, opening and closing the umbrella to check the spokes. 'Here, you use it so you don't get soaked.'

It took a while for Jane to pick up the potatoes as they, along with the now bruised apples, had rolled into the gutter. Her hands were soon cold and muddy, and she had to wipe her face which was wet from the torrential rain.

Holding up her umbrella the woman gestured impatiently. 'Just put the cans of soup in, never mind the vegetables … Oh, don't tell me, the bread's split open as well.'

'I'm really very sorry. I'll pay for everything that's damaged.'

Far from being disgruntled, the woman gave a wan smile.

'No need. Besides, all this new decimal stuff confuses me. It was much easier when everything was in shillin's.'

'Are you sure? I don't want to see you go short.'

'Don't look so worried, luv. I do office cleaning and the bread was only to make a sandwich for work.'

Eager to be on her way, Jane stepped a few paces back and, clutching her now wet and bulging handbag, wondered what state her police hat would be in.

'I have to go – I am so sorry.'

The woman suddenly started gasping and heaving for breath.

'Are you all right?' Jane asked with concern.

'No, gimme a minute … it's … me asthma.'

'Do you live nearby?'

'Ashburn House.'

'That's off Homerton Road on the Pembridge Estate, isn't it?'

The woman nodded and took more deep breaths. 'It's the shock … you runnin' into me.'

'Long way to walk, you sure you'll be all right?'

'Let me … get me … breath back first.'

'I'll help you home.'

The Pembridge was a notorious council estate built in the 1930s. Jane had been to it a few times on incident calls. It consisted of eight five-storey blocks of grimy brick and contained a thousand flats. The residents were of different ethnic backgrounds, but predominantly white. Families of six lived in two-bedroom flats. Drug dealing, fights, vandalism and graffiti were part of daily life, and the stairwells served as urinals for drunks.

Jane carried the groceries over one arm as the woman leaned heavily on the other, constantly stopping to catch her breath. By the time they had walked up to the third floor of Ashburn House and along the landing leading to Flat 44, the woman was breathing so heavily that Jane thought she was going to faint.

On entering the flat she helped the woman out of her mac and gave it a couple of swishes outside to get rid of some of the water before hanging it over the folded wheelchair that was leaning against the wall in the hallway. Jane asked where the kitchen was. The woman pointed to the room on the right.

'You go and sit down and rest and I'll pop these groceries in the kitchen for you,' Jane told her with a warm smile.

'Would you be a luv and make me a cuppa tea with milk and three sugars?'

'No problem,' Jane said, although she was desperate to get a move on as she was already late for work. She hooked her handbag over the wheelchair.

Entering the kitchen Jane was surprised by the amount of expensive modern equipment. In one corner there was a Hotpoint front-load washing machine with a matching tumbler-drier on top of it. Next to that stood a dishwasher and an upright fridge with a separate freezer compartment. The room itself was spotlessly clean with a Formica-topped table and four matching chairs to one side.

Having filled the kettle Jane put it on the gas cooker which, like the other appliances, looked fairly new. She got the teapot, sugar, cup and saucer from the cupboards, then took the milk from the fridge and placed everything on the kitchen table. She noticed that there was a council rent book in the name of Mrs Irene Bentley on the table. Under

it there was a Green Shield Stamps Gift Collection catalogue, along with some other magazines. Jane picked up
the gift catalogue and flicking through it saw that it was
filled with the latest kitchen appliances, televisions, entertainment systems, sports goods and clothes. It struck Jane
that it would take more than a few Green Shield Stamps
books to purchase any of the electrical goods on offer.

The sudden whistling of the kettle made her jump.
Replacing the catalogue she noticed that there was a
brochure for Wolf power tools, and another for Hilti
power tools, which made her suspect that the woman's
family were in the building trade.

'Oh ta, luv, just what I need after me ordeal … a nice
cup of Rosie.' The woman was lying down on the large
sofa and she sat up as Jane handed her the tea.

'You're looking a lot better, Irene.'

The woman laughed and a drop of tea dribbled from
her mouth. 'Cor blimey, I haven't been called that in years.
Been known as Renee ever since I was a nipper.'

'Sorry, I saw your rent book and just assumed.'

'Did you now? Bit nosy of yer, and never assume, luv,
always ask.' She slurped at her tea.

The lounge was modern and comfortably furnished.
The thick fitted carpet was a maroon colour with swirling
yellow rings, and there was a wing chair that matched the
sofa. Against the wall on one side of the room there was a
large teak storage cabinet, and a matching dining table
and four chairs.

'You have a very nice flat.'

'Me boys look after me.'

Jane heard the front door being opened, then slammed
shut, followed by a few seconds' silence and then the
sound of heavy footsteps.

'Ma? Eh, Ma? Where you at?' a man's voice bellowed.

Jane turned and saw a tough-looking dark-haired man in his thirties swaggering towards the living room with his hands deep in the pockets of his black donkey jacket. He stopped abruptly just inside the door and looked at Jane. She could see from the way he filled the doorframe that he was big and muscular. His nose resembled a boxer's and he had a square-set, unshaven jaw.

'What's going on, Mum?' he asked, looking Jane up and down with disdain. She noticed his eyes were dark and penetrating.

Renee was sipping her tea so Jane took the opportunity to explain her presence.

'I bumped into your mother and she had a bit of a shock, so I helped her home. My name is Jane Tennison.' She put her hand out politely for him to shake.

He didn't reciprocate, but gave her a cold arrogant glare and asked his mother brusquely if she was all right.

'I had one of me asthma attacks, John,' Renee said, a nervous tremble in her voice as if she was afraid of him.

Jane picked up on the uneasy atmosphere and tried to break the tension. 'I made a pot of tea, would you like a cup?'

'Really … moving in now, are you?' he replied, and coming closer gripped Jane by her elbow.

'Go on, get out … get the fuck OUT! Move it, PISS OFF NOW,' he snapped, and virtually frogmarched her out of the room.

Pushing her hard in the small of her back he propelled her onto the communal landing, barely giving her time to grab her bag before he slammed the door behind her. Tempted to ring the doorbell to give him a piece of her mind, Jane then thought better of it. It wasn't so much that he was large and intimidating, but she was already late for work and if things got out of hand she had no means of calling for backup.

John went into the lounge, pulled off his jacket and threw it onto the wing chair. He clenched his fist at his mother.

'What you think you're fuckin' doing, you stupid old cow? I could slap you so hard right now.'

Renee cringed away from him looking terrified. 'I'll put the kettle back on and make a fresh cuppa ... '

He poked his finger at her. 'I'd like to pour the boiling water over your stupid head. Don't you know a bloody rozzer when you see one?'

Renee shook her head in fear.

'Her fuckin' handbag was in the hallway. I had a quick look and there was a police hat in it, you stupid bitch. She was wearing black tights and shiny black shoes – it all sticks out like a sore thumb. What in Christ's name do ya think you were doin'?'

'I'm sorry, son, I—'

'She's bloody snoopin' around, that's what she's doing.'

'I didn't know, I swear before God I didn't know! She almost knocked me off me feet in the street.'

He sighed as he went to the kitchen and got himself a can of beer from the fridge. Taking a large swig, he began to calm down. Maybe it was just his paranoia kicking in, but seeing the police hat had really infuriated him. His hand was shaking as he swigged down the rest of the can, crushed it and threw it into the bin. Feeling more relaxed he made a fresh mug of tea and took it through to his mother.

'Here you go, I've sugared it. I'm sorry I kicked off,

Ma, but I'm upset about your cleaning job and I don't want you doing it no more. Besides, you're getting your state pension now so ya don't need to work anyway.'

'But I like working and I got friends there—'

'No buts, Ma, just do as I say. You stay put and no more visitors. You got everything you need and more right here.'

She cupped the mug in her hands and sipped. 'I get lonely, John, and with you not working why can't I carry on doing what I've done for most of your life?'

'Listen to me. I'm not going to be staying here for much longer, and when I leave you can do what you like, but for now you do as I tell you. And if you see that bitch rozzer around here again, you tell me.'

By the time Jane arrived at the station she was an hour late. Her hair was bedraggled and dripping wet, the uniform under her coat was damp and her shoes were soaked through as well. She knew she would have to report to the duty sergeant, but wanted to smarten herself up a bit before the inevitable dressing down for being late and missing parade.

She stood outside the front of the imposing four-storey redbrick-and-white-stone building and realized that she'd have to pass the front counter and duty sergeant's desk if she went in via the main entrance. She decided to go through the rear gates, so she could sneak down the stairs to the ladies' locker room to tidy herself up. To her relief there was no one in the yard as she scuttled across it: the Vauxhall Viva panda cars must have all been out on patrol.

'Tennison! Stop right there!' a voice bellowed from the canteen window on the third floor.

Recognizing the voice of Sergeant Bill Harris, Jane froze on the spot.

'What bloody time do you call this?'

Jane looked up slowly. 'I'm really sorry, Sergeant, but I—'

'No excuses. You've got two minutes to be in front of my desk in full uniform for inspection.'

Jane wished she had access to a hairdryer, but she didn't have time to do anything with her hair. She tied it in a ponytail with a thin black band and pushed the sides up under her hat before running upstairs to the front office to present herself. Sergeant Harris, he of 'thirty years' experience', as he constantly liked to remind everyone, was a hardened old-school copper who thought the recent amalgamation of the women's police force with the men's was 'an outrageous bloody disgrace!'

Jane was certain that he would, as usual, find some tedious job for her. More often than not she found herself in the communications room processing calls and dispatching the patrol officers to incidents over the radio. Even when she got to go on patrol, if anything of interest came up she was bypassed, or worse ignored, thanks to Sergeant Harris's hold and influence over the junior male constables below his rank.

As she stood to attention in the front office Harris walked around her shaking his head in disapproval.

'Have you been using your hat as a cushion? You look like a drowned rat, you've got a filthy face, and what's that all over your hands?'

'Mud, Sergeant, from picking up potatoes.'

He leaned forward, his face close to hers. 'Don't be funny with me, Tennison.'

'I was helping an elderly lady and—'

'I don't want to hear it. I've got officers helping the CID with a dead body, one who's gone sick and I've had to post someone else to your beat. And to top it all, I'm havin' to answer the duty desk phone and deal with the public at the front counter myself. I should be directing, not doing, Tennison.'

'Sorry, Sergeant. Can I still go on patrol?'

'No, you missed your chance by being late. I expect better, Tennison, and this incident won't go unnoticed on your next probationer's report. Now, get your backside into the comms room and help Morgan out. All the incoming message forms from the weekend and this morning need to be filed away.'

Jane scurried into the small stuffy communications room where WPC Kathleen Morgan was on the phone speaking to a member of the public, recording the details on an incident message pad. She smiled, gave a wave and mouthed 'Hello' to Jane, who waved back.

Kathleen, or Kath as she was commonly known, was a curvaceous brunette with hazel eyes and thick, unruly, curly hair. She had a habit of wearing too much make-up, contrary to police regulations that stated it should be 'subtle and discreet', but she didn't care and was more than capable of coping with her male colleagues' flippant or derogatory remarks. She would stand firm, hands on her hips, ready for any of the macho banter:

'You've got too much lipstick on, Morgan.'

'Oh really? Well, kiss it off then – that is if your belly can even let you get that close.'

Kath was twenty-six and had joined the police aged nineteen. She was a London girl from Canning Town and was used to the chauvinistic ways of many of her male counterparts. She took no stick from anyone. She was the only other woman on 'B Relief' with Jane, and had shown her the ropes from day one.

The teleprinter in the corner was clicking away and rolling off messages from Scotland Yard and other stations. Beside two wooden desks, facing each other, was a small telephone switchbox with a radio communications set. On the desk where Kath was sitting was the latest piece of technology, a visual display unit computer, or VDU as it was commonly known. It allowed fast access to centrally held records at Scotland Yard, including information on stolen or suspect vehicles, wanted or missing persons and registered-vehicle owners. The wall adjacent to the desks was covered with collator's cards showing pictures and details of local wanted criminals and those suspected of habitual and recent crimes. Next to these were a number of missing persons appeal leaflets.

'Jane, can you check the teleprinter for any urgent messages while I put this call out to one of the panda cars?' Kathleen asked and Jane nodded.

'Panda Five Two, can you attend the scene of a suspect's disturbed break-in at 22 Wick Lane ... Golf Hotel, over.'

'Five Two received and on way,' the reply came over the loudspeaker.

'I'm sorry I was late, Kath.'

'No problem, darlin' – what kept you?'

Jane started to give a condensed version of the earlier events, causing Kath to laugh out loud when she told her about the apples and potatoes rolling into the road.

'I dunno, Jane, it always happens to you, don't it?'

'I thought she was going to faint, so I ended up taking her home to Ashburn House on—'

Kath raised her eyebrows and interjected. 'The Pembridge Estate, another of Hackney's delightful areas.'

'Actually her flat was surprisingly well furnished and the kitchen had some really new appliances. She must've got the stuff from the Green Shield Stamps catalogue.'

Kath looked bemused. 'What sort of stuff?'

'A front-load washer, tumbler-drier, dishwasher, cooker—'

Kath laughed at Jane's naivety. 'The stamps are a rip-off. It would take years, not to mention spending a fortune, to get the thousands and thousands of stamps needed to buy that lot. More than likely the stuff was nicked off the back of a lorry, or taken from a warehouse break-in and then sold around the estate. You'd be surprised how many villains live on estates like the Pembridge. What was her name?'

'Irene Bentley – although she asked me to call her Renee – and her son was called John. He was an aggressive sod, not even so much as a thank-you for helping his mum. He didn't want me in the flat so frogmarched me out.'

'Villains can smell the Old Bill a mile off. You need to be careful, Jane. Never go on the rough estates without backup.'

'It was a lesson learned, Kath. Anyway, what's this about a dead body? Sergeant Harris mentioned something.'

Kath said that she didn't know too much, but handed Jane a copy of the teleprinter message sent to the Yard.

'Poor thing was—' Kath began before breaking off to answer the phone.

Jane sat down behind the desk and started to read the message. The body was found early morning on the recently built Hackney Marshes Adventure Playground, close to the Kingsmead Estate. The victim was an unknown white girl with blonde hair, believed to be fifteen to eighteen years old, wearing hot pants, a white blouse and blue platform boots.

Kath finished dealing with the phone call. 'You read it? Poor kid, just awful, so young.'

'It doesn't say how she died,' Jane noticed.

'They're waiting for the post-mortem, but I heard it was pretty obvious ... the bastard used the girl's own bra to strangle her to death.'

'How horrible.'

'From the way she was dressed, and the junkie tracks on her arms, they think she was on the game and may have been turning a trick at the playground. They're setting up the crime squad office as the incident room for the murder.'

The door to the comms room opened and Sergeant Harris stuck his head in. 'DCI Bradfield wants to see me in his office about the murder and he'd like a cup of tea, Tennison, milk and two sugars with some digestive biscuits. Same for me as well, and when you've done that take over from me on the duty desk and cover the front counter as well.' He left, banging the door shut behind him.

'Pleasant bugger, isn't he?' Kath said, giving Jane a smile.

'Key to getting on his good side is to keep your head down and "Yes, Sarge, no, Sarge, three bags of grovel, Sarge."'

The canteen was closed so Jane went to the small kitchen annexe instead. As usual it had been left in a mess and she was revolted by the state of it. Above the sink there was a water-splashed, hand-written notice taped to the wall: 'Leave it as you'd expect to find it … TIDY & CLEAN!' She shook her head in disgust. The sink was full of old tea bags, dirty mugs, cutlery, and plates caked with crusted HP and tomato sauce. She put the kettle on the gas cooker, rolled up her sleeves, picked out the used tea bags, tipped out the greasy cold water from the plastic bowl and filled it with hot water and washing up liquid. As she washed the dirty dishes a male officer walked in, dropped three dirty mugs and plates in the sink, said, 'Thanks, love,' and walked out. Jane sighed, finished the washing up, dried the dishes and then stacked them on the open shelves.

Jane carried the two mugs of tea and the biscuits on a tray to the DCI's office and, balancing it on one knee, she tapped the door which immediately swung open, almost causing her to drop the tray. Cigarette smoke billowed from the room and the stench was repulsive.

'About bloody time, I thought you'd gone AWOL again.' Sergeant Harris grabbed the tray from her. 'Take these Polaroid photos of the murder scene back to the incident room next door and give them to Sally the indexer.'

Outside the DCI's office Jane had a quick look at the six small pictures Harris had given her. She hadn't yet been to a murder scene. She had attended a non-suspicious death of an eighty-year-old man with angina. He'd been found dead in his bed from a heart attack, but that was nothing compared with this. The pictures of the young female victim shocked her, particularly the close-up shot of the heroin-needle marks on the girl's arms. Worse was the close-up of the victim's face, with the bra wrapped round her neck. Her bulging eyes were dotted with red spots and her swollen tongue protruded from her mouth. Blood trickled down from where she must have bitten it whilst being strangled.

Jane felt queasy as she walked into the incident room, only to find it empty. She assumed that the detectives must be down at Hackney Marshes or out making enquiries near the scene. The medium-sized room looked cramped with eight old wooden desks and chairs taking up most of the floor space. There were two telephones and a large carousel on top of one of the desks, with a pile of indexing cards next to it. On the wall a map of Hackney Police Division was dotted with different-coloured pins denoting where robberies, burglaries, assaults and other incidents had taken place in the last few months. Next to the map was a large sheet of white paper with a description of the victim, the location, date and time of the discovery of the body, and the name of the lab sergeant dealing with the forensics. A note pinned to the wall stated that the post-mortem would be at Hackney Mortuary.

Worried about leaving the Polaroids on the desk, Jane decided to take them downstairs to the front office and return them to the incident room later when Sally was there.

Sitting down at the duty desk she put the photographs face down. She noticed that one of the red lights on the phone console linked to the comms room was flashing and another was white, which meant Kath Morgan must be using that line.

'Don't stare at it, woman ... answer it.'

Jane jumped and snatched up the phone. She hadn't seen Sergeant Harris approach from the side. 'Hackney Police Station, can I help you? Just one moment, please. I will need to take some details. Can you state your name?'

17

Aware Harris was watching over her shoulder she took a pen from her shirt pocket and drew the message pad towards her, writing down the caller's name. At the same time she checked her watch to note exactly what time the call came in.

Jane listened as Harris breathed heavily beside her. She then placed her hand over the mouthpiece explaining that it was a Mrs Hardy reporting that her purse had been snatched outside a pub.

'She sounds drunk,' Jane said.

'Give it here,' Harris said, grabbing the phone.

He leaned his elbows on the desk. 'Mrs Hardy, this is the duty sergeant. You will need to come to the station so WPC Tennison can take a full crime report. Good day,' he said bluntly, and flicked the call button off. 'There, job done. Let's see if she can be as bothered when she's sober.'

Then Harris saw the crime scene pictures. 'What are these doing here? I told you to take them to the incident room.'

'I'm sorry, Sergeant, but there was no one there and I didn't want to leave—'

'I'll bloody do it myself.'

Jane knew he was using it as an excuse to get away from the duty desk and that he probably wouldn't come back for ages, which in some ways was a blessing.

An hour later it was five o'clock and, as Jane had suspected, Harris still hadn't returned. She wondered if he was in the snooker room or playing a game of gin rummy for money in the canteen. She popped into the comms room to get her handbag and told Kath she'd been in the incident room but hadn't been able to glean much more about the case than they already knew.

'The crime scene pictures were horrible, Kath. How could someone do that to her?'

'You'll get used to it, Jane, you have to in this job. The proper large photographs will be developed by tomorrow and they'll be even more graphic.'

Jane kept the comms-room door open so she could see the front counter in case anyone came in. She pulled out a form from her handbag.

'What have you got there?' Kath asked.

'I decided to sign up for the Dr Harker lecture, the one you told me about,' answered Jane.

Julian Harker was a renowned forensic scientist who would be discussing in detail a complicated murder inquiry he had been involved in. As a probationer Jane was allowed to attend lots of courses and she was keen to take advantage of any opportunities to learn more.

'He's a snazzy guy, quite attractive, which is a plus. He's really clever and you'll learn a lot.'

Kath leaned close to Jane – she wore a distinctive heavy perfume that Jane found rather overpowering – and whispered that it was always good to get one over the other plods.

'You never know who's watching and listening, love. The more you learn the better you'll become at the job. You know what they say … knowledge is brains …'

'I think you mean power, Kath.'

'Whatever, I've been to two of his lectures, and believe me he knows his stuff.'

'I have to give this form to Sergeant Harris first and I doubt he'll recommend me. He hates the fact women are integrated now and can do the same jobs as the men.'

Kath snorted. 'Integrated, my arse! The blokes still get paid more. Anyway, stuff Harris. Take it straight up to

19

Bradfield now, he can only say yes or no. I'll keep one eye on the counter and I'll tell Harris you nipped to the loo if he comes back.'

Jane was nervous of DCI Bradfield. His impatient manner was intimidating and although Kath insisted he had a kinder side, Jane was yet to see it. Looking towards his closed office door she wondered if perhaps her timing, due to the murder investigation, was not great. Suddenly the door swung open and Bradfield walked out. He was well over six foot tall, handsome and raw-boned, with red curly hair, and as usual had a cigarette dangling between his lips. He looked smart in his neatly pressed dark grey suit with shiny black polished brogues.

It was now or never, she thought to herself. 'Excuse me, sir.'

'What?' he snapped impatiently.

'Could I possibly have a word?'

'It'd better be quick because I'm starving and about to get a sandwich from the canteen,' he said, causing a lump of ash to fall from the cigarette still in his mouth.

Jane had a sudden thought. 'I'd be happy to get that if you're busy, sir. In the meantime I wonder if you could read and approve my application to attend Dr Harker's forensic science lecture.'

He clicked his fingers twice for her to hand the form over, which she did. He had just started to read it when one of his detectives, Constable Mike Hudson, came running up the stairs with a look of excitement on his face and his CID notebook in his hand.

'Got a possible, guv! Young girl aged seventeen, a patient at the Homerton Hospital Drug Dependency Unit – she matches the description of our victim. Her details are in here, as well as her boyfriend's.'

Bradfield looked enthused as Hudson handed over his notebook. He had a quick look and handed it back. 'Good work, son. I want every available detective in the incident room for a meeting in ten minutes.'

Bradfield grabbed a pen from the detective's breast pocket and signed Jane's application without reading it any further and passed it to her with a smile.

'Pay attention at the lecture. Harker is the best scientist in the forensic labs.' He stubbed his cigarette out in the overflowing ashtray attached to the wall.

'Don't bother with the sandwich – I've got no time to eat it now.'

'Thank you, sir,' Jane said, as she looked at his signature on the application form with a beaming smile.

CHAPTER TWO

'Right everyone, listen up,' Bradfield said assertively as he strode into the incident room, which was a hive of activity.

'Thanks to DC Hudson we have a possible name and some background details for our victim. Julie Ann Maynard, aged seventeen. Criminal records show one arrest and previous conviction for prostitution earlier this year. She was a heroin addict, as is her boyfriend Eddie Phillips, aged nineteen, both patients at the Homerton Drug Dependency Unit. When was their last attendance, Hudson?'

'Two weeks ago, sir, and neither of them have turned up for their appointments since.'

Bradfield frowned. 'She's seventeen, a junkie, and the hospital didn't bother to report her missing? Did you ask them why, Hudson?'

'The hospital said they attended the drug unit on a voluntary basis and assumed that Julie Ann and Eddie had decided to just up and leave.'

Bradfield lit a cigarette. 'Did they have addresses for them?'

'Yes, sir, the same one for both Eddie and Julie Ann.' Hudson nervously flicked through his notebook.

'Which was?' Bradfield asked impatiently.

'Uh, it was ... 32 Edgar House on the Pembridge, sir.'

'It's important Eddie is traced and arrested for questioning without delay.' Bradfield gestured towards Detective Sergeant Gibbs.

'Spencer, you and two detectives go to Edgar House after the meeting. Kick the door in, search it and nick Eddie Phillips if he's there. If he ain't, get a surveillance unit to keep an eye on the address in case he returns.'

'Yes, guvnor, be a pleasure, and I take it you will be authorizing any overtime we may just happen to incur?'

Bradfield smiled and nodded. 'Even if it means you have to work through the night, Spence. We have to consider Eddie Phillips might have been Julie Ann's pimp and maybe murdered her after an argument over money. He may even be on the run by now, so, Sally, I want Phillips' name and description circulated via the teleprinter to all police stations across London and—'

'Yes, sir,' Sally the indexer said, frantically taking notes as Bradfield continued.

'Circulate Julie Ann Maynard's details as well. I want an address for her parents, or any next of kin, asap, so that a formal identification can be made at the mortuary.' Sally nodded.

'Right, get out there, keep knocking on doors and asking questions on and around the Kingsmead. Hold off on the Pembridge until DS Gibbs searches Edgar House and hopefully brings in the little shit Eddie Phillips.'

DS Spencer Gibbs was a tough and often unruly officer, tall and gaunt with thick, brushed-back hair on top of his head and an almost crew cut to the sides. He had a keen eye for fashion and when off duty liked to wear skinny trousers and winkle-picker shoes, which Kath Morgan loved to tease him about. Gibbs enjoyed being part of a rock band, but his commitment and loyalty to his day job made him a popular member of the team.

Gibbs went to 32 Edgar House accompanied by two young DCs, Ashton and Edwards. They were all wearing heavy raincoats due to the continuing downpour. The young officers were surprised to find the address was a boarded-up squat. Gibbs wasn't.

'It's what you'd expect from junkies – they sleep rough cos no one's stupid enough to take 'em in. Nip back to the car, Edwards, and get a couple of torches out the kit bag in the boot.'

Gibbs found a loose piece of wood on the landing and used it to prise open enough of the boarded-up door to the squat so he and his colleagues could get in.

'Are you following all this Watergate and President Nixon stuff on the news, Sarge?'

'No!' Gibbs answered tersely as he led the way inside, shining his torch around the rooms and booting old drinks crates out of his way. The place stank of urine and dirty blankets, and amidst the numerous crushed cans of lager and broken bottles of cider, torn sleeping bags lay beside rotting food. They searched the bedrooms where used hypodermic needles littered the bare boards. Gibbs swore and kicked out at the disgusting mess and then straightened, gesturing for them to keep quiet. They could hear shrieks and laughs coming from the stairwell outside. Gibbs went out the front door onto the landing and picked up the bit of wood he'd used earlier.

Eddie Phillips was walking up the stairs with his friend Billy Myers. The two nineteen-year-olds looked manky: they both had dirty long hair and wore filthy stained T-shirts, flared jeans and Cuban-heeled boots. Gibbs and the two DCs approached them. They resembled three thugs with their coat collars turned up and Gibbs swung the stick like a golf club as he shouted.

'Which one o' you is Eddie Phillips?'

Billy looked terrified and pointed to Eddie who tried to make a run for it, but Gibbs was quick on his feet and caught him by his hair, then kicked his legs from under him. Eddie cowered as he lay on the floor and Gibbs pushed the piece of wood into his chest.

'We found your girlfriend, Eddie, but she looks a lot worse than you do!'

Jane sat by herself in the canteen eating a cheese and mushroom omelette. The canteen was buzzing and everyone was talking about the murder investigation, including the four detectives at the table opposite her, who she couldn't help overhearing. One said how frustrating it was that they still hadn't been able to locate Julie Ann Maynard's family, but now that her boyfriend had been brought in for questioning the case might be solved quicker than expected. She listened intently as Edwards, who'd accompanied DS Gibbs, described the arrest and then what had happened in the CID car on the way back to the station.

'Gibbs gave him a good dig in the ribs and forced him to look at a picture of the dead girl's body. The little wanker burst into tears and said it was Julie Ann but her real surname was Collins.'

'Why'd she use a false name?' the youngest detective asked.

His colleague slapped him across the back of the head. 'Because she's a tom, thicko, and they use false names if they get arrested for soliciting.'

The detective rubbed his head. 'Did he say anything else?'

'Not really, but you could see he was bricking it. Gibbs

tried to get him to cough, but he was such a blubbering emotional wreck that we couldn't get anything out of him.'

DC Edwards then gave his opinion. 'Bradfield's taken Phillips to his office for an interview with him and DS Gibbs. If he did it, believe me those two will break him.'

'Or fit him up,' his colleague said, and they all burst into laughter.

Having finished her meal Jane started to hurry down the stairs: Harris wanted her back on the duty desk, probably so he could return to the snooker room. But, hearing raised voices, she stopped on the first floor by DCI Bradfield's office. She moved a bit closer to his door to listen and could hear a person she presumed to be Eddie Phillips sobbing profusely.

'Don't bloody lie to me, son,' Bradfield shouted.

'I swear on my life I'm not lying,' came the response.

'You bloody well are – we both know you strangled her to death.'

'No … No, I would never hurt Julie Ann, I loved her.'

'That's it, that's why you killed her, because you loved her.'

Eddie was snivelling. 'I don't understand what you mean.'

'You found out she was getting shagged for money and drugs and you didn't like it. You had a fit of jealous rage and squeezed the life out of her.'

In floods of tears Eddie still protested his innocence. Then there was the sound of a hand banging repeatedly on a desk, followed by the gravelly toned voice of DS Spencer Gibbs.

'Stop lying! It'll be a lot easier for you if you tell us the truth.'

'I am, I am! The last time I saw her she was getting into a red car ... a Jaguar, I think, and it looked newish. I was high on heroin so it's hard to remember.'

'When was this?'

'What?'

'When did you see Julie Ann getting into a fucking red Jaguar, Eddie?' Gibbs asked.

'The last time I saw her.'

'When was that, Eddie?'

'How do you mean?'

Bradfield's calmer voice took over.

'Come on now, son, you are saying that the last time you saw Julie Ann she was getting into a red Jaguar.'

'Yeah, yeah, that's right. I've not seen her since then, I swear before God.'

'So when exactly was it?'

'I dunno, maybe a week or so ago. I don't remember exactly.'

'Keep lying and you'll find a slap round the head might help you remember,' Gibbs said.

Jane hurried back to the front office. Harris was his usual miserable self, accusing her of taking her time on her refreshment break, when she'd actually only had half an hour. He said that he would be in the sergeants' room writing up some reports. It irritated her that he was so lazy, but she was pleased that he would be out of her hair for a while.

Another hour passed and Jane only had a couple of incidents to deal with. Then she saw DCI Bradfield and DS Gibbs taking Eddie Phillips into the custody area. He was thin and scrawny and it was clear his heroin addiction had taken a toll on his body. He looked much older than nineteen. His face was covered in red scars and his shoulder-length black hair was dirty and matted.

A few minutes later Bradfield came out of the charge room and strode towards her. Jane started to stand to attention and winced as she felt her tights catch on the rough wooden handle of the desk drawer.

'You ever been on a bereavement visit?'

She swallowed and coughed.

'Pardon, sir?'

'Obviously not. My lads have their work cut out here, so get your skates on – you're coming with me to see the dead girl's family. The address is 48 Church Mount, Hampstead Garden Suburb. You know how to read an A–Z street map, I take it?'

She didn't dare tell him that she had only recently passed her driving test, and had only used an A–Z to find her way on her beats in Hackney. She used public transport to get around London itself, as it was free for police officers.

'I need to tell Sergeant Harris, sir. He said I had to cover the front office until end of duty.'

'Don't worry, I'll deal with him. Now get a move on, WPC …?'

'Tennison, sir, Jane Tennison.'

Bradfield left and Jane went into the comms room. She checked her tights, only to find that the snag had turned into a ladder.

'Oh my God! I don't believe it, this is the second pair in a week. Those ruddy desks need sandpapering. Look – I've got a ladder on the knee now!'

Kath smiled. 'Like I said, Jane, it always happens to you, don't it?'

Pulling her skirt down in the hope the ladder wouldn't show, Jane booked out a personal radio and asked Kath for directions, which she quickly jotted down in her note-book. She hurried to the ladies' locker room, grabbed her uniform jacket and hat and went upstairs to Bradfield's office, only to be told by DS Gibbs that he was waiting for her in the rear yard.

'Get a move on, he's waiting.'

She was heading across the yard when she heard Bradfield's voice and saw him standing by the snooker room, holding the door open and remonstrating with Sergeant Harris.

'Covering the duty desk and front counter is your problem, Harris, not mine. As the DCI and your superior officer, I decide who I take with me, not you.'

He slammed the door shut and as Jane walked past she saw Harris glare at her through the window. Bradfield was wearing a long black raincoat with the collar turned up. She could see that he had shaved and changed his shirt to meet the victim's parents. The sooner they had the dead girl formally identified the faster they could move on to issuing press releases and appealing to the public for information.

Bradfield got into the driving seat of an unmarked red Hillman Hunter CID car. As Jane got into the passenger seat he threw an A–Z street map onto her lap, which she thought was rather rude of him.

'Christ, I hate death notices, but you gotta do what you gotta do. I guarantee it won't be pleasant, never is. When we get there, you stay quiet, but if the mother has a meltdown take her to the kitchen, or wherever, so I can chat to the father in private. Right, which way?' he snapped as he started the engine and reversed out of the parking bay. He was such a big man his shoulder almost touched hers when he changed gear and drove out of the yard at speed.

Jane had her notebook open beside the A–Z. 'Dalston Lane, Balls Pond Road, Holloway Road, Archway Road and er ... it's off Aylmer Road.'

'Good knowledge. You must be a London girl.'

'Maida Vale, sir.'

'Posh place,' he remarked.

It was a nerve-wracking drive as Bradfield hurtled down the streets and swore profusely at every red light. The rain was still pouring down, making it difficult for Jane to see the road signs and street names through the windscreen wipers. The car didn't have 'blues and twos', just a tinny-sounding bell, which she had to keep pressing so they could get through the heavy traffic and red lights. Clinging on to the handle of her passenger door she found it hard to concentrate enough to locate their destination, and now it was dark she had to use her pocket torch to see the street map.

'Are we on the right bloody road?' he asked impatiently.

'Yes, sir, left here into Winnington Road, then right, and the address is the next left ... Oh sorry, it was first right you wanted.'

'Jesus Christ, get it together.' Jane took a deep breath and tried not to react to Bradfield's brash manner.

'Sorry, sir, it was the first right.'

Bradfield did a fast three-point turn and at last they found Church Mount. He slowed his pace as they approached number 48 and peered from the car window.

He jerked on the handbrake. 'Looks very upmarket ... if I've been given the wrong fucking address somebody's head is going to roll.'

He got out of the car then leaned back in, clicking his fingers.

'Envelope ... back seat, grab it for me.'

Whilst reaching over to the back seat Jane felt the ladder in her tights split open even further. She got out and hurried to join the DCI as he walked up the path, lighting the way with her pocket torch. Bradfield coughed repeatedly and straightened his tie before taking a deep breath and ringing the doorbell. There was the sound of a dog barking from somewhere in the house. He waited briefly and then rang the bell again. Lights came on in the hall, and through one of the glass panels beside the front door a man peered out.

Bradfield already had his black warrant card in his hand and held it up. The door was unlocked and opened by a tall, hawk-nosed man, his thinning hair standing up on end.

'Mr Collins?'

'Yes.'

'Good evening. I'm DCI Leonard Bradfield and this is WPC Tennison. Do you mind if we come in, sir?'

The door opened wider, revealing Mr Collins wearing pyjamas under a thick dressing gown, and slippers.

'What is this about?'

'Is there somewhere we can sit down and talk, sir?'

George Collins closed the front door behind them, as a pale-faced woman, also wearing nightclothes and with her hair in clips, came from the lounge.

'What is it? Has another house been broken into?'

As they were led into the comfortable living room Jane kept tugging at the hem of her skirt. Mr Collins sat with his wife on the sofa and Bradfield sat on the armchair opposite. Jane remained standing to one side; she could see the Collinses looking very confused.

On a piano was a large photograph of a smiling, innocent-looking girl, aged about fifteen. She had glorious blonde wavy hair and wide blue eyes. With a jolt of recognition, Jane could see similarities to the murdered girl in the Polaroid pictures, although the photograph on the piano had obviously been taken before Julie Ann had become a drug addict.

After what seemed an eternal, uncomfortable silence, Bradfield cleared his throat. 'Do you have a daughter called Julie Ann?'

After a slight pause, Mr Collins spoke. 'Yes. Is she in trouble again?'

'I am very sorry to have to tell you that a girl we believe to be your daughter has been found dead. She—'

'No, no, you are wrong, it can't be my Julie,' wailed a distraught Mary Collins as she moved closer to her husband.

The usually brusque Bradfield now spoke softly, clearly and quietly.

'The body of a young female was found earlier today at an adventure playground in Hackney. She was murdered and we need to have her formally identified as soon as possible.'

Jane watched as Mr Collins reached across to hold his wife's hand, gripping it tightly.

'But you can't be sure it is Julie?'

'Sadly I believe it is, sir. I don't want to distress you by showing you photographs of her, but having seen the picture on your piano I am almost certain that the victim is your daughter.'

Mrs Collins began to cry uncontrollably and her husband put his arms round her. He gently kissed her head and stroked her hair. Bradfield said nothing for a minute or two as he let them share their grief. Eventually Mr Collins slowly released his wife, and stood up saying he would go and change. His body was taut and he clenched his hands beside him. He moved robotically to the double doors of their living room, and Bradfield rose quickly realizing what was going to happen. He was directly behind Mr Collins when his legs gave way, and he caught him in his arms.

'It's all right, sir, I'm here. I'll help you up the stairs and WPC Tennison will stay with Mrs Collins.'

The wretched man sobbed and clung to Bradfield as they left the room.

Jane was unsure what she should do, and found her eyes brimming with tears. She pulled some tissues out of her handbag and handed one to Mrs Collins, then dabbed her own eyes with another.

'She hasn't been home for over a year. We tried to help her but she kept running away, so it became pointless reporting it in the end. She broke George's heart, you know, and we always knew the drugs might kill her, but for her to be murdered ... it's ...' Mrs Collins couldn't finish her sentence as she broke down again.

Bradfield returned and leaned close to Mrs Collins, who sat with her hands pressed against her knees and was rocking back and forth.

'Your husband needs you upstairs. If you wish, you can accompany us, or if you want to stay here I can call some-one to be with you.'

Mary Collins looked up at Bradfield and again Jane could see the kindness and gentleness in his face and manner. He helped Mary Collins to her feet with his arm around her, and assisted her from the room.

Jane was wiping her eyes and blowing her nose when Bradfield walked back in.

'What are you crying for? You didn't know her. This is all part of the job – you need to pull yourself together. He's getting dressed, but she's in the bathroom and I think she's wet herself, so go and see what you can do.'

'I'm sorry, sir.' Jane hurried from the room as he opened the envelope and took out the Polaroid crime scene pictures. Finding a close-up of the victim's face he moved to the piano and held it against the silver-framed photograph. There was little doubt it was their daughter.

Mary Collins could not face attending the mortuary to identify the body, so Bradfield spoke with a female neighbour who was a close friend, and she agreed to stay with Mary and look after her. The drive to the mortuary was solemn and silent with Mr Collins sitting in the back seat staring out of the car window. Out of respect Bradfield drove at a steady pace, without using the police bell this time.

He broke the silence asking Mr Collins if he drove, and he said that he did, but mostly at weekends as he used the Underground to and from work. He was a chartered surveyor and owned his own company.

'I will organize a police car to take you home after the identification.'

'Thank you, that is very kind.'

'What car do you drive?' Bradfield asked casually.

'A Bristol. It's rather old now, but it used to belong to my father.'

Remembering Eddie mention that he'd seen Julie Ann getting into a red Jaguar, Jane noted the DCI's subtle way of handling such an important question.

Hackney Mortuary, a dank building constructed in the late nineteenth century, was situated across the church square from the station. The head mortician, who lived in a flat above the premises, unlocked the reception doors and they were instructed to wait whilst he finished preparing the body for viewing. They sat on hard-backed chairs, under ghostly strip lighting that flickered and gave the corridor a yellowish hue.

Bradfield checked his watch and Jane could see he was getting impatient, which in turn made her apprehensive about asking any questions or speaking to the distraught Mr Collins. Bradfield stood up and, excusing himself, went off to find out what was causing the delay, striding through the swing doors into the examination area of the mortuary. She noticed that although he was a big man he moved with agility and was obviously very fit. For all his brashness and impatience with her she'd been surprised by how gently he'd handled the wretched disclosure of Julie Ann's death.

Jane didn't know what to say to Mr Collins. She had never been to a mortuary before, and at nearly eleven o'clock at night there was an empty, chilling feel to it. Mr Collins sat with his bony hands clenched together, the whites of his knuckles showing as he pressed his hands tighter. Jane asked if he would like a glass of water, but he shook his head and surprised her by breaking his silence.

'She was the most beautiful little girl, never any trouble when she was younger. Clever, and she could dance, very light on her feet, spinning like a top. She wanted to be a ballet dancer one day ... I have some cine film of her dancing.'

Suddenly the swing doors opened and Bradfield gestured for them to follow him through to the examination area and the numbered refrigerated storage drawers. The room smelt of disinfectant and the young mortician was waiting by drawer 6. When he opened it Jane felt the cold air waft around the room and up her nostrils. The sliding tray was slowly pulled out and the body was covered in a white shroud. The mortician gently pulled it down to enable Mr Collins to see the face of his daughter. Jane could see red indented welt marks around Julie Ann's neck. The swollen bitten tongue had been pushed back in her mouth, but it caused her lips to bulge slightly, and her eyelids had been closed.

'Is this your daughter, Mr Collins?' Bradfield asked.

There was hardly any pause as he looked down.

'Yes, this is my daughter,' he whispered.

It was over quickly and the drawer slid back into position. They returned to the reception area and Jane radioed the station asking for a panda car, on the instructions of the DCI, to take Mr Collins home.

As they waited in the corridor a terrible grief-stricken rage erupted from Mr Collins. He let out a howl like a wounded animal and gripped a chair. He then picked it up and hurled it towards the glass windows.

'YES, THAT IS MY DAUGHTER!' His voice rasped as he turned his fury towards Bradfield, swearing and gesticulating at him with his bony finger.

'She was the light of our lives and you tell me she was murdered. What caused those marks on her neck? Who killed her? Who is to blame? This isn't OUR fault! We loved her, gave her everything a young girl could want, and she rejected us, rejected all we had done for her. WHY? I need to know WHY.'

It looked as if Mr Collins was about to throw another chair, so Jane stepped back, but he crumpled and fell to his knees sobbing.

Surprised, Jane watched as Bradfield knelt down beside the broken, weeping man, speaking softly to him whilst gently rubbing his hunched shoulders. He told Mr Collins that they had arrested a suspect who was still in custody and would keep him informed of the progress of the investigation, and that detectives would visit his home in the morning to take a statement from him and his wife. Eventually Mr Collins was calm enough to be helped outside to the waiting police car.

'I didn't expect that,' Bradfield said as Jane followed him back inside.

'Thank you for taking me with you, sir. It was a good learning experience for me.'

'You can show a couple of hours' overtime and I'll sign it off. Have you ever been to a post-mortem?'

'No, sir, not yet,' she said, not relishing the thought but excited at what she hoped he was about to say.

'It's arranged for midday tomorrow, so meet me here.'

'Yes, sir, thank you, sir.'

'One word of advice though.' Jane listened intently. 'Always carry a spare pair of tights in your locker or handbag,' he said and winked.

As it was well after midnight, and public transport sparse, a uniform night-duty patrol car gave Jane a lift home to the flat in Maida Vale. She was relieved neither her parents nor her sister were up so that she could sneak into her bedroom and crash out. She looked round the familiar room. Above her bed was a large poster of Janis Joplin which she'd bought after the concert as a reminder of how much she had admired her. She was pleased to be home after the experience in the mortuary and had just changed into her nightdress when her sister, Pam, walked in.

'You know you should ring Mum and Dad if you are going to be so late. They were worried about you and you should have more respect. Have you tried it on?'

'What?'

Pam turned and pointed to the large black-plastic zip bag hanging on the back of the door.

'You can hardly miss it, but you have to make sure all the alterations have been done; she's finished all the dresses now, and done lovely puffed sleeves. You know she used to make dresses for Alma Cogan?'

'Sorry, I'll try it on in the morning.'

'Make sure you do. You seem to forget I'm getting married in a few days and you'd better not forget the rehearsal at the church either.'

'Pam, I'm really tired out,' Jane said as she got into bed.

Pam started to walk out and then stopped and did a childish little twirl, flapping her hands. 'Wait till you see my wedding gown – it's amazing; and I've got a long veil edged with lace – it's so beautiful.'

'Goodnight, Pam.'

As soon as the door closed Jane shut her eyes. Pam's dance reminded her of Mr Collins' memory of his daughter. She could see the pale white face of Julie Ann in the mortuary and suddenly her mind was filled with images from the crime scene pictures. The hot pants, the platform boots and the way her bra had been tied in a knot around her slender throat. Julie Ann wasn't beautiful any more. Her face was bloated and her purple swollen tongue made it look as though she was wearing a grotesque mask.

As Jane thought of Mr and Mrs Collins' loss, the soulful words of her favourite Janis Joplin song came into her head, and suddenly seemed so poignant.

> *Take another little piece of my heart now, baby!*
> *Oh, oh, break it!*
> *Break another little bit of my heart now, darling . . .*

CHAPTER THREE

Jane got up early and had a shower. She decided to try on
the dreaded bridesmaid dress. She unzipped the black bag
and the salmon-pink taffeta skirt spilled out: just looking
at the dress made her feel ill. The boned corset had a
sweetheart neckline and there were now puffball sleeves.
The huge satin bow and wide sash were pinned to the
hanger. She sighed. The frock was hideous. She pushed
the skirt back and zipped up the bag. She quickly dressed
and made her escape without waking her parents or sister.
She left a note to apologize for being so late home and left
it on the breakfast counter.

Jane arrived at the station early; she didn't want to miss
the post-mortem of Julie Ann Collins. She knew how
lucky she was to be asked to attend, as most probationers
got to attend only run-of-the-mill, non-suspicious post-
mortems.

The detectives on the murder investigation had worked
hard until the early hours of the morning. With the assistance of officers from the special patrol group, they had
made enquiries in the vicinity of the playground, on the
Kingsmead Estate, and at Edgar House on the Pembridge
Estate where the victim was known to have squatted.

Sadly they had not uncovered any witnesses who had noticed anything unusual or who had seen Julie Ann with anyone the previous day. She and Eddie Phillips were known on the estate, as was the fact that they sometimes squatted in one of the empty flats, but it seemed that they never caused any problems or bothered anyone. Eddie, the detectives discovered, had a grandmother called Nancy Phillips who lived on the estate and he stayed with her when he wasn't shooting up or high on drugs.

Shortly before midnight, while the SPG officers were still on the estate, they stopped a young male drug addict, Billy Myers, just outside the block where Julie Ann had squatted. It transpired that he knew the victim and, along with another drug addict, had spent the previous night with Eddie. He told the officers that Eddie was so spaced out on heroin he wouldn't have known what time of day it was, and when he had asked him where Julie Ann was, Eddie had said he didn't know and hadn't seen her since she'd gone off with a punter in a car. The officers traced the other drug addict and he gave the same story without any prompting.

The police divisional surgeon had examined Eddie. He had a number of needle marks from injecting heroin in his left arm, but no marks on his body that suggested he had been involved in a violent struggle.

Bradfield and DS Gibbs had re-interviewed Eddie, who still protested his innocence, and when asked if he was with anyone on the night Julie Ann died he said he couldn't remember as he was high on drugs.

Eddie's description of the last time he'd seen Julie Ann was still vague, as it was at least two weeks ago. He blamed drugs and methadone for his memory loss, and when asked about the red car he'd seen her getting into he said he was 'pretty sure' it was a newish Jaguar as it was shiny and he liked them. Eddie was unable to give a description of the driver, saying that he only saw the car from behind and didn't take any notice as he thought it was probably some punter picking Julie Ann up for sex.

Bradfield was beginning to doubt Eddie's involvement in Julie Ann's murder, but couldn't rule out the possibility that he was hiding something or knew someone who might be involved.

During the interview Eddie had been asked who their drug dealer was. He told them that Julie Ann used to get drugs for both of them, but he didn't know who from. Evidently, Julie Ann used to let her drug-dealing punters have sex in return for heroin, instead of cash. Bradfield found it repellent that Eddie allowed his so-called girl-friend to sell her body in order to feed their heroin habit. When asked if Julie Ann had a pimp, Eddie said he didn't know but Bradfield suspected he was lying. However, there was no incriminating evidence to charge Eddie or keep him in custody, so Bradfield had him released pending further enquiries. He warned Eddie to stay with his grandmother and that at some point he or one of his detectives would want to speak with him again.

Without any witnesses, they had no clear time of death, only that Julie Ann's body had been discovered at 9 a.m. the day before by some kids. It was clear that she had been strangled, but they needed to know what time she was killed, and whether the murder had happened in the playground or elsewhere.

Bradfield demanded that his officers push any inform-ants they had to find out who had supplied Julie Ann and Eddie with heroin. He instructed them to check all the red-light districts in Stoke Newington, Holloway, King's Cross and Soho for any toms who might have known Julie Ann or seen a red Jag loitering for pick-ups. He wanted the car and driver traced, even if it meant speaking to everyone in London who owned a red Jaguar, which could run into thousands.

Jane went to the parade room in the back yard to check her tray for any internal mail or notices. She opened an envelope with her divisional number and station code. It contained the results of her latest continuation training exam and she had passed with an overall mark of 85 per cent. With plenty of time to spare Jane decided to have a coffee and a Chelsea bun in the canteen. She was just heading up the stairs when she saw Kath Morgan coming out of the CID office dressed in flared jeans, a T-shirt and denim jacket.

'You're in early,' they both said in unison.

Jane explained about the invite from DCI Bradfield to attend the post-mortem.

'You lucky so and so, Jane. I've never been to a proper murder one, only a routine natural-causes death. Anyway, after that DS Gibbs gave me a tip and told me to use some Vicks VapoRub – you put a bit under each nostril to avoid the stink. In fact I've still got the unopened pot I bought. It's in me parade-room tray, help yourself to it.'

'Oh, thanks, Kath, I will. Why don't you ask if you can come as well?'

'I'm busy already. I got a bit of info about a burglar working the Holly Street Estate over by London Fields. He's turning over the old folks' flats and nicking pension books and cash. DS Gibbs said I could do a plain-clothes shift with the crime squad to try and nick him on the plot. I hope it pays off, Jane, as I really want to get onto the crime squad and then get selected for detective.'

'It would be a first for this station, Kath, a woman detective.'

'I know! There's only a couple of other WDCs in the Met, but I'm determined to prove myself.'

Jane smiled. 'He of the thirty years' experience would have a heart attack. A woman detective ... what a bloody disgrace.'

'Pissing Harris off would be a bonus,' Kath replied and they both laughed.

Kath's tone became serious as she continued.

'Listen, about that bloke you mentioned, the one that threw you out of his mother's flat. Was his name John Bentley?'

'Well, I'm pretty sure it was. Irene Bentley was the name on the rent book and he called her Mum.'

'Before I went off duty last night I had a quick look through the collator's criminal index cards. There's a Bentley whose description matches but he lives at a different address. Bit of a nasty sod from a nasty family: he's been done for GBH.'

Jane smiled saying she was glad she hadn't tried to dig him in the ribs with his mother's umbrella.

'Lucky you didn't. From his record he'd have likely walloped you one.'

The CID office door flew open as DC Edwards came out. 'Come on, Kath, get a move on. We need to get the obo van parked up before the suspect gets there,' he said as he rushed past her.

'I'm friggin' ready so keep your hair on,' Kath shouted and turned back to Jane. 'I know why he wants to make a quick arrest ... there's a game of shoot pontoon followed

43

by three-card brag in the CID office tonight and his fingers are twitching to lose his weekly expenses.'

Kath started to follow the disgruntled detective down the stairs, but stopped.

'Listen, there's a place coming up soon at the section house in Mare Street. It's just down the road and would save you loads of time travelling, but you got to make it snappy or the room will go. It's only a fiver a month as well.'

'Thanks, Kath, I appreciate it.'

'And have a word with the collator about the Bentleys – he'll probably know a lot more – always good to get to know who the villains on the patch are.'

Jane went to the collator's office on the ground floor. The post was held by PC Donaldson. Rather overweight and with thinning grey hair, he had worked at Hackney Police Station for over twenty-five years. There wasn't much Donaldson didn't know about who was who in Hackney's criminal underworld. He received and collated information about criminals on the division and dispersed intelligence to the beat officers about crime trends and people wanted or suspected of a crime. His knowledge was invaluable, and he was highly respected by everyone in the station as a genuinely nice man who had time for everyone, male or female.

Donaldson flicked through the index-card drawer marked 'B'. 'Here it is, full name John Henry Bentley, aged thirty-seven.' He withdrew the three cards from a plastic sleeve and handed them to Jane who looked at the black-and-white mug-shot picture on the front.

'That's him,' she said.

PC Donaldson drew out two further cards from the 'B' drawer.

'They're a well-known family who've lived in Hackney all their lives. All of them villains and all hard as nails, apart from the mum Renee, bless her. John's got a council house on Middleton Road and his younger brother David, who's thirty, lives with his mother on the Pembridge.'

Jane noticed that amongst John Bentley's convictions there was grievous bodily harm, burglary and theft. 'Middleton Road is by London Fields, isn't it?'

PC Donaldson nodded.

'WPC Morgan's doing an observation on the Holly Street Estate for a burglar nicking pension books. Do you think it might be ...?'

'No way. Nicking pension books or snatching old ladies' handbags isn't their style, plus John Bentley's been clean for quite a few years. They have their own code of honour, his kind, the number one rule being you don't grass to the police and two you don't turn over old people. If they caught someone doing that they'd beat the crap out of them and break their fingers for good measure. That's how John got his conviction for GBH.'

'The victim grassed on him?'

'No, CID heard him screaming – they caught John breaking the poor bloke's fingers with a hammer.'

Jane winced. 'I got the impression his mother was frightened of him.'

PC Donaldson handed Jane another index card for a Clifford Bentley, aged seventy-two. He explained her fear probably stemmed from her old man, 'Cliffy' as he was known, knocking her about before he got a ten-stretch in Wormwood Scrubs.

'He's real handy with his fists, but more as a renowned bare-knuckle fighter. At one time he associated with the Kray twins as a bag man collecting protection money.'

'What did he go to prison for last time?'

'The Sweeney got a tip-off from a snout and nicked him on the pavement,' he said.

Seeing the look of puzzlement on Jane's face Donaldson explained that 'snout' meant informant and 'the Sweeney' was the Met's flying squad nickname from the Cockney rhyming slang 'Sweeney Todd'. The unit had no boundaries and operated all across London investigating commercial armed robberies. Clifford Bentley was arrested whilst trying to rob a security van during a bank-cash collection and he'd have got a much longer prison sentence if the gun had been real and loaded. Donaldson remarked that it wasn't Clifford's usual style, but rumour had it he urgently needed cash to pay the Krays off on a gambling debt.

'What happened to the informant?'

'Don't know, but word has it he's part of a concrete pillar somewhere.'

'Is John Bentley a builder?' Jane asked, recalling seeing the power tools brochures in Renee's kitchen.

'Could be, but like I said he's been clean for a while and can turn his hand to anything.'

'What does the brother David do?'

Donaldson handed Jane his index card. 'Not a lot after he smashed his legs up. Good few years back he was out with his dad and brother nicking lead off a church roof when night-duty CID caught them red-handed. David tried to do a runner: silly bugger jumped off the roof and broke his legs badly. Big sob story at the trial as he was in a wheelchair. His barrister played the sympathy card, the soft judge fell for it and David got a light sentence.'

Jane looked at David Bentley's card and saw that the

arresting officer was the then Detective Sergeant Bradfield.

'Can I take these cards with me to have a look-over?'

PC Donaldson explained that no one was allowed to remove the cards from his office, but she could make notes if she wanted. The other alternative was to order copies of their criminal records on microfiche from Scotland Yard. Jane said not to bother and that she had just been curious after meeting the over-aggressive John Bentley the day before.

'Well, good on you. Always good to do research for yer knowledge, and any time you want to know who's who, you come to me.'

Jane got the Vicks VapoRub from Kath's tray. She was making her way to the mortuary when DCI Bradfield sped into the station yard in his light blue Ford Zephyr, causing her to jump out of the way as he pulled up abruptly into a parking bay. He got out of the car, said nothing to her, but simply nodded. She could see from the look on his face that he was not in the best of moods. He strode ahead of Jane forcing her to hurry in his wake, and she was almost clipped in the chest as he pushed open the door to the mortuary and went towards the coroner's assistant's office. He held up his hand in a gesture for her to wait behind him, then opened the door and peered in.

'DCI Bradfield. Are they ready to go with the PM on my murder victim?' he asked.

Jane heard a murmured reply, and then Bradfield closed the door.

'Follow me,' he said abruptly, walking down the corridor and banging open the swing doors to the examination room as if he was on some sort of mission. He patted his pocket for his cigarette pack and stuck one into his mouth then paused to light it, leaving a trail of smoke behind him.

The awful putrid smell in the room hit Jane instantly and made her gag. The head mortician was finishing stitching up the decomposing body of an elderly man on a white porcelain examination table. She had been warned about the smell by Kath, but hadn't expected it to be so bad. Opening Kath's jar of Vicks she put some on her finger and rubbed it below her nostrils.

'That's not a very bright idea, luv,' the mortician said with a touch of sarcasm.

Jane noticed Bradfield raising his eyebrows and shaking his head as if she was dim.

'Sorry, what's not a bright idea?' she asked, wondering what was so amusing.

'The menthol in the Vicks clears your nasal passages so you'll be able to smell even better now.'

'She's a probationer ... first PM,' Bradfield said, grinning, and the mortician laughed, saying he thought as much.

Jane felt silly and realized that she was the butt of the joke Gibbs had initially intended to play on Kath.

To distract herself she looked around the small room. The walls were lined with white brick-shaped tiles and the stone-flagged floor was angled to a gulley which ran down to a drain area. The other porcelain examination table was clean and dry and on it was a large wooden chopping board and round plastic bowl. To one side were two steel trolleys which were covered with an array of different-shaped cutting instruments. On one trolley there was a white butcher's scale with a steel meat tray resting in its holder. Then the doors swung open and a tall dapper man in his mid-forties with swept-back blond hair walked in. He was wearing a brown wax Barbour jacket, white shirt, blue-and-white-striped tie, grey slacks and brown zip ankle boots. He was carrying a large black doctor's-style case which he put down on the clean examination table. Jane thought he must be the forensic pathologist as DCI Bradfield greeted him with a friendly smile and firm handshake.

'I'm glad I got you on this case, Paul. The Chief's breathing down my neck and pressing for results, but right now we've still got bugger all,' Bradfield said.

'Who's the wooden top?' Paul asked, using a detective's term for a uniform officer.

'WPC Tennison, meet Detective Sergeant Lawrence, best lab liaison officer in the Met. Any suspicious death or murder scene, he's the man you want working it,' Bradfield said and patted him on the shoulder.

DS Lawrence gave him a suspicious glance. 'You after a loan of money for the office card game or something?'

'You can't even take praise now?'

Jane realized this was the first time she had seen Bradfield smile: it made him appear quite boyish. She had been made aware of the highly respected role of a lab sergeant during training at Hendon, and Bradfield and Lawrence obviously rated each other highly. There were only twelve lab sergeants in London and they were all experienced detectives with twenty years-plus service. They worked alongside forensic scientists at crime scenes and at the Met's laboratory in Lambeth. They didn't make arrests as this could detract from their invaluable input.

'You got any thoughts on the scene, Paul?' Bradfield asked, his cigarette dangling from his lips.

'It's a bit of a minefield. There were lots of footprints but it is a kids' adventure playground.'

Lawrence added that some were 'plod-issue boots',

referring to the footprints of the uniform officers who trampled over the scene, but he had concentrated on the footprints near the body, and had taken some plaster-cast lifts to examine in the lab. It was hoped they might get a possible size and be able to compare them to any suspect's shoes. DS Lawrence said he had been to the station and visited Eddie Phillips in the cell, but he was wearing Cuban-heel boots which didn't appear to match any marks at the scene.

'What about prints?' Bradfield asked.

DS Lawrence shook his head. 'We concentrated on anything metal, but due to the recent heavy rain we only managed to get a few lifts. I've had them sent to fingerprint branch to look at.

The mortician finished on the old man, wrapped a shroud round the body and placed it on a metal trolley. As he picked up a shower hose Jane hadn't noticed that Bradfield and DS Lawrence had stepped into the side corridor leading to the fridges. The mortician turned on the hose and started washing down the examination table and floor. The force of the spray sent dirty bloodstained water splashing onto Jane's skirt, shoes and tights, causing her to squeal and jump back out of the way. The mortician then threw a bucket of water onto the floor, and gave it a quick once-over with a mop. From the smell the water contained a large measure of disinfectant. She didn't say anything to him but strongly suspected it was an intentional initiation to the mortuary for probationers.

The assistant mortician wheeled a shrouded body into the room, and Jane could see from the blonde hair hanging loosely over the edge of the trolley that it was Julie Ann's. The assistant handed DS Lawrence some paper bags containing the victim's clothing and then wheeled the old man's body out to the refrigerators. Lawrence had a quick look in the bag that contained Julie Ann's white socks and her boots.

'We got quite a few red fibres on the soles of these socks, probably from a carpet of some sort. I'll get the scientist to check all the clothing for any similar or other foreign fibres. Her platform boots are blue cloth and patent leather so we might get a fingerprint off them if he dragged her.'

DS Lawrence then took out her underwear. 'Looks like there might be some semen-staining on the gusset.'

'She was a tom so there's probably bucket loads of it,' Bradfield replied sarcastically. He patted his pockets for his pack of cigarettes and lit up a fresh one.

'Look out, here comes the miserable munchkin,' DS Lawrence said as the swing doors opened.

A small stumpy man entered the room carrying a clip-board and paper. He was in his fifties, with grey thinning hair and half-moon glasses perched unsteadily on the end of his bulbous red nose.

Jane observed that his green mortuary gown and black wellington boots were stained with blood and body tissue, and deduced that he must be the pathologist. The two morticians slid Julie Ann's shrouded body from the trolley onto the table.

'Try and keep your fag ash off my instruments today, DCI Bradfield. DS Lawrence, you're doing exhibits and photographs, I take it?' the po-faced Professor Martin said as he wrote their names in his notes. He turned towards Jane, lowered his head and peered over the top of his glasses. 'And you, young lady, are ...?'

'Probationary WPC 517 Golf Hotel Tennison, on B Relief Hackney, sir.'

Martin sighed. 'This is a mortuary, not a courtroom – I

can see you are a WPC and an unusually pretty one ... name and number is all I require. I'm Professor Dean Martin, and not to be confused with the crooner.'

Seeing Jane staring at the red spider-web marks on the Professor's face, DS Lawrence leant towards her and whispered, 'He drinks like Dean Martin though ... that's what too much whisky does to your skin.'

Professor Martin put a black-rubber apron over his gown and pulled on some green-rubber gauntlet gloves. The apron had two metal link-chains at the neck and waist to hold it in place.

'I wasn't needed in court this morning so I've already done my external examination of the body. Gather round, please,' Martin said as he moved towards the body and then, like a magician, pulled off the shroud in a theatrical flurry to display the naked girl.

Jane gave a sharp intake of breath. Julie Ann's body was alabaster white, stretched out with her hands placed at her sides. DS Lawrence got a camera out of his kit bag and took some photographs.

Martin looked at Jane as he spoke. 'Time of death is the question most consistently asked by detectives in murder investigations. However, due to many variables, it is extremely difficult to determine, and can never be one hundred per cent accurate.' He flicked over a page on his clipboard.

'He's showboating for her benefit,' Jane heard Bradfield mutter to DS Lawrence.

'So, as to time of death for little missy here: the body was found at 9 a.m. in the open. Livor mortis, which is due to the settling of the blood after death, was well developed, thus indicating the victim had been in the same position for six to twelve hours. At the scene at 10.30 a.m., I took vaginal swabs and a rectal temperature. I have considered the overnight external air temperature, which in turn influences the rate of heat loss from the body and affects the onset of rigor—'

Bradfield sighed. 'Can we just have it in layman's terms, Prof?'

Martin puffed out his chest indignantly. 'By my calculations she was killed on Sunday the 13th of May sometime between 6 p.m. and midnight.'

'It didn't get dark until just after eight and it's unlikely she was killed outside in broad daylight,' DS Lawrence remarked.

'Do you think she was killed at the playground, or elsewhere?' Bradfield asked Martin.

'I don't know, it's impossible for me to say.'

'She could have been murdered indoors somewhere nearby, carried on foot in the early hours and dumped,' DS Lawrence speculated.

'OK, Sherlock, how's that explain her bra still being round her neck?'

Martin spoke before Lawrence could answer. 'It was tied in a double knot and so tightly neither I nor DS Lawrence could unpick it at the scene. In the end I had to cut it free with some scissors.'

DS Lawrence removed the bra from the paper bag and showed it to DCI Bradfield so he could see the knot for himself. He then removed the blouse and laid it on top of the bag.

'The two upper buttons on the blouse are missing and they weren't found at the scene.'

'They could have come off at any time, even accidentally,' Bradfield said.

Lawrence pointed to the chest area of the blouse.

'There's tear damage where the buttons were, which suggests a struggle.'

Jane stepped forward so she could get a better look at the bra.

'Excuse me, sir, but the bra's strapless, so he could have removed it at the scene while she still had the shirt on during a bit of foreplay.'

There was a sudden silence in the room as all three men looked at each other and Jane thought she was about to get a dressing down.

DS Lawrence glanced at Bradfield, nodded at him and whispered, 'It's a good point.'

Professor Martin tapped his clipboard with his pen to get their attention.

'We're going round in circles and the fact is I have to consider both possibilities: was she murdered at the scene, or dumped there? Now can we get on with the post-mortem, please?'

Professor Martin peered down at his clipboard as he walked round the table to Julie Ann's left side. 'I have had a close look using a magnifying glass and cannot find any hypodermic needle marks that appear to be recent.'

He lifted up her left arm and pointed to the black and blue track marks around her inner elbow joint, which Lawrence photographed.

'As you can see there is bruising around all these injection sites, which indicates they are old. It's difficult to determine the exact age of the bruising as veins in junkies start to collapse after repeated heroin injections. However, I would estimate the most recent to be anywhere between one to two weeks old.'

'So that suggests she was off heroin just before she was murdered?' Bradfield remarked.

'Possibly, but I believe your victim was attending a treatment centre for help, so she may well have been pre-scribed methadone as an opiate substitute.'

Bradfield made a note in his pocket book to ask the treatment centre about the methadone. Martin lifted Julie Ann's right arm and they could see that the whole of the inside of the lower arm was badly bruised.

'You can see there is blue and yellow coloured bruising to the inside length of the lower arm caused by severe blunt-force injury, which has ruptured blood vessels in her skin.' Martin asked the morticians to turn the body over.

The extensive bruising and welt marks to Julie Ann's back and buttocks were quite horrifying, even Bradfield and DS Lawrence were visibly shocked. Jane shuddered at the thought of the pain the poor girl must have suffered during the beating. Professor Martin explained that ini-tially the injuries would have appeared dull red to blue, but over time the red blood cells would have been broken down, releasing the yellow-brown hue seen on the edges of the blue-bruised areas on her back.

'So the bruising's old?' DS Lawrence asked.

'Yes, the yellow colour does not appear until a few days after the initial injury and you can see the clear differ-ences from the red marks round her neck caused by the strangulation. In this poor girl's case I'd estimate the beat-ing injuries are at least six to ten days old. The type of surface and force that impacts on the body will have an effect on the intensity, size, shape and pattern of the bruis-ing as well.'

'Any idea what caused them?' Bradfield asked, brushing cigarette ash off his jacket.

Martin said that due to the time lapse since the injuries were inflicted, it was hard to tell. However, it was clear that whoever had inflicted them must have been in a rage, and some of the welt marks still had a faint curved pattern that could have been caused by something like a walking stick.

Martin looked at Jane. 'WPC Tennison, would you mind crouching down in a side-on foetal position and raising your right arm, palm outwards, as if you were cowering and trying to protect your head?'

Hesitantly Jane did as requested so Martin could act out his theory.

'The assailant stood in front of the victim's right side and raised the weapon. This in turn caused the victim to hold up her right arm to protect herself from the beating,' Martin said as he swung his arm in a backwards and for-wards motion. 'She was hit three or four times on the lower arm before falling over and being repeatedly struck across the back and buttocks.'

Jane followed Martin's cue and fell to the cold wet floor. There was silence in the room as she peered up and saw the three men staring down at her with a look of bewil-derment.

Bradfield shook his head in disbelief. 'The Prof didn't mean for you to actually do that bit, Tennison, so get up.'

She felt embarrassed, yet relieved, as the floor smelt of disinfectant and the tiles were not that clean.

Bradfield looked at her impatiently as she stood up and raised her hand as if in a classroom.

'Excuse me, Professor Martin, is it possible to tell if the attack occurred when she was fully clothed or naked?'

'Very good question. We have a bright little probationer amongst us, and one not keeling over for a change. But then again we've not got to the fainting part yet.' Martin chortled and then cocked his head to one side, looking at Jane.

'I may have been able to give you a clearer answer had the beating taken place up to seventy-eight hours before death, as marks from the clothing are sometimes visible on the surface of the skin.'

'Was she raped?' Bradfield asked, becoming even more impatient.

'There's some old bruising on the inner thighs, but nothing recent or unusual for someone who worked in the sex trade.'

Professor Martin said he would now start the internal examination. Jane knew she had to keep calm, and decided that the best thing to do was to try to think of it as a biology lesson in human anatomy. Bradfield then took her by surprise as he gently patted Julie Ann's right foot: it was a gesture a father might give to his sleeping child.

As Martin stood over the body a mortician handed him a scalpel from the instrument tray. He proceeded to make a deep incision in the shape of a Y from the front of each shoulder to the bottom end of the breastbone, and then down from the sternum to the pubic bone. The skin and muscle from the cut was peeled back, with the top flap pulled over the face of the body. A mortician then sawed the ribs off exposing the internal organs. Jane noticed the smell, but it was not as pungent as the smell of the elderly man's body. DCI Bradfield got out his packet of Woodbine non-tipped cigarettes and lit one up from the butt of his previous one, handing another to DS Lawrence. He hesitated and proffered the pack to Jane. She declined, but she did find that the smell of the cigarette smoke helped mask the stench from the body.

Martin now cut into the bladder and took a urine sample. Together with a blood sample from an artery he handed it to DS Lawrence for toxicology tests at the lab.

The assistant mortician placed a large plastic bowl between the legs of the victim. Professor Martin cut away the internal organs, sliding them in one block into the bowl. Then he carried it over to the other table to do a closer examination and take some samples for micro-scopic study.

Jane took a few deep breaths, exhaling the air from her mouth as she started to feel queasy.

The mortician used a saw to cut a circle around the top of the skull, and then removed it with a T-shaped bone chisel and hammer. Next came the brain, which he took over to Professor Martin who was still examining the internal organs and weighing them.

Oh my God, Jane said to herself, and unable to watch shut her eyes. She took a few more deep breaths and sniffed. Contrary to what she had been told the VapoRub did in fact help keep her standing upright, but the over-powering smells and sights were making her feel sick.

'There may be another reason your victim wanted to get herself off heroin. I have discovered a dead foetus in the uterus. She's about 2.9 inches long, weighs .81 of an ounce and some teeth have started forming – so I would estimate Julie Ann was twelve to fourteen weeks pregnant. The child could have died at the same time as the mother, or possibly as a result of the earlier beating.'

Hearing this new information made Jane open her eyes, and she was so taken aback by the fact that the victim was pregnant her dizziness went. Martin placed the foetus in an airtight container filled with formaldehyde, and although Bradfield and Lawrence both looked, Jane could not bring herself to do so.

'My God, it doesn't even look human, more like a baby monkey,' Bradfield whispered in shock.

'It is human, believe you me, and sadly perfectly formed for the time of the gestation,' Martin said quietly.

The post-mortem examination of Julie Ann Collins lasted nearly three hours and DS Lawrence took extensive photographs of all her injuries. As he packed his camera in its bag he leant over to Jane.

'You did well, luv. Most probationers keel over as soon as they see the body on the slab – and good spot about the bra being strapless.'

Jane smiled. Bradfield told her to get a move on and she dutifully followed him out of the mortuary. She thanked him for letting her attend the post-mortem.

He stopped and cocked his head to one side, looking down at her.

'Congratulations, Tennison. You impressed me – very attentive and you asked intelligent questions. But I've never had anyone thank me for allowing them to attend a post-mortem before.' He hesitated before he asked what she felt about the fact that their victim had been pregnant.

'So sad – perhaps she didn't even know?'

'Maybe, but it makes me want to catch the bastard even more. She was only seventeen years old, and now it's a waste of two lives, not just one.'

'Do you think Eddie Phillips killed her?'

He didn't reply and remained deep in thought as they crossed the station yard. Jane asked him if she could be excused now the post-mortem was over as she was on late shift.

'What time is it?'

'Three o'clock, sir.'

'Is Sergeant Harris on duty?

Jane nodded. Bradfield handed her a £1 note and told her he needed to talk to him. In the meantime he wanted her to go to the canteen and get him a coffee and a ham sandwich then bring them to his office.

Jane went to the washroom first as she could smell disinfectant on her hands and clothes. It was so strong she realized she'd have to get her jacket and skirt dry-cleaned and her shirt washed. She scrubbed her hands over and over, but the smell persisted and she wished she'd kept some decent soap in her locker.

Looking in the washbasin mirror Jane smiled at herself and swore she'd never be silly enough to lie down on a mortuary floor again. She removed the Vicks VapoRub from her handbag and, deciding to forget about the two embarrassing incidents altogether, dropped it in the bin. But she could not forget the sight of Julie Ann on the mortuary table, nor the terrible beating she had suffered.

CHAPTER FOUR

In the station yard a Leyland Sherpa 'paddy wagon' parked up. Kath climbed out of the back with a detective, escorting a young man who was clearly under arrest and, with his frizzed hairstyle and clothing, obviously a fan of Marc Bolan. He was dressed in high-heeled platform boots, skin-tight flared jeans and a Moroccan-style fur-and-embroidered sleeveless jacket. The uniform driver of the van assisted the detective with the prisoner while Kath, who had a chuffed-to-bits look on her face, went to get some paperwork from the CID office.

Jane took Bradfield his coffee and sandwich, but after the post-mortem the sight of food made her feel queasy. He barely looked up as he was reading a report. Twice she started to ask him if she could go, but he held his hand up and told her to be quiet, so she just stood and waited for him to finish reading.

Two detectives had spent the morning with Mr and Mrs Collins taking a background statement. It transpired that Julie Ann was three months from her eighteenth birthday and had not been living at home for a year and a half. During that time they had not seen or heard from her. They explained that their daughter had started to abscond from school at the age of fourteen, and that no matter how hard they tried to reason with her she still played truant. She had started to mix with an unsavoury group of boys she'd met in the West End one weekend. They discovered her smoking cannabis and constant arguments followed as she became more and more difficult to handle. She had run away numerous times since she turned fifteen and had either been brought back home by the police, or turned up dishevelled and belligerent.

Her mother described how she had discovered injection marks on Julie Ann's arm whilst she was sleeping, and how the heroin usage had made her a totally different girl. The Collinses' grief and shock were compounded when they were told by the detectives that Julie Ann had been arrested and convicted for prostitution six months ago. Mrs Collins could not understand why her daughter would do such a thing, but it was explained that it was to feed her heroin addiction. When asked if they knew Eddie Phillips and were shown a Polaroid picture of him, they responded that they had never seen or heard of him before, nor did they know anyone who owned a red Jaguar.

Bradfield looked at Jane. 'You still here? Do me a favour and get me a fresh pack of Woodbines, will you, as I'm out of cigarettes.' He placed a 50p coin on the desk.

Jane wished she'd just left the sandwich and coffee on his desk. She begrudgingly picked up the coin and set off for the newsagent's opposite. On her way downstairs she bumped into Kath, who was in a buoyant mood.

'How did it go at the post-mortem? I can smell you from here – I bet it wasn't very pleasant,' she said.

Jane told Kath how interesting it had been, but decided not to mention the dead foetus in case it was something

Bradfield didn't want people outside his team to know about yet. However, she did explain how DS Spencer Gibbs's Vicks-up-the-nose was a practical joke intended for Kath.

'The little shite! Typical – but I'll get him back somehow.'

'You got your burglar then?' Jane asked, having seen Kath in the yard.

'It was bloody brilliant, Jane. We were parked up on the estate watching from the spy hole of the obo van when the little scrote burglar turned up. He saw an old lady come out of a flat, waited till she'd gone and then knocked on her door. When he got no answer he pulled out a jemmy from under his swanky jacket and prised the door open. I was shaking with excitement and we caught him red-handed in the bedroom with notes in his hands, and more stuffed in his pockets. She kept her life savings in a shoe-box and we recovered the lot for her. I'm even listed as nicking him on the arrest sheet and I'm going to be interviewing him with a detective. There's been quite a few old people's flats turned over and I reckon he's done 'em all. You know what really makes me sick? He had a wedge this thick.' She indicated with her finger and thumb before continuing.

'He'd got hundreds on him he'd nicked ... Still, the cocky bugger won't be swaggering around like he's some rock star any more. Stealing from an old lady like that is real sicko, Jane.'

'Well done, Kath! That's got to be a bonus for you, and a big step towards becoming a detective.'

'Fingers crossed, Jane, fingers crossed,' Kath said as she hurried off to the custody room.

*

Jane got the Woodbines and was returning to Bradfield's office when Sergeant Harris came out with a face like thunder. He glared as she approached.

'You might think you can get round Bradfield by fluttering your eyelashes, but you can't fool me, Tennison. Your cards are marked, so I suggest you watch your step if you want to pass your probation and be confirmed as a WPC.'

As Harris stormed off Jane couldn't believe that he was so riled simply because she had been to a bereavement notification and a post-mortem, things she was expected to do during her probation anyway.

She knocked on Bradfield's door, and when he told her to come in she handed him his Woodbines and his change. He thanked her, inviting her to sit down.

'How do you get on with Harris as your reporting sergeant?'

'Fine, sir, he's very helpful,' she replied unconvincingly, not daring to be honest in case Bradfield and Harris were friends.

'What are you like at indexing?'

'I'm not very good, sir,' Jane said, wanting to get back to the front office before Harris boiled over.

Bradfield flicked open a file on his desk. 'Funny that. Your application says you went to the Central London Polytechnic and did business studies, and you used to help in your father's company during the holidays, so you must have some experience of indexing?'

'Yes, sir, but not in murder investigations.'

'My indexer Sally is three months pregnant. Under police regulations it means she's due to go on maternity leave, so I need a replacement.'

Jane thought about Harris's threat. She realized

Bradfield had already told him he wanted her to do some indexing, and that was why he was so annoyed with her. 'I'm honoured that you have asked me, sir, but I am still a probationer and—'

He interrupted her, patting a vast file on his desk.

'It's only temporary. Take this with you and do a few hours here and there until I find a suitable replacement. As you know, Julie Ann may have been murdered nearby and dumped, so I need to concentrate on the area close to the scene, and that means the Kingsmead Estate. There's no way a magistrate will give me a warrant to search each and every one of the bloody flats down there. I need someone to check off all the names the occupants give in the house-to-house enquiries against the electoral register, and also check with the collator for anyone with a criminal record living down there.'

'Yes, sir. Do you want me to start now?'

'What a good idea, and do the same for the residents of Edgar House on the Pembridge where the squat was,' he said with a smile.

Jane stood up to leave, and although she knew she should feel pleased with herself, she worried about Harris. But if she let Bradfield down it could jeopardize her career even further.

'One last thing – you're not the only one who thinks Harris is over the hill and a lazy waste of space, and I don't think he was too pleased I just told him as much. If he gives you any hassle let me know; for now you work for me.' He took a bite of his sandwich and pulled a face.

'Jesus Christ, this is tuna.'

'Is it? I'm sure I asked for ham.'

'Never mind. Sally will give you a run-through on indexing and what to do, but first I want you to type up what Professor Martin told us at the post-mortem.'

'Yes, sir, thank you.'

She started to go, then realized she hadn't picked up his file. He watched her as she returned to his desk to collect it. She blushed as he smiled at her, and was so flustered she almost tripped and only just managed to hold on to the file.

'I'll get on to it straight away.'

'Good, thank you.'

As she closed the door behind her, Bradfield opened his new pack of Woodbines.

Jane went to the small PCs' writing room, next to the parade room, to type up the post-mortem report. When she'd finished she took it up to DCI Bradfield to check over, but he wasn't in his office. She left the report on his desk and went down to the collator's office to talk to PC Donaldson about the residents of the Kingsmead and Pembridge estates.

'Bloody hell, are you telling me he wants you to check out every address and person on the estate? You do realize that on the Kingsmead alone there are nearly a thousand flats and over four thousand residents? I'm happy for you to look through my criminal index cards, but like I said before, you can only do it in here. If you want microfiche copies of any files then write the name and criminal-record number in my book here and I'll order them from the Yard.'

'Can I take the voters' register with me, please?'

'Go on then. I've got a spare one in my desk drawer so you can keep that one for now. If you get any suspect names run them by me and I'll see if I can find out any more about them from my various sources.'

'Do you know anything about Jaguar cars?'

'Not really, way above my wages. I'm a Ford Cortina man myself. Why?'

'DCI Bradfield said the victim of his murder investigation was last seen getting into a Jaguar and I don't know much about cars myself.'

'You could try the black rats.'

'Who?'

'Traffic police. A black rat is an animal that will eat its own family, which equates to a traffic officer having no compassion for uniform patrol and CID officers when it comes to drink driving or other vehicle offences. There isn't much they don't know about different makes of cars. Try the unit at Bow.'

On her way to the incident room Jane knocked on DCI Bradfield's door to see if he had read her report on the post-mortem, and to ask if she should now index and file it. The door was opened by a huge man in his early fifties with a ruddy, stern-looking face. He was at least eighteen stone and wore a blue pinstriped suit, light blue shirt, tie and black brogues.

'Sorry, I was looking for DCI Bradfield,' she said, wondering who he was.

'So was I, young lady, and as the Divisional Detective Chief Superintendent I expect to be addressed as "sir" or "Mr Metcalf".'

Jane stood to attention. 'Sorry, sir, I didn't realize—'

'Do you know where DCI Bradfield is?'

'He said he had a meeting with you in the uniform Chief Superintendent's office, sir.'

'Ah, I thought it was in his office. Do you need to see him urgently or can I pass a message on?'

'No, sir, I just wanted to ask if I should file the report I typed up for him on the post-mortem of Julie Ann Collins.'

The DCS held up Jane's report. 'I've just been reading it. DCI Bradfield's report is very detailed, to the point and interesting. Poor thing was pregnant and used as a punchbag, I see. Anyway I'd best get on – this report can be indexed and filed.' He handed it to Jane.

She knew it would be a bad move to say she had actually compiled as well as typed it, but didn't want to upset Bradfield or get him into trouble.

Jane had hoped to find Sally in the incident room, but there was no one about. She looked around. There was a piece of paper with 'Indexer' written on it stuck to the side of a desk and on top of it was the carousel index-card holder. Also on the desk were two trays. The one marked 'IN' was overflowing with paper while the 'OUT' one was empty.

Just as Jane was wondering where to start, there was a howl as Sally ran in crying.

'Are you OK?' Jane asked.

'Honestly, it's like working with a bunch of school kids! I mean what childish idiot thinks it's funny to do that?' Sally said, exasperated.

Jane was confused. 'Do what?'

'Somebody's put cling film under the toilet seat. I sat down to pee and the next thing I know it's bouncing back at me and soaking my knickers and skirt. It's so stupid! I just thank God I wasn't throwing up.'

Jane and the other women officers, alongside the female clerical staff at the station, were sick to death of the male officers' childish behaviour. It was only because they couldn't be bothered to walk down to the basement where the men's toilets were situated. Kath had complained on more than one occasion to Sergeant Harris, not only about the fact that the seats were constantly being left up, but also about the fact that there was always urine all over the floor because of the male officers' inability to aim properly. In retaliation, there had been another 'prank' incident where the black-plastic toilet seat had been smeared with fingerprint ink and it had taken days to wear off the backside of the poor WPC who had sat on it.

Jane calmed Sally down and the indexer looked relieved when told that DCI Bradfield wanted Jane to be a temporary stand-in for her.

'Thank God, because I have a mountain of stuff I should have got done but it's been so difficult – I just feel sick all the time. They should have got someone to help me out weeks ago. I warned Bradfield, and he's the worst of the bunch when it comes to indexing as he stuffs everything into a file, and it's all jumbled up and in no kind of order.'

Sally began explaining the indexing system and gave Jane a crash course on what to do.

'The first forty-eight hours of a murder inquiry are always the most hectic, but after a few days if they haven't charged anyone it slows down and you get a chance to catch up.'

'It's very quiet in here – are all the detectives out on enquiries?' Jane said, looking around.

'Mostly yes, but the local ones tend to use their own desks in the main CID office to write their reports. They only come in here to hand them in, or if they want you to do something for them. The briefings and meetings are all held in here, though.'

Sally went on to explain that if DCI Bradfield or DS Gibbs wanted tea or coffee she was expected to make it for them because they were senior officers, but if a detective constable asked she should tell them to get their own.

'Believe you me, they'll all try it on when you're new, but don't let them get away with it. Really you should have another indexer working with you. I've been complaining for months, but nothing has been done to help ease the load. Bradfield said he would ask the DCS for extra staff and another indexer, but when it comes to more female officers they frown and think one is more than enough.'

Jane was trying hard to take on board everything she had been told, and could hardly believe it when Sally started to put her coat on.

'Are you leaving now?'

'Yes.'

'Will you be coming back tomorrow?'

'No, love, I am officially on maternity leave and I want to go and lie down at home. They knew I was leaving today and I am not staying here another minute, especially after that bloody stupid thing in the toilets.' She started removing her personal items from drawers, picked up a small pot plant with bedraggled leaves and put everything into a paper carrier bag.

'You have to make sure you keep all the information up to date on the sheets of paper hanging on the walls.'

Sally jotted down her home number and handed it to Jane, saying that if she ran into any problems, or was confused as to what to do, she could ring her. Jane thanked Sally and wished her well.

Left alone, Jane sat trying to assimilate everything. She put the thick file from Bradfield to one side thinking she should start on the trays. She took out her notebook and flicked through to the last page where she had made a note when speaking to Donaldson about the red Jaguar. She decided that she would get that done straight away.

Jane phoned the Bow traffic office and was put through to the garage sergeant. She gave her name and number and said that she was working on the Julie Ann Collins murder investigation. She explained that the witness could only say that he'd seen the car from the rear and thought it was a fairly new red Jaguar.

'Well, I doubt it would be the E-type Jag as they are sports cars, much lower to the ground and a very different shape all round, especially at the rear. You'll probably be looking for an XJ6, and although your witness said fairly new I'd allow a bit of leeway and go back to September 1968 when the XJ6 was first manufactured, so anywhere between and including an F to L suffix index plate. Also there are different shades of red, like regency, signal ...'

Jane was making notes in her pocket book. 'OK now, the engine will be a 2.8 or 4.2 litre with six cylinders, which is the more popular, and they all have twin exhausts as well as a petrol cap on both sides of the upper boot. Have you got that?'

'Yes, almost – just a second, and er, don't they all have a small cat on the bonnet?'

The sergeant laughed. 'It's a statue of a leaping jaguar. It was never on the XJ series, though some people did fit one themselves, but anything like that on a front bonnet became illegal in 1970 because of the injuries it can cause to pedestrians.'

'What about the inside?'

'Wood and leather upholstery is standard on both models.'

'And what colour would the upholstery and carpets be on a red XJ6?' Jane asked, remembering DS Lawrence pointing out the red fibres on Julie Ann's socks at the post-mortem.

'As standard the leather interior would be magnolia or biscuit with matching light-coloured carpets.'

'Could the boot carpet be red?' Jane asked, feeling she was clutching at straws.

'All the carpet could be red if you pre-ordered the car and specifically asked for it to be customized.'

Jane felt a buzz of excitement and wondered if the fibres came from the red Jaguar the victim was last seen getting into. She thanked the garage sergeant for being so helpful and informative and was about to put the phone down.

'Hang on, I haven't finished. There's also the possibility it was an XJ12, with a 5.2 litre engine, but that only came out in July last year. Same shape as the XJ6 except it has two small front grilles either side of the large one.'

Jane licked the tip of her pencil as she realized just what he had said.

'So we could be looking at thousands of Jaguars across the country?' she asked with trepidation.

'Let's have a look in my production book here ... roughly to date the 2.8 is around nineteen thousand vehicles, 4.2 fifty-nine thousand and the XJ12 just short of three thousand, so that's—'

She gasped. 'Eighty-one thousand Jags ... bloody hell ... sorry, Sergeant, I didn't mean to swear.'

'It's a lot, but you can narrow down your search and start with red and variant-coloured cars registered from '68 onwards.'

'Could you list those for me?'

'No way, I can't help you with that. But the manufacturers should be able to, and can give you the registration details so you can track them to the current and any previous owners. Anyway, I need to go as there's been a fatal accident down by the Blackwall Tunnel. Good luck with your search,' he said, and ended the call.

Jane realized the enormity of the task facing Bradfield, even assuming the Jaguar was red. She looked in the Yellow Pages for the nearest Jaguar sales garage. She called them, giving her details to the receptionist and requesting brochures for the XJ6 series models and the XJ12. The receptionist said she'd stick them in the post on her way home.

Jane was about to type up her notes on the cars when she remembered what Sally had said about keeping the information sheets up to date. She used a black marker pen to put up some brief details about the post-mortem and Professor Martin's conclusions.

'Hello, darlin'.' The male voice startled her and she dropped the pen.

She bent down to pick it up and in doing so suddenly felt her backside being squeezed. She turned round sharply in anger.

'You shouldn't do that,' she said defensively.

'Do what, darlin' ... what did I do?'

'You put your hand on my bottom – it's unacceptable.'

'Come on, sweetheart, I'm just showing my admiration for a very neat little arse.'

The officer who had touched her was wearing a black-leather jacket, flared trousers, white shirt with the top button undone and a wide, garish kipper tie. His colleague was similarly dressed but wearing a black roll-neck sweater. Both men were in their early thirties and had side-burns and collar-length hair.

'What do you want?' Jane asked nervously.

'Well, apart from you, sweetheart, we're after DCI

Bradfield. We're from the Sweeney and need to tip him the wink on something.'

Jane realized they were flying squad officers and explained that the DCI was at a meeting with the DCS and said she could pass on any information to him. The two detectives looked at each other as if she couldn't be privy to what they knew.

'Don't worry, as his indexer I'm the soul of discretion,' she said sarcastically.

The one who had touched her shrugged his shoulders. 'Well, we're pretty busy so you'll have to do. Word has it you're trying to trace a red Jag in connection with a murder.'

'Yes, that's right.'

'We had an armed robbery on Saturday just gone at a Yid jeweller's house up the road in Stamford Hill.'

The detective explained that the suspects were seen to make off in a red Jag and a witness got a part registration. The suspect vehicle had since been recovered in Chatsworth Road, Hackney on Monday afternoon. Jane knew this was not too far from either the Kingsmead or the Pembridge Estate and realized the importance of the information.

'Where's the car now?' she asked.

'We had it taken into the lab at Lambeth. Anyway, the owner is Italian and said he didn't even know the car was stolen until we knocked on his door. Said he'd been ill in bed for a few days and hadn't even noticed it was nicked off the driveway.'

'You think he was involved in the robbery and dumped the car?'

'Ten out of ten, Inspector Clouseau . . . and maybe even involved in your murder. We nicked him and turned over his drum but found nothing from the Yid shop.'

Jane was irritated by his Clouseau remark, and confused by his jargon. 'Excuse me, but a Yid and a drum?'

'You're fairly new Old Bill, ain't ya? A Yid's a Jewish person, a drum's a house and we searched it. The Eyetie's on an ID parade 11 a.m. tomorrow morning at Stoke Newington nick, so if Bradfield has any witness he wants to eyeball the line-up then bring 'em over.'

She scribbled the information down as fast as she could. 'I'll make sure he gets these details.'

Jane watched as the two flying squad officers walked away. The one who'd touched her had a strange gait, a sort of slow swagger, his hands cutting across the front of his body.

Kath came into the room just as they neared the door.

The detective in the kipper tie stopped and stood in the doorway. 'Hello, Kath, you're looking as lovely as ever. You doing anything tonight ...?'

Kath brushed him aside. 'Piss off, Duke,' she said and the two detectives laughed as they went.

Kath sat down opposite Jane. 'Bloody flying squad, they think they're movie stars. The gobby one's called Duke because he swaggers around like the actor John Wayne. He used to work here before he went on the flying squad. You gotta watch him as he's got WHT.'

Jane smiled, realizing the significance of his walk for his nickname, and asked Kath what illness WHT was.

'Wandering-hand trouble, very touchy-feely, and if he tries anything on with you, confront him.'

'I already have. He squeezed my backside and I told him it was unacceptable behaviour.'

'Be firmer next time – they think they can get away with anything so if he tries it again tell him you'll report him.'

'Right, I will.'

'And at the same time give his wandering hands a good swipe. There's a few times I'd have liked to have slapped his face, I can tell you.'

'How's it going with your burglar?'

'Brilliant. We searched his house and he had a big wedge of cash stashed in a tin box under his bed. He admitted it was stolen from various OAPs' flats on different estates. Looks like he's going to cough to a good few burglaries when we interview him, and the detective working with me reckons Bradfield will be well impressed.'

Jane congratulated Kath on her good work and told her how Bradfield had asked her to do some indexing for him.

'You're kidding me! That poor Sally was run off her pregnant feet – they should have replaced her weeks ago. I'd hate to be doing Bradfield's indexing because he's a lazy sod when it comes to paperwork. Listen, I've already heard Sergeant Harris moaning about it downstairs and that's why I came to see how you're getting on.'

As they spoke DCI Bradfield walked into the room and glared at Jane. 'Why did you give the post-mortem report to DCS Metcalf before I read it?'

'I didn't, sir, I left it on your desk and he found it when he was looking for you.'

'The DCS likes to snoop about, so in future put stuff for me in a sealed envelope with my name on it. Get me a coffee and a *ham*, not tuna or egg, sandwich,' he said sternly and turned to Kath.

'I've been hearing about your successful arrest and the recovery of a large sum of money, WPC Morgan. Good work. Tell me, what uniform shift are you on at the moment?'

Kath explained that she worked alongside Jane and was also on late shift, but had booked a few days' leave as from tomorrow to visit her sister in Brighton.

'Listen, Kath, I could do with an extra pair of hands helping on this investigation as I'm short-staffed.'

'OK, guv, I'll cancel my leave, but I'll need to sort it with Sergeant Harris first.'

'Leave him to me – you're on board as from tomorrow.' He turned to leave the room.

Jane raised her hand. 'I've been making some enquiries about Jaguar cars, sir, and I—'

'Later, Tennison, I'm busy – remember I don't want tuna or egg, just straight ham and a black coffee.'

Tired out, Jane returned to Bradfield's office with a coffee and sandwich. The room was filled with clouds of smoke and the smell of the pungent Woodbine cigarettes he favoured. He pulled at his tie to loosen his collar, and handed her back the post-mortem report, telling her to index and file it. She felt as if she was invisible to him and thought he might have at least thanked her or complimented her on the report, like the DCS had done. He also wanted her to write up on the team noticeboard that an office meeting would be held tomorrow morning at ten o'clock, and everyone was to be present without fail. One of his detectives had been back to the Homerton Hospital's Drug Dependency Unit and made enquiries, speaking to a doctor, nurses and some of the drug-addict patients. Although Julie Ann Collins was known to them no one had seen her for two weeks and, even more surprisingly, nobody knew she was pregnant. The doctor assigned to her case was not forthcoming, stating that patient confidentiality was of the utmost importance when treating drug addicts. The detective had, however, spoken briefly with a social worker at the hospital, a large, mixed-race woman called Anjali O'Duncie, who said she had known Julie Ann well, and Eddie. Bradfield said O'Duncie was being brought into the station at 6.15 p.m., having agreed to be interviewed about the last time she saw Julie Ann.

'I want you to be present when I interview her. You need to take notes of what O'Duncie has to say and then type them up.'

She nodded and he gave an open-handed gesture.

'Have you got all that?'

'Yes, sir.'

'What are you waiting for? Go on, hop it.'

Jane went back to the incident room and slumped onto a chair. She was near to tears and bit her lip. Kath put an arm round her. 'You all right, darlin'?'

'I am so exhausted, Kath, I've been working flat out. Why do I get the feeling I'm just being used?'

'Cheer up, I'll be "on board" as from tomorrow, so I can help you,' Kath said. She understood how Jane was feeling as she'd been through it herself, though she'd been much more savvy than Jane when she'd first joined.

'I've just got so much to do, and he keeps on giving me more things. It's typing up one report after another and then all the indexing that Sally didn't do.'

'Take it easy, luv. At least Bradfield's trusting you to sit in with a possible witness, so although he may not say it something must have impressed him.'

'Well, I hope you're right because I'd rather be in the front office covering the counter and putting up with Harris than being the CID's general dogsbody.'

Kath cocked her head to one side. She gently hooked a stray strand of Jane's hair away from her face.

'No you wouldn't. But just stay focused, do what you can, and if there's a problem you have to learn how to handle it. What you mustn't do is get tearful and act all stressed out. Don't give 'em any ammunition. If you feel like havin' a bit of a meltdown do it out of sight in the ladies' locker room. You'll see a few dents on the front of the roller towel – that's where I've punched the hell out of it when I've been really pissed off. Now, you go and wash your face and then get ready to interview this woman – and take it from me, you're doing just great.'

'Thanks, Kath,' Jane said and left the room.

In the locker room she washed her hands and splashed cold water over her face. She crossed to the roller towel and dragged it down to pat herself dry. She couldn't help but smile as she saw the dents, and then after a moment stepped back and threw a punch. It hurt like hell and she sucked her knuckles but she felt a great deal better.

CHAPTER FIVE

An overweight woman in her late thirties was waiting at the front counter. She wore a flowing multicoloured hippie dress, bangles on each wrist and big gold looped earrings. Her dark hair was braided into long dreadlocks and a headband encircled her forehead.

'Anjali O'Duncie?' Jane asked and the woman, who appeared anxious and nervous, nodded. Jane introduced herself and took Anjali into the small public interview room and fetched her a glass of water.

Jane thought it best not to speak about Julie Ann without Bradfield being present, and in an effort to make pleasant conversation asked Anjali how she was.

She shook her head and let out a big sigh. 'Not been great recently, officer. I ended up having an operation in the very hospital I work in.'

'Oh, I'm sorry to hear that.'

'I was in terrible discomfort before they discovered it was my appendix, and they only just caught it in time. It were about to burst and could have killed me. The pain was shocking! I was in terrible agony, worse than childbirth.'

'Well, I'm glad to see you're better now,' Jane said.

'That's not the half of it ... I was recovering fine until

the scar became infected and I was given these antibiotics which I then had an allergic reaction to. I came out in the worst rash you've ever seen – looked like a Dalmatian but with red spots and dark skin.'

'I'll go and see where DCI Bradfield is,' Jane said and stood up.

Anjali put her hand on Jane's arm so she sat back down. 'They were penicillin, you see, awful … I was in a terrible state, kept me in for another two weeks, agony, it was, all that time in hospital.'

Jane wished she'd never started the conversation as Anjali couldn't stop talking, going into great detail about her bad reaction, and repeating herself. Jane felt forced to listen without interruption simply because she couldn't get a word in edgeways. Something struck Jane as rather strange – if O'Duncie was in hospital with appendicitis she'd have been on a different ward and not in the Drug Dependency Unit with Julie Ann.

'Were you on the same ward as Julie Ann?' Jane asked curiously.

Anjali looked at Jane as if she was stupid. 'You must be jokin', of course I wasn't. I didn't have a drug problem. I'm no junkie, it was me damn appendix. I just told you, I had it taken out last year, and I've been back at work nearly three months now.'

'Right, I see, sorry, I misunderstood you.'

'Obviously I knew her, otherwise I wouldn't be here, would I? Poor thing had been in and out of our clinic for weeks and I spent quite a bit of time counselling her.'

'That must be hard work with drug addicts.'

'I'm not a doctor or anything medically trained – I work for the clinic on a sort of social level. I mean we obviously have professionals dealing with medication as I'm not

81

trained to do that either, but we have an area where they can have a cup of tea and biscuits.'

Jane could sense something wasn't quite right. 'What does your job entail exactly?'

'I look after the area, keep it tidy, counsel the addicts with a nice chat, a hot drink and biscuits.'

Gradually Jane deduced that Anjali O'Duncie was basically a cleaner cum tea lady who had no training whatsoever in addict rehabilitation or counselling. It transpired she was paid a small hourly wage and would be there on a daily basis, but liked to sit and talk to some of the kids as it made her feel she was doing some good.

'So how well did you know Julie Ann?'

'I suppose I knew her quite well. I recognized her from the picture the detective had when he come to the hospital the second time and that's why I said I'd come in here.

'Terrible thing to have happened to her, but drug addicts do live dangerous lives.'

'Was Julie Ann on methadone?'

'Yes, but I don't handle any drugs meself. It's all monitored and prescribed by the doctors. Some of the addicts are very strung-out when they come in and need the methadone as a substitute for heroin to calm down.'

'Can I get you another glass of water, cup of tea?' Jane asked.

'A tea would be nice, two sugars, but I have an allergy to cow's milk, brings me out—'

'In a red rash.' Jane smiled.

'That's right – do you get it as well?'

Jane shook her head.

She was making her way upstairs to the canteen when she came across Bradfield on the stairs. He stopped and ran his hand through his curly red hair making it stand up on end as he asked if O'Duncie had turned up.

'You might find her a bit trying.'

He frowned. 'Why, have you been questioning her?'

'I haven't, sir, but she doesn't stop talking, although I did try to stop her. I had her own personal medical history before she moved on to Julie Ann.' Jane told him everything O'Duncie had said so far.

'Well, looks like I won't be long with her.'

'I don't think she works in any actual medical or counselling capacity at the hospital. I'd say she was just a cleaner or a tea lady.'

'So it looks like she's trying to big herself up and waste our time.'

'Yes, could be. Would you like a coffee?'

'Nope, I'll go and talk to her.'

Jane returned to the interview room with a cup of sugared black tea. O'Duncie was leaning on the table and repeating her appendix experience to Bradfield who was sitting opposite. He had a look of impatience on his face and gestured for Jane to sit down.

She passed the tea to O'Duncie who peered into the cup, smiled and made a slurping sound as she took a big sip.

'Ahhh, that's better. Dairy products play havoc with my stomach and give me diarrhoea, but this is just how I like it.'

Jane sat to one side as he tapped his open notebook.

'Julie Ann was missing for two weeks ...'

'I know, but I didn't see her at the Drug Dependency Unit and she didn't turn up for appointments so I just thought she'd gone off the rails or was going to another hospital elsewhere. They do that, you know, get signed up at different hospitals in different names to get more methadone and just abuse the system. We try and monitor it, well, not me exactly, but one of the staff will try to make contact with other hospital drug units.'

'Did she ever mention she was pregnant?' Bradfield asked quietly.

'Oh, I didn't know that. What did she have, a boy or a girl?'

Jane felt Bradfield's impatience and coughed as O'Duncie sat back in her chair.

'She didn't. The foetus was only twelve to fourteen weeks and died with Julie Ann when she was murdered.'

O'Duncie looked horrified and close to tears. 'I don't know what to say ... I really can't believe it, I feel as ...'

He glanced at her and lifted his hands to say he understood she was shocked and didn't have to explain her emotions.

'Miss O'Duncie, Julie Ann Collins was strangled, but she also suffered a severe beating a few days before her body was found. Can you recall anyone who visited, or came to the hospital with her, that you think we should know about?'

'Did you say Collins? I thought her name was Maynard.'

'She fed her drug habit through prostitution so she used a false name.'

'That's quite common, you know, Officer Bradfield. Anyways there was a lad called Eddie, her boyfriend, I think. They were often together, now let me think, what was his surname ...?'

'Phillips?' Bradfield asked, getting impatient.

'Yes, that's him – thin, weedy little chap with acne. I think he stays with his grandmother, when he's not stoned or injecting, that is. Him and Julie Ann were at the clinic together as in-patients originally. In fact that's probably how they met, and then they would come together on day visits. I'd have a cup of tea and chat with them as we like to keep a sort of open house and I try and be helpful, you know, by talking to them. But I found it hard when I was feelin' so ill meself with a terrible agonizing pain down me right side, which I knew wasn't menstrual.'

Bradfield closed his notebook and glanced at Jane. It was obviously going nowhere, and he'd had enough of listening to O'Duncie prattle on.

'Thanks for coming in.'

'I didn't have much option, did I, as the police officers told me I had to come in as I wasn't around when they first came to the clinic, I was having terrible pains again and—'

Bradfield glanced at Jane and interrupted her. 'WPC Tennison will take your full details for our records.' He left the room.

Jane started to take down Anjali O'Duncie's details and home address. She slurped the rest of her tea before pushing the cup away. 'I regret telling her off now. It was the last time I saw her, but she was naughty.'

Jane looked at her. 'What was naughty?'

'I caught her in one of the doctors' offices. Eddie was standing outside keeping lookout and I thought maybe she was after methadone, but she was using the phone. The door was open and I heard her speaking to someone, having a big row, shouting and swearing.'

'What time was this?'

'I remember I was about to go home, so it would have been three o'clock, or maybe around four thirtyish. I mean, like tonight, I was there until I come in here.'

'Was this recent? Can you recall what day it was?'

'Erm, well, let me think …' She paused for a few seconds. 'At least two weeks before they found her murdered. I remember it because it was against the rules to be in that office, even I'm not allowed to use the doctors' phones. They got a call box in reception but it's always out of order.'

'Do you remember who she was phoning?'

'No, I don't know who it was.'

'Think hard, try and remember – every little detail is important.'

There was a silence as O'Duncie closed her eyes and touched her forehead with her hand.

'I'm sure I heard her asking for money. I think she said the name Paddy but whoever it was she swore at them and when she saw me she hung up. I told her she wasn't allowed to use the doctors' offices and she said sorry and just walked out.'

'Did you report it to anyone at the hospital?'

'No, I didn't see any need to.'

Jane hurried Miss O'Duncie out and then went in search of Bradfield. He was in his office with DS Spencer Gibbs and four other detectives, all playing cards and chain-smoking whilst drinking whisky and beer.

'What do you want, Tennison? Can't you see we're busy?' DS Gibbs said, a cigarette between his lips as he poured Bradfield a stiff Scotch.

'Sir, just after you left O'Duncie recalled Julie Ann making a phone call in a doctor's office to someone while Eddie Phillips was keeping watch outside in the corridor.'

'What?'

'It was two weeks ago. She was a bit unsure but she thought she heard her say the name Paddy and something about money. Apparently she was very angry and was swearing and shouting.'

He inhaled deeply, sipped his whisky, and let the smoke drift from his nose.

'Is O'Duncie still here?'

'No, sir, I let her go.'

'Well, that's no use to me right now, is it? Type up a report and leave it in an envelope for me and I'll deal with it tomorrow morning.'

'I'm off duty in an hour, sir, but if you need me to visit the drug clinic this evening to check their phone records I can ...'

He glared at her. 'What? If I need you? What the fuck are you inferring, if I need you? Jesus Christ, I've had it up to here today and I'm trying to relax now, so go home ... hop it.'

Having typed up the O'Duncie interview report Jane collected her belongings from the incident room and went to the ladies' locker room. There was now a printed notice: 'LADIES ONLY – NO MEN ALLOWED!' on the door. Having washed her hands she was about to dry them when she noticed a new dent in the metal roller towel. She smiled realizing someone must have upset Kath. She suddenly heard Bradfield's voice in the corridor outside.

'Listen, Spence, I want that screwball junkie Eddie Phillips brought back in and given a rough time. He must know something about that phone call, or at least who it was made to. Get the night shift out there looking for him.'

'If that's what you want. Wearing out the carpet though, isn't he?' Gibbs said.

Jane dried her hands, still listening, easing down the roller towel.

'Get someone down to that hospital tonight and see if

they keep phone records for calls made. I'm interested in the day she was last seen and three days prior. O'Duncie's a bit dim, and I doubt she can tell the bloody time, so I want every call checked from between 1 to 6 p.m. for that period.'

'No problem, guv, and it shouldn't be difficult to link a number to this Paddy guy ... if he's not ex-directory, that is.'

'I feel like I'm losing the plot, Spence, and I'm totally knackered. That young Tennison is as sharp as a tack, maybe too sharp for her own good.'

'Me and the lads are going for a few pints down the Warburton Arms and then for a curry in Brick Lane. Why don't you join us?'

'I might take you up on that.'

'Have you seen this?'

'What?'

Gibbs pointed to the notice on the locker-room door. 'Any money it's Kath Morgan having a moan – "LADIES ONLY" I'm taking that down ... Better still, I'm gonna take a crap in there and not flush it.'

Bradfield laughed. 'Come on, let's finish the card game and get down to the pub.'

Jane sighed with relief as she heard them leave. She waited a few more moments before she eased the door open to make sure the coast was clear.

CHAPTER SIX

Jane was in work early the next morning, in order to try and clear the investigation 'IN' tray before the office meeting at 10 a.m. She checked her own tray in the PCs' writing room and was surprised to see the Jaguar brochures there. There was a note saying that the sales garage receptionist had dropped them off on her way home, rather than posting them. Jane left the brochures, along with the reports about the Jaguar cars and the flying squad information, on DCI Bradfield's desk and managed to get a big pile of indexing done before he walked in at eight thirty.

'Good morning, sir,' she said politely.

'No, Tennison, it's not a good morning,' he replied gruffly.

His grey suit was badly creased, his Windsor-knot tie loose and top shirt button undone. He had a face like thunder, and it was obvious he was very hungover from the previous evening's gambling and drinking session.

'Can I help you with anything?' Jane asked.

'Not unless you can conjure up more staff or know where Eddie Phillips is!' he snapped.

'I could make some enquiries about Phillips with—'

Jane was about to say the collator but was cut off by Bradfield.

'No, you can get a "Wanted" telex circulated Met-wide with his details and description. Also, put it out over the local radio to all the uniform patrol officers. There's a bottle of Scotch up for whoever finds and nicks him first – two bottles if it's before midday.'

Jane selected Eddie's index card from the carousel and started to copy his details down onto a message pad when she was interrupted by Bradfield handing her a £1 note. He said he'd be in his office with DS Gibbs and they both wanted coffee and a bacon sandwich.

Jane wasn't happy about being used as a personal waitress, but she'd already been warned by Kath that when a senior officer told you to do something you did as asked or your cards were marked. First she went to the control room and sent out the telex and radio message regarding Eddie Phillips. Next Jane got the bacon sandwiches and coffees, then with a forced smile took them into Bradfield's office. Gibbs was also hungover and stank of stale booze. For once his manic energy had been stifled – he wasn't even tapping on the table, playing drums as he usually liked to do.

Once back in the incident room Jane continued with the indexing. The eight detectives on the squad gradually came in to book on before wandering off for some breakfast. Most of them were polite, asked who she was and introduced themselves, but there were two or three who seemed to turn their noses up at her and didn't have the courtesy to even say good morning. One of them even had the cheek to ask her to get him a cup of tea, but she fibbed and told him DCI Bradfield had said that she wasn't to be the tea lady for junior officers. It had the desired result as the detective grunted and walked off without a word. She was learning fast.

Two detectives were in the office when Kath came in with a face like thunder.

'Which one of you lot thought it would be amusing to draw on my notice?' she bellowed and waved the sign from the ladies' locker room above her head.

Jane could see a drawing of testicles and a large penis, the head of which had a smiley face on it.

'If it happens again then I will be taking fucking finger-prints. Yours are all on file and I'll easily find the culprit, so leave my notices alone.'

The two detectives laughed and said it was nothing to do with them.

'Just like cling film on the toilet bowl, I suppose? Use your own bloody loo, or next time I'll have your tackle hanging from the door.'

'Ouch,' they both said as they left for the canteen.

Although Jane agreed with Kath, and thought it was a very childish prank, she had to force herself not to giggle. She suspected the drawing was DS Gibbs's work, having heard him chatting to Bradfield outside the locker room the previous evening, but she kept quiet.

'Good for you, Kath.'

'Bloody detectives are supposed to be experienced and mature, but they behave more like a bunch of kids. They even come on duty and go straight off to the canteen for breakfast.'

'I know – in uniform we don't even get a cuppa after parade because we have to go straight out on patrol.'

Kath shook her head and having calmed herself down said she'd help Jane with the indexing before the meeting.

*

The team gathered in the small office, some sitting on chairs whilst others perched on the edge of desks. When DCI Bradfield entered with DS Gibbs everyone stood up and the DCI motioned with his hands for them to sit down. He pointed in the direction of Kath and Jane.

'I'm sure most of you already know WPC Morgan. She'll be working with us for a few days and—'

A detective interjected. 'If you can't see Kath, you'll always be able to hear her coming, guv.' He then made the sound of a foghorn which caused ripples of laughter round the room. Kath refrained from responding and simply smiled.

Bradfield continued, 'And this is WPC Tennison, who's filling in for Sally for a bit whilst she's on maternity leave.'

'How's the father feel about that?' a detective asked.

'How should I know? I've never met Sally's husband,' Bradfield remarked irritably.

'I didn't mean Sally's old man, guv … I meant DC Ashby.'

There was more laughter round the room and Jane wasn't sure if Ashby's face was red with anger or embarrassment at the remark. DS Gibbs told them all to shut up and behave. Kath leant over to Jane and whispered that everyone thought DC Ashby was having an affair with Sally as they had once been caught coming out of the ladies' locker room together on a night shift.

Bradfield proceeded by asking what the hell had gone wrong with the re-arrest of Eddie Phillips. Jane now realized why he had been so mad when he came in that morning. DC Ashby explained that Eddie wasn't at the squat or his grandmother, Nancy Phillips' flat when nightshift officers turned up there at midnight. Nor was he there at 6 a.m. when Ashby and a colleague visited the flat. She was a tough lady with iron-grey hair who told them to fuck off and stop harassing her and her grandson. Then, whilst searching the place, they had taken further abuse about causing her angina to flare up.

Bradfield took a deep breath and exhaled loudly. 'Bloody marvellous, so it looks like the lying little shit has done a runner.'

The office door opened and DS Paul Lawrence walked in. He apologized for being late and explained that he'd been busy discussing some forensic results with the scientist and they had both worked in the lab until after midnight on the case. He handed Bradfield an envelope and said it contained photographs of the scene and post-mortem.

'Has anyone checked Homerton Hospital drug unit for Phillips?' DS Gibbs asked.

Everyone looked at each other blankly until a detective spoke up and said that he went there yesterday evening to make enquiries about the phone call Anjali O'Duncie allegedly heard Julie Ann make, but no one had mentioned anything about Eddie returning to the hospital.

'Sir, if Eddie overdosed he could be in a hospital casualty unit or on a normal ward being treated,' Jane commented.

The room went quiet and she felt as if everyone was staring at her because she had had the audacity to say something. She noticed Bradfield nod his head slightly as he looked at her. However, he said nothing and let Gibbs continue.

'Right, Tennison, after the meeting phone the Homerton. If Phillips isn't there then ring round every casualty hospital in London if you have to.'

Jane nodded to Gibbs and saw Kath give her a sly wink and thumbs-up for her suggestion.

Bradfield returned to the officer who had been making enquiries at the Homerton about the phone call.

'Is there any good news on that front?'

'Well, guv, it's sort of yes and no.'

He explained that on the last day Julie Ann had been seen at the clinic a telephone switchboard operator recalled a lady on the internal line saying she was a nurse and needed to contact the parents of a patient. The nurse then asked for a directory enquiry to be made and the operator thought she sounded rather distressed.

'You get the details, name, address, etc?' Bradfield asked.

'The hospital operator did get a number and gave it to the woman, but she didn't keep a record and can't remember any details about it. Also the hospital don't list every call from every phone.'

'One step forward, two back,' Bradfield remarked, shaking his head in disappointment.

'Maybe not. Whoever asked for the number would probably have written it down. If the doctor had a notepad on his desk the unknown lady, who could have been Julie Ann, may have written the number and address down,' DS Lawrence suggested.

'But she would have torn the details off the pad,' Gibbs remarked.

'Yes, but when you write on something like a notepad the pressure of the pen, or pencil, carries through to the pages underneath the top one. We can light the pages below the original document from different angles, use some multiple-exposure photography and hopefully bring up the indented writing left behind.'

'But it was two weeks ago,' Gibbs said, shaking his head.

'So what? For one we don't know how many pages of the pad have been used since, it could be none if the doctor's been away, and besides, nothing ventured nothing gained,' Lawrence retorted.

Bradfield sighed. 'Ashby, get down to the Homerton now and ask O'Duncie to show you the doctor's room Julie Ann used to make the call. If he's got a notepad take it up to the lab pronto.'

Ashby grabbed his jacket and hurried out the door.

'Any more gems of wisdom for us, DS Lawrence?' Bradfield asked.

'Maybe, just depends how you look at it. Regarding the child Julie Ann was carrying, the foetus was too young to do any reliable blood grouping.'

'Terrific – we got another dead end,' Gibbs said.

'No, we tested her knickers with benzamine, made a slide and examined it with haematoxylin ...'

'You're beginning to sound like Prof Martin – give it to us straight and simple, please,' Bradfield instructed him.

'We found semen and a blood smear on her knickers, and on the vaginal and anal swabs. A person's ABO blood group can be detected in body fluids, and in this case the blood was all from the same group, but a different one to Julie Ann's blood group. The scientist obtained Pep A 2 from the stains which is common in Race Code 3 individuals and not found in other races ...'

'For Chrissake, what have we got?' Bradfield shouted.

'She'd had anal sex with a black man, but of course it may not have been with consent. In forcing himself on her he could have torn and bled from the small piece of skin that joins the foreskin to the penis, which is called the frenulum. Also the semen could have come from sex some hours before she was murdered, or from the suspect at the scene before he killed her.'

'So either way our killer could be the black geezer who left the blood and semen in her?' Bradfield asked.

DS Lawrence nodded and added that the question of exactly where Julie Ann was murdered was still unanswered. Another detective pointed to his groin and asked if they should ask any suspects if they had, figuratively speaking, 'a sore head' and get them to drop their trousers for an inspection.

Everyone laughed loudly, even Jane and Kath.

After a brief pause Bradfield flicked through his notes.

'We got any update concerning the red fibres on Julie Ann's socks, Paul?'

'Well, we got a few off her hot pants and blouse as well, but the majority were on her socks and inside her boots. The scientists at the lab were of the opinion they were probably from some sort of cheap carpet, but couldn't give the exact origin.'

DS Gibbs raised his hand. 'Just a thought, but Jaguar cars are fitted with carpets, right? Would they be similar?'

Lawrence shrugged his shoulders. 'Not sure, never dealt with a body in an XJ, or been in one for a ride.'

Bradfield rubbed his chin. 'We need to start doing a bit more to trace this red Jag Eddie Phillips saw Julie Ann getting into. The punter could have had sex with her in the car, then strangled and dumped her.'

'Are the seats the same sort of fabric as the carpets in a Jag?' Detective Edwards asked.

'I think leather is standard, but she could have had sex in the back of the car, taken her clothes off and they came in contact with the carpet,' Lawrence replied.

Jane realized that Bradfield hadn't as yet read the

reports about the Jaguar cars she'd left on his desk. She held her hand up but Bradfield ignored her. Kath could see something was troubling Jane.

'What's up?' she whispered and Jane told her he couldn't have read the reports yet and the flying squad ID parade was at 11 a.m.

'Don't worry about that – Eddie Phillips didn't see the driver,' Kath replied.

'He'll be mad with me if I don't say anything,' Jane said anxiously.

Kath stuck her hand in the air. 'Excuse me, sir, but WPC Tennison has made some enquiries about Jaguar cars and I totally forgot to tell you about a red Jag the flying squad recovered yesterday.'

There was tutting and head-shaking from the male officers in the room, and one even commented that 'plonks', a male derogatory term for WPCs, were bloody useless.

'Kath pointed me in the right direction for the Jag enquiries,' Jane said, trying to ease the situation.

'Make that your first and last mistake on my squad, Morgan, or you'll be directing traffic for the rest of your career. Tell me about the flying squad first,' Bradfield snapped.

Kath recalled as much as she could from what Jane had told her the previous day.

Jane added that the garage sergeant had told her that roughly eighty-one thousand Jags had been manufactured since 1968.

'Jesus Christ, eighty-one thousand,' DS Gibbs exclaimed and there were looks of disbelief round the room.

Jane pointed out that the search could be narrowed down if they started with red and variant-coloured cars registered from 1968 in London, and those that were specially ordered with red carpets. She also mentioned that she had contacted a Jaguar dealer for brochures on the two models concerned. Bradfield told her to get on to the manufacturers and make enquiries after the meeting.

DS Lawrence spoke next. 'You need to consider the Daimler as well.'

'Why? We're looking for a Jag,' Gibbs said, exasperated.

'Jaguar own the Daimler brand and the car is essentially, in size and shape, the same as the Jag, but more luxurious. A lot of people mistake one for the other and the only differences, as far as I'm aware, are the shape of the front grille and the badge.'

Bradfield remarked that with the Daimler now being a possibility it could mean another few thousand vehicles and owners to try and trace. He told Kath to help Tennison regarding the car enquiries and to get some Daimler brochures as well.

'That little junkie, Phillips, could be lying but either way he needs to be found asap and leant on. I want more detail about the car he saw Julie Ann getting in. We can show him the brochures and take him out on the streets to point out a bloody car that looks the same. If he was the lookout when Julie Ann made the phone call then there's a good chance he knows who this "Paddy" is.'

'Paddy doesn't sound like a black person's name,' a detective remarked.

'Neither does Anjali O'Duncie,' Bradfield fired back.

'Could Julie Ann have said something else that sounds similar to Paddy?' Gibbs suggested.

'For Chrissake, cut all this crap with names. Bloody well get out there and find Eddie – that's the only way we'll trace who she called,' Bradfield shouted, and started to delegate tasks to his team.

He told one of them to go over to Stoke Newington and speak with the flying squad detectives about the Jag they had recovered, and the Italian who had been arrested for robbery. He also wanted the house-to-house enquiries extended to all the blocks of flats on the Pembridge Estate and told Gibbs to organize it.

DS Lawrence asked if there was anything else DCI Bradfield needed him for as he'd like to get back to the lab and have a look at the red XJ6 that the Sweeney lads had sent up, to see if the carpet fibres were a match.

Bradfield concluded the meeting and returned to his office to ring George Collins, the victim's father, and ask him to come to the station as there were a couple of developments regarding the investigation that he needed to discuss in private with him.

While Bradfield was still on the phone to Mr Collins, Jane took him his coffee. She could see that he had now opened the envelope containing her typed reports and had them laid out in front of him. She was about to turn and leave when he held his hand up, palm facing her, to indicate that she was to stay put. A few seconds later he ended the call with Mr Collins.

'Good work with the Jaguar enquiries, but I would prefer to be told about this sort of information prior to an office meeting.'

'Sorry, sir, I thought you wanted me to leave the reports in an envelope for you.'

'As you can see I am very busy and have a pile of paperwork, case files and envelopes on my desk. If something is important I need you to communicate it to me verbally as well.'

'Yes, sir,' Jane said, feeling he was blaming her for not reading the reports himself. She turned to leave.

'I haven't finished,' he said, and held up the report concerning the flying squad arrest of the Italian and the recovery of the Jag. 'If WPC Morgan forgot to relay this information to me, why did you type up the report?'

Jane paused, unsure how best to answer his question, but Bradfield didn't wait for an answer and she felt her stomach churn in anticipation of an angry outburst from him.

'As I thought ... you both lied. However, loyalty to your colleagues is what the CID is all about, but don't let it happen again. Now go and get on with your work.'

'Yes, sir, thank you.'

'One more thing, come here.'

She hesitated and edged closer to his desk. He sniffed, leaning further towards her.

'You smell of Dettol.'

'I'm sorry, sir, I still haven't got my jacket and skirt dry-cleaned from when I was on the floor at the mortuary and—'

'All right, all right – go on, get back to work.'

Jane went to the incident room and told Kath what Bradfield had just said to her about them covering for each other. They both smiled cheekily, realizing they had been lucky to get away with it. Kath remarked that maybe he had a lighter side to him, and Jane replied that next time it was just best they told the truth and took the flak for their mistakes.

As they sat going over what they had to do, and who would do what, Sergeant Harris walked in with a smirk of satisfaction on his face. He announced that two of his uniform officers had been doing the murder squad's job for them while they sat and drank coffee. Kath asked what he meant and Harris replied that Eddie Phillips had been seen wandering aimlessly on the Pembridge Estate, and having been arrested by his officers was now in a cell downstairs.

Kath suggested that Jane go and give Bradfield the good news, but she hesitated.

'What's up?'

'Do I smell of Dettol?'

'Yeah, I noticed it, why?'

'I must be getting used to it – my jacket and skirt need dry-cleaning.'

Kath went to her bag, took out a perfume spray, and before Jane could refuse gave her a few squirts. It was an expensive perfume she always wore herself.

'There you go. It's called Ambush, Goddess of Fragrance.'

Jane was about to go to Bradfield's office when DS Gibbs walked in and sniffed.

'Bloody hell, smells like somebody shat in a pine forest in here.'

'Piss off,' Kath mumbled under her breath.

'What did you say, Morgan?' Gibbs said with a glare, wondering if she was being insubordinate.

'It's off.'

'What's off?'

'The search for Eddie Phillips. He's been nicked and is in the cells downstairs—'

Gibbs was out of the office to tell Bradfield the good news before she could even finish the sentence.

Jane couldn't believe how much Kath had pushed her luck, but was pleased not to have to see Bradfield when she was reeking of Kath's perfume.

CHAPTER SEVEN

As soon as Bradfield heard they had arrested Eddie Phillips, he went down to the cells with DS Gibbs to get him out for an interview. True to his word he took down a bottle of whisky for each of the arresting officers from the crate stashed in his office.

Eddie was asleep on the thin mattress when Bradfield threw open the cell door and kicked his feet to wake him, but he just lay there moaning like a belligerent child who didn't want to get out of bed. Gibbs grabbed Eddie by the scruff of his neck and dragged him off the mattress. He was like a rag doll and it didn't take long to realize Eddie was still stoned and could hardly string two words together, never mind stand upright. Bradfield got straight to the point and asked him who Julie Ann had phoned from the doctor's office while he kept lookout. Eddie mumbled something about the police harassing his grandmother and picking on him. Bradfield told him he hadn't even started yet and instructed one of the uniform officers who'd arrested Eddie to ply him with coffee for the next two hours in order to wake him up so that he could be interviewed.

Jane ushered a pale-faced George Collins upstairs to Bradfield's office. He was wearing a dark navy pinstriped suit, and he was so thin that the shoulders appeared to be padded. Underneath the suit jacket was a pristine white shirt, with a tie that had a small crossed golf-club monogram on it.

He was cordial as he shook hands with Bradfield and apologized for not being able to come to the station earlier due to a meeting with the vicar about his daughter's funeral. Bradfield explained it might be some time before the body was released, but he would speak with the coroner whose decision it would be. He then invited Mr Collins to sit opposite him and offered refreshments. He declined, and still standing reached into his inside jacket pocket and produced a cutting from a newspaper which he unfolded and placed on the table for Bradfield to see.

'This morning's paper describes my daughter as a drug addict and prostitute. Why did you tell them that, Mr Bradfield?' he asked calmly, but with a look of hurt in his eyes.

Bradfield scanned the article. 'I can assure you, Mr Collins, that I said nothing of the sort to the newspapers.'

Collins took a deep breath. 'My wife is beside herself. She's inconsolable and feels ashamed.'

'I would very much doubt that it was one of my officers who spoke to the press. It's possible the leak may have come from one of the mortuary staff and I will investigate the matter, Mr Collins.' He refolded the article and held it up. Collins shook his head, so Bradfield threw the cutting in the bin and asked him to sit down, which he did.

'Have you charged the man you arrested with the murder of my daughter?' Collins asked nervously.

'Not as yet, and it's looking more likely that he may not be the person responsible.'

'But he must know something if you arrested him, so why aren't you—'

'We are doing everything possible to find Julie Ann's killer, Mr Collins. I can assure you we are following up on some leads that we hope will be very productive ... However, there are also a few questions of a delicate nature I need to ask you.'

'I'll do whatever I can to help.'

'Firstly, and regrettably, I have to inform you that Julie Ann was twelve to fourteen weeks pregnant at the time of her death.'

Bradfield paused to let a shocked-looking Mr Collins digest the information. Jane was struck once again by how gentle Bradfield's manner was, but she felt deeply sorry for Mr Collins, who was struggling to speak.

'How can you be sure ...? Could it be some kind of mistake?'

'I won't go into specifics, but suffice to say the pathologist has confirmed it, Mr Collins, and I am sorry but I have to ask if you and your wife were already privy to this information?'

'Dear God no. If Julie had told us we would have done everything possible to make her come home.'

'Did she make contact with you when she was upset or in any kind of trouble?'

'The first few times she ran away – once or twice. My wife and I begged her to come home, but she'd accuse us of trying to control her life. We just wanted to get her away from the drug dealers and addicts.'

'That's totally understandable, and you and Mrs Collins must have been under immense stress. Do you know who any of her dealers or drug-addict friends may have been?'

'No, but believe you me if I did I'd swing for them.'

It suddenly occurred to Jane that behind Bradfield's soft tone and calm manner there was an underlying purpose to his line of questioning, but she wasn't sure exactly what it was.

'I understand that you cared for your daughter deeply, but may I ask why you stopped reporting her missing?'

'I have already explained this – she kept running away from home and your lot got fed up with us and Julie, so there was no point in reporting it any more. One officer virtually accused us of being terrible parents who had spoilt our daughter. We loved her and thought she loved us, but it seems she came to love drugs more.' He was pressing his bony hands together and twisting them round in agitation.

'Did you look for her yourself?'

Jane thought the question a bit harsh and could see that Mr Collins was angered by the insinuation behind it, but was also close to tears.

'Of course we did, day and bloody night all over London, in some of the most unsavoury places imaginable, but to no avail. Some people recognized her photograph so we knew she was alive, but as time went by we eventually realized we'd have to wait for her to make contact. The weeks and months passed but she never did ... and now she never will.' His voice was filled with emotion as he finished his sentence. He stared forlornly at the floor.

Jane listened intently as Bradfield changed tack. 'It must be of some solace to know that Julie Ann had voluntarily checked herself into a drug dependency unit.'

Mr Collins looked up with sadness, tears welling in his eyes. 'Your detectives told me yesterday, but didn't say when.'

'About ten weeks ago. She may have been trying to kick the habit for herself and the baby she was carrying. However, two weeks ago she suddenly stopped attending after she made a phone call from the drug unit. Did you receive a call from your daughter two weeks ago?'

Mr Collins ran his bony hand through his thinning hair. He was shaking.

'No, no, I did not. I've already said that we hadn't heard from her for almost eighteen months.'

Bradfield paused, took a deep breath and flicked to a page in his notebook. 'She was last seen getting into a red car near the hospital, possibly a Jaguar XJ6 or 12. Do you know anyone who may own a red Jag?' he asked and closed the notebook.

Mr Collins shook his head.

'Did Julie Ann ever call you for money?'

Mr Collins gave a slight snort of derision and leaned forward.

'At first, yes, a couple of times, but you clearly have no idea what hell it is to live with a heroin addict, do you, Mr Bradfield? Of course they ask for money ... and if you don't give it to them they will steal it from you, and pawn your prized possessions to feed their habit.'

Jane watched, mouth open, as a very tense Mr Collins sat upright in his chair waiting for an irritated-looking Bradfield to say something.

'Do you recall if your daughter associated with anyone called Paddy?'

Mr Collins was becoming frustrated. 'She never mentioned or used the name in my presence ... and before you ask I only know it as a colloquial term for an Irishman.'

'Do you know if your daughter had any black male friends?'

'This is getting ridiculous, DCI Bradfield. She was at an all-girls' school, and I can assure you there are no blacks living in any streets near us.'

'But as a heroin addict she probably did mix with black drug dealers and addicts, you'd agree?'

'Dear God, I keep telling you, I hadn't seen my daughter in over a year so I have no idea who she'd been mixing with recently.'

Jane thought, from the way the interview was going, that Bradfield was going to be heartless and reveal the fact that Julie Ann had had sex with a black man, and that there was a possibility of rape.

'I'm just trying to do my job, Mr Collins, and I am sorry if what I ask you is upsetting. To try and find who murdered your daughter I need to know as much as possible about her, even details that may seem unpleasant.'

Collins stood up. 'What do you want from me? Everything you tell me rips me further apart. I refuse to be subjected to any further questioning. I came here to help, not to be interrogated like this. I would like to go home now, please. Surely you have the decency to understand that all my wife and I want to do now is bury our daughter? Everyone here refers to her as Julie Ann but we always called her just Julie ... Sometimes it feels as if you are describing another girl, but it isn't ... She was my beloved child and now all we want is to be left alone to grieve for what could have been ...'

'Excuse me a moment, Mr Collins,' Bradfield said, then got up and walked out into the corridor, closing the door behind him. He gave a short whistle to attract DS Gibbs's attention, who came out of the incident room and joined him in the corridor.

'Spence, bring Eddie Phillips into my office as Tennison takes Collins out.'

Bradfield returned to his office. 'Thank you for coming in, Mr Collins. I will inform you of any developments in our investigation. WPC Tennison will show you out.' He gestured for Mr Collins to leave as Jane followed.

As Mr Collins opened the door Eddie entered, and they had to squeeze past each other through the narrow space. Bradfield watched closely and was sure he saw an expression of surprise on Mr Collins' face, as if he'd seen Eddie before. As the door closed Bradfield pointed to the seat Collins had used and told Eddie to sit down.

'Fuckin' hell, this is like musical chairs from one room to another. You got me coming in and out of here – it's not right when I ain't done nothin'.'

'Shut up and stop moaning,' Gibbs said and dragged him across the room by the collar before banging him down onto the chair.

Bradfield stood over him. 'Right, you piece of scum, I want some answers, and by that I mean the truth … no lies. Do I make myself clear?'

Eddie pointed at DS Gibbs. 'He's just given me a hard time in an interview and I don't know nothing more than I already told ya. I wanna speak to a solicitor. I know my—'

Eddie's head flew forward from the unexpected slap Bradfield gave him to the back of his head.

'Don't start quoting Judge's Rules and arrest rights to me or next time it'll be more than a gentle tap I give you. Do you understand me?'

Eddie was rubbing his whiplashed neck. 'Yes, all right.'

'That man in the suit who just left, you know him?'

'No.'

'He acted as if he'd seen you before.'

'I've never seen him in me fuckin' life.'

Gibbs, who was taking notes, leant over to Bradfield and whispered that the detectives who visited Mr Collins yesterday for a statement had shown him a picture of Eddie.

'Why the fuck didn't they tell me in the meeting so I didn't waste my time!' Bradfield snarled.

Eddie was still rubbing his neck. 'This is all makin' me grandmother sick, you lot showing up in yer patrol cars is frightnin' the life out of her – she's seventy-eight years old and got angina … it's doin' her head in.'

'That the same granny that told my detectives to fuck off, is it? Taking in a junkie like you must be what's doing her head in. Did she also take in Julie Ann, did she stay with you at your grandma's?'

'No. Me gran don't like drugs and I respect that so I never does them in her flat. I also don't take other addicts in cos I know they'll try and nick stuff.'

Gibbs laughed. 'Yeah, like you never have, Eddie.'

Gibbs explained to Bradfield that Eddie had told him Julie Ann either used squats or slept rough, and that the squat on the Pembridge was where he'd 'shoot up' heroin and had first met Julie Ann. He had only known her for a few months and never seen her around Hackney before that. Bradfield asked Eddie if he knew where she'd been staying before he met her and he said that he didn't know, but from what she did say he thought she had run away from home.

'Did she speak about her parents?'

'Her mum sometimes. She said she missed her but didn't want to go home.'

'Why not?'

'I don't know and I didn't ask.'

'Did she ever talk about her dad?' Bradfield asked and Eddie shook his head.

'Who did she call from the doctor's office on the last day you saw her?'

'I don't know.'

Bradfield nodded to Gibbs who slapped the back of Eddie's head. 'That's a lie – you were keeping lookout while she was in the office and got caught,' Gibbs said.

Eddie squealed. 'OK, OK, lay off with the slaps as I can't think straight.'

He admitted that he was keeping watch, walking up and down and checking round the corner that no one was coming, so he didn't hear who she called or what was said, and then O'Duncie the tea lady had caught them.

Bradfield asked if Julie Ann had ever mentioned anyone called Paddy who she wanted money from.

Eddie said the name wasn't familiar and Bradfield asked if it could be a drug dealer or pimp she was using.

Eddie paused and looked nervously at Bradfield who could sense he was hiding something.

'Cough it up, Eddie.'

Eddie picked at his spots, refusing to look up. 'I can't.'

'Then I'll charge you for withholding evidence in a murder investigation, you'll be remanded in custody and do cold turkey in prison. I'll also make sure your cell mates think you're a grass and use you as a punchbag.'

Eddie was shaking like a leaf and couldn't look them in the eye.

'Not to mention some inmates like to shag young boys,' Gibbs added.

Eddie looked up at Bradfield. 'There was a dealer she spoke about called Big Daddy, but I don't know if it was him she called. Sometimes she paid him cash and other times she let him have sex for drugs.'

'What's he look like and where can I find him?'

'Honestly I don't know ... I've never met or seen him. She said he had a mate called Dwayne and Big Daddy made her do sex with them both at the same time. I'm being honest – that's all Julie Ann told me.'

'Did Big Daddy or Dwayne drive a red Jag like the one you saw her get into?'

Gibbs interjected and said that Eddie had been looking through the Jag brochures just before he brought him into the office. Bradfield asked if the car was like the XJ6 or 12.

'Shit, I only saw it for a few seconds. I dunno now for sure if it was a Jag, but it was definitely red and as I've said over and over I didn't see the driver and I've never seen Big Daddy or Dwayne. It's not like me and Julie Ann was together all the fuckin' time.'

Bradfield rocked back in his chair, lit two cigarettes and handed one to Eddie who thanked him and took a long slow drag.

Bradfield stood up and indicated for Gibbs to join him in the far corner of the room. Eddie puffed on the cigarette, hunching his shoulders and staring at their backs, but he couldn't hear what they were saying.

'What you reckon, Spence? Is Big Daddy real or a name he's made up to appease us?'

'Probably real, but I think he knows more about him, and understandably he's scared shitless ... especially if Big D murdered our victim. We could slap him round the room all day but for fear of his life I doubt he'll give us more.'

'Well, let's call his bluff, make him think we know more and see what reaction we get.'

They returned to their seats and Bradfield stubbed out his cigarette and lit another for Eddie before continuing.

'Come on, Eddie, what kind of boyfriend are you that just watches his girl get into a car and doesn't even look to see who she's with? What kind of prick are you that knows she's missing for two weeks and does nothing about it?'

'Listen, I was just her friend, right, I never shagged her.'

'So you're a little poofter who likes it up the arse then,' Gibbs interjected.

'No I'm not, but she was pickin' up blokes to pay for drugs.'

'Smack for you as well, obviously,' Bradfield said. He deliberately paused and stared at Eddie.

'Yeah, she gave me some – so what?'

'So you're her pimp and living off immoral earnings.'

'Jesus Christ, I didn't force her to do anything ... it was me that took her to the clinic to get her off the hard stuff.'

Bradfield leaned across the table and dragged Phillips' arm towards him, rolling up his denim-jacket cuff.

'That looks like a fresh track to me ... you back using, are you?'

'Only cos you bastards are houndin' and harassin' me and it ain't right at all.'

'Let me tell you what is right, Eddie. We know Julie Ann was shagging a darkie and three months up the duff. You were with her when she made that phone call – she was overheard asking for money. How long after that call did you see her get into the red Jaguar?'

'I dunno – an hour or so, maybe more.'

'She was pregnant with Big Daddy's baby, wasn't she?'

Eddie didn't look up, his hands and body shaking as he inhaled the smoke from the cigarette.

'This Big Daddy, describe him to me. Is he black, white, big, small—'

'Black and big.'

'Tell me more about him or I'll rip your grandma's flat apart on a drugs search and leave her to clean up the mess.'

'You bastards leave her alone ... I only seen him a few times ... he's huge and a flashy dresser, two-tone shoes an' a big felt hat, and he's always wearing shades. You can slap me all you want but I don't know nuffink else.'

Bradfield opened the envelope containing the crime scene and post-mortem photographs. He got up and stood beside Eddie placing the most graphic ones from the post-mortem on the table.

'Look at her, Eddie, LOOK AT WHAT WAS DONE TO HER!' Bradfield shouted as he pushed Eddie's head forward so his nose was virtually touching the gruesome picture. Eddie was horrified and gasping for breath as he began to heave and gag.

Jane was writing up some further details on the sheets of paper on the wall. Kath took a sip from her mug of coffee and checked her watch.

'They've been in there with Eddie Phillips for ages. Wonder if they got anything out of him about the phone call that fat woman O'Duncie overheard Julie Ann making?'

As if on cue Bradfield walked in and tossed the crime scene and post-mortem photographs onto Jane's desk.

'Stick these up on the wall and get someone to empty the waste bin full of Eddie Phillips' puke in my office. There's a bit on the floor that needs cleaning as well.'

Kath frowned. 'Eh, by someone do you mean us, sir? No cleaner will be around at this time. We had a drunk in the cells the other night that shat on the mattress and—'

'I don't care, just get me a coffee first and then get it cleaned up.'

Kath huffed as she left to get him a coffee.

'How did it go with Eddie Phillips, sir?' Jane asked.

'We made some progress and got a couple of black drug dealers' names out of him, but by his description of one of them he's seen too many movies.'

Bradfield lit a cigarette and told Jane he wanted her to ring the drug squad at Scotland Yard to see if they knew them. He said the main man was described by Eddie Phillips as a huge bloke nicknamed Big Daddy. The other was his mate Dwayne and according to Eddie they passed Julie Ann round like a rag doll, screwing her in return for heroin.

'The phone call from the hospital ... maybe she was calling Big Daddy, not Paddy ...'

Bradfield raised his eyebrows and Jane realized her comment was a bit like telling him to suck eggs.

'Maybe, but it was rather strange that when I mentioned to Mr Collins that his daughter made a phone call he never asked who to.'

Jane now realized why Bradfield had paused when he mentioned the phone call to Mr Collins.

'You think she may have phoned her father for money?'

Bradfield tapped his nose twice and it reminded Jane of Shaw Taylor on *Police 5* when he used his catchphrase 'Keep 'em peeled' when asking viewers to be observant.

Jane continued, 'Thing is, if she was calling her father then you'd expect she'd know her home phone number and wouldn't need to ask the switchboard for it. She could maybe have wanted money for an abortion.'

'Might not have been approved by a registered practitioner, but a back-street abortionist would do it for cash,' he said, and cocked his head to one side at her concerned expression.

'It's so tragic, and it just gets murkier and murkier – every chance in life and she goes off the rails. Do you think something drove her to go against her parents and turn her back on them?'

He shrugged his shoulders: Jane seemed so naive. It got murkier all right, and sometimes it weighed you down. The upside would be when they found the killer, and he knew they would start a fresh round of enquiries now. The case had at last warmed up.

'Trying to sort out the time frame isn't easy – three months pregnant, calls from the hospital wanting money ... Eddie sees her getting into a red Jag about an hour later and swears it was the last time he saw her. She then goes missing for almost two weeks. I dunno – can you type it all up in chronological order for me?' he asked politely.

'Yes, certainly, sir.' She flushed as she looked at him. Something she hadn't noticed previously was how blue his eyes were, and unlike most red-headed people, his eyelashes were incredibly dark.

'Is there something else?' he asked.

'No, sir.'

Kath returned with a coffee and handing it to Bradfield told him there was a clean bin in his office but she'd need Dettol to sort out his carpet.

'Thanks for the coffee,' he said, and left the room.

Kath followed him out muttering under her breath, 'Right, sir, every single DC's done a runner which just leaves me, so I'll go get an effing bucket and mop.'

Jane set to work on the time frame, as Bradfield had asked her to do. Kath eventually reappeared wearing yellow Marigold gloves and grinning.

'Christ, now *I* stink of Dettol. There was more than just a bit of puke on the floor and boy did it smell.'

'I'm sorry, I should have helped you.'

'Don't be, all done and dusted and at least he didn't

crap everywhere ... I wouldn't clean that up for anybody. DS Gibbs is taking a shower – the kid puked over him and his pointy shoes.'

'Not his winkle-pickers?' Jane remarked, knowing how upset he'd be.

'You want a laugh, come with me ... come on.'

Jane smiled, put some carbon paper between two blank sheets of paper and popped them into the typewriter.

'Come on, hurry up.'

Curious about what Kath was so eager to show her, Jane followed her out of the room.

'By the way, Kath, I'm going to the continuation training centre tomorrow for that lecture by the forensic scientist, so I won't be in.'

'Ah pity. It's one of the detectives' thirtieth birthdays, so you'll miss a big piss-up in the office. God, they can pack it away. Why don't you pop in after CTC for a drink and get to know the team a bit better?'

They headed down the stone stairs to the basement, Kath leading the way.

'I'll see how I feel,' Jane said.

'Sometimes letting your hair down is good for releasin' all the bloody tensions, Jane, but it's up to you.'

Kath stopped outside the men's locker room, inched the door open and leaned in.

'Ah pity, I think we missed it.'

Jane was still confused as to why they were there.

Kath looked at her. 'He was givin' a rendition of Gerry and the Pacemakers before, you know he sings in this band ... no, hang on ... shush and listen.'

Jane was anxious to get back to finishing the time frame, but Kath waved her hands for her to be quiet. From the gents' shower room wafted the unexpectedly clear voice of DS Gibbs loudly singing the Moody Blues song, 'Nights In White Satin':

> *'Nights in white satin*
> *Never reaching the end*
> *Letters I've written*
> *Never meaning to send ...'*

Kath gave a gleeful shrug of her shoulders and whispered that when she could afford it she was going to buy one of those new small tape recorders. Gibbs continued singing:

> *'Beauty I've always missed*
> *With these eyes before*
> *Just what the truth is*
> *I can't say any more ...'*

'Kath, I should get back to my desk,' Jane said, turning to the stairs, but Kath grabbed her arm.
'No, listen, listen ...'

> *''Cause I love you*
> *Yes I love you*
> *Oh how I love you ...'*

Kath started mimicking Gibbs quietly in a sing-along, but the more she got carried away the louder her voice became. As Kath's reached a crescendo Gibbs's suddenly went silent and she sang solo on the next few lines:

> *'Gazing at people some hand in hand*
> *Just what I'm going through they can't*
>   *understand ...'*

Jane laughed when the disgruntled voice of Spencer Gibbs bellowed out, 'Eh, who is that ... is it you, Morgan?'

'Sing that at my funeral, will you, Spence?'

'Shut the fuck up, Kath.'

'"'Cause I love youuuuu ... Ohh how I love you ..."'she finished.

Jane and Kath were holding back the laughter as the shower door opened and Gibbs stepped out with a towel wrapped around him. They both beat a hasty retreat hoping he hadn't seen them, and Jane wondered if there was something going on between Gibbs and Kath – if so, they certainly kept it quiet.

At the end of her shift Jane left the typed time frame and interview notes on Bradfield's desk and decided to go home.

On the bus she sat in her usual rear seat on the top deck and read through some of her study notes for next month's probationary exam whilst listening to her radio, which helped divert her mind from the events of the last few days.

There were four teenagers screeching and laughing up at the front, and they began banging on the window when the bus stopped to let passengers on and off. She pushed the earpiece further in and looked down to the pavement to see a teenage boy mouth 'Fuck off' and give a two-fingers gesture to the kids on the bus. Jane shook her head and thought that in a poor area like Hackney they probably had nothing better to do.

She was about to continue reading her study notes when she saw Renee Bentley walking slowly towards the bus beside a wheelchair that was piled high with Co-op bags filled with groceries and cans of beer. Holding the handles of the chair was a chiselled-faced man in his early thirties. He had blond shoulder-length hair and walked with bowed legs, dragging one foot slightly, but he had a big chest and wide athletic shoulders like a weight-lifter. Jane remembered PC Donaldson telling her about David Bentley falling from the church roof. She had seen the chair when she took Renee Bentley home, and wrongly presumed it was for her, but it was obviously for her son.

Mrs Bentley's pale face made her look worn out, but she was quite well dressed in a smart coat with a fake-fur collar. The boy on the street who had been gesturing to his friends on the top of the bus was walking backwards when he accidently banged against the wheelchair. David Bentley reacted instantly with speed, pushing the kid aside with one sweep of his right arm. The kid almost stumbled off his feet, and David lost his balance, but Renee caught his arm to steady him. The boy ran off laughing as David gripped the wheelchair handles and eased it down the kerb to cross the road. As the bus pulled away Jane stood up to look from the back window. She could see Renee and David standing in the gutter and she realized how close they were to being knocked over. Jane could see the frustrated fury on David's face from when the boy had laughed at him, and as Renee put a protective arm around her son he shrugged her away.

Jane sat back in her seat remembering how John Bentley had scared her, the way he had shouted and frog-marched her out of the flat. David in comparison looked rather pitiful, but recalling the tired face of Mrs Bentley she felt sorrier for Renee.

CHAPTER EIGHT

Jane had forgotten to switch her alarm clock on and was woken by her mother gently shaking her shoulder.

'You said you wanted to be away by half seven, dear.'

Jane sat bolt upright. 'Oh my God, what time is it?' she asked, rubbing the sleep from her eyes.

'Don't panic, it's only seven. When you didn't appear for breakfast I thought you might have already left, but then I saw your hat and jacket in the hallway. Do you know it smells of disinfectant?'

'Yes, I know,' Jane said with a sigh.

'Anyway I've ironed a clean uniform shirt for you.' She held it up proudly and hung it on the back of the door.

'Thanks, Mum.'

Mrs Tennison picked up Jane's uniform shoes.

'I'll give these a clean as they're very dirty. What on earth is sticking to them?' She took a sniff and wrinkled her nose. 'They smell of something – not dog dirt, is it?'

Jane leapt out of bed and grabbed her dressing gown.

'I'll have a quick shower, but I haven't time for break-fast.'

'You should eat something. Would you like some toast or a sandwich for the journey?'

Jane told her mother not to worry, and said she'd get

something at the training-centre canteen. She took fifteen minutes to get showered and dressed into her nicely pressed skirt and fresh white shirt. Her mother was finishing pressing her uniform jacket when Jane walked into the open-plan room and saw two slices of toast and marmalade on the breakfast bar, along with a coffee. She took a bite of the toast and a sip of coffee to wash it down quickly.

'Your shoes are nice and clean now and I've sprayed some freshener on this jacket, but that smell is still strong – how on earth did it get there?'

'I was at the mortuary and they swill down the floors with disinfectant, which permeates your clothes.'

'Oh goodness me! Anyway, about this evening – it's all been arranged and you'll need to be there by six,' her mother said.

'What are you talking about?' Jane asked. She fastened the top button of her shirt and began to put her tie on.

Her mother handed her a piece of paper with the address of the local church.

'The rehearsal for the wedding, Jane. You, as chief bridesmaid, the other bridesmaids, the groom and the best man have to be there and you have to practise taking Pam's bouquet and—'

'Oh my God, the lecture doesn't finish until five so I don't think I can make six.'

'But you told me it would end early afternoon.'

'I'll try and get there as quickly as I can, Mum. I have to go now as I'll be in trouble if I'm late,' Jane said, pulling on her jacket before taking another bite of toast and sip of coffee.

'You'll be in trouble if you don't get there on time.'

Jane wiped her mouth and kissed her frazzled mother's

cheek, almost getting poked in the eye by one of her rollers. In the hallway she put her hat in a carrier bag, grabbed her coat and checked her pocket radio was in her handbag. As she opened the front door she heard her younger sister Pam.

'Don't forget the rehearsal, Jane.'

'No time to chat, byeeeee,' Jane called, and shut the front door behind her.

Pam, who was still in her pyjamas, shook her head in annoyance as she approached the breakfast bar.

'Don't let that coffee and toast go to waste – your sister had to leave it.' Mrs Tennison took the half-eaten piece for herself while Pam picked up the other slice and took a bite.

'Did you make sure she'll be at the church, Mum?'

'She said she'd do her best to get there on time, but her lecture finishes—'

'Honestly, Mum, Jane should have sorted it weeks ago like my other bridesmaids did.'

'She'll be there, Pam.'

'She'd better be, Mum. Have you seen her in her bridesmaid's dress?'

'I know you're anxious, dear, but she's up and down to Hackney every day so I never know whether she's coming or going or even what shift she's on next. I hardly get a word out of her because she's always so tired. You know sometimes I wish she'd never joined the Met, especially when she's on nights. I worry myself sick. She said she'd been at the mortuary and that's why the smell on her uniform was horrible. God only knows what was sticking to her shoes. I don't know, I do worry about her.'

'She can take care of herself, Mum, she always has.'

'I know, I know.'

'Jane can be so selfish at times, though, and she must know how important my big day is to me!'

'She knows. Now, do you want me to make you some scrambled eggs on toast?'

'Yeah, I'll go and have a shower first.'

Mrs Tennison fetched a bowl, broke the eggs and was giving them a good whisking when her bleary-eyed husband shuffled in.

'Been like Piccadilly Circus this morning. Went to go to the bathroom and Jane was in there, now Pam's having a shower,' he said and perched himself on a stool.

'Did you clean her shoes?' he asked.

'Yes, shocking smell, and her jacket stank of disinfectant. She told me she'd been to a mortuary and they swilled the floor with something.'

Although the Tennisons' large flat in Maida Vale had three good-sized bedrooms, an open-plan lounge, dining room and kitchen, complete with breakfast bar along one wall, it only had one bathroom, and with three women living there Mr Tennison was always last in line.

'You have to have a quiet talk with Jane. I know she's never wanted to be a bridesmaid, but this Sunday is Pam's big day and I won't have Jane spoiling it with a sour face,' Mrs Tennison said bluntly as she broke two more eggs into the bowl for her husband's breakfast. She was a very pretty woman, even in her satin quilted dressing gown, furry slippers and hair in small pink rollers.

'She won't let her sister down,' Mr Tennison said.

'She tried to get out of being a bridesmaid when it was first discussed. As the elder sister Jane has a duty to be chief bridesmaid.'

'Well, Jane's work must be very stressful and—'

'I want everything to be organized to the last detail so the wedding day will run smoothly. She could have waited a few months more, but she's always been headstrong.'

'You can say that again, dear. I know you were upset when she signed up to the Met without telling us, but I'm proud of her, and if it's the career she wants then she should—'

'Not Jane, I was talking about Pam. And as for a career, well, it sounds to me she's mostly making tea and coffee.'

'Well, the hair salon isn't what I'd call a classy joint, just local and temporary, I suspect.'

'I was talking about Jane's job, and besides, Pam is a fully qualified colourist now so she isn't making clients tea and coffee.' Mrs Tennison finished whisking the eggs and poured them into a cooking pan.

Mr Tennison sighed. 'Either way as long as they're happy, but to be honest I do worry about Jane patrolling the streets in a rough area like Hackney. Maybe after she's finished her probation she'll move into something else like the mounted branch. She used to like riding when she was younger – or maybe the traffic police.'

Mrs Tennison smiled. 'The thought of her directing traffic makes me laugh, especially as she failed her driving test twice before finally passing it.'

She was already placing two plates of scrambled eggs on the Formica-topped bar, and inserting the bread into the toaster.

'Are you having eggs?' he asked, sitting on one of the stools.

'No, darling, I'm watching my weight for the wedding. I'm going to John Lewis this afternoon to collect my outfit.'

'You will look ravishing.'

She gave him a playful slap on his shoulder and then leaned in close.

'You will too in your Moss Bros top hat and tails ...'

'Am I in a top hat and tails?'

'You know you are, so don't start to tease me.'

He sighed and said that it was going to cost him a fortune, but she had already gone down the corridor to call Pam for breakfast.

Jane arrived at the training centre above the large post office in Holloway Road, Islington, just as her classmates were being ushered into the classroom, meaning she didn't have time to get herself anything from the canteen. The room was basic and cold, with twenty desks made of wood and metal, laid out in five rows of four. In the centre of the classroom was a Kodak carousel slide projector facing a white screen behind which was a large blackboard.

The sergeant standing at the door pointed to a desk that had a stack of identical files with 'Dr J. Harker. Lecture Files. Confidential' stamped on them.

'Stop chattering, take a file and sit where you want. Fill out the name card on your desk and then stand by it ready for inspection,' he said in a monotone.

There were twenty probationary officers present, all in their early twenties, and only Jane and one other were WPCs. As the sergeant inspected them he told some of the male officers that they needed haircuts, hadn't shaved properly, or their uniform trousers didn't have neatly pressed creases. He told the other female officer present to remove her hooped earrings, and she apologized saying she had meant to do so before class but had forgotten. The sergeant gruffly remarked that if a violent prisoner grabbed them she'd never forget her ear lobes being ripped off.

Jane felt good when he commented to the rest of the class that he expected to see all their uniforms in the same neat and well-pressed condition as hers. She knew it was all thanks to her mother and realized she'd have to get some tips from her if she was going to move into the section house. Looking after her uniform, washing and ironing her clothes would then become her own responsibility.

'Sit your backsides down,' the sergeant shouted out.

The room was filled with the sound of scraping chairs and whispered conversation as they all sat down.

Jane found herself at the front. She looked round the classroom and saw a couple of people she knew from training school. She raised her hand slightly and gave them a wave, which they returned.

The sergeant suddenly shouted out, 'Class!' and everyone stood to attention as the Inspector entered with a man whom he introduced as 'one of the foremost and renowned forensic scientists in the UK ... Dr Julian Harker'.

Harker acknowledged the polite applause and gestured for everyone to be seated. The room was full of expectant energy as everyone waited eagerly to hear him speak.

Jane was surprised by how young Dr Harker looked: he appeared to be not much older than the rest of the class. She flicked open the front of the file and, seeing from his CV that he had a PhD in biology, realized his youthful appearance belied his actual thirty-eight years.

Harker clicked his fingers in her direction. 'Please do not open the file yet. I will tell you when to do so.'

Jane flinched, mumbled an apology and noticed he had

cold, slate-grey piercing eyes. Kath had said he was attractive, interesting and worth listening to, but in his stiff white-collared shirt, bow tie and grey, creased trousers, Jane found him rather pompous.

Harker took his time, placing his folder on the lectern before turning to an officer and asking him to close the blinds and turn off the neon strip lights. He had a very cultured, aristocratic tone.

'In your folders are some of the relevant statements from a major investigation, such as the pathologist's and my forensic report. There are copies of the crime scene photographs, but I will be showing you slides of the scene and bodies as well. Some of you may find them disturbing, but at some time in your career you may well find yourself attending scenes of a similar nature. I hope you have enquiring minds as there will be a Q and A session at the end of my lecture for me to clarify anything you feel necessary. However, I will be asking you questions relating to the murders during my talk as it will show me whether or not you are paying attention.'

Curious to see what was in the file, Jane sifted through the paperwork in front of her, while Harker placed a sheet of acetate paper on the overhead projector, then covered it with a blank piece of paper so as not to reveal all the contents. He switched on the overhead and, as if conducting an orchestra, used a broken telescopic radio antenna to point at the words projected onto the wall. Jane settled back in her seat, listening intently as the lecture began.

At the station Kath was at the front desk dealing with an irate Nancy Phillips who was demanding to speak with someone in authority about her grandson being slapped about. She wore a crossover apron under her cardigan, and a pair of fur-lined ankle boots. Her thick stockings fell in folds around her swollen ankles.

'You bleedin' lot don't have any idea what happens when you keep nosyin' around and drivin' up in yer patrol cars. There's some nasty villains livin' around me, and God forbid you'd ever take them in. Instead yer just harass my poor Eddie when he's done nuffink wrong. He's entitled to a solicitor, you know, like me he knows his rights. I know he's got drug problems, that's why he's livin' with me, so I can keep an eye on him, unlike his bleedin' mother ... the no-good bitch, and—'

Kath slapped the desk with the flat of her hand.

'Mrs Phillips, if you would just let me get a word in edgeways I can write down the particulars and deal with your complaint appropriately.'

'That's what I'm fuckin' here fer, you dozy cow.'

The duty sergeant walked in behind Kath.

'Hello, Nancy, what are you creating about?'

'I want to speak to that Detective Birdbank that's dealin' with me grandson.'

'It's DCI Bradfield,' Kath said.

It took a while longer to placate Nancy Phillips before she was taken in to speak with Bradfield. At first he had refused to talk to her, but Kath said that perhaps he should just have a few words to appease her as she was a tough old broad who knew that her grandson should have had access to a solicitor.

'We've only had him in for questioning, for Chrissake! We've not pressed any bloody charges, and he was withholding evidence about the phone call, Big Daddy and another dealer Dwayne somebody or fuckin' other. I've got a hundred and one things to do so send her packing.'

'Just a short chat, guv. You never know, she might even be able to help us.'

'I've got officers from the drug squad coming here in a quarter of an hour so I'll give her ten minutes, that's all – bring her up.'

Jane was frantically scribbling down notes as Harker explained that a mother in her seventies and a daughter in her forties lived together in Biggin Hill and were murdered in their home. He brought up different slides as he described entering the victims' premises. The class were shown small blood drops on the living-room carpet and blood smears on some of the objects removed from drawers. There were also blood drops in the hallway and some blood smears on the walls leading to the three bedrooms at the back of the cottage.

Jane felt as if she was the first officer at the scene, moving slowly and cautiously through the house, her adrenalin pumping as she feared the worst for the two female occupants.

'Can any of you tell me about Locard's principle of exchange?' Harker asked, but there was silence in the room.

He sighed and glibly remarked, 'I see that forensic awareness still isn't taught at Hendon Police College.'

He walked to the blackboard and wrote, 'Dr Edmond Locard, 1877–1966, French criminologist and forensic scientist – Contact Equals Trace'.

He turned back to the class. 'He was a pioneer in forensic science and stated, "Every contact leaves a trace." His theory is that when two objects come into contact with one another, each will take something from the other object or leave something behind. So what does that mean in the context of our unfolding crime scene?'

Jane got in first. 'That the killer will have left traces of themself behind and taken traces from the house with them.'

'Correct, but what I'm interested in is the wider meaning for the officers who first entered this horrific scene.'

There was a brief pause for thought in the room before a constable suggested that it meant the police officers had also left traces of themselves as they searched the victims' cottage. Harker nodded and stated that was why you always needed to be careful about where you stood, what you touched, how you opened something like a door, so as not to damage or destroy any evidence the suspect had left behind. He told them that they should make a note of everything they did at a scene as soon as possible after the event.

Jane flicked to an empty page in her notebook and wrote down, 'Red fibres, Julie Ann's socks'.

Kath got a coffee for Bradfield and a cup of tea for Mrs Phillips before taking her to his office. Bradfield told Kath to stay and as the disgruntled Mrs Phillips sat on the chair in front of him she took a few deep sniffs, her nose twitching up and down like a rabbit's.

'It smells of Dettol in here,' she remarked as she took out a cigarette from a packet in her apron pocket and lit it.

Bradfield gave her a cynical grin. 'That's thanks to your precious grandson, Mrs Phillips, he puked—'

She was shaking her finger at him before he could finish his sentence. 'I know he's got troubles, I know he's been a pain in the backside, but he's been on that substitution stuff methalene.'

'I think you mean methadone,' Bradfield said, raising his eyebrows in despair.

'Metha ... lene, dean, done, whatever ... He's been trying to get clean and been out lookin' for work. I got to keep me eyes peeled for him cos his mother's a tart and my son wouldn't even put his name on the bleedin' birth certificate. I'm all he's got and I got to stand up for him. You lot are harassin' him – he didn't do anythin' to that bloody girl they found.'

'Did you know her?'

'Who?'

'The girl that was found, Julie Ann.'

'She was a pack of trouble, hoity-toity stuck-up little tart. I threw her out, I said to him not to ever bring any bloody junkie back to my flat. You turn your back on 'em and they'll soon have their fingers in the biscuit jar looking for the housekeeping money.'

'So you did know her?'

'Twice he brought her to my place, and I warned him, but he was besotted. She treated him like he was her servant, wanting the crusts cut off her bleedin' toast.'

'When was the last time you saw her?'

'Weeks ago ... there I am encouraging him to keep going to the clinic to stop the drugs, warning him over and over that if he doesn't stop I'll have no alternative but to throw him out. She wanted to make a phone call, the cheek of her. I told her I didn't have a phone and to get out. She asks me, all posh like, where the nearest hotel is, and I told her that if she had cash for a hotel she could bloody well leave me some money for the bed and food she had off me.'

'A hotel?'

'Probably lyin', but I knew she was making money as a tom.'

'How did you know?' Bradfield asked.

She touched the side of her nose twice. 'When you been around as long as I have, dear, you know these things.'

'Do you know who her pimp was?'

Her laugh had a guttural tone to it. 'Not personally, no, but I saw her talkin' with a big black guy just outside the estate one day.'

'Do you know his name?'

'No I don't. We've enough of them on the estate, their kids left to run riot.'

'Did you ever see her in a red Jaguar?'

'Believe me if I did I'd remember that. Like I told you, she stayed at mine twice and that was a while back.'

Bradfield had heard enough and was eager to get rid of her.

'Well, Mrs Phillips, WPC Morgan has taken notes about your complaint, but your grandson was re-arrested because he lied to us, and he has been assisting us with our enquiries.'

'Well, now you got to assist me.'

'As I said, WPC Morgan will process your complaint through the appropriate channels.'

'You got no right to keep him here and I want to see him before I go.'

'Your grandson was released last night, Mrs Phillips,' Kath said.

'Well, where is he then? You lot picked him up, he obviously puked because you treated him so badly, and now I dunno where he is.'

'You can report him missing to WPC Morgan,' Bradfield said, wishing she'd stop yapping and leave.

'No, I just want to know where he is.'

Bradfield thought the same, wondering if Eddie Phillips had done a runner, or worse, was going to tip off Big

Daddy that the police had been asking questions about him. He stood up and said he would circulate Eddie's description on the Met radio. He didn't say the real reason was he wanted Eddie arrested again as he'd lied about Julie Ann staying at his grandmother's. He ushered her to the door and opened it, eager to talk to two drug squad officers who he hoped could shed some light on the dealers Julie Ann had scored from. As Kath was about to step into the corridor he leaned over and whispered to her.

'Let her sign the complaint forms then bin them, and tell everyone I want that little shit Phillips found asap.'

Kath wasn't happy about his instructions, but as he was her superior officer she felt obliged to do as he told her.

Bradfield shut the door behind them and sitting at his desk he sighed. He ran his hands through his hair and then lit a cigarette, inhaling deeply and letting the smoke drift up into two circles above his head. Eddie had lied yet again. Bradfield reckoned it was more than likely fear, but at the same time something really bothered him. Where was Julie Ann for those missing two weeks? Not with Eddie, it would seem, and not staying at his grandmother's. She had to have been somewhere, and someone had to know. He began to think that all the searching for the driver of the red Jaguar was possibly a waste of time and manpower. After the first wave of excitement it felt like the investigation was flat-lining and if it continued that way the case would end up in the dead files. Bradfield needed a result, because without one it would be his career in the doldrums.

CHAPTER NINE

Jane was enthralled as Harker continued his lecture, even when he said that the pictures he was about to show the class may be quite distressing and he understood if anyone felt the need to look away. Jane reckoned everyone was so worked up about what was coming that no one would be able to resist the urge to look, no matter how gruesome the slides were.

'Every crime scene is different and, like a roll of film, tells a story with a beginning, middle and an end. We all like a happy ending, but if you fail to deal with a crime scene properly, in a slow, methodical manner, you will make critical and irreversible mistakes.'

He walked over to the carousel projector and brought up the slide which he said was of the mother's bedroom.

There were gasps round the room. A woman wearing a nightdress, dressing gown and slippers was on a wooden chair in the corner, tied up with a white sheet that was stained crimson red from her blood. Bloody footprints were all over the floor and blood splatters covered the two corner walls and ceiling area either side of the seat. Harker explained that the blood had come from the beating she had received, which had also left her face black and blue and totally unrecognizable. Brown packing tape was wrapped round her mouth and hands.

He then moved on to the next slide which was taken in the daughter's bedroom. On top of the bed there was a woman lying face down. As Jane scanned the body she noticed that the woman's legs were apart, her dress had been lifted up over her bare buttocks, and her underwear had been ripped in half. Harker didn't need to say anything as it was clear from the photograph that she had been raped and murdered. There was a stunned silence and Jane could see some of her fellow officers looked horrified. She didn't feel squeamish, more fascinated by the scene and eager to hear from Harker about the items and clues recovered for forensic examination.

Harker continued, 'The pathologist estimated that both women had been dead since early to late Wednesday evening. The mother in the chair suffered a repeated beating to her head and face with a blunt object, but that didn't actually kill her. She was physically sick, but the packing tape round her mouth forced her to try and swallow her vomit back down and she choked to death. Her attacker stabbed her in the heart after death and further multiple injuries were also discovered at the post-mortem. She had many minor stab injuries to her neck, chest, arms and legs, none of which would have killed her, but would have caused intense pain.'

He took a long pause before he continued.

'The daughter's hands were taped together at the front and her mouth gagged as well. She was strangled from behind, most probably while the assailant raped her, though this may have occurred after the strangulation. There were no traces of semen so the suspect either failed to ejaculate or wore a condom.'

There were more gasps around the room at the suggestion of necrophilia.

Harker moved on to the next slide which was a close-up of the daughter's face and neck revealing her bulging, bloodshot eyes.

'The red pinpoint-type marks in her eyes are petechial haemorrhages and this is a classic sign to the pathologist of asphyxiation due to obstruction of the airway. The haemorrhages occur when blood leaks from the tiny capillaries in the eyes, which can rupture due to increased pressure on the veins in the head when the airways are obstructed. The red abrasions on her neck were caused by the assailant's fingers and you can also see some fingernail marks. However, these can sometimes be caused by the victim themselves when trying to pull the attacker's hands from their throat.'

Jane held up her hand. 'I was wondering about fingerprints.'

Harker looked at his watch. 'I was going to cover that after lunch, but seeing as you ask I'll do it now. A fingerprint at a crime scene *could* be evidential gold, especially if whoever left it already had a criminal record meaning their fingerprints were previously taken and retained on file. We then have something to physically search against, and hopefully get a match providing us with a suspect's details.'

Jane raised her hand again, and he glanced towards her.

'Could some people's prints be at a scene innocently? I mean what if they'd just visited the premises for—'

'Yes, yes, I am just coming to that.'

He went on to explain to the class that every fingerprint recovered from the scene was sent to the fingerprint bureau at Scotland Yard and manually searched against the many thousands of criminals' fingerprints on record. Prints were also taken from everyone known to have visited the premises for elimination purposes.

'We discussed fibres from a suspect's clothing.' Harker stared at Jane. 'If his clothes are covered in blood he would probably burn or throw them away, so what use are fibres then?'

Jane thought he was testing her knowledge, but he didn't know what she had learned so far on the Julie Ann Collins case.

'Well, if the suspect went to and from the scene in a car there may still be traces of the car fibres at the murder scene and traces of the victim's and suspect's clothes in the car. There may even be traces of the victim's blood in the car.'

'That is a good point, because I did find a large amount of blue cotton fibres on the daughter's top, skirt and legs, which could not be traced back to anything in the cottage and therefore must have come from the suspect's clothing when he lay on top of her and committed the rape and murder.

'As you can see, the interpretation and assessment of a crime scene is constantly evolving as more evidence is uncovered and examined at the forensic lab. At the time we actually knew quite a bit about our suspect, but sadly not who he was. We considered, from the evidence, the possibility of a tradesman that owned, or had access to, a car, wore size 8 Gazelle trainers and a blue boiler suit. While shoe size is a poor predictor of exact height, there is a relationship between the two and without going into mathematical detail the suspect could have been between roughly five foot six to five ten, assuming he had stopped growing. I should also add that we did find *one* fingerprint that we were sure was the suspect's and in doing this we did something that was quite unique.'

Like the rest of the class, Jane was transfixed. She was enjoying testing herself and applying her new-found knowledge to the Collins case.

After a couple of pints and a chat with the drug squad officers in the Warburton Arms, Bradfield and Gibbs went for a late lunch in the canteen. Their shepherd's pie and chips was greasy, and even with heavy dollops of HP sauce the food was still unpalatable.

'I can't eat this shite,' Bradfield said, pushing his plate to one side.

Gibbs ploughed on, shovelling forkfuls into his mouth, but both were frustrated as the drug squad officers had not heard of a Big Daddy, or a sidekick called Dwayne.

Gibbs wiped his mouth with his napkin. 'Looks like that little turd Eddie Phillips was lying about Julie Ann Collins again ... and has done a runner.'

'Yeah, I know that, thank you, Spence, but the drug squad guys will keep digging and hopefully they'll find out something positive for us. I want that little bastard Eddie found and dragged back in here.' He stood up and replacing his chair under the table gripped the top of it. 'I'll be in my office going over everything, but I got to tell you, Spence, it's not looking good and DCS Metcalf is constantly wanting updates.'

'I thought he was supposed to be running the investigation,' Gibbs remarked.

'He's busy on another case so he's overseeing it and entrusting me with the investigation, but I'm telling you, Spence, right now this case is flat-lining.'

*

'Now comes the most fascinating part of today,' said Harker as they settled back into their seats after lunch. 'The ever charming and helpful suspect Brian Hall agreed to come into the station. Meanwhile, two officers attended his uncle's premises making enquiries about Hall's movements during the week of the murder. Low and behold his work records revealed he'd delivered and assembled a new double-sized wooden bed and mattress on the Wednesday morning to the two women's address.'

Everyone in the class sat bolt upright, listening intently as Harker put up a slide of the mother's bedroom and pointed out that, although the wooden headboard was new, no one had noticed or thought about it at the time. When asked if he had heard about the murder Brian Hall had looked totally shocked and said that he hadn't, but he could have been to the premises on a delivery but wasn't sure as it was months ago. Hall was confronted with the delivery and cash payment invoice that his uncle had given the police, but he remained calm and said he must have been to the premises, but had totally forgotten about it as he did so many deliveries every week and could not remember every person he met.

'It was as if butter wouldn't melt in his mouth. He wasn't at all nervous and had an answer for everything. He accounted for his movements after work by saying that he was at home all evening with his father, who just happened to be suffering from early onset Alzheimer's, thus his alibi couldn't be disproved beyond doubt. The DCS decided to arrest Hall on suspicion of murder, and obtained a warrant to search his house and car and go over everything with a fine-tooth comb.' Jane yet again put up her hand and asked about the blue fibres and if they came from Hall's boiler suit.

'Good question. I recall you brought up the fibre possibility earlier,' he remarked.

Harker continued by saying they were a match, but sadly the suit was very common and the one Hall wore didn't have any blood or fibres from the victim's clothing on it, and both his company van and car were spotlessly clean and the latter had new seat covers and rubber mats. Hall was also asked if he owned Gazelle trainers and he said he didn't. It seemed that he had every angle covered and their only hope was he'd slipped up or was being too clever for his own good.

He indicated for the next slide to be brought up. It was a large colour close-up of a smiling Brian Hall, a keen angler, on a riverbank. He was crouching down and proudly holding up a first-prize cup with a very large freshwater carp on the ground by his feet.

'Taken two weekends before the murders and found hanging in his living room – this was mistake two. Remember I told you every picture tells a story, but can you spot it?'

There was total silence as everyone looked at the picture, tilting their heads this way and that to try and see it from different angles, but no one was forthcoming with an answer.

Harker dropped another clue. 'He said he'd never owned a particular type and brand of trainer?'

Everyone's attention was instantly drawn to Hall's feet and there were repeated echoes around the room of the words 'Gazelle trainers', which he was wearing in the photograph.

'Also note the good condition the trainers are in, which means they were fairly knew. We also found a ratchet screwdriver in his tool kit, and although it fitted for the murder weapon on the older woman there were no forensic traces whatsoever on it and we think it was obviously thoroughly cleaned. Mistake three was the real nail in his coffin and the discovery of evidence by myself that I am particularly proud of. I was able to match a section of the tape used to gag the victims with a reel I discovered at his premises. However, when Hall was asked about it he refused to answer any further questions from that moment on. He never admitted or said another word until he appeared for trial at the Old Bailey.'

Harker looked at his watch and closed his file. 'The jury unanimously convicted Brian Hall of both murders. Although we were pretty certain he stole money from the two ladies no large sums were ever recovered from Hall's home. It may have been they didn't have much money on the premises, which makes their torture and murder even more senseless.'

The class applauded Harker as the lights flickered back on and the lecture ended. For Jane it had been an excellent and informative day and she couldn't wait to talk to Kath about everything she'd learned. Harker reminded everyone that cracking a case was a team effort: police, forensic scientists and crime scene officers all working together and sharing information was what resulted in success.

'I hope you have all found today useful and that you can take away something beneficial from it, maybe in how you approach a crime scene as the first officer attending, or a murder investigation for those of you who aspire to becoming detectives. That's it. Good work, everyone – would the spokesperson for each group please stack the files on the desk by the door as you go?'

The rest of the class had gone when Jane approached

Harker, who was placing his acetate and projection slides into his briefcase.

'Excuse me, Dr Harker,' she said as she neared.

He clicked his briefcase closed and looked up at her.

'May I ask you a question?'

He sighed and nodded.

'I was interested in how people react in stressful situations.'

'You can probably answer that question yourself to an extent. If you think about it, most of us at some time in our lives have experienced the range of feelings that accompany traumatic experiences, such as depression, denial and so on.'

'You said Brian Hall was shocked and concerned when told about the murders. I just wondered what it was in his manner during the interrogations that convinced you even more that you had the right person.'

Harker lifted his briefcase from the desk. 'As a scientist I deal with and advise on questions relating to the crime scene and forensics. Detectives always carry out the interviews with a suspect.'

'Oh right ... I didn't realize, I thought from your talk that you were present, but thank you ...' Jane thought from his demeanour and answer he wasn't interested in talking to her. She started to walk off.

'That's not to say I can't help you as I'm well versed in every aspect of the Brian Hall case, and working alongside experienced detectives I've often discussed a suspect's guilt and behaviour with them.'

'What are the reactions that give the suspect away and make detectives think they are guilty?'

'In the case of Brian Hall it was quite clear his concern was a cover to make it appear he felt sympathetic and upset about the two victims and was not connected to their deaths.'

'Did he ever get angry or lose his temper during the interviews?'

'Sometimes a suspect, even an innocent one, will show rage and aggression towards the interviewing officers, but Hall was different. He was arrogant; he looked down his nose at them with contempt and thought they were fools. For the first time in his life he was the focus and centre of attention, and even when confronted with the packing tape as damning evidence he believed he was too clever to be caught. He had an answer for everything, never showed any remorse and I honestly believe he would have killed and raped more women if he hadn't been caught.'

Jane thought about how best to put her next question before continuing.

'Say a person killed someone close to them, like a loved one, relative or friend, could they react with anger at any stage?'

'From what I have learned from other cases the answer is yes, but where and when the anger will manifest itself is often variable and could be in private. Anyone who has committed a serious crime like murder is under a great deal of stress. Behavioural reactions like a sudden out-burst of anger, in or out of a police interview, can be the result of inner turmoil and remorse about the crime com-mitted, but it doesn't mean the suspect is inherently guilty.'

Jane persisted. 'So, losing a loved one under any cir-cumstances must create all sorts of dreadful emotions and confusion?'

'Yes, but sometimes emotion can give a suspect away, so you need to watch their reactions closely. They may shed a few crocodile tears in a false display of grief to try and hide their guilt.'

'But how can they force themselves to cry like that?'

'Like an actor they draw on their own emotional experiences and trauma. The only difference is the suspect's emotional experience is a real murder they committed. Sometimes the tears may be regret for what they have done or even self-pity,' he said, and looked at his watch.

'Thank you for your help, Dr Harker, and I really enjoyed your talk ...'

'Listen, it's after five, would you like to join me for a drink?'

She gasped. Hearing the time, she realized that she would be late for the wedding rehearsal.

'Oh no, I have to go! I'm sorry, I would have liked to, but my sister's getting married.'

He gave her a confused look.

'There's a church rehearsal and I'm chief bridesmaid and I can't be late for it.'

She hurried to collect her bag from beside the desk she had been sitting at.

'Another time then – I'm sorry, I don't know your full name.'

'It's Jane Tennison,' she said, hurriedly pulling her jacket off the back of her chair and putting it on.

'Where are you stationed?' he asked as he opened the classroom door.

'I'm a probationer at Hackney.'

'I'll know where to find you then.' He let the door close behind him, leaving her alone in the classroom.

Realizing the Underground would be her quickest option Jane ran to the Holloway Road station. She showed her warrant card at the barrier and the guard let her through. She rushed down the escalator onto the Piccadilly Line train. It wasn't until she changed at Piccadilly Circus for the Bakerloo Line and was heading for Maida Vale that she thought about Dr Harker asking her to have a drink with him. As she sat back in her seat she thought he must have appreciated her attentiveness and constructive comments regarding the fibre traces. It never entered her head that he might also have found her attractive.

Jane looked at her watch as she ran from Warwick Avenue Underground station, across Edgware Road and into Hamilton Crescent towards St Mark's Church. She was already late, and arriving at the church she had difficulty in opening the large wooden doors. Frustrated, she twisted and turned the big metal-ring door-handles. Finally the latch on the inside lifted and she was able to push the heavy door open with her shoulder. Through the glass vestibule doors she could see her sister, Tony the groom, the best man, the bridesmaids and her parents standing in front of the altar. The vicar was rehearsing the vows and was interrupted mid-sentence as the doors clattered loudly behind Jane as they closed. In unison everyone turned and looked to the back of the church.

'I'm so sorry,' Jane said in a loud voice which echoed round the church. She hurried down the aisle removing her raincoat and shoulder bag, which she threw down on a pew, before standing next to her mother in police uniform.

Mrs Tennison glared at Jane and whispered that she had missed most of the rehearsal. She told her to take off her uniform jacket and stand with the other bridesmaids.

Pam looked at her parents and Jane. 'About time, Jane! Mummy, you won't be standing there, you will be sitting in the first pew, and at this point so should you be, Daddy.'

'I was just standing in for Jane, dear,' her mother replied and pushing her husband scuttled with him to the pew.

The vicar made a deliberate coughing sound to get everyone's attention before continuing with the wedding vows. Pam was wearing a small makeshift veil, and on hearing the vicar say, 'You may now kiss the bride,' she lifted it, but wasn't smiling as she was still upset about Jane being late.

The vicar then showed them the anteroom and register the 'newly married, happy couple' would sign. Pam turned to Jane and put her hands out towards her.

'Hold these.'

'Hold what?' Jane asked, as there was nothing in Pam's hands.

'I'm miming handing you my bouquet of flowers before we sign the register, then you hand them back afterwards.'

'Right.' Jane nodded her head dutifully, holding out her hands to accept the imaginary bouquet.

'And remember when we enter and leave the church you need to be far enough behind me so you don't step on my veil.'

'Right,' Jane repeated and pretended to hand the bouquet back.

Jane and her mother walked home as it wasn't very far. Mrs Tennison slipped her arm through Jane's. 'You should have gone with your sister and the other bridesmaids – a few of the girls from the salon are joining them later as well for her hen night.'

'Well, for one she didn't ask me. Anyway, I doubt they'd appreciate me being in uniform, unless they were having one of those silly, haw-haw, dress-up-as-policewomen hen-party evenings.'

'No. She's booked a table at the Clarendon and Daddy's paying. I hope Tony doesn't let him have too much to drink, you know how belligerent he can get when he's two sheets to the wind, insisting on doing his Greek-dancing routine.' Tony, rather ill at ease, had asked Mr Tennison to join him and the best man for a few beers.

Jane laughed, recalling how much her father had enjoyed his holiday in Corfu a few years ago. She couldn't picture him with his soon-to-be-son-in-law doing something so frivolous.

'How was the lecture? Run over, did it?' her mother asked pointedly.

'Dr Harker was absolutely fascinating and I learnt so much. The case was a vicious double murder where a—'

An anxious-looking Mrs Tennison interrupted. 'Yes, well, I'm glad you were in a classroom and not out patrolling a rough area like Hackney where vicious crimes like that happen.'

'The murder took place in a cottage in Biggin Hill. That's in the Kent countryside, Mum.'

When they arrived home Mrs Tennison hung up her coat alongside Jane's uniform jacket.

'Let me see you in the dress, Jane, because you know Pam will have a fit if it doesn't look perfect.'

Jane reluctantly went to her bedroom, took off her uniform shirt and looked at the black zip bag hanging ominously on the back of the bedroom door. It reminded her of a body bag as she slowly unzipped it to reveal the bridesmaid dress. The layers of salmon-pink taffeta burst out again below the corseted waist. Taking it off the hanger she unpinned the wide cummerbund-style belt that had an over-large satin bow round it, but worse still for Jane were the dreadful puff sleeves. 'Oh my God,' she said to herself as she held the dress up to her body and looked in the mirror.

Her mother walked in and clapped her hands together with a delighted smile. 'Oh isn't it beautiful? You and the other bridesmaids are all in identical dresses, and wait until you see Pam's wedding gown! Come along now, put it on, let me see you in it. I hope it won't need any last-minute alterations. I'll just put our supper in the oven and be back in a minute,' she said and picked up Jane's dirty work shirt to put in the laundry basket.

Jane closed her bedroom door then billowed out the skirt before unzipping the back of the dress to step into it. With trepidation she pulled it up; thankfully it was the right length. She twisted the bodice round and zipped it up as best she could before putting her arms through the awful puff sleeves. She looked in the mirror. 'Shit,' she muttered, noticing the sweetheart neckline was embarrassingly low and the corset pushed up and accentuated her 34DD breasts. She sighed: there was nothing she could do about it now. She held her hands up in front of her breasts as if holding the imaginary bouquet and thought the flowers might just cover the revealing neckline. She really didn't want to go to the wedding in what she considered a monstrosity of a dress, and all she could hope for now was that all police leave would be cancelled that day. She had to twist the dress round to get out of it. She hung it up, pulled on her old dressing gown and left the room, calling to her mother,

'It's a perfect fit, Mum. Nothing needs to be done.'

CHAPTER TEN

Bradfield was putting on his suit jacket, ready to call it a day, when he heard the knock at the door and Sergeant Harris entered.

'Sorry to bother you, but I've just had the control room from the Yard on the blower. There's a possible crime scene at Regent's Park and—'

'That's not even on my patch. Tell them to call the local DCI out,' he said tersely as he put on his coat.

'Sergeant Paul Lawrence, lab liaison, has requested you attend. Apparently a woman walking her dog along the canal towpath saw a body in the water trapped between two stationary barges.'

'What the hell has that got to do with me?' Bradfield snapped.

'DS Lawrence fished the body out and thinks he might be that Eddie Phillips bloke you were looking for.'

'Jesus Christ, that's all I need. Can you arrange for a blues-and-twos car to run me to the scene?'

'Already have, they're waiting in the yard.'

Bradfield was so tired that he fell asleep in the back of the car, even with the siren blaring away. When he arrived a uniform officer took him down to a stretch of the canal towpath between Regent's Park Road and Gloucester

Avenue. The area was dimly lit with towpath lights. As Bradfield approached he saw DS Lawrence holding a clipboard and writing some notes. He was standing beside the body which was face down on a large white plastic sheet and still dripping wet.

'Sorry to call you out to this, guv. I'm not sure if it is your boy – his face is a bit bloated so I'd say he'd been in the water for a good few hours – but there are similarities to the description you put out for Eddie Phillips. Luckily for us he was wedged between two barges otherwise he'd have sunk to the bottom and probably not surfaced for a few days, and then he would have been totally unrecognizable.'

Bradfield looked around, sighing. 'It would help if we had a bit more light for a start – you need to turn him over and shine a torch on his face.'

'I was just making a sketch and some notes about the injury on the back of his head – there's a big lump and cut.'

Bradfield borrowed a torch from a uniform officer, then knelt down and closely examined the injury wondering if it was from an intentional blow or accidental fall. DS Lawrence shone his torch onto the shirt. Bradfield followed suit and they could both see that it was pale blue with a floral print and frilled cuffs and had water-diluted bloodstains on the collar and some drops down the back.

Lawrence shone his torch further along the body and Bradfield saw that the trousers were purple velvet and the shoes suede and high-stacked.

He looked up at Lawrence. 'Well, that's a relief.'

'What is?'

'I don't think this is Phillips as he doesn't wear this type of poncey gear. Last time I saw him he was dressed in shitty, puke-stained clothes and dirty scuffed boots.' He folded back the collar to see the make of shirt and Lawrence peered over his shoulder.

'It's a Mr Fish, they—'

'I'm not in the mood for silly ironic water-related jokes after schlepping all the way out here for nothing.'

'I'm being serious. Mr Fish makes and sells upmarket, fashionable clothes for elite customers like Mick Jagger and David Bowie. He's got a boutique in Clifford Street, Mayfair. That shirt would probably set you back fifty quid and the velvet trousers at least forty.'

'How do you know these things?' Bradfield asked, still wondering if Lawrence was having a laugh at his expense.

'I've dealt with a few rich people in my time. A Mr Fish suit would set you back over a hundred or more, unlike an off-the-peg from Horne Brothers for a few quid.'

Bradfield shook his head and sighed. 'Can we just get this over and done with so I can get a pint before the pub closes? Flip him over so I can see his face.'

DS Lawrence grabbed the feet and asked the uniform officer to help. Together they slowly turned him over. Bradfield noticed there was also a frill down the front of the shirt. He moved the torch light towards the face. It was slightly bloated, with long, shoulder-length wet hair, and there was a fine white froth covering the mouth and nose. He knelt down again to get a closer look.

'What's that stuff round his mouth?'

'The frothy foam is a mixture of water, air and mucus, whipped up by respiratory efforts to breathe, and indicates that the victim was still alive when he went in the water.'

Bradfield rolled up the left sleeve of the frilled-cuffed shirt and saw the faint injection mark.

'Fuck it, this is Eddie Phillips,' he said, shaking his head.

'I'm glad I called you then,' Lawrence remarked with a sigh of relief.

Bradfield looked puzzled as he stood up and looked at Lawrence. 'Baffles me where he got this expensive gear from when he hasn't got a pot to piss in. And what's he doing over here in Central London?'

'Maybe he was doing a bit of dealing,' Lawrence suggested.

'Was there anything in his pockets?'

'Loose change and a soggy bus ticket from Hackney, dated yesterday,' Lawrence said, holding up a clear plastic property bag with wet items inside.

'Have you any signs as to where he might have gone into the water?'

DS Lawrence pointed to two barges a few yards away. 'He was wedged in there and a bit further up by the bench under the bridge I found some blood drops, and these.'

He held up another property bag and shone his torch on it. The bag contained the paraphernalia used to inject heroin; a syringe, a darkened burnt spoon, lighter and a trouser belt. Lawrence took Bradfield over to the bench where he'd found the items and suggested a possible-case scenario was that Eddie sat on the bench, shot up, and once the drug kicked in fell, hitting his head on the ground. He shone his torch on the concrete pavement before continuing.

'As you can see there are some blood drops in one area, then a trail towards the canal. Those coupled with the blood on his shirt collar and back suggest he might have fallen, banged his head, stood up then staggered forward and fallen into the water between the barges.'

Bradfield said nothing as he followed the blood trail, shining his torch onto the murky water between the barges. He then returned and looked at the body's arms.

'I hear you, but I can't see a clear fresh injection site and there's no empty heroin bag, which could mean he got a whack round the back of the head and was dragged over to the canal and thrown in.'

'Yeah, that's possible. But the empty bag could have been blown into the canal and if he was dragged on his back I'd expect to see a smear of blood on the pavement. Any fresh needle marks would be hard to distinguish on a dead body, especially in light like this,' DS Lawrence explained.

'Shit, I need this like a hole in the head.'

'Sorry to spoil your evening, guv, but it could turn out to be an accidental OD that caused the chain of events leading to his death.'

'I bloody well hope so, Paul, but I need to bottom this out quickly so get his body taken to Hackney Mortuary and call out Prof Martin. I want a full post-mortem done tonight and toxicology done asap.'

'I don't think he'll be pleased. I'll see what I can do about the tox results, but usually it's at least two weeks.'

'I couldn't give a toss about Martin. If he gets bolshie find another pathologist.'

Bradfield contacted DS Gibbs from a payphone near the scene. He told him to visit Nancy Phillips with WPC Kath Morgan to inform her that Eddie's body had been found in the Regent's Canal. He also instructed him to bring her down to the mortuary to do a formal ID before the post-mortem began.

'Bloody hell, guv, you know what time it is an' I got a gig with me band over at Greenwich.'

'Can't you get someone else to do it?'

'I'm the singer and—'

'Just effing get on with it, Spence.'

'OK, never mind – it's just a poxy gig in a pub anyway.'

It was nearly eleven o'clock when a rather irate Professor Martin began the post-mortem on Eddie Phillips' body. He wasn't at all pleased about being called out so late at night, but made out he was doing everyone a favour. However, Bradfield suspected he hadn't attended out of interest in the case, but rather for the extra money involved in an out-of-hours PM. Bradfield and Lawrence both noticed Martin smelt of whisky and was slurring his words. They knew Martin had a reputation for liking a drink and Bradfield would have been within his rights to get a replacement, but he didn't want a stand-up argument and calling out another pathologist would delay everything.

Martin was given some strong black coffee as the body was washed and prepared for the autopsy. It was a long PM, as Martin took short breaks during which he consumed more coffee and a packet of ginger nut biscuits. It was over half an hour before Martin finally cut the body open to examine the internal organs. A short while later he looked up at Bradfield and Lawrence.

'Right, my friends, there's a considerable amount of water in the lungs and stomach of our chappie, which is obviously consistent with drowning. I would estimate, from body discolouring and slight bloating, that he'd been in the water since early morning.' He burped loudly and excused himself with a loud, 'Beggin' your pardon, gentlemen.'

Bradfield was becoming irritated: he'd had a long, tiring day. 'How could it take so long for anyone to notice the body?' he asked DS Lawrence.

'Well, because it was trapped and partially hidden between the two moored barges,' Lawrence said, yawning.

Growing ever more impatient Bradfield lit another cigarette and looked at Professor Martin.

'How do you think he got the injury to the back of his head?'

'Well, in my opinion it occurred shortly before death and he may well have been unconscious when he hit the water. However, as we sometimes have to say in the trade ... I can't give you a definitive answer as to the exact mechanism of injury, but I can say he drowned.'

'You've already told me that, Professor, but I need to know if the injury was deliberate and led to him drowning. Have I got a murder or an accident?' Bradfield said, beginning to seethe.

'Well, he could have received a deliberate blow from a blunt object, but pathologically I have no bloody way of being sure.'

Bradfield clenched and unclenched his fists as Martin, slurring his words, sprayed him with ginger biscuit crumbs as he spoke.

DS Lawrence gestured with his hand for Bradfield to calm down.

'Len, my theory from the blood trail is that Eddie shot up, fell backwards, cracked his head open, got up and staggered—'

Bradfield shook his head and interrupted. 'But it doesn't rule out somebody else picking him up and throwing him into the canal whilst he was unconscious or in a drug-induced state, does it?'

Martin gave a long sigh. 'Looks like he tired of injecting in his arm, even though the vein's not collapsed. I found an injection site in the boy's left groin and have taken blood and urine samples for drug and alcohol testing.' He wafted his hand towards his samples tray.

Bradfield remembered using Eddie's recent injections in his arm against him during interview. He watched as Martin prodded the dead boy's left groin with his finger.

'It's fresh and the only one in this area, so if injecting drugs caused him to fall over he had time to pull his pants up.'

Lawrence glanced at Bradfield as he squeezed his cigarette out and put the fag end into his pocket.

'Then that fits with how I saw it happening at the scene. I know it's all speculation, but it seems logical to me.'

Martin took off his apron and chucked it aside.

'If you don't mind I would like to go home to bed,' he said, and walked out.

Lawrence put his arm around Bradfield's shoulder.

'You look knackered, Len. Why don't you take off and get some shut-eye?'

'I'll grab some kip back at the station. I'm gonna have to get all this down in a report for Metcalf, who's already breathing down my neck.'

'You can handle him, Len.'

As they were leaving the mortuary assistant pulled the green sheet over Eddie's naked body.

'What are the odds Metcalf lumbers me with Eddie's death investigation because of the connection to Julie Ann's murder?' Bradfield turned, looked at Eddie and shook his head. 'What a waste, and only nineteen years old.'

CHAPTER ELEVEN

Early the next morning John Bentley pulled up in a mark 1 white Ford transit van outside a row of garages off Masons Street at the far end of the Pembridge Estate. He unlocked the heavy-duty padlock he'd fitted to the garage door and, grabbing the handle, heaved it up on its metal rails. He had a quick look around before returning the few yards to his van and reversing it up to the open garage door. He got out and had another cursory look around before squeezing between the van and garage pillar. Opening the transit's rear doors he removed a sledgehammer, pickaxe and spade, then placed them in a large empty metal storage box at the back of the garage. Returning to the van he leaned in and started to drag out a heavy-duty electric Kango hammer drill, which caused a loud scraping sound as it slid along the van's metal floor. 'Bloody thing weighs a ton,' he muttered to himself as he decided to try and lift rather than drag it. He heaved for breath as he grabbed it with both arms and slowly walking backwards looked over his shoulder at the metal box and realized that it was too long to fit in. Unable to hold the Kango any longer he placed it on the ground and removed the concrete drill-bit so it was shorter. He lifted it into the metal box and stood with his hands on his hips, taking deep

157

breaths before locking the box and covering it with an old tarpaulin. As he was closing the van doors he was startled when he heard a voice.

'You heard what's going down?'

John looked to the side of the van and saw his brother.

'Jesus Christ, Dave, what you doin' creeping up on me like that?'

'I wasn't creepin', I just came to warn ya that the Old Bill's been nosing round the Kingsmead Estate and Edgar House since that young girl got murdered in the playground.'

John glanced at his brother. He was using his walking stick, his twisted leg making him lean over at the waist.

'I already know that, but if I'd known she was gonna get herself killed before I rented this poxy garage then I wouldn't have bothered, would I?' he replied sarcastically.

'I just wanted to warn you to be careful, that's all.'

'I am. Besides, if the rozzers are all busy looking for a murderer over on the Kingsmead they ain't gonna be sniffin' around here so much and that's better for us, isn't it?'

'Suppose so. You know that old big-mouth Ma Phillips?'

'Mum's friend, what about her?'

'She was in the street earlier, screaming her head off and accusing some detectives of murdering her grandson Eddie. She wants to form a protest group outside the nick.'

'She's always liked the sound of her own voice,' John said, jumping into the van.

He turned the engine on and moved the van forward six feet before getting out with the padlock and key.

'Did you get the Kango?' David asked.

'Yeah, bloody thing weighed a fuckin' ton,' John replied as he replaced the padlock on the garage door.

'Should have asked me – I'd have helped carry it in.'

'I was out early cos I had to drive out through the Blackwall Tunnel to a dealer in Kent for a cash buy. He assured me it's untraceable, but he was a nasty sod and didn't even help me lift it.'

'Maybe it might be better to take it back and exchange it for two smaller ones,' David suggested.

'Are you havin' a laugh or just bleedin' plain stupid?' he asked scathingly as he secured the padlock.

'No, stands to reason they'd be lighter and do the same job, only a bit slower, but if you are using two together then—'

'Shut up.'

'You got the cutting gear organized?'

John glared at his brother and whispered through gritted teeth, 'Keep your mouth shut – you wanna telegraph what we're workin' on?'

'There's nobody about, and I was only askin'.'

'I don't want to use the same fence for everything on the job, it's too risky. So I'm goin' even further afield for that – believe me I'm lookin' out for you and me. By the way are you comin' to visit Dad this afternoon?'

'Yeah, of course I am. Gimme a ride back to Mum's wiv you?'

John got into the driving seat and his brother moved round to the passenger side. It never ceased to infuriate David, the way he had to lean heavily on his walking stick to swing his gammy leg onto the foot-panel of John's van to get in. His strength was in his upper body, which he demonstrated when he was able to lift his body weight by gripping onto the side of the door. He plonked himself down on the passenger seat. He was glad the garage was only a short distance from the flat as he hated using his wheelchair. Some days, though, he had no choice, particularly as he couldn't walk far or stand up for long.

John drove from the rented garage onto a side road that skirted the Pembridge Estate. Passing Edgar House he suddenly slammed on the brakes causing David to lurch forward and nearly hit his head on the dashboard as the van came to a halt.

'What was it, a cat?' David asked as there was no other traffic and no one crossing the road.

John banged the palm of his hand on the steering wheel. 'How many times have I asked her to stay away from those old cows? All they do is gossip and yak about nothing.'

At first David wondered who his brother was talking about, but looking up and across the road he could see their mother, her hair in rollers, and wearing her wraparound apron and carpet slippers. She was standing with her arms folded and nodding her head as she talked to a group of women standing next to a police 'Appeal for Information' notice about the Julie Ann Collins murder. They were all gossiping and giving a mouthful to a group of kids who were playing and shouting abuse at each other.

'She misses doin' her cleaning and having someone to chat to,' David said in her defence.

'You know why I stopped that. To top it all the stupid bitch came home with a fuckin' policewoman the other day. I can't wait to find another place and get out of this dump. When I'm gone she can go to her bingo and do whatever she friggin' wants. But until it's over she stays put, and you are supposed to be keepin' an eye on her while I'm out graftin'.'

'Lemme go and get her,' David said as he pulled the door-handle.

'No, just leave it. The old man says we should put her in

a nursing home, and if she's any more trouble that's where she's bloody well going.'

'You can't do that to her – she's our mother.'

'Yeah, but if she screws this up for us I'll break her soddin' neck.'

David ignored John, got out of the van and, using his walking stick to lean on, limped towards the group of women.

John leant over and lowered the passenger window. 'She's not getting in here, so you can walk her home,' he shouted as he drove slowly past his brother.

Watching David walk made John apprehensive about using him on the job. He had mentioned his worries to his dad on a previous prison visit, but his father took the view that families should stick together and that David should be the lookout. His dad had also told him to keep the team numbers to a minimum, and only bring in people they knew they could trust with their lives. John just hoped that David's lameness wouldn't be a liability.

When David and his mother returned to the flat a few minutes later John was sitting in the kitchen working out the finances in a small black notebook. Hearing the front door slam he snapped it closed.

David walked into the kitchen. 'Mum said Ma Phillips had to identify her grandson's body last night. Apparently his face was all black and blue and she reckons the Old Bill done him in and dumped him in the Regent's Canal.'

John yawned. 'Can't see why they'd bother to take him all the way there when there's the River Lea right on their doorstep.'

Renee walked in, picked up the kettle and started to fill it with water. 'You were out early this morning – do you want a cup of tea?'

David nodded, but John didn't even acknowledge his mother.

'John?' she asked.

'No, and what did I tell you about staying away from them women, Ma?'

'I was, but then the police started knocking on doors looking for Eddie Phillips and asking questions about the murder. A detective even came round here and—'

John banged the table hard with his fist. 'You didn't say I was livin' here, did ya?'

'No, course not, I said it was just me and David, who was a cripple, and he left. There was so much going on I wanted to find out a bit more so I went to see Nancy Phillips. She lives at the far end of the estate. Her grandson knew the girl who was—'

'I really don't care,' John interrupted, wishing she'd shut up.

'Turns out he was the last to see her alive. They arrested him and then he ends up dead and in—'

'The Regent's Canal. I know already.'

'Did she tell you as well?'

'No!' John snapped back at her. 'Shut up, mind yer bloody business and stay indoors. You got a new colour TV now instead of that black-and-white one, so just sit and watch it.'

'Did you want a cup of tea?'

'I said NO! Why can't you remember from one thing to the next? And listen up, we're gonna see Dad this afternoon and I can't take you cos I've only room for two in the van and David's coming with me.'

'Dave and I can go on the bus.'

'No you bloody can't, so for Chrissake listen to what I tell you. I'm gettin' sick of repeating myself – you got short-term memory loss, that's what you got.'

'Leave her alone, John. I'll have a cuppa with you, Ma,' David said as John stormed out of the kitchen saying he'd be in his room.

Renee got out a teapot, opened the caddy and started spooning in the tea leaves. 'He should be out lookin' for a job, not being nasty to me all the time. Where did he go this morning? He was out before I got up.'

'He's sorting some delivery work out, Ma.'

'Well, since he moved back in here he's been like a bear with a sore head. He should spend more time trying to sort out his marriage to Sandra. She never comes round to visit me no more.'

'That's his business. Don't tell him I told ya, but from a letter I saw I think they're getting a divorce.'

'That's terrible – no matter how badly your dad treated me I never even considered divorce. I just put up with him. John really needs to sort out his life. It was fine here before he moved back in, you know, when it was just you and me. You want a cup of tea?'

'Yeah, yeah, I said I'll have one. You keep forgetting stuff, Ma, and John worries about how you'll cope when you're on yer own.'

She pointed her finger at him. 'When am I gonna be on me own? And you listen to me, I coped with you two each time your dad was in the nick. I've bloody coped all me life. He'll be out soon and don't think I'm looking forward to it. He's seventy-four and I just hope to God he's calmed down. Besides, you'll be here wiv me, won't cha?'

David shrugged. 'Well, you know I got to think about my future, and it's not easy getting up and down the stairs here any more. I'm livin' on my disabled handouts and benefits, and you know how Dad likes his space round the flat. Maybe it's time for me to look for a place.'

'Have you found a girl then?' she asked, wagging her finger at him.

'No I haven't, and I'm not likely to, livin' here. Besides, Dad's worse than John with his moods. I've always been scared to death of him.'

Renee poured two mugs of tea and sat down. 'No need to remind me what your dad's like – I've lived with him and his temper for nearly fifty years. But where will you go? I mean you can't get a proper job, can you? Maybe the council will rehouse you if you complain about the stairs hurting your leg?'

David spooned sugar into his mug. 'I've always wanted to go to Florida.'

'Florida? You mean in America? How could you ever afford to go there?'

'Might get lucky one day. Where's the milk?'

'Oh I'm sorry.' She went to the fridge and brought out a pint bottle, pouring a drop into her own mug before passing the bottle to David.

'You know, what you really need is one of them NHS three-wheeled invalid cars. I've seen a bloke doing his grocery shopping in one, scoots along in and out the traffic, and he's got to be seventy or eighty.'

'Yeah, well, I'm not that handicapped or old yet, and I'm not gonna be holed up here for the rest of my life.'

Renee got up and opened a kitchen drawer. She pulled out a plastic bag containing David's medication. 'You're not up to somethin' with John, are you?' she asked quietly.

Ignoring her, he tipped out the pill boxes and containers, selecting one pill after another and laying them in a line on the table: antidepressants, painkillers and some for his kidney problems. He was also in constant pain from arthritis in his crippled leg, and his back throbbed like mad after his workouts with his weights.

Renee watched him and sighed. 'I'm not stupid, you know, David. Living with your dad I always knew when he was up to no good. He could never sleep, paced round the bedroom, and then going out at all hours with a pocket full of loose change. I knew he was going to the telephone box on the corner. The closer it got to him doing a bit of illegal business the more he'd be snapping at me. That time you fell off the church roof, I said to him don't take the boys with you and he slapped me one, but I was right. I mean look what happened to you.'

'Don't start on that again, Ma.'

She reached out and patted his hand. 'I wish I could do something, son. You've always been the handsome one, and you can still turn a girl's eye, so there's got to be a nice young lady out there for you.'

'If I can't fuck her she ain't gonna be interested in me, and I'm not going out with some old dog that feels sorry for me. Now go and watch telly and leave me alone.'

Renee was shocked at his language, but she said nothing and carried her mug into the lounge where she sat cupping it in her hands. She wanted to weep for David. He had always been her favourite and now he was an impotent cripple – all because her husband and his brother took him up onto that church roof.

Clifford, John and David had all received prison sentences after the botched church job. Living alone while they were all inside was the first time in her life she had found peace: no threats, no arguments, and no fear of the cops knocking on the door was bliss. Eventually, due to his injuries, David had been released early on parole and returned home where she cared for him. Having him dependent on her was not a burden: after all, he was her little boy. Without his father or brother around to influence or pick on him David was placid and they had enjoyed each other's company.

Renee sighed, sipping her tea. She was now almost certain something was going on, and that both her boys were involved.

David washed his mug and placed it on the draining board. He then scooped up his pills, tipping them into the plastic bag before putting it back in the drawer. As he began to feel the effects of the painkillers he decided to go and lie down. He used his stick to steady himself and edged past the folded wheelchair that he hated with a passion. He could hear the TV on loud and saw his mum in the lounge fast asleep, with her eyes closed and her mouth open. On the way to his room he thought he'd see how his brother was and went into the small box room, which contained a single bed, a wardrobe, an old sewing machine and boxes of clothes and junk. John was sitting thumbing through his small black notebook.

'Mum's asleep,' David said.

John looked up and stared at his brother. He realized from the dozy expression on his face he'd recently taken his medication.

'Are you all right, Dave?'

'Sure, just going to lie down. Get me up this afternoon when you're ready to go to Pentonville.'

'OK. Finances are really tight for the job. We still got a lot of stuff to store and need a good walkie-talkie set. The guy in Kent told me they got some at the Army barracks in Woolwich.'

'What, they sellin' off equipment?'

'No, I'm gonna have to nick 'em unless we can bribe a squaddie.'

'We? Are you taking me with you?' David asked nervously.

'No, I meant Danny Mitcham. He knows where the barracks is and being an ex-squaddie has a contact so I'll take him with me to suss it out.'

'Danny? So Danny's gonna be in on it as well then?' David frowned.

John nodded and went back to looking at his notebook.

'Are you sure about him? I mean he was discharged because he's a head case.'

'Danny whacked a military copper who was asking for it. Besides, he's reliable and as strong as an ox. He was on bomb disposals and there's nothin' he don't know about electrics. Now you go an' lie down, and sleep off your painkillers cos you know how Dad hates you lookin' dozy.'

David shuffled to his room and awkwardly lowered himself onto the bed. He thought about what his ma had said and wished he'd kept his mouth shut about Florida, but that's where he'd always dreamed of flying to. Not only for the sun and sea, but also the specialist treatment he'd been reading about. He had been given very little information or medical advice on his badly broken legs either in the hospital or the prison. The doctors and wardens said he deserved what he got for thieving. Whilst he was in prison the plaster cast on his right leg had been cut off and replaced twice due to the agonizing pain it caused. The doctors had attempted to straighten his leg, but it became deformed and twisted along the bone and knee joint. It had been eighteen months of torture until he could stand unaided, but his foot was permanently arched, the leg bent and he was in constant pain.

David eventually started to work out at a men-only gym, and the trainer encouraged him to concentrate on his upper-body strength. He soon became hooked on the high he got from working out hard and enjoyed the release that the physical exercise gave him from his daily stress and depression. At home, in the privacy of his bedroom mirror, he would proudly display his six pack and muscular arms to himself, but no amount of pornography lifted his flaccid member.

David remembered with humiliation the time he'd decided to pay a prostitute, but found himself unable to get an erection. His doctor told him that his inability to have an erection, and his depression, were physically and mentally linked to his accident and lame leg. He had left his local doctor's surgery refusing to believe he was impotent. Walking home he recognized some of the slags off the estate who he knew were toms that used a squat to do their business with clients. He had foolishly tried again, paying a blonde prostitute upfront, but this time the anger at his inability to perform made him physically abusive towards her. She threatened to report him to the police but he knew she never would, never could, as she was a cheap junkie selling her body for sex.

Feeling a fresh rush of frustration he thought instead about how he'd like a joint now, so he could dream about Florida. If they pulled the job off, it was going to be a reality – first class all the way. As he slowly drifted off to sleep he thought about the risk of them being caught. He knew that he would never survive another prison sentence. It was a sad comfort, but nevertheless a decision he had made – if they failed he would take his own life.

CHAPTER TWELVE

On her journey to the station Jane couldn't stop thinking about Dr Harker's lecture. Her quiet evening at home with her mother after the wedding rehearsal had ended on a note of amusement when a drunken Pam had returned home, picked up a wedding magazine and started moaning that she was unsure about her choice of wedding dress.

Mrs Tennison had had to persuade Pam that it was too late now to change her mind.

'It's gorgeous and you've made the right choice. It's just pre-wedding nerves.'

Jane had laughed and said to herself, wait until you see the state of my cleavage in my tight bridesmaid dress!

She had gone to her bedroom, leaving her mother and Pam to discuss the final details, bouquets and veils. For the first time in weeks she had not, as usual, gone straight to sleep. Instead she lay on her bed and thought about how she could use what she had learnt from the Harker lecture on the Julie Ann Collins case, especially as it helped to take her mind off the hideous bridesmaid dress.

Refreshed and eager to get back to work, Jane arrived at the station at 8 a.m. She was unsure whether DCI Bradfield would still want, or need her, to continue with the indexing of statements and information on the Collins investigation. She was about to knock on his door when Kath saw her in the corridor and scooted out from the incident room.

'Shush, Jane, don't wake him up. He's having a kip in his armchair.'

They both went into the incident room and Kath continued to update Jane about Bradfield.

'He didn't finish in the mortuary until 2 a.m., and then he had to write up his report cos the DCS is on his back. He's been here all night and God knows what time he eventually got to sleep. I've had a pretty rough night of it – Spencer Gibbs had me looking after Mrs Phillips after she threw a wobbly, but mind you I don't blame her under the circumstances.'

Jane had a puzzled look on her face. 'Kath, can you please slow down and start at the beginning as I don't have a clue what you're talking about regarding Mrs Phillips.'

'Sorry, I totally forgot you were at Harker's lecture yesterday. Bloody brilliant, isn't he? Did you spot the crucial clue with the suspect's trainers?'

'Yes to the talk and no to the trainers. Tell me more about what's been happening here.'

'Well, it wasn't exactly here, over at Regent's Canal to be exact. Anyway get a couple of coffees and a bacon roll for us both, an egg in mine as well, and then I'll give you the whole story,' Kath said, handing Jane some money.

She returned from the canteen fifteen minutes later and listened intently as Kath told her everything that had occurred the previous evening concerning Eddie Phillips and his grandmother.

'She was in tears but calm at first, well, more in a sort of catatonic shock, I'd say. Then when she ID-ed Eddie's body at the mortuary she really went off on one, screamed her head off and went for poor old Spencer. Her personality change was unbelievable.'

'Did she hit DS Gibbs?' Jane asked with surprise.

'Tried to slap him and then kicked him in the shins. It was quite funny as he was hopping about on one leg because it hurt so much!'

'Why did she react like that?'

'Do me a favour, Eddie's face was bloated and discoloured from being in the water. Anyway she was convinced Bradfield and Gibbs had beaten him to death then dumped his body in the Regent's Canal.' Kath went on to explain how she'd had to restrain Nancy and get the police surgeon out to sedate her.

'I felt so sorry for her I took her home and stayed the night with her. The drugs calmed her down, but she still had tears spilling down her cheeks and kept saying, 'My poor little fella, what a waste.' Eddie was all she had and even though he was a druggie she obviously loved him. She even told me that looking after him was what kept her going. Eventually she fell asleep, but when she woke up at the crack of dawn the drugs had worn off. She saw me as the enemy cos I was connected to Bradfield and Gibbs. She screamed that she'd tell the papers and get a petition up from everyone on the estate about how the police had murdered her grandson.'

'What happened then?' Jane asked.

'She told me to eff off out of her flat, so I did before she went for me as well.'

'Regent's Park is a bit off Eddie's usual patch for shooting up, isn't it? From what I read he normally used the squat on the Pembridge,' Jane remarked.

Kath cocked her head to one side, noting Jane's use of

'shooting up', proving that she had picked up the drug lingo Kath had explained to her.

'A dog walker found him face down between two barges, more towards Camden than by the Zoo side. Who knows what he was doing over that way. In fact Mrs Phillips came to the station yesterday morning as she thought he was still in custody, but he'd been released the day before.'

'I think it's really strange. I mean do they reckon he died where they found him, or elsewhere and was dumped?' Jane asked.

Kath shrugged. 'Gibbs told me they don't know for sure, but they think that whatever happened to him occurred on the canal path. So far there are no witnesses. All he had on him was a few coins and a bus ticket from Hackney, bought shortly after he was released from here.'

'How long had he been in the water?'

'No idea as I didn't get to stay for the post-mortem. But you know they got those two big markets in Camden and they're both fairly new, very trendy and the sort of place drug dealers might hang out.'

Jane remembered something. 'Didn't Eddie Phillips give DCI Bradfield the names of some dealers?'

'Yeah, and the drug squad came in and were with him for a couple of hours. They were going to do some digging and speak to informants and see what they could find out, but I don't think he's heard back from them.'

Jane sifted through the indexing carousel and finding the card she was looking for showed it to Kath.

'Eddie said two men, one nicknamed Big Daddy and someone called Dwayne.'

Kath nodded, 'Yeah, that's right.'

'Do you think Eddie got scared and went to see this Big Daddy?'

Kath had a drip of egg yolk on her chin and she wiped it off with her paper napkin before answering.

'Why would Eddie go see someone he's scared of?'

Jane shrugged. 'He might tell him about being arrested as a murder suspect, or that the police were asking questions about Julie Ann's dealer. He could say he kept quiet and didn't tell the police anything so—'

'He wouldn't look like a grass? I dunno, Jane, it's possible, but what I do know is the poor little bastard ended up dead.'

'We should have had him followed after he left here.'

'Yeah maybe, but I wouldn't go saying that to Bradfield. He was really pissed off last night because he still thinks Eddie was withholding information.'

'And I'll be more pissed off if you two don't get on with some work!' Bradfield said.

Kath and Jane were so engrossed in their conversation that neither of them had seen him standing in the doorway. He was rubbing his hair dry with a towel and had obviously just had a shower in the men's locker room. He threw his Eddie Phillips death-scene and post-mortem reports down on the desk and told Jane to get them typed up and indexed. He then turned to Kath and asked her to call the drug squad and tell them to pull their fingers out, as it was now possible that this Big Daddy character, or his sidekick Dwayne, had murdered Eddie Phillips.

Jane got out some blank index cards, placed two sheets of plain paper and carbon in the typewriter and began typing. Kath was straight on the phone to the drug squad whilst Bradfield asked Jane if Kath had updated her on the death of Eddie Phillips.

'Yes, sir,' she replied nervously, wondering how much he'd heard of her conversation with Kath.

'This case is going from bad to worse. Tell the team as they come in that I want an office meeting at 10 a.m. I'm going to the canteen for some breakfast,' he said gruffly.

Kath put the phone down. 'Two drug squad officers are already on their way from the Yard to see you, guv.'

He said nothing, simply raising his hand in acknowledgement as he left the room.

'Do you think he'd been standing there for long?' Jane asked.

'Na, otherwise he'd have had you over the coals for the remark about tailing Eddie. So tell me, how did it go with Dr Harker?'

'It was really interesting and informative when he discussed fibres being left behind and picked up at a scene by suspects. Especially as there were red carpet fibres on Julie Ann's socks. Dr Harker was very nice and I liked him ... he even asked if I would like to go for a drink.'

'Wow! Teacher's pet! So where did you go?'

'I didn't – I had a rehearsal for my sister's wedding.'

'So you turned him down? Couldn't the rehearsal have waited?'

'No way – you have no idea how obsessed my family have been with it all – the church arrangements, the reception venue, the invitations ... My sister is behaving like a prima donna and I can't think of anything worse than being a bridesmaid.'

'Ah well, she's your sister and it'll be her big day.'

'The only hope I have is of some major incident happening so that my leave gets cancelled and I have to come to work.'

'Don't be so cruel! You never know, you might get a leg-over with the best man.'

'For goodness' sake, Kath, if he's anything like the guy

she's getting married to that is definitely not going to be on the agenda.'

'Well, maybe you'll get another date with Harker – mind you, rumour has it he's married with kids.'

'What?'

'It's only what I heard. You gotta watch these forensic scientists – they're all smooth talk and touchy-feely. I think he's attractive in a sort of public-school way. Why not put yourself down for another one of his lectures?'

'I wouldn't mind another lecture but there's no date if he's married.'

Kath pursed her lips, smiling.

'Well, you're quite a prude, aren't you, Jane Tennison?'

'I don't think not dating a married man, children or not, has anything to do with being a prude. Why get into something that isn't going to do anything but cause hurt and emotional stress?'

'You're not gay, are you?'

'No I am not! Honestly, Kath, you're really embarrass-ing me.'

'Well, I don't know, you could be, as I've never seen you out with any of the guys from this station. Mind you, I can't say I blame you as most of them are only interested in havin' a quick shag. Are you dating a fella or shacked up with anyone?'

'You know that I live at home with my parents.'

'Oh Christ yes, I forgot. Did you fill in that request form for a section-house room?'

'Yes, but I haven't heard back yet.'

'I know there's a space coming up, and you'll have your pick of three floors of guys. Lotta drinking and sex goes on, but there's a uniform sergeant in charge who's like Godzilla. Heaven forbid if he catches you going in or coming out of one of the men's rooms, and vice versa for the blokes. Mind you I suppose living at home is not conducive to having a hot fling.'

'Kath, for heaven's sake!'

'My God, don't tell me you're a virgin?'

Jane had her back to the door. She was about to reply when she realized there were two men listening in behind her. They were both dressed scruffily in jeans and T-shirts and one had long, manky-looking hair and a droopy moustache. Kath burst into giggles, as Jane flushed bright red having been caught out twice in the space of minutes. The younger of the two detectives winked at Jane and said he lived in room 12 at the section house on the first floor. His mate commented that unfortunately he was married and lived at home, but having heard what Kath had just said he was now thinking of moving to the section house. They both laughed loudly and asked where DCI Bradfield was. Kath, still laughing, said he was in the canteen and they left the room.

'I'm sorry, Jane, but you should have seen them with their jaws wide open.'

'Who were they?' Jane asked.

'Drug squad guys by the looks of it.'

'Does the one with the scruffy hair really live in the section house?'

'No, but I wish he did,' Kath replied with a leering smile.

Jane was unsure how to rebuff the giggling Kath as she didn't like the way she had drawn her into discussing her private life. As always she could never remain uptight with Kath, who now hooked her arm around Jane's shoulder.

'Don't pay any attention to me, darlin'. With those big tits you got I'm sure you had a lot of guys panting after you at Hendon Police College. I know I did – lost my virginity to the PTI sergeant. The positions he could get into were unbelievable – he had a body like Burt Reynolds in *Deliverance*, and like the film he took me on a trip into unknown and dangerous territory,' she said with a cheeky grin and another giggle.

Jane didn't feel like laughing. In fact she felt rather disappointed in Kath, but she nevertheless laughed, acting as if it was all a joke.

Jane continued typing Bradfield's report. She couldn't stop thinking about the elderly Nancy Phillips' reaction when she'd seen her grandson's body. Although Jane felt sorry for her something niggled in her mind. Once she'd finished the typing she opened her handbag and got out the small notebook she had used during the lecture. She flicked through it until she came to the bullet points she'd made after her last conversation with Harker. She'd written and underlined 'Grief causes emotion = stress & anger = real or fake guilt?'

Jane hurriedly picked up a pen from the desk and wrote 'Julie Ann' next to her last entry and then put a circle round her name.

Pentonville Prison's visiting times were always crowded and noisy occasions. Families with children were usually kept over to one side, and the inmates were brought in by officers in groups of four to five. John and David sat at a table looking around the room to see if there was anyone they recognized as they waited for their father to be brought in.

'Here he is,' John said as he nudged David.

As their father strutted towards them he nodded to the

officer sitting in a high chair overlooking the room. Clifford Bentley had thick grey hair and his son John resembled him. Although John was slightly shorter they both had the same square jaw and dark hooded eyes.

Clifford sat facing his sons. He nodded hello to both of them before drawing a plastic pouch filled with tobacco and some Rizla papers from his trouser pocket. Opening the pouch he removed some tobacco and dropped it onto a paper and nonchalantly made a roll-up with one hand.

John reached into his pocket, slowly pulling out a box of matches. He held them up so the watching officer could see what he was doing, struck one and his dad leant forward with the roll-up in his mouth.

'Got everything for the new kitchen organized, have you?' Clifford said through the side of his mouth and took a deep drag before blowing the smoke in the air.

'Yeah, just a few more items needed but they're expensive. I've rented a garage, cash payment under a false name, and we're storing stuff there until we're ready to begin,' John said softly as he glanced round the room.

'Is it secure?' Clifford asked, and John nodded as he continued, 'Good, yer don't want anything nicked before you're ready to go.' His voice was gravelly from years of smoking and he had to cough frequently to clear his airways of phlegm. He handed John the roll-up and started to make another for himself.

'You'll have to work flat out when you start.'

'Yes, Dad,' the two sons said in unison.

'Good, but make sure you always do it in the right hours. Don't want locals complaining about the noise and calling the filth, do we,' he said, referring to the police, and the boys shook their heads.

'As soon as I'm released on parole I'll help if you need

me, but me joints ain't what they used to be,' Clifford said, putting the new roll-up in his mouth.

As he patted his pocket for a box of matches two young kids started fighting and screaming at each other. Clifford looked at the officer in the high chair and caught his eye.

'Letting kids in this effing place does me eardrums in, officer, it shouldn't be allowed ... Can't you sort 'em?'

The officer in the high chair nodded to his colleague on the floor to deal with the kids. Clifford used the opportunity to remove the palmed matches from his pocket and secretly place them on his lap under the table. John caught his father's eye and nodding picked up the box of matches he had used to light their cigarettes. He held up his hand and rattled the box again towards the floor officer for permission to hand them to his father. The officer nodded and went over to speak to the mother of the screaming kids. Clifford took the matches from John, lit his roll-up and then switched them for the box on his lap.

'So, who've you got to help decorate?' Clifford asked and made a show of tapping the box on the table whilst puffing at the thin cigarette he had rolled so expertly.

'Danny, the ex-Army bloke. He's good with electrics and well up for it.'

Clifford realized Danny would be the 'bell man'. He inhaled, slowly letting the smoke drift from his nose. 'Boxer, weren't he?'

John nodded. 'Yeah, he fought middleweight in the Army. Tough son of a bitch.'

'Well, if he's up for it then you got to make sure he knows exactly what the job entails, but more important what I expect from him.'

'He knows, Dad, he knows,' John replied.

Clifford flicked the ash into a tin ashtray on the table, palmed John's box of matches, and picking up his tobacco pouch folded it over, tucking the matches inside before putting it in his pocket. He looked at David.

'You've not said a thing yet, son. You OK?'

'I'm fine, Dad.'

'Is he, John?'

'For Chrissake, Dad, I can answer for meself!'

'I'm sure you can, son, but your eyes look squiffy. You ain't getting addicted to the painkillers, are yer, cos I warned you about them.'

'No, Dad, I only take what I need.'

Clifford wagged his finger at David. 'Are you on that wacky-backy shit? Loads of 'em use it in here and you can tell cos of their squiffy eyes.'

'No, I was out with Ma in the rain the other night and got a bit of arthritis in me leg. It's been real sore and keeping me awake so I'm just knackered, that's all.'

'How is she?'

John leaned forward. 'She's forgettin' stuff all the time. If she gets any worse she'll need to go in a nursing home. She's not cleanin' offices no more and I don't like her goin' out on her own.'

David glared at his brother. 'She's all right, I look out for her.'

'Well, I'll be out soon enough to check yer mother over and decide what's best for her ... but keep her indoors, and for Chrissake don't let her have so much as a smell of the decorating job. There's a pal of mine in here who'll need a slice of bread. He's got eight more years but he wants his missus and kids to have it while he finishes his stretch.'

'What's he got to do with it?' David asked.

180

'Let's just say he put the decorating job our way and don't question my decisions, son.'

'Sorry, Dad,' he said, looking dejected.

'Are you going to be able to handle it, David?' Clifford asked, having no worries about John.

David swallowed and nodded as he clasped his hands tightly together beneath the table. His leg was really throbbing and he started to rub his thigh.

'We need him,' John said, then leaned close to his brother and ruffled his hair.

'He's gonna be just fine, Dad. That's right, isn't it, Dave?'

'Yeah, I'll be fine. We've not got all the gear yet but I'll help John work on it.'

Clifford nodded and then looked directly at John. 'You take care of him, understand me? I want him taken good care of – don't want the smell of paint gettin' on his chest, do we?' He gave a crackling laugh, and then looked round the room.

'Do you need anything, Dad?' John asked.

'Yes, son, a nice hot tart.' Again he laughed, then with the roll-up now just a small thin wet paper he flicked it into the ashtray.

As the visit continued he asked John about Sandra and if they were going to get back together or divorced. John said he didn't want to even try to move back in with his wife: he'd had enough of her whining and moaning and was better off unattached so he could plan for the future.

His dad frowned. 'So, John son, who are you shaggin' now?'

David sat silent, still rubbing at his throbbing leg. To him John and his dad were not like father and son, but more like two blokes swapping sexual banter and conquests.

181

He'd always known his father had other women and never really even attempted to hide it from their mother. John was laughing about a woman who ran a local brothel in Chatsworth Road and had two black chicks who were turning tricks faster than a greyhound out the traps. The prison officer passed by their table and their father gave him a cordial nod as he leaned close to his sons, whispering that the bastard was on the take as he had a wife and four kids to support. He rubbed his thumb and fingers together to indicate the officer took money for illegal goods.

David was eager to leave and glad when he heard the bell, indicating that visiting time was over. They watched their father strutting away, turning to wave to them as the officers herded him out with five other inmates. You could tell by the way the other inmates gave their father distance that he was a king pin inside. God forbid if any of them nudged him or invaded his space.

John took hold of his brother's arm and helped him out of his seat to the security gates where he was handed his walking stick. It wasn't until they were sitting in the van that John opened the box of matches his father had so cleverly switched. The Izal toilet paper was folded and refolded into a thick wedge under a row of matches. John eased out the paper and David glanced at his dad's small neat handwriting as his brother slipped the note into his breast pocket.

'Ain't you going to read it?'

'Not here, I'll wait till we're home. We can pick up a few beers with fish and chips on the way ... yeah?'

David nodded, staring from the window. John didn't mention the 'decorating job' but spoke about football and his favourite team, West Ham. David wasn't really listening, he was just thinking about 'the job' and it made his stomach churn.

John slowed down and pointed across the road. 'There it is.'

David looked up: it was as if his brother had read his mind. He was frozen to the spot, his eyes transfixed on the small Trustee Savings Bank in Great Eastern Street.

'That high-rise car park there has a 360 view from the top ... You don't mind heights, do ya, Dave?' John said, and smirked as he drove on across Great Eastern Street and turned the van radio on.

Somewhat ironically the DJ announced the Adam Faith song 'What Do You Want'. John looked at his brother and began to sing along, deliberately substituting one of the words:

> 'What do you want if you don't want money?
> What do you want if you don't want gold?
> Say what you want and I'll give it to you, DAVEY,
> Wish you wanted my love, baby!'

John had a big grin on his face as he turned and looked at David, who couldn't help but smile as well.

Everyone on the murder team gathered together in the incident room and listened attentively as Bradfield brought them all up to speed concerning the discovery of Eddie Phillips' body and the post-mortem.

'As you can see, exactly how he died is still up in the air and we need to bottom it out fast.'

The detectives in the room looked surprised and DS Gibbs spoke out.

'We're busy with the Collins case and strapped for staff

already, guv – can't another team take the Phillips case?'

'I've said exactly that to DCS Metcalf, Spencer, but he says we're to investigate both cases as in his opinion they are linked, but he's giving me five more staff.'

'It'll be like a sardine tin in this poky office,' one detective said, to Bradfield's annoyance.

'If you don't like it, son, then piss off back to uniform and deal with shoplifters!'

There was complete silence in the room as everyone realized the DCI was not in the mood for frivolity or to be argued with. He lit a cigarette and told DS Gibbs that he was to concentrate on the Phillips case, get a team together to spend up to midnight working a mile stretch of the Regent's Canal, both directions from where the body was found. He wanted every stroller and dog walker stopped and shown a picture of Eddie Phillips in case anyone recognized him, and they were to be asked if they had seen anything suspicious on the canal path in the last two days.

Kath mentioned the markets at Camden Lock and the possibility of drug dealers.

'Good call, Morgan. Spence, cover the markets as well and get as many uniform as you can from the local nick to help you.'

Gibbs glared at Kath. Even though he knew she'd made a good suggestion it meant more work for him.

'Did the drug squad guys have anything useful for us to go on?' Gibbs asked.

'Yes and no. They did some digging around and it's believed Big Daddy originates from Moss Side in Manchester. No name for him as yet, but he's black, about six foot four and built like a brick shit house – wears a draped blue suit and fedora, with two-toned brown-and-white shoes. We got no address as apparently he keeps on the move. He's Jamaican like his sidekick Dwayne Clark, who's known as "Shoes", not because of the surname connection to the well-known brand, but because he apparently takes delight in stamping on people's heads. A search on criminal records on his name was also negative, but the drug squad did get an address.'

Gibbs asked if they should get a warrant and spin Dwayne's place, but Bradfield informed him the drug squad had done it early that morning. 'It was a squat in Chalk Farm, clean as a whistle drugs wise – not even a bottle of aspirin. Dwayne's girlfriend and her three young kids were at the address; our suspects weren't. Apparently she was a right gobby cow and said Dwayne, and a black bloke called Josh, ran a window-cleaning business together ...' He paused to let the laughter in the room die down before continuing.

'You may laugh but the drug squad found a load of new ladders, sponges and buckets at the address – even an MOT for an old van, but nothing for a Jag.'

Everyone in the room knew the window cleaning was probably a front for dealing drugs.

Kath commented that Chalk Farm was a stone's throw away from Camden Town and Jane asked if Dwayne's girlfriend knew where the two of them were. She heard some sniggers in the room and someone whisper, 'She's so naive.'

'Yes she did,' Bradfield said, and frowned at the whisperer, which brought a chuffed smile to Jane's face.

He continued, 'She said they were both in Coventry and had been there for well over a week, which conveniently puts them both out of town during Julie Ann and Eddie's deaths. And before you ask, she doesn't know where this

Josh lives and was adamant he's not Big Daddy, but the drug squad officers said it was obvious she was talking a load of bollocks.'

'What the hell are they doing in Coventry?' Gibbs asked.

For the first time Bradfield smiled. 'Apparently the window-cleaning slash drugs business is doing so well, they are looking to expand and set up there as well. Big Daddy is most probably this Josh, and if originally from Moss Side that's a real tough drug area, so my guess is he still has contacts there and he runs drugs from Manchester to London, with drop-offs in Birmingham and Coventry on the way – all whilst *cleanin' windows*, haw haw.'

'What a load of cock,' Gibbs replied.

'I know that, Spence. Dwayne's tart is obviously lying through her teeth about the alibi, but we've no bloody evidence to disprove it at the moment. The drug squad showed her a picture of Julie Ann, but she said she'd never seen her and, "Dwayne don't mix with white trash". She'd never heard of Eddie Phillips either.'

'If she's been primed as to what lies to tell us maybe they know we are looking for them, which means Eddie Phillips must have blabbed,' a detective commented.

'Stop telling me the bloody obvious as it's really beginning to piss me off! What I want to know, but clearly don't, is exactly where Big Daddy and Dwayne are right now,' Bradfield said, and lit another cigarette from the one he was just finishing.

'Are the drug squad making enquiries in Coventry?' DS Gibbs asked.

'No, Spence – you are. Go up there and—'

'I thought you wanted me to cover the canal?'

'I said organize a team to do it, then you can link up

with the Moss Side and Coventry drug squads. If you find Big Daddy, Dwayne and or this Josh bloke, nick 'em and transport them back down here for questioning.'

Gibbs sighed. He didn't fancy schlepping all the way to Coventry, but he had no choice.

Bradfield told everyone that now the drug squad knew about Eddie's suspicious death they'd put pressure on known hard-drug users and informants in and around a square mile of where his body was found, in an effort to get more on 'Josh' and Dwayne Clark. They had also organized a team to keep surveillance on Dwayne's flat and Bradfield had agreed that if any drugs were seized when they were arrested the drug squad boys could deal with that after he'd interviewed them.

'So far we've got Jack Shit on this case and I'm getting it in the ear from the DCS to get results. You need to start pulling your fingers out of your backsides and work harder. I want those two black bastards found and banged up in a cell downstairs within the next twenty-four hours. Overtime is not a problem – now get out there and graft.'

As everyone went about their business Bradfield approached Jane.

'I need you with me this afternoon now that Spence is off to Coventry,' he said irritably.

'May I ask where we are we going, sir?'

'It's a memorial service for Julie Ann.'

Jane thought he may have made an error. 'Do you mean funeral, sir?'

'If I did I'd have said funeral, wouldn't I, Tennison? Her parents were informed that it'll be at least eight weeks, maybe more, before the coroner releases the body. So they decided to have a memorial service in the meantime.

Get yourself spruced up then meet me in the yard in ten minutes.'

Jane grabbed her jacket from the back of her chair and a roll of Sellotape from the desk before hurrying down to the cloakroom. She wrapped a load of tape round her hand so the sticky side was facing out and brushed down the back of her jacket removing the bits of fluff and cotton. Having put the jacket on she did the same with the front and then combed her hair. She was about to retie it back with an elastic band when it suddenly snapped.

'Shit, shit.'

She didn't have another one so grabbed her hat from her locker and putting it on pushed her hair up inside it, but strands of it slipped out. Frustrated, she recombed it and tucked it behind her ears before giving her cheeks a pinch and doing up the buttons of her jacket. She did a quick check of her tights, and with her handbag over her shoulder scurried out towards the station yard where Bradfield was waiting impatiently in the driver's seat of an unmarked red Hillman Hunter. She opened the passenger door.

'Get in, get in,' he said tetchily.

She was still shutting the front passenger door as he pulled away at speed.

'We are just going to make an appearance out of respect, sit at the back, give our condolences and be visible for as long as necessary. Then we get back here – I've got a lot to do.'

Bradfield drove in silence and Jane wondered if she should make some polite conversation or if it was best to keep quiet. Eventually Bradfield started talking, not turning towards her but staring directly out of the windscreen.

'God, I hate these things. Whoever killed Julie Ann and

her baby is still out there. If I'd got something to tell them like we'd caught the bastard responsible it might have helped soften their grief. I don't know – pregnant and a junkie at her age: I'm surprised she didn't want an abortion.'

There was an awful pause, before Jane decided to say something.

'Apparently drugs can disrupt menstruation, especially heroin. So even if she missed some periods she might not have connected it to being pregnant. Then there was that phone call Anjali O'Duncie overheard. If Big Daddy was her dealer and the father, maybe she was asking for money for an abort—'

Bradfield turned and stared at her. 'You think he'd give a shit? He's got kids littered all over the place by God knows how many women. Why would he bother to help a teenage hooker who was passed round to his cohorts to feed her addiction? All she cared about was the next fix.'

There was another lengthy pause before Jane tried again.

'Do you think that Eddie was murdered because he'd told you about this Big Daddy character?'

Bradfield sighed and ruffled his hair. 'I dunno. The toxicology results might show he overdosed on heroin which caused him to accidentally fall into the canal and drown. Who knows – maybe he was so high he thought he'd swim upriver and sneak into London Zoo,' he said with a hollow laugh.

Jane continued, 'It's another no-witness case like Julie Ann. Although it is different because we know he was at the station the day before and if this Big Daddy did kill Eddie then I guess you have a possible motive. Eddie was the last person to see her two weeks before her body was found. Professor Martin said she had bruises from a bad beating prior to her murder, so if we could find out where she was for those two weeks it would really help because—'

He interrupted her. 'Thank you, WPC Tennison – I'm aware of the time frame and have been doing everything possible to trace her movements and whereabouts during that missing period.'

'Sorry, sir,' Jane said, deciding it was best to keep her opinions and thoughts to herself.

The church was already half full of mourners by the time they arrived. Bradfield and Jane were surprised to see a white coffin on a plinth in front of the altar. It had a long plaited wreath of white lilies and a picture of Julie Ann on top of it. Mr and Mrs Collins entered arm in arm. They glanced towards Jane and Bradfield who were standing side by side in the back row. As they passed Mr Collins gave a small bow of his head to acknowledge their presence and then continued along the church aisle to sit in the front pew. A vicar in a black cassock, white surplice and black tippet that hung down to his knees entered from the vestry and stood at the lectern as the organ played an unrecognizable short piece. He gave a light cough before he began the service.

'I'm sure you are all aware that the body of Julie Ann cannot, for legal reasons, be here with us today and a full funeral service will be held at a later date. However, we look not to the things that are seen but to the things that are unseen; for the things that are seen are transient but the things that are unseen are eternal. I welcome George and Mary Collins, family and friends, to this special service for God's beloved child Julie Ann, who is here with us in spirit. A regular at our Sunday service she enjoyed singing with the church choir, a delightful spontaneous young girl, who was blossoming into a beautiful young teenager. We all share the grief of her parents at a young life so tragically cut short.'

The vicar continued and Jane could sense Bradfield's impatience as he stood beside her sighing and shuffling his feet and twice looking at his watch. The vicar announced the hymn 'All Things Bright and Beautiful', which they sang before Mr Collins stepped up to the lectern.

'I thank you all for coming today. My wife and I have been touched by the care and kindness so many of you have shown us. Your words, cards and letters of sympathy are helping us both come to terms with our tragic loss, although I am unsure if we will ever recover fully from losing our only daughter. We have been able to recall and keep in our minds the joy Julie Ann brought to us. She was an adorable little girl, always full of fun and with so many gifted talents. She especially loved to dance and we were proud beyond words to watch her progress through her dance classes and grade exams, but the sadness that ...' He faltered and took a moment before he continued, recalling how much hope they had had for her future and how they believed that one day she would dance professionally on stage.

Bradfield turned over the page of the order of service card, trying to estimate in his head how long it would be before it ended. Two more hymns and a psalm to be read by a relative, and a solo hymn by one of the girls in the choir. Jane kept on flicking glances at him and he leaned close to her.

'I reckon we won't get out of here for at least another half-hour!'

It was longer, three quarters of an hour later, when the vicar ended the service with a bidding prayer and he and Mr and Mrs Collins left the church to stand outside and thank everyone for coming. Mrs Collins was visibly upset, her eyes red-rimmed from weeping.

Jane and Bradfield were the last to exit the church and George and Mary Collins were just getting into a friend's car. The vicar approached Bradfield with a weak smile.

'Thank you for coming to pay your respects to Julie Ann. It meant a lot to Mr and Mrs Collins. They are having a small gathering at home, family and close friends, and they asked me to say that you're both welcome.'

'Well, I'm not sure—' Bradfield started to say.

'I think it would be most helpful to their state of mind if you were there. I know they are finding it difficult to cope with the fact Julie Ann's body has not yet been released for burial, and they feel there are still so many unanswered questions.'

'Yes I understand, but—'

'Good. I've a few things to attend to, but I will see you there,' the vicar interrupted and sauntered off.

'Shit, I suppose we have to show our faces now,' Bradfield said belligerently.

'Well, if it helps Mr and Mrs Collins through the day it can't be a bad thing,' Jane said.

'All right, we stay no more than ten minutes and I'm only speaking to them about the case. You can fend off anyone who's nosy and wants to know how the investigation is going.'

'But what should I say?'

'That it's *sub judice* to talk about it with anyone other than the parents.'

'I thought that only referred to a case already under judicial consideration?'

'I know that, but they don't. If you don't like it then you can stay in the car for all I care.'

It took a while to get to the address as Bradfield made a wrong turning, which didn't help his already irritable mood.

Cars were parked in the Collinses' drive and on the road. Bradfield parked opposite in the street, got out and ran his hands through his hair before heading towards the house. He stopped and turned to see where Jane was and she was still sitting in the car. He walked back and tapped on the passenger window, which she wound down.

'What are you doing?' he asked.

'I thought you wanted me to wait in the car.'

'I was being sarcastic, Tennison, but please yourself. I won't be long anyway.' Bradfield walked off.

Jane was upset by his attitude and, feeling she'd be a hindrance rather than a help, stayed put.

The front door of the house was wide open, people going in and some still parking outside. Jane sat looking from the car window, watching the mourners walking sedately up the path. Ten minutes passed and Jane crossed and uncrossed her legs as she desperately needed to go to the bathroom. She began to feel uncomfortable and eventually couldn't wait any longer.

She left the car and entered the house where she saw the young girl who had sung the solo holding a tray of white wine ready for the guests to take into the living room.

'I need to use the bathroom,' Jane said, feeling embarrassed.

The young girl grinned. 'The vicar just went into the

downstairs one. He'll probably be a while, what with his cassock and surplice to contend with, but if you go straight up the stairs there's a bathroom just along the landing.'

'Thank you,' Jane said and hurried up the stairs.

Bradfield felt cornered as Mr Collins stood close to him. Everyone else was talking quietly and Mrs Collins was sitting on the sofa crying profusely. Mr Collins was eager to know if there were any developments in the police investigation. Bradfield told him that they were still trying to track down whoever supplied Julie Ann with drugs and they had a couple of positive leads they were currently following up on. Mr Collins asked what had happened to the young boy they had arrested. Bradfield knew he was referring to Eddie Phillips and not wanting to distress Mr Collins further just said he had been released pending further enquiries, but it would seem he wasn't involved in her death.

Bradfield saw Jane attempting to attract his attention from across the crowded living room. She was surreptitiously raising her hand, but when he didn't respond she threaded her way through the guests and moved to stand just behind him.

'Sir, could I have a word with you, please?'

He turned to face her, and excused himself to Mr Collins.

'Can't you see I'm busy talking with Mr Collins, and take your ruddy hat off inside the house,' he whispered.

'Please – it is very important I speak with you in private.' Jane removed her hat, causing her hair to fall loose.

'I'll be with you in a minute,' he said sternly and turned back to Mr Collins.

He made his excuse to leave and shook hands with him

and then spoke briefly with Mrs Collins telling her how nice the service for Julie Ann had been.

At last he made his way to the front door, placing his empty wine glass onto the young girl's tray as he edged past her.

'That was a very nice solo,' he remarked as Jane trailed behind him feeling something akin to a lap dog.

As they walked down the front path towards the car Jane tapped his arm.

'I think you need to look in the garage at Mr Collins' car before we leave, sir.'

He stopped and turned abruptly.

'What on earth for, Tennison?'

'It may not have been a Jaguar XJ6 or 12 we should have been looking for.'

He glared at her, but at the same time he was curious, and gestured for her to move out of the way as he crossed the small section of grass towards the garage door which was closed. Jane stepped in front of him. She had a quick look round before grabbing the handle and pulling the door halfway open. She ducked underneath and into the garage followed by Bradfield who saw the only thing in it was a vehicle covered by a fitted tarpaulin. The garage was dimly lit by the natural daylight filtering in. He looked at Jane in a manner that made it clear she'd better get to the point quickly as he was beginning to lose patience. She lifted back a section of the cover over the offside front wheel, pulling it back further for him to clearly see the dark maroon colour. He snatched the tarpaulin from her and whipped it back to reveal the front registration plate and maker's badge.

'It's a two-door 1960s Bristol?' he said.

'Eddie Phillips only ever saw the car from behind, sir.

We may have been wrongly assuming that it was a four-door Jaguar.'

Bradfield pulled even more of the cover back onto the car roof to reveal the driver's door and offside of the vehicle. He tried the door-handle but the car was locked.

'Can you see the colour of the carpet?' Jane asked.

He shaded his eyes with both hands and peering into the car could just about see the matching maroon carpet surrounding the gear stick. He stepped away, chewing at his lips. He checked his watch.

'Right, we need to get back to the station and get a search team organized and a warrant before we come back here,' he said, pulling the tarpaulin over the car. He slid out under the garage door followed by Jane.

As they headed towards the patrol car he stopped and cocked his head to one side.

'You have very nice hair, but keep it tied back when on duty.'

He didn't ask how she had come to suggest he look in the garage, or even say well done, but he did hold open the passenger door for her to get into the patrol car.

CHAPTER THIRTEEN

On the return journey to the station Bradfield stopped at Old Street Magistrates' Court. Jane waited in the car whilst he spoke with one of the magistrates who, after hearing his information on oath, signed and issued a search warrant for the Collinses' house and car.

Bradfield got back into the driving seat and handed Jane the search warrant. 'OK, what made you suspicious about the car?' he asked.

'To be honest I wasn't actually sure if there would be a car in the garage.'

'Just answer the question.'

She started to explain about needing the bathroom, and how she had gone upstairs because the vicar was using the one downstairs. He impatiently pushed her to get to the point.

'At first I went into the master bedroom by mistake, and I noticed a few framed photographs on the dresser. One was of Mr Collins standing beside a red car which at a glance looked like a Jaguar, but when I took a closer look I realized it wasn't. Then I remembered you asking him what vehicle he drove.'

'He said it was an old Bristol that belonged to his father.'

'I'd never seen a Bristol car before today, and it made me think that, maybe, Eddie Phillips was mistaken.'

'Listen, I'd appreciate it if you kept this between us – I should have asked him what colour his car was and I should have picked up on the similarities in shape when Mr Collins told me he owned a Bristol.'

Jane nodded in agreement to his request and he remarked that it would be a positive move forward if they got a match on the Bristol car's carpet to the fibres on Julie Ann's body.

Jane hesitated before continuing. He'd leaned over so close she felt the need to move away from him a fraction.

'There's another bedroom next to the master bedroom which must be Julie Ann's.'

'You had a look in there as well?' he asked, somewhat surprised.

'No ... I really needed the bathroom.'

'Is there a point to this apart from your bladder?'

'Yes, sir, there's a box room, which I thought would be the bathroom, but it wasn't.'

'Get on with it.'

'The box room contained a small single bed and a wardrobe, but I didn't have the time to look round. As I closed the door I noticed four screw marks on the outside and two sort of straight-line indentations. Also on the doorframe at the same height were two more screw marks. I had a closer look and—'

'Don't tell me, you couldn't hold it in any longer and had an accident?' he said, exasperated by her waffling.

She was offended by his remark as she was being serious. 'No I did not. I wondered if there were similar marks on the inside as well so I had a quick look. No screw marks but quite a few rubber scuff marks and scratches, like someone had been trying to kick the door open.'

He looked at her. 'From the sound of it that door had a lock on the outside at some time.'

'Yes, that's exactly what I thought, sir. Most likely to keep someone locked in. I wondered if that's where Julie Ann had been kept while she was missing for the two weeks before her body was found.'

He leant back against the seat. 'Well, that puts a whole new perspective on the case. George Collins was really having a go at me about not finding his daughter's killer or coming up with any new evidence. I never got so much as a hint that he or his wife could be involved. If they are they've both lied from day one.'

Jane thought of her discussion with Dr Harker. 'Sometimes the guilty use anger, criticism or confrontation to detract from their guilt and the suspicion of others. They are even capable of weeping, not for the crime they have committed but for themselves.'

Bradfield smiled. He knew she was repeating Harker's words.

'Don't treat everything you read or hear as gospel – people don't all react in the same way and I find it hard to believe his wife's grief is in any way a cover.'

'What about his, though?' Jane asked cautiously.

Bradfield said nothing. He made no acknowledgement of her input and sat staring ahead as he drove, mulling over his interaction so far with George Collins. He suddenly turned, took his hand off the gear stick and patted Jane's knee.

'When I told him we believed his daughter was dead he seemed shocked and distressed. Then when he left the room to go upstairs I thought he was going to collapse and I just got to him before he toppled over. If he was acting it was an Oscar-winning performance. Also there's that scene at the mortuary, hurling the chair? If you are right he had to have known all along she was dead, which means he fucking locked her up in the bedroom, gave her a good beating with something then strangled her before dumping the body.'

'Do you think he raped her as well?'

'God forbid, but it's possible. I have to say that was the most opportune piss you ever needed.'

She didn't find it amusing, but had no time to reply as he pulled into the station yard, screeched to a halt, grabbed the warrant from her hand and was out of the vehicle like a shot, heading for the incident room.

Striding in, Bradfield asked Kath where everyone was. She replied that they were all out on enquiries by the Regent's Canal, or on their way to Coventry. As Jane came in behind him he told her to go back downstairs and arrange for a uniform officer to be on standby to drive them to the Collinses' house. He also wanted her to use the control-room radio and get two detectives to park up near the Collinses' house and notify him when the guests were all gone.

'Yes, sir. Which two officers do you want?'

'I don't give a toss – any two will do. I'll be in my office and get someone to bring me a coffee,' said Bradfield, raising his voice, impatient now to search the house.

Just over an hour passed before all the guests were gone. Jane was about to inform Bradfield when he walked in snapping an elastic band between his fingers as he approached her.

'I want you on the search to deal with Mrs Collins as she's likely to have a nervous breakdown when she hears why we're there. Here, for you – tie your hair back, Veronica.'

He flicked the elastic band onto her desk and she looked at him, puzzled.

'Veronica Lake was a movie star who always had her long hair loose. Oh never mind, she was well before your time anyway,' he said, and went to his office to get his jacket.

Kath looked over with raised eyebrows.

'Getting on well with the guv, I see? Sergeant Harris's nose will be even more out of joint. What exactly is the big development?'

Jane was collecting her bag from the drawer and was about to explain everything to Kath when she heard a loud whistle from the corridor and Bradfield's voice.

'Come on, come on, let's go, Veronica!'

When they arrived at the Collinses' house there were no cars in the drive and the garage door was shut. Bradfield spoke with the two detectives assisting him and they all walked up the path together. He rang the doorbell and stepped back with the warrant in his hand. The sound of a dog barking went on for a few moments before George Collins opened the door. He was wearing an apron and rubber gloves, and looked taken aback. Bradfield explained that he had a search warrant and that he needed to speak to him.

'It really isn't convenient – my wife is sleeping and I have to finish the washing up. We're both very tired—'

'I'm sure you'd rather I spoke with you here than down at the station, Mr Collins,' Bradfield said in a stern manner as he stepped into the house forcing Mr Collins to move backwards.

'What's happening? Is this to do with my daughter? Have you got some new information?' Collins asked nervously.

Bradfield didn't answer his question but introduced the two detectives and told the uniform officer to remain by the front door. Jane thought it strange that a clearly agitated Mr Collins didn't even ask why they wanted to search his house. He just led them into the living room which had now been cleared of all the glasses and dirty plates.

He started to remove his apron. 'I won't be a moment. I need to let the dog out as he scratches at the door.'

Bradfield made him even more uneasy as he followed him into the kitchen where there was a small white elderly terrier who yapped for a moment before he was put out into the garden. Mr Collins removed his rubber gloves and tossed them onto the side of the sink. Rows of wine glasses had been rinsed and neatly placed on the draining board ready to be dried.

As they both returned to the lounge Mr Collins rolled down his shirtsleeves, buttoning the cuffs.

'My wife is sleeping,' he repeated, looking as if he didn't really understand what was going on.

'My officers need to search Julie Ann's room.'

He looked surprised. 'Why?'

'We didn't do it before because she hadn't been home for over a year. It's just in case there are any little notes, bits of paper, etc – anything that might help us track down her killer as it could have been someone she's known for years.'

Collins said her room was second on the left upstairs and sat nervously on a wing chair by the fireplace, his bony hands clenched together.

A relaxed Bradfield gestured for Jane to sit on the sofa as he stood in front of the fireplace. She was interested as to how he was going to approach questioning Mr Collins and the news that he was now a suspect in his daughter's murder.

DS Lawrence popped his head into the living room and Bradfield introduced him to Mr Collins before taking him to one side and saying he wanted Paul to start on the Bristol car which was in the garage. Lawrence said he'd have a cursory look at the carpet, but to give it a thorough examination he'd need to have it removed to the lab.

Bradfield turned back to Mr Collins. 'DS Lawrence will need to take a carpet sample from inside your car, so if you could give him the keys we can make a start.'

'What on earth for?'

'We have a witness who saw your daughter getting into a vehicle of a similar colour and shape to yours, and we also found red carpet fibres on her clothing,' he said, and paused to gauge Collins' reaction.

'They could have got on her when she was last home,' Mr Collins said defensively.

'Well, according to you and your wife that was well over a year ago and it would be unlikely any fibres from your car would still be on her,' DS Lawrence remarked.

'Then why do you need to examine it?'

Bradfield spoke quietly, lying. 'It's just for elimination purposes and standard procedure in this sort of case. Now if you would kindly give us the keys to your car we can make a start.'

Collins replied that the keys were in the cutlery drawer in the kitchen. He also expressed great concern about any of the carpet being cut as it was in perfect condition and he would like to be present to witness any damage, should it occur.

Bradfield looked at DS Lawrence who was experienced enough to realize he wanted to be on his own with Mr Collins.

Lawrence produced a roll of clear Sellotape from his

bag and said that he would take tape liftings of the car's carpet fibres, and that way there would be no need for a cutting. Lawrence turned to Jane and told her she could assist him to see how it was done. She would like to have stayed and listened to Bradfield question Mr Collins: since the post-mortem and Harker lecture forensics had fascinated her and she was loath to miss the opportunity to learn something new.

'Can you let the dog back in, please, and shut the kitchen door so he can't get out?' Mr Collins requested as Jane left the room.

Bradfield opened his notebook and began flicking back through the pages.

'Had you in fact seen your daughter Julie Ann more recently?'

'No,' Collins replied unconvincingly and his Adam's apple moved up and down his neck.

'That's a lie, isn't it?'

Collins twisted his head, but did not respond.

'Don't make this difficult for me – for your own good it's time you started telling the truth, so no more lies.'

'I am telling you the truth.'

'Did you pick her up outside Homerton Hospital about two weeks ago?'

'I swear to you I didn't! I don't even know where Homerton Hospital is.'

'Well, how do you explain the same colour fibres from your car getting onto her clothes?'

'I don't know. Maybe she got into another car with the same type of carpet.'

Jane walked back into the room as Bradfield was about to challenge Mr Collins on his remark.

'Excuse me, sir ...'

'I'm busy talking to Mr Collins, Tennison,' Bradfield said sharply without even turning to look at her.

'I'm sorry, but—'

'Wait outside,' he said, raising his voice as he glared at her.

His abruptness made Jane nervous, even though she was only doing as asked. 'DS Lawrence wants to speak with you.'

Bradfield was irritated, but he knew if Paul Lawrence wanted him he must have discovered something important.

'Stay with Mr Collins,' he said as he stomped out of the room.

DS Lawrence was standing by the car in the garage. He had a magnifying glass in one hand and was examining a single strip of taped fibres he had lifted from the boot carpet.

Bradfield spoke as he approached. 'I know the bastard's lying – he started bricking it when I asked him about the last time he saw his daughter. They're a match, are they?'

DS Lawrence looked up slowly; he didn't need to say anything. Bradfield could see from the look on his face that the fibres didn't match.

'Don't you need to look at them under a proper microscope to be sure?' he asked with concern.

'Yes, but I'm ninety-nine per cent certain the fibres from the Bristol are not the same as the ones we found on Julie Ann – the type of weave looks different. It's a lovely car, 1962 Bristol 407 with beige hide seats in immaculate condition.'

'Shit, this can't be right. I know he's hiding something from me. Could she have got in this car without picking up fibres from it?'

'Yes, like I just said the seats are leather and if he brought her back here and killed her he may have borrowed, or had access to, another car to dump the body.'

'Good point. But only he can answer that so I'm going to ratchet it up a notch with him.'

'If you want to make him sweat then call his bluff, tell him you got a phone number off the doctor's notepad at the clinic.'

'But we drew a blank on that.'

'He's not to know – just see what he has to say. In the meantime, I want to have a look in her bedroom and the box room as well.'

'OK, there's two officers already up there now.'

'Remember the red fibres were mostly on her socks and in her boots. Well, if she was walking around on a carpet up there then—'

'I hear you, and I'll spin the phone number, see what reaction I get.'

They went back into the house and DS Lawrence went up the stairs as Bradfield checked the phone on the hall table, jotting down the number in his notebook.

He was about to return to the living room when DS Lawrence peered over the banisters.

'I think we may have got lucky up here – the carpet in the box room has red fibres that are much more similar in weave and colour to those on Julie Ann.'

Bradfield hurried up the stairs to join him. DS Lawrence pointed to the screw marks on the box-room door and said they were not very old, and in his opinion a clasp for a padlock had been screwed to the hallway-side door and frame.

'The tiny splinters in the screw holes are still fresh and the straight-line indents were probably caused by the clasp being forced against the door when it was being kicked from the inside. Have a look at this.' He stepped into the room followed by Bradfield and pointed to the lower half of the door.

'A shoe print from the sole of a boot, and scuff marks.'

Bradfield knelt down beside Lawrence to take a closer look. 'I can see scuff marks, Paul, but not any from boots.'

The room's thick curtains were already closed, so DS Lawrence flicked off the light, crouched down and shone a torch at an oblique angle onto the door, lighting up the outline of a boot print. He then got out a jar of black powder and a fingerprint brush which he dipped in the powder and began to lightly apply to an area of the door.

'Add a bit of magic powder and hey presto,' Lawrence said.

Bradfield was transfixed as the outline of a boot mark and the sole treads slowly and clearly appeared.

'I thought that only worked on fingerprints.'

'A little something I discovered recently after a nothing ventured, nothing gained situation. There's more there, but from memory they look the same size and sole pattern as Julie Ann's boots, although I can't confirm that until I do a one-to-one comparison back at the lab. Someone definitely wanted to kick their way out of this room.'

'There are times when I could kiss you, Paul.'

'A mere thank-you and a few pints will suffice,' Lawrence replied.

A smiling Bradfield calmly went back to the living room to confront Mr Collins with the new evidence.

'Well, it looks like the fibres from your car are not a match to those we found on Julie Ann.'

George Collins said nothing, but the look on his face was a mixture of relief and surprise. Jane was also surprised and felt bad that they had both jumped to conclusions and got it all so terribly wrong.

'The box room upstairs clearly had a padlock and clasp on it recently – why was that?'

'I put it on to keep the dog in there when we entertained in order to stop him begging for food at the table. It didn't work as he just howled for attention, so I took it off and threw it away.'

Bradfield shook his head. 'That's another lie, isn't it, George? A lie to cover up what really happened.'

Mr Collins said nothing but Bradfield was determined to break him.

'It gets better; for me, that is, not you. You see, the carpet fibres in your box room are the same as the fibres on your daughter's socks. They probably got there because you made her take her boots off after she kept kicking the door you'd put a padlock on to keep her in.'

Jane felt a surge of elation and paid close attention to Mr Collins. His hands clenched and unclenched, a muscle at the side of his jaw was twitching in agitation.

'You see, George, we now know that Julie Ann, contrary to what you have stated, did call you. She left an imprint of a phone number she rang from the clinic on a doctor's notepad. I've just checked it against your phone in the hallway and they match.'

Jane knew they had no result from the notepad, and leaned forwards frowning as she watched Mr Collins become even more agitated. Bradfield tapped his notebook and repeated the phone number. He then spoke very quietly.

'Come on, this is your opportunity to tell me the truth, George. If you and your wife were keeping Julie Ann here to get her off the drugs and you lost your temper with her and lashed out then get it off your chest and tell me.'

'Oh God, but please, my wife has no knowledge of any of this.'

'I understand that you don't want to implicate her, but she didn't just turn a blind eye, did she? I'm starting to lose my patience. Do you want me to go and wake her up and bring her down here?'

'No, please no. She was with her sister in Weybridge for the week, she wasn't at the house – I swear to you she was not here.'

'Tell me everything, George. It'll be better for you in the long run.'

Collins took a deep sigh, his hands knotted together and his head bent down as he stared at the carpet.

'I'm sorry, Julie called my office and they contacted me to say she'd rung. I'd normally have been at work, but I'd taken most of the day off to play in a golf competition. I'd just returned home when they called but I had no contact number for her so I couldn't call her back.'

'We have a witness who heard her making a call to you.'

Jane glanced at Bradfield. He appeared totally relaxed leaning back in his chair.

'Yes, I did speak with her. I'd only been here about half an hour when she rang. She was hysterical and crying, and said she wanted to come home. You have to understand how difficult it was for me.'

'So what did she say to you?'

'Well, as usual she was belligerent and asking for money so I put the phone down on her. I was upset – she always made me feel wretched. Then she rang back again a while later reversing the charges from a payphone. She was calmer this time and begged me to help her, repeating over and over that she needed me, and wanted to come home. The truth is I didn't want to talk to her, but I still loved her and so I relented. I told her she could come home, but she had no money for a bus so I went straight out and picked her up near a hospital in Hackney. She looked terrible, and was shaking and crying.'

'What time was this?'

'Erm, she called just after I got home from a game of golf. I'd not played a good round so I didn't stay on and it would have been perhaps five or five thirty in the afternoon I picked her up.'

He paused and took a deep breath, clearly distraught at recounting what happened, and he continued to look down at the floor.

'I heated up some soup for her. Her nose was running and she was shaking, her face was gaunt and her body so thin she was hardly recognizable as my daughter. And the clothes she was wearing were awful. I was glad her mother wasn't here to see her.'

Bradfield was taking notes, but thought Mr Collins was being evasive and considered putting pressure on him to reveal exactly what he did do to his daughter. Realizing it could make him clam up Bradfield thought better of it and flicked through his notes before tapping a page with his pen.

'So this was roughly about two weeks or so before her body was found?'

Mr Collins nodded and replied that it was a Thursday.

'When she first called you, what exactly did she say?'

'I just told you, she wanted money and—'

'Sorry, yes, you said that, but did she call you "Father" or use any familiar term?'

Mr Collins looked perplexed and shrugged his shoulders.

'She shouted and was very abusive and I believe she said, "Daddy, you have to help me."'

Bradfield flicked a page of his notebook and Jane saw him underline something.

'So what happened when you both got back here?'

Collins straightened up and leaned forwards in the wing chair. 'On previous occasions when she had turned up unannounced she would make promises, but then steal from her mother's purse, or take the housekeeping money, not to mention anything else of value that she could sell for drugs, then she'd disappear again. This time I was not going to be hoodwinked by her, so I said she could sleep in the box room. I wanted to make sure she couldn't leave so I took my screwdriver and put a clasp and padlock on the door. All the while she was making promises: if I helped her she would straighten out and get her life back together. She promised to go back to school and sit her A levels – something I had heard many times before. She agreed to be locked in the box room for her own good, but only if I helped her.'

Bradfield doubted Julie Ann would have agreed to be locked up.

'Why the box room, and what did she want from you?'

'There was less in there for her to smash up as she came off the heroin and mostly she wanted money. She told me she had been raped, was now pregnant and had been to see someone in Brixton who would give her an abortion for a hundred pounds. It was hard to believe she was telling me the truth because she looked so wasted and undernourished. However, she said I could go with her so I would know she wasn't lying.'

He paused and took a deep breath, still leaning forwards staring at the carpet with his hands held in front of him.

211

'Go on, Mr Collins,' Bradfield said, encouraging him to continue.

'Well, I was shocked, but still wondered if she was telling the truth or after money. I told her that an abortion was wrong and if she had the baby then her mother and I would stand by her and help raise the child.'

His voice cracked as he continued and slowly explained how Julie held his hand, kissing it and promising to be everything he had ever wanted. Tears trickled down the side of his nose. He described how he had sat with her in the box room until she had fallen asleep exhausted. He had then padlocked her in the room before going downstairs.

'About an hour later I went to see how she was and ask her if she wanted something to eat. I removed the padlock, went in and realized what a fool I'd been.'

'How do you mean?'

'I should have checked the rucksack she had with her, but with all the stress I didn't think to. She was lying on the bed and I saw the syringe on the floor. She must have heard me coming, but it was as if she didn't care she was so high. I couldn't believe it. I felt sick and angry with myself for trusting her again.'

He became agitated, wringing his hands as he described how he got a glass of water and threw it in her face before shaking her shoulders to rouse her.

'What happened next?'

'I told her how disgusted I was and said that if she really was pregnant what she was doing was appalling and that her baby would be born a heroin addict just like her. She spat at me, screaming that she didn't care as she didn't want the baby. Then she said that it was a black bastard who had raped her.'

Jane could see that Mr Collins was becoming highly emotional, but there was also anger in his eyes as he recounted what happened. He said that he had been afraid that he would lose control, so he had grabbed her ruck-sack and the syringe and then locked the door.

'She started kicking and screaming to be let out, but I had to keep her in there. I waited for what seemed like ages until she stopped and then I unlocked the door. She came at me in a fury, lashing out and hitting me. In a panic I ran down the stairs to call the police and picked up the phone, but she ripped the line from the socket and went for me again. It was hard for me to believe that she could be so violent, so terribly angry.' He searched in his trouser pocket, brought out a handkerchief, blew his nose and started crying.

'Why didn't you run outside and call for help?'

'I don't know. On impulse I followed her into the kitchen where she started pulling all the drawers out look-ing for the housekeeping money. I was worried she'd find it so I tried to drag her away, but she pushed me back-wards kicking out at me with such terrible anger and hatred it really frightened me. I stumbled backwards and she pulled open another drawer, found an envelope, took it out and opened it. I shouted at her to put it back and leave the house but—'

Bradfield put up his hand to stop him. 'It can't have been that much if it was just housekeeping, so why didn't you let her take it and leave? Then you could have called the police without being scared.'

'No, no, you don't understand. It was my staff's weekly wages. I couldn't just let her take it.' He began to cry even more.

'Why on earth do you keep such a large sum of money

in the house?' Bradfield asked in surprise. Mr Collins told him that he always got the cash from the bank on a Thursday and made up the pay packets on the Friday morning at work, but he usually took the money back to the office and locked it in the safe.

Bradfield asked why he hadn't done so this particular Thursday and Collins seemed exasperated, explaining that he'd been to the bank before he went to the golf club and had come from the bank to change into his golf clothes and collect his clubs.

'I tucked it away in the kitchen drawer and hadn't thought any more about it because after her call I had been in a hurry to collect her.'

'Did Julie Ann know you always went to the bank on a Thursday? I mean could she have called you at your office that day because she knew you'd have money?'

Collins' body sagged as he lifted his hands and shrugged.

'Yes, she could very well have remembered, but she had not been to the office more than a couple of times and a good few years ago.'

'So you say she attacked you and then you ran down the stairs?'

'Yes, then she was in the kitchen pulling out the drawers, and I honestly had not thought about it until I saw her find the envelope. She tried to leave with the money, but I couldn't let her take it as my staff would have nothing to live on for the week. I tried to stop her leaving but she pushed past me into the hallway.' He started to sob and looked up at Bradfield. 'I didn't mean to do it, I swear I didn't, they were just there.'

'What was there?' Bradfield asked.

'My golf clubs. They were still in the hallway where I'd

left them earlier. I can't even really remember exactly how it happened – I was so angry with her. She tried to open the front door so I just grabbed a club from the bag and hit her.'

As he began to sob and shake profusely Jane was shocked that even in anger he could do this to his pregnant daughter. Bradfield waited for him to calm down and asked how many times he struck Julie Ann.

He wiped his nose. 'I don't know, two or three times maybe ... She fell to the floor and was rolling around moaning. I suddenly realized what I'd done and begged her to forgive me ... but she screamed that she'd report me to the police and have me arrested. Some of the money had scattered on the floor so I picked it up, and I was so disgusted with what I'd done that I told her she could have it. But she said nothing, went limp and just lay there curled up in a ball.' He paused, then shaking his head he said repeatedly, 'I thought I'd killed her.' Jane watched as the man broke down, sobbing wretchedly.

Bradfield waited for him to regain some composure, feeling little sympathy for George Collins; he should have controlled himself and never have hit Julie Ann, but it never ceased to amaze him how people could turn on those they loved the most. To make matters worse Collins had never even considered trying to call an ambulance, instead going into the living room and pouring himself a brandy to calm his nerves.

'Julie Ann was clearly not dead, so what did you do?' Bradfield asked, masking his revulsion for the man in front of him.

Mr Collins continued in a pained low voice, 'I suddenly heard the front door slam and ran back into the hall. I couldn't believe it. She'd gone, leaving the few notes that had fallen out of the envelope on the floor. She'd taken the rest of the money and her rucksack was gone. When I realized I rushed outside, but she was already running off down the road.'

'Did you chase after her?'

'No, I had nothing left in me to go after her, but I wish to God that I had. I had never raised a hand to her before that day and I am totally ashamed of what I did.'

'Did you hear from her again?'

'No, but I now know for certain she only came here looking for money that day. She faked being unconscious and I felt betrayed as everything she said was lies, even the fact she was pregnant. It wasn't until you told me at the station that the pathologist discovered she really was pregnant that I knew she's told me the truth about that. I wish to God I'd never played golf that day, then I would have taken the money back to the office safe and there would have been nothing for her to steal except the housekeeping.' Collins' grief had turned to anger.

Bradfield tapped his notebook. 'So you say she took her rucksack. Was there anything she left in the box room that might help us?'

'I don't know, I just removed the padlock so my wife wouldn't know Julie had been here and threw the hypodermic needle and some dirty clothes into the bin, then shut the door.'

'She definitely never tried to contact you again?'

'No, I swear to you. And my wife was away and has no knowledge of Julie being here. I am too ashamed of what I did to tell her. The first time I knew any more about what happened to her was when you came here to tell us she was dead. I have been consumed with guilt and worst of all I never got the chance to tell her how sorry I was and that I still loved her, no matter what.' Jane watched as Collins started sobbing again, his head in his hands.

'On the day and evening before her body was discovered, where were you?' Bradfield asked quietly and calmly.

'Where was I? Surely you don't still think that I could have had anything to do with her murder?' Collins looked up, surprised. 'I was at work and afterwards I was here with my wife all night. We actually had our neighbours over for dinner, so you can ask them to verify it.'

'I will do that, Mr Collins. Exactly how much money did she take?'

Collins stuffed his handkerchief back into his pocket.

'It was about £2,000, well, minus the notes she left behind, which I think were maybe about a hundred.'

Bradfield let out a slow whistle. 'New notes?'

'They were sequentially numbered £5, £10 and £1 notes. Whenever possible I always use the same teller and ask for the cash like that as it makes it easier to count off and check the individual pay packets are correct. I had to go back to the bank on Friday morning to withdraw more cash. The teller was surprised to see me and she asked if there was a problem. I didn't tell her what had happened, but said that I'd had an unfortunate situation and she jumped to the conclusion I'd been robbed. She gave me a list of the serial numbers for the notes I had withdrawn.'

'Do you still have it?'

Collins looked confused.

'I think so. I came home with it in my pocket.'

'I would like a copy of the serial numbers, Mr Collins.'

'Will it help your investigation?'

'The fact that your daughter had so much money makes her vulnerable and may be another motive for her murder. There wasn't a penny on her when we found her body and she obviously didn't have an abortion. I doubt she blew two grand on heroin in just over a week, but the serial numbers may help us to trace Julie Ann's movements after she left here, and hopefully trace the person who killed her.'

Mr Collins nodded. Bradfield tipped his head at Jane to indicate that she should accompany Mr Collins. She followed him to the kitchen; the dog was asleep in a scruffy old basket. Mr Collins pulled out a drawer that was crammed full of receipts.

'It's the odds-and-ends drawer so I may have put it in here.' He tipped the contents out onto the kitchen table, seeming much calmer now that he'd confessed.

Bradfield walked slowly up the stairs and could see that DS Lawrence had unscrewed the box-room door from its hinges to take back to the lab for further examination. He asked Lawrence if he or the detectives searching Julie Ann's room had found a rucksack or anything else of interest.

Lawrence held up a small quilted shoulder bag with worn cotton and velvet patchwork squares, on which some of the stitching had come loose.

'This is a typical hippie-style bag and was hidden under the mattress in the box room. There's a sort of concealed side bit in it, a bag within a bag, containing some drugs paraphernalia and other stuff. I'll log everything back at the station and take anything useful for examination at the lab.'

He handed it to Bradfield who glanced inside and saw an unopened clean syringe, matches, used spoon with burn marks and a rubber tourniquet for tying round the arm when injecting. There was also a small empty plastic bag with tiny traces of white powder left in it.

'Looks like she forgot this in her hurry to get out of the house,' Bradfield said, and nodded towards the master bedroom. 'Mrs Collins stirred yet?'

'No, and we still need to look in there,' Lawrence replied.

'I'll get her downstairs and then you can have a discreet look round without her knowing,' Bradfield said, and checked his watch. He told his two detectives they could go back to the Regent's Canal to search for any witnesses to the Eddie Phillips incident.

'Are you arresting Mr Collins?' Lawrence asked, but Bradfield didn't answer as he walked towards the master bedroom.

He tapped on the bedroom door and waited. He tapped again and slowly opened the door to peer into the room. The curtains were closed and Mrs Collins was wearing a sleeping mask with the plum-coloured eiderdown pulled up to her chin. He moved quietly across the room towards her and noticed the photographs of Julie Ann on the bed-side table. There were more photographs of her at various ages along the dressing table and on the chest of drawers. One photograph showed her in a tutu and ballet shoes, her tiny hands holding the edge of the net skirt. It was almost incomprehensible that this sweet angelic child, with beautiful eyes and a small Cupid's bow mouth, had become the ravished junkie they'd found strangled on the playground nudging one of the roughest estates in Hackney.

He went over to the curtains, swishing them back. Mrs Collins remained asleep so he nudged the bed with his knee, but there was still no response. He turned as Jane walked in and handed him the list of serial numbers which Mr Collins had found.

Bradfield looked at Mrs Collins and whispered, 'It's like she's in a coma. I've opened the curtains and nudged the bed. You'd better wake her as I don't want to give her a heart attack. Just verify exactly when she went to her sister's and when the neighbours came for dinner.'

'She's probably exhausted after the memorial service. Should I tell her about her husband's confession?'

'No, that's up to him. Besides, it will come out in the long run.'

'What are you going to do?' she asked.

He paused at the bedroom door.

'About what?'

'Mr Collins – are you arresting him?'

He shrugged. 'I don't condone what he did to his daughter, but he's suffered enough with her death and he and his wife need each other right now.'

Jane was touched by Bradfield's compassion. She looked round the room and wondered if the many pictures of Julie Ann had in some small way influenced his decision not to arrest George Collins.

Jane leant over the bed. 'Mrs Collins ... MRS COLLINS.' She gently nudged Mrs Collins' shoulder.

When she'd finally awoken, Mrs Collins confirmed everything her husband had said about her being in Weybridge on the Thursday and the neighbours coming for dinner. She was understandably concerned as to why the police were at the house so soon after the memorial service and Jane said they were just following up on some information and that her husband would tell her all about it. The reality was that Jane didn't have a clue what George Collins would say to his wife or how he'd explain the missing box-room door, but that wasn't her problem.

As she left the bedroom she saw DS Lawrence in the hallway.

'I hear you impressed Dr Harker with your knowledge on fibre transfers – he said you were the only one in the class who thought of it. Now, I wonder where you got that from?' he said with a cheeky grin.

Jane blushed; it hadn't crossed her mind that Harker and Lawrence might actually work together.

'Don't worry, I didn't tell him you were at Julie Ann Collins' post-mortem, or that you got it from me. Harker was very impressed, though, and not just with your knowledge,' he said with a wink, making her blush again.

'Take a bit of advice from an old sweat like me. You're a sharp cookie, Tennison, and the stuff with the Bristol and the screw marks on the door was a good spot. But never try to run before you can walk, not in this job. As a probationer it's always best to keep your eyes and ears open and mouth shut, or you'll fall into a heap of shit before you know it.'

During the journey back to the station in the uniform patrol car Bradfield sat in the front passenger seat flicking the pages of his notebook back and forth and going over everything George Collins had said.

'That's a shedload of money his daughter nicked. It meant she was flush with cash for the two weeks before her body was found.'

'Do you think the serial numbers can help trace where she was over that period?' Jane asked.

'Be a bloody lucky stroke if they did. The money could be anywhere by now, especially if she was buying smack with it. That cash will have been moved around faster than a ferret. Two grand is a lot of bloody money, and

221

scumbag drug dealers like Big Daddy and Dwayne "Shoes" Clark are probably the sort of people who'd kill to get their hands on it.'

'Interesting that she told her father she'd been raped – do you think that was true?'

He sighed. 'I dunno. She lied about most things and slept with punters for a living, so even if she was alive nobody would believe her, or would just think that rape goes with the risky territory, so to speak.'

'If we find who strangled her he's guilty of a double murder because he killed her child as well.'

He slowly turned in his seat to look at her.

'Sadly, no. If an unborn child dies because of injury to the mother rather than injury to the foetus it's neither murder nor manslaughter. You could never prove the intention to kill, or transfer of malice. Even child destruction under the Infant Life Act wouldn't stick as the foetus was too young.'

'How do you know all that?'

'CID course when I was first made detective. We had to learn all the different acts and offences off by heart. Fail an exam and you were out – back to uniform.'

'Sounds pretty intensive.'

'It was, and still is,' he said, and paused.

'It's not easy to become a detective then …'

'We need to find the bastard, or bastards, who killed Julie Ann. So far we seem to keep moving one step forward and then end up back at square one. Now, I'd really appreciate it if you kept quiet and let me concentrate.'

'Yes, sir, I'm sorry,' she said, surprised, as he'd done most of the talking.

At the station they joined DS Lawrence, who'd returned before them and was now checking over and listing the items taken from the Collinses' house. The contents of the patchwork shoulder bag were laid out on a table, the drugs paraphernalia to one side and the rest to the other. Lawrence stood beside Bradfield as they looked over some thin, cheap-looking silver bracelets, elasticated beaded necklaces, some plastic toy animals and an unused Tampax. DS Lawrence made a joke about it being effing useless considering her condition. There was also a cheap bright pink lipstick, and an empty purse made of Moroccan leather with a broken clasp. A medical card in the name of Julie Ann Maynard was for the Homerton Hospital Drug Dependency Unit, and then there were scraps of paper with names and contact numbers. Bradfield told Jane to copy all the names and numbers down and start making criminal-records enquiries on them, and DS Lawrence could then take the paper for fingerprinting, along with the empty plastic bag of what had most probably been heroin.

Jane looked down at the items on the table – the bracelets reminded her of Janis Joplin who had worn so many bangles on her wrists. Some words from Joplin's 'Piece Of My Heart' began to sing out in Jane's mind:

> *You're out on the streets looking good,*
> *And baby, deep down in your heart I guess you*
> *   know that it ain't right,*
> *Never, never, never, never, never, never hear me*
> *   when I cry at night,*
> *Babe, and I cry all the time!*

CHAPTER FOURTEEN

The café's front window was filled with cheap Greek travel brochures and photographs, as well as a planning order and notice to customers that the café was to undergo refurbishment. The door had a broken blind with a 'Closed' sign on it. As John knocked on the door he was encouraged by the fact that it was difficult to see into the café from the street. At first there was no answer so he knocked again and a few seconds later the door was unlocked and inched open. The man who answered was a fifty-year-old muscular Greek with iron-grey hair. He had a hard, lined face with a jutting chin and bad teeth, along with bulging thick-set hairy arms and a barrel-shaped chest. The top four buttons of his white shirt were open revealing a gold chain and coin pendant engraved with an owl with oversized piercing eyes, not dissimilar to the man's own.

'You Silas?'

'Who wanna know?'

'You do souvki takeaway?' John asked, using the pre-arranged introduction his father had given him. The scribbled notes had been hard to read as they were written in pencil on Izal toilet paper and were badly creased, due to being refolded so many times in order to fit into the small matchbox.

'You mean souvlaki?' Silas spoke with a strange accent, a mixture of Greek and Cockney.

'Yeah, I'm John Bent—'

'No last name, first only, you come in,' he said in a staccato manner.

John stepped inside as Silas looked outside, quickly glancing up and down the road before relocking the door. They shook hands and Silas jerked his head for John to follow him. The interior of the café was small and shoddy, with six tables covered in plastic red-and-white-checked sheets. A refrigerated display counter contained a number of plastic bowls with different sandwich fillings and olives, while cakes and Greek pastries were arranged to one side next to baskets of sliced bread and rolls. There was a large espresso machine, and an array of bottles and sauces on dusty shelves behind the counter.

Silas led John to a back room; the doorway had a greasy multicoloured plastic strip curtain hanging across it. Inside there were boxes and boxes of what appeared to be tins of tuna, vine leaves and assorted vegetables stacked on unsteady-looking shelves.

'You wanna a coffee or sometink, or shall we just get on wiv it?'

'I'd like to see where we start, and do you have a back yard so we can bring in the equipment or does it all have to come in via the front?'

'I have yard, but maybe good if decorating stuff come in front way during first day to make it look real. I still open café in day and you work at night so look like I still keep business going. Anyone ask I say basement being converted for more seating as I expanding, so there should be no problem.'

Silas flicked on a light switch and John followed him down stone stairs into a large dank basement.

'You got a power source down here?'

'I got big set of cables with long leads, plenty power for down here.'

They stood side by side facing an old whitewashed brick wall. Silas slapped his palm against it. 'This also bank's wall. You smash through here, dig tunnel and vault is on other side, but you gotta thick concrete floor base that is gonna take hours of drilling – they say it supposed to be impenetrable.'

'Bloody hell, it's a lot of work,' John said quietly.

'Yeah and we only work through night and stop 5 a.m. before light and people about on streets. I open café at seven but only during week. I close weekends cos no local business open.'

'I'm going to have to get some wooden RSJs and Acro props for that wall if we want to knock through it.'

'What you mean?'

'The wall here will not be that difficult to get through, but it's a supporting wall so I need to put up support planks where we remove the bricks, which we'll have to do slowly. Last thing I want is the whole lot collapsing in on us.'

'Too bloody right,' Silas said, looking concerned.

'You know how thick the concrete floor is below the deposit vault?'

'I hear is plenty thick, built three years ago. If we can't drill our way in, we might need explosives to blast through.'

'Blasting is a last resort. I've got a heavy-duty Kango hammer drill but I reckon it will be too weighty and awkward for even two of us to lift and drill upwards.'

226

'So what you do?'

'Get a smaller one which is more fucking cash out of my pocket.'

'I also hear the concrete floor has gotta thick metal mesh in it for extra strength and security.'

'Are you serious?'

'Course I serious – why I make joke about such things?'

'Cos it means more expense and I'm virtually out of cash as it is.'

'Why more expense – you trade big Kango for small?'

'I'll think about it, but I'll need an angle grinder to cut through the mesh.'

'No problems, I give you more money, you pay me back when job done.'

'What about alarms?'

'I don't have any.'

John was beginning to wonder if Silas was stupid, but realized it was just the language barrier. 'I mean in the fucking bank. I've got someone on board who's a good bell man but he needs to know what he's up against to disarm it.'

'Alarms inside of bank, plus all windows and doors. The vault has big steel entry door, but as we go up through vault floor from below it no trigger it.'

'Of course it will …!'

'No, listen to me. I hear there no alarm inside vault as they think nobody can get in.'

'Whoever you got all this info from, does he know what we are going to do and is he safe to keep his mouth shut?'

Silas let out a deep guttural laugh, but John was not so amused and wanted to know if the alarm informant would have to be paid off.

Silas held his pendant towards John. 'My father give this to me many years ago. Is the Owl of Athena from ancient Greece, a symbol of knowledge, wisdom and how you say ... shrewdness. I have no informant, I hear the bank staff talk when they come in my café for food and drink, and the young ones they yap, yap, yap.'

John felt relieved and more confident about Silas who could have lied and said he did have another man who needed paying.

They both stood staring at the whitewashed wall. Silas explained that one of the safety-deposit boxes contained at least £100,000 in untraceable notes. John knew this, but he was curious as to how Silas knew. Silas explained the man used to be a regular at the café, and after too much ouzo one night he said he had put some nicked money in the vault.

'Silly sod then get himself arrested, but added to de cash there'll be Christ only knows what. People who use these deposit boxes stuff in jewellery and uninsurable stuff along with a lot of antique silver and dodgy gear – millions could be had for the takin',' Silas said grinning and then offered to make John a coffee.

They left the basement and went up the stairs into the café. Silas made some Greek coffee in a small copper pot that he said was called a *briki*. He poured one for himself and one for John into two clear glass demitasse cups with saucers. John took a sip out of politeness, but it was like tar and tasted far too strong for his liking.

'This other guy you bringin', you know him well?' Silas asked, taking a sip of his piping-hot black coffee.

'He's the bell man, name's Danny Mit—' he began to say and Silas wagged his finger rapidly reminding him it was first names only.

'Danny's kosher and I'm using me brother to keep watch from up on high. Any sign of the cops, anyone passing, anything suspicious, or if we're too noisy, he'll be able to radio us to stop.'

Silas sighed. 'I tell you, I gonna be very glad to get out of this shithole as soon as job is done.'

'What will you do?'

'I will have to get out of England, but I gonna disappear to Katakolon in my country. Get me a nice villa overlooking the Ionian Sea, a small fishing boat, then I'm just gonna relax.'

'No family then?'

'Yes, wife and three kids, but I already send her back to live with her sister a month ago. I gonna tell her I win big on horses so she no suspicious. I won a packet on the Grand National with Red Rum, what a horse. Besides she's no complainin' if living well in nice place. You can come and visit, you'll soon be able to afford it.' He grinned.

John smiled back. Looking round the dingy café he could understand why Silas wanted to return to his homeland.

Silas lit up a small cheroot and tapped John's arm. 'So you all set?'

'Yeah ... just one thing ... can we trust this geezer in prison who set it all up? I know he's got a long stretch inside, but what if he's trying to get on the side of the cops? You know, settin' us up and grassin' to get early parole.'

Silas shook his head and rubbed his pendant. 'Listen to me and the wise owl, I trust him cos he gotta trust me good. I know more about him an' could get him banged up for a fifteen stretch. This is a payback, and if he is fuckin' us over I will grass him up. That dough in the safety deposit was the takin's from a robbery where a young rozzer got shot in the legs with a sawn-off. You understand me? Don't think I'm some damned ass-stupid Greek that works tables.'

John nodded and looked at his watch. He'd been with Silas for nearly an hour and any worries he'd had were now allayed. He was confident that not only could they trust him, but also he was a shrewd man eager to get on with the job.

'OK, let's start the ball rolling, I'll begin bringing the decorating gear over tomorrow night,' he said with a sly grin.

Jane had arrived at work just before midday. She and Kath were sitting in the incident room updating the index cards, proofreading and filing statements.

'I can't believe how much my sister is carrying on about the wedding. She'll no doubt have a fit when she sees me in the bridesmaid outfit – makes me look like Jayne Mansfield because of the corset.'

'Can't you get it altered?'

'No time, it's all been so rushed.'

'She's not up the duff, is she?'

'No, she is not,' Jane said indignantly.

'Is she a virgin like you then?' Kath said, grinning.

'Don't start on that again, Kath. I'm not in the mood for it, I mean what with my cleavage, the puffball sleeves and this huge sash with a big bow and the most awful shade – salmon-pink – I will look terrible.'

Kath tried hard not to laugh at the thought. 'Not with a figure like you've got. Besides, look on the positive side – the sleeves might distract from your boobs hanging out.'

'Shut up,' Jane said as she threw a paper clip at Kath.

'Do you two ever stop pissing about?' Bradfield said as he entered the room.

'We weren't, sir. I asked her to throw me a clip to hold these statement pages together,' Kath replied sheepishly.

'Has Spencer Gibbs called in from Coventry?'

'Yes, sir, about three hours ago. They arrested Dwayne Clark at an address this morning,' Kath said and handed him notes she'd made of an earlier phone conversation with DS Gibbs.

'That's brilliant. What about the bloke known as Big Daddy, or Josh?'

'Neither of them was there.'

'Bollocks, so we're still no further forward. What else did Gibbs say?'

'He's bringing Clark straight here. He should be back soon.'

'Well, let's hope he persuades Dwayne to see the light before they get onto the North Circular.' He was about to leave when he turned to Jane.

'All those bits of paper in Julie Ann's patchwork bag – you get anything from them?'

Jane held up some sheets of paper from the desk next to her.

'I've copied everything down, sir. I am still working on them, but nothing of interest so far. I've made a note that Anjali O'Duncie was wrong about overhearing the name "Paddy", and Julie Ann actually made the call to her father so it was "Daddy" and not connected to Big Daddy the drug dealer.'

Bradfield grabbed Jane's notes from her hand and had a quick glance-over before dropping them down on her desk. 'Well, pull your finger out, Tennison. I've got the

DCS on my back and he wants results. If DS Gibbs returns in the next hour tell him I'll be in the canteen.'

Jane waited until he left the room and looked at Kath who was checking her watch. 'Kath, can you help me with this? There's initials, odd names and phone numbers ... but I just haven't—'

'No can do, Jane. I've got to go over to Old Street Court. That burglar I nicked screwing the old people's flats is appearing. I shouldn't be too long as he's pleading guilty and asking for a number of other burglary offences to be taken into consideration.'

'That's a great result, Kath, and good for your career.'

'Kind of odd because he's a nasty little sod and then there was all that cash we found hidden under his bed. He must have done way more jobs than he's admitting to. Then again maybe he's being a bit savvy as he was caught bang to rights. If he was found guilty by a jury at a trial he'd get an even heavier prison sentence. Still, either way at least he'll be behind bars where he belongs, and the old 'uns will feel a bit safer.'

Jane had just started to go through the names and numbers from Julie Ann's bag when a sharply dressed DS Gibbs walked in singing 'Nights In White Satin'. He asked where Bradfield was and she informed him the DCI was in the canteen before asking if Dwayne Clark had said anything on the journey back. Gibbs told her briefly that he had denied knowing Julie Ann and Eddie Phillips and didn't know any Big Daddy or where Josh lived, but thanks to a Coventry drug squad informant they now had various possible names for him.

'Josh Richards, Jenkins, Rankin – all bullshit, no doubt, so Christ knows what his real name actually is. Do me a favour while I speak with the boss – can you go through

all the index cards, statements, information, in fact everything we have and check if the name "Tod" appears
anywhere?'

'Well, he asked me to check off Julie Ann's stuff asap,'
Jane said.

'Make my request the priority, and don't look so worried, he'll agree with me.' Gibbs did a quick drum beat on
the desk then resumed his singing as he left the room.

Bradfield was just finishing his bread-and-butter pudding
with custard when Gibbs put his coffee and sandwich
down on the table and sat opposite him.

'We got Dwayne.'

'I heard, but not Big Daddy, which is what I would have
preferred.'

'I know, but I'm pretty certain that Josh is the first name
of Big Daddy. There are different surnames he uses, but I
need to do a bit of digging on them.'

'Did Dwayne say anything in the car?'

Gibbs finished a mouthful of his sandwich. 'Nope, just
repeated word for word what his girlfriend told us about
expanding the window-cleaning business and being out of
London for over a week at the material times. The bloke
at the place he was staying alibied him – not even a used
spliff in the place. Dwayne admitted working in the
window-cleaning business with a Josh, but conveniently
doesn't know where he lives as he recently moved. He
also denied either of them were dealers.'

'You're losing your touch, Spence.'

'What do you mean?'

'Over two hours in a car with a suspect and you
couldn't break him to get a full name and address.'

'I tell you he's a tough one, and I got the impression he's

233

frightened of Big Daddy like Eddie Phillips was. I gave him a slap and even locked him in the boot of the car for nearly an hour. He was sweating like a pig but he still didn't crack.'

'Get him out of the cell and bring him up to my office so I can interview him,' Bradfield said, pushing his dessert bowl to one side and standing up.

'He's not in the cell. I released him on the North Circular.'

'You effing did that without even consulting me!'

'I tried to get hold of you but you weren't available. Come on, it isn't as bad as it sounds. I'd already stopped and called the central surveillance unit at the Yard while he was in the boot. They were ready and waiting to tail Dwayne when I kicked him out the car, so no doubt he should lead us to Big Daddy.'

'They'd better bloody well not lose him.'

'Even if they do we still know where he lives with his girlfriend, and he's unlikely to do a runner,' Gibbs said, getting out his notebook and flicking it open to the last page. 'I searched through Dwayne's gear and there was a bit of notepaper with "TOD" in capital letters and a Primrose Hill dialling code on it, and sort of dots and ticks beside it. Might be a good lead so I didn't take the actual note as I didn't want to give away I'd seen it. But you know dealers do use their own forms of made-up code.'

'Primrose Hill,' Bradfield said thoughtfully, then clicked his fingers and gestured to Gibbs to follow him.

As they entered the incident room Bradfield pointed his finger at Jane.

'Tennison, that list you were working on – let me see it.'

Jane handed it over and nervously asked if there was something she'd missed.

'Did you write down everything exactly as it was on the notes in Julie Ann's bag?'

'Yes, I'm pretty sure I did.'

He looked through the list closely and then stabbed his finger at it. 'There it is, that's the bloody link.'

Jane and Gibbs looked at each other wondering exactly what he was referring to.

'I knew there was something she was hiding.' He looked at Gibbs. 'Spence, get round to the hospital and drag that fat woman in here now.'

'Who are you talking about?' Gibbs asked.

'The big black woman that works at the drug unit – the appendix-obsessed one who never stopped talkin'.'

Jane pulled an index card from the carousel. 'Do you mean Anjali O'Duncie, sir?'

'Yeah, that's her – did she ever mention any relatives to you, Tennison?'

'Not as I recall.'

'Where does she live?'

'Gave an address in Stoke Newington; it's on her index card,' Jane said.

Gibbs looked somewhat baffled. 'Is there something I'm missing here?'

Bradfield held up Jane's notes. 'Are you positive you've recorded correctly what was on the pieces of paper in Julie Ann's bag?'

'Yes, sir.'

Bradfield pointed to an entry and showed it to Gibbs whose eyes lit up when he saw 'TO'D'.

'That's the same three capital letters Dwayne had on a bit of paper, but without the apostrophe after the "O".'

'I'm sure there was a slight gap between the "T" and the "OD" on Julie Ann's bit of paper,' Jane added.

Bradfield held his hand up for them to be quiet as he paused briefly to think before continuing.

'OK, this might be a long shot or a blinder, but I'll bet my wages the "T" is an initial for a Christian name, "O" apostrophe "D" is a surname and our Anjali woman may be related.' He picked up the phone, rang the comms room and asked for a name check to be run on criminal records against black males with the surname O'Duncie aged between twenty-five and forty. He also said he was specifically interested in O'Duncies with Christian names that started with a 'T' and he wanted any results printed off and brought up to him immediately. He then told Jane to get on to the council offices that covered Primrose Hill to see if they had any tenants or residents under the name O'Duncie.

He put the phone down. 'If Josh is a false name for Big Daddy used by Dwayne, then this "TOD" might be who we should actually be looking for, or at least connected to the drugs or murders in some way. Is there a home phone number on Anjali's card, Tennison?'

'No, she said she didn't have one.'

Gibbs chipped in, 'If she thought Julie Ann was speaking to Big Daddy on the hospital phone then she may have deliberately misled us by saying it was someone called Paddy.'

Bradfield nodded. 'Exactly. We now know Julie Ann called her father but this O'Duncie woman's in a perfect position to refer the drug addicts who attend the Homerton unit to a dealer so they can buy more drugs.'

Bradfield was feeling certain that at last they might have a positive breakthrough. Even more so when an hour later they had information that a Terrence O'Duncie, aged thirty-two, had previous convictions for drugs offences dating back five years. His criminal record showed he was black, over six foot tall and had an address in Stoke Newington, the same address Anjali O'Duncie had given, and it was suspected he was her younger brother.

Bradfield was eager to interview Anjali, especially as he was now more confident that Terrence O'Duncie was a strong suspect for murder, and might even be 'Big Daddy' himself.

Anjali was brought into his office later that afternoon. She was belligerent and accused them of harassing her, and denied knowing anyone called Big Daddy or a Terrence who had the same surname as her. Bradfield and Gibbs could tell from the beads of sweat running down her forehead that she was nervous and obviously lying. Bradfield slowly put pressure on her and asked if she knew a Dwayne Clark, but yet again there was denial.

He snarled at her. 'I'm not a bloody fool like you! Clark works with Terrence O'Duncie, who's on our records for possession of drugs, possession with intent to supply and supplying, and he's done time in Brixton Prison.'

Anjali still denied knowing either man, but Bradfield had got an officer to bike Terrence O'Duncie's file over from Scotland Yard before the interview. The mug shot showed a good-looking, lighter-skinned man with short waxed hair. He was six foot two inches and had deep, penetrating dark eyes and high cheekbones. He slowly pushed the mug-shot photograph in front of Anjali. 'Terrence O'Duncie – the home address on his arrest sheet five years ago is the same as yours. He's your brother, isn't he, so don't you dare say again you don't know him or I'll have you charged and in court so fast—'

'What for? I've not done nothing wrong,' she said, wiping her forehead on her sleeve.

He banged his hand on the table. 'Aiding and abetting drug supply, assisting a murder suspect, conspiracy to obstruct justice in a murder investigation, which carries a sentence of life imprisonment.'

She sat in silence, shaking and wringing her hands, beads of sweat now falling onto her dress.

Bradfield leaned closer. 'God knows what the hospital will think of you when I tell them.'

Anjali froze, her eyes bulging open with fear. 'Please don't, I really like working there counselling and helping those poor kids get off drugs.'

'Don't lie – you're nothing more than a tea skivvy who uses the job to direct the addicts to your brother who then supplies them and pays you for the introductions.'

She began to cry. 'On my life I don't, honest I don't, I just wanted to help them. Yes, Terrence is my brother, but mostly everyone calls him Terry. I haven't seen him for weeks and I've never met anyone called Dwayne or Big Daddy. I knew Terry had a drug problem but he told me he was off the stuff and was living with a crowd of ex-junkies who were all helping each other through cold turkey. He said that if I knew any kids who needed support and a place to stay then I should send them to him.'

'Did you send Julie Ann to him?'

'Yes, but I didn't tell Eddie about Terry, though Julie Ann might have.'

'OK, now tell me where this brother of yours lives, Anjali.'

'I dunno the exact address, I never been there. All I know is it's a big four-storey squat in Primrose Hill.'

Gibbs leaned over and slapped the table.

'Oh right, so you just send your junkie kids over without a street or a house number, stop fuckin' lying.'

Anjali chewed at her lips, then opened her large bag and after sifting around brought out a small address book.

'This is the truth, I am tellin' you the God's truth because I dunno the address. I send them like my brother said to 24 Court Road in Chalk Farm so someone there can tell them where to go.'

Gibbs leaned across and spoke quietly to Bradfield. 'That's Dwayne Clark's address. Maybe he's a middle man and that's the reason we didn't find any gear stashed there.'

'Bloody well organized, isn't it?' Bradfield turned back to Anjali as Gibbs rocked in his chair.

'Why did you lie about who Julie Ann was talking to on the phone in the doctor's office?' Bradfield asked.

'I swear before God that I heard her say "Paddy" or something like it. My brother is doing good by them kids, but if I'd told you about him you're all a racist lot an' would think he was involved cos he was black and fit him up him with her murder.'

'I don't need to fit him up, sweetheart, he's in it up to his eyeballs. If what you say is true then your precious brother used you to entice young girls into his set-up. Then he plied them with drugs and passed them round like rag dolls to be raped and abused. Problem was he got Julie Ann pregnant and she probably threatened to expose him so he murdered her. Eddie Phillips was another weak link and he had to die as well, so tell me, how does it feel to be responsible for sending two youngsters to their deaths?'

Anjali O'Duncie was now a gibbering wreck, sobbing and wailing whilst continually claiming that all she was doing was trying to help down-and-out addicts by giving them somewhere safe to stay. She was adamant her brother was a good honest man since he was clean.

'What will happen to me now?'

'That depends on what your brother has to say when I nick him, but for now you ain't going anywhere until I find him. DS Gibbs will take you down the cells.'

No sooner had Bradfield finished the interview with Anjali than he received a phone call informing him that the surveillance unit had lost Dwayne Clark and he hadn't returned to his address in Chalk Farm. DS Gibbs had expected Bradfield to be livid with him but was surprised at how calm he was under the circumstances. The reality was he knew they'd find Dwayne again, but his priority was to find Terrence O'Duncie and hopefully collar the so-called 'Big Daddy' for the murder of Julie Ann and Eddie. He told Jane to get on to Camden Council and ask where all the squats were located in Primrose Hill and in particular any old four-storey houses. They knew by now that the phone number attached to the note DS Gibbs had copied from Dwayne was that of a call box located in Primrose Hill.

It didn't take Jane long to get a result. There was a four-storey terraced house that had been occupied by a number of 'hippie types' for eighteen months. The premises were in King Charles Road and had been empty and boarded up for five years before the squatters moved in. The street was expensive and fashionable, the local residents all very wealthy people, and although many had complained to the council there was nothing they could do under 'squatters' rights'. Also the previous occupant had died and no known next of kin had as yet been traced. The local uniform officers had visited the premises a couple of times due to loud-noise complaints, but the squatters had always been apologetic and polite. The house had even been raided on one occasion after an anonymous drugs tip-off but nothing had been found.

'Where's WPC Morgan?' Bradfield asked Jane.

'She's in court this afternoon with the burglar she arrested.'

'Right, you'll have to come with us then. No doubt be a few women and kids in the place so I'll need a plonk for the gentle touch if it starts kicking off.'

Jane hated it when her male colleagues referred to female officers as 'plonks'. It was insulting, and even more so to think that only the women should have to play nanny to kids. However, she bit back a retort, glad to be able to gain further experience by going on the raid to arrest a suspect for Julie Ann's murder.

CHAPTER FIFTEEN

The tall grey-bricked Victorian terraced house occupied by the squatters was close to the Regent's Canal, where the body of Eddie Phillips had been found. The building, with its sash windows and black wrought-iron fencing, was the same shape and size as all the others in the street. The only things that marked it out from its neighbours were the cracked, peeling paintwork and the unwashed windows.

Two rake-thin young white males were sitting outside it on the grimy steps leading up to the front porch and smoking cigarettes. One had bright, red-dyed hair like David Bowie, and was wearing skintight flared trousers with patches and embroidered flowers, and a floral shirt with frills. The other pasty-faced kid had frizzy hair, and his skintight cat suit, worn with high wedged boots, made him look as if he had just left the stage of the musical *Hair*. Two young girls came out and sat with the boys, sharing the cigarettes. Their hair was braided and one girl had flowers either side of her head. They were equally pale-faced, with heavy dark mascara and black liner round their eyes. Their floating long dresses had layers of beads and their wrists were covered in cheap bangles. Both girls had filthy bare feet. Two small children in dirty vests, and one in a sodden towelling nappy, were playing with coloured marbles on the pavement.

Blasting out from an open window on the top floor was the Jimi Hendrix song 'All Along The Watchtower', and it was obvious some of the youngsters were stoned. They laughed as Bradfield, followed by Gibbs then Jane, headed up the steps to the front door. When Bradfield showed his warrant card they applauded and started making grunting noises like a pig. He wasn't in the mood for their bad attitude and lack of respect.

'Unless you all want to be nicked and your kids taken into care I suggest you shut up, behave and answer my questions, starting with ... Is Terry O'Duncie in?'

No one said anything.

'You might also know him as Big Daddy? So, last time I'll ask ... Is he in the house?'

A child no older than six spoke up and said that Terry was in bed sleeping and his mother pulled him towards her and told him to shut up.

'Out of the mouths of babes,' Bradfield said and laughed as he pulled out two photographs from his inside jacket pocket then held them up for the group to see. One was of Julie Ann and the other of Eddie Phillips.

'Any of you ever seen these two kids here?'

They all looked at each other and shrugged their shoulders. The young boy was about to say something, but his mother tugged at his arm and he said nothing. Their attitude annoyed Bradfield even more, especially as they hadn't made a real effort to look at the photographs. He flung them down on the lap of the David Bowie lookalike and ordered two of the uniform officers accompanying them to round everyone up and contain them in the front room of the house. He told the group that he would be searching the premises for some time so they could all take a good look at the photographs to see if they helped jog their memories.

The hallway had bare floorboards and the rooms leading off it had nailed-up makeshift curtains made from tatty old bits of sheets and other badly stitched-together materials. Threadbare mattresses, stained sleeping bags and broken furniture littered every room; beer and Coke cans lay in corners and takeaway cartons of rotting food spewed out of old plastic bags. Jane shuddered and gagged slightly as she saw a plate of rancid food crawling with maggots. Gibbs laughed and said they'd be good for fishing. She could see he and Bradfield had become hardened to searching disgusting slums. The smell of incense from smouldering joss sticks permeated the air, but still failed to disguise the heavy scent of marijuana.

In one room a young girl with silk flowers pinned to her long blonde hair was sitting cross-legged peeling potatoes, the multitude of bracelets on her arms jangling as the peel fell onto the soggy newspaper between her legs. She looked no older than sixteen, had eyes like a panda's and wore a pretty torn floral smock which made her appear innocent.

'Looking for Terry O'Duncie. Which room is he in?' Gibbs asked, showing her his warrant card.

'I don't know,' she replied nonchalantly as she sliced a potato into quarters and dropped it into a plastic bowl of water by her side.

Gibbs had another set of photographs which he held in front of her. She continued peeling a potato and said in a very upper-class voice that she didn't know who had stayed at the squat previously as she'd only been there a couple of days.

Jane followed Bradfield as he checked out the kitchen. It was full of used pans and plates piled in a big sink full of greasy water and broken mugs. A large, filthy-looking disconnected old cooker had a Calor gas stove from a VW camper van on top of it and a big pot of vegetable stew was bubbling away. The windows had newspaper stuck over the broken glass and a bedraggled cat was up on the draining board scavenging for food and licking dirty plates. The numerous open black bin bags stank of rotting food. Jane had been disgusted with the mess left in the station kitchen by the officers but this was far beyond anything she had ever come across, and to think that the squatters were cooking for and feeding the young children, never mind themselves, was shocking. She held her breath as she gave a cursory glance around. Through the cracked window in the back door she could see even more open bags of rubbish left to rot, and presumed there were no dustmen collecting from the house. She couldn't wait to get out of the foul kitchen. She took a deep breath: if her mother knew where she was and what she was doing she would have heart failure.

The Jimi Hendrix song continued at a deafening level, and having no luck downstairs the team headed up to the first-floor landing. The stairs were strewn with cigarette butts and empty cans of beer. Wine bottles on every other step held different-coloured candles; wax had dripped down the sides of the bottles and onto the stairs.

Posters and prints were pinned up on the yellowing, damp-stained landing walls. The floor was covered with a heavily soiled fitted carpet, which appeared to have once been dark blue and good-quality shagpile. Jane pushed open a bedroom door and undid the wooden shutters of the large double bay window to let in the light. She saw that the walls had been painted bright blue and were patterned with white stars and yellow moons and sprinkled with glitter. Sleeping bags and tatty blankets were strewn over the floor along with tin plates and ashtrays overflowing with cigarette stubs and old marijuana roaches. The smell in the room was a mixture of stale sweat and damp and the heady incense gave off a sickening flowery perfume. Candles of every shape and size stood in pools of hardened wax and a lit amber-coloured cone candle flickered in one corner.

Bradfield stared in disgust. 'Christ, how many kids are dossing down here? It must be a bloody fire hazard with all these candles.'

Jane bent down to pick up a plastic bag and look inside but Gibbs pulled her hand back. He took a pen out of his pocket to flick the top of the bag open and it was full of used hypodermic needles.

'You prick your hand on one of those and the next thing you know is you'll be really sick with hepatitis.'

'What's that?' she asked.

'You need to read General Orders more often: there was a warning about it. You can get hepatitis from an infected person's blood, semen, or other bodily fluids, and it will badly damage your liver. The stupid bastards are sharing and reusing the same needles. If you see any of them with yellow, jaundiced-looking faces, sure bet is they've got it.'

A relieved Jane thanked him for his timely intervention. In reality she was so taken aback by the squalor she was unsure what she should or should not be doing.

Bradfield had seen enough and eager to get his hands on O'Duncie headed out into the corridor to go up to the next floor. Jane checked out a bathroom: the smell was worse than that of the decomposing body at the mortuary. She retched as she saw that the toilet was filled with unflushed faeces and urine, and the bath full of vomit. From the rust-stained taps and filthy washbasin it was obvious the water had been turned off for some time.

Jane went onto the landing as DS Gibbs came out of another bedroom and jerked his thumb back towards the room. 'Two more teenagers out for the count in there. Looks like they were making clothes or something – lot of cut-up material and sewing stuff. I told 'em to get dressed and go down to the front room with the others.'

The music was still blaring from the room on the top floor, though the song was now Hendrix's 'Voodoo Child' and the volume had been turned up slightly.

'That's my favourite of all his hits – the guitar licks are just unbelievable. He could even play the thing with his teeth, you know,' Gibbs said and started to do a bit of air guitar, making Jane smile. She was getting to like him more and more: he was quite a character.

They both heard a short shrill whistle and looked up to see DCI Bradfield leaning over the balcony crooking his finger for them to come up to the top floor. As they joined him Jane noticed the carpet was much cleaner and the landing window had old red drapes like theatre curtains still hanging on the original rail. Bradfield told them he had checked out two of the three rooms and found them empty. When the first Hendrix song had stopped he had heard a male and female voice in the room at the end of the corridor.

Bradfield crossed to the closed door. It was fitted with a Yale lock, but it didn't look like a professional job. He turned to Gibbs. 'Come on, stuff this softly-softly approach. Do your Bruce Lee bit and kick the door in, Spence.'

Gibbs took three paces back then two quick steps forward and, raising his right foot, kicked hard on the Yale causing the door to fly open and the lock to splinter away from the frame.

'What the fuck do you think you're doing?' a deep voice said from inside the inky dark room.

As the natural light from the hallway filtered in they could make out a naked black man lying on top of a young white girl with blonde hair braided in two long plaits.

'Police, stay where you are,' Gibbs shouted above the music as he ran over and pulled the curtains open letting the light flood in.

They all recognized O'Duncie from his mug shot, even though his face was contorted with rage. He rolled off the woman and stood up. She screamed and instantly pulled the orange bed throw over her naked body.

O'Duncie in the flesh was a very handsome, broad-shouldered man with a well-defined muscular body and collar-length wavy Afro hair tied with a multicoloured bandana, Jimi Hendrix style. A heavy silver neck chain attached to a black studded cross hung from his neck and his wrists and fingers were covered in silver bangles and gold rings.

'Sit down on the bed now,' Bradfield shouted as Jane blushed at the sight of his naked body.

'It's not true what they say: my dick's bigger than that,' Gibbs said in a demeaning way.

'Get the fuck outta here!' O'Duncie shouted.

'I hope you're talking to the teenager,' Bradfield said, nodding at the girl lying on the red-velvet-framed bed. She was terrified and pulling on some underwear and a kimono under the bed throw.

Bradfield went over and turned the stereo off. It had two large speakers and seemed expensive and new. He could see a power cable extension lead that went up through an open hatch into the loft and he suspected O'Duncie was stealing the neighbours' electricity.

Jane looked round the room. The ceiling was black with stuck-on gold stars, the walls painted in psychedelic colours and adorned with pictures of rock stars like Jimi Hendrix, The Rolling Stones, Led Zeppelin and Deep Purple. Sheepskin rugs were scattered over the floor; crimson and blue silk throws hung from a pole at each end of the bed so that it looked like a sheikh's tent. There was an array of expensive candles stuck in various gilt candle-holders more suited to a church and a wooden cross was fixed to the wall above the bed's headboard.

Bradfield whispered to Jane to take the terrified teenager downstairs and find out how old she was and if she knew anything that could help them. Jane nodded and told the girl to come with her, but she also suspected Bradfield didn't want her to be present while he and DS Gibbs spoke with Terrence O'Duncie.

'You can put some clothes on, O'Duncie, or be taken to the nick stark bollock naked. Either way I don't care because you are in fuckin' big trouble.'

'What ya want to arrest me for? I ain't done nothing wrong,' he said in an angry tone whilst pulling on some underpants.

Bradfield paid him no attention and started to look around. There was a large wardrobe in one corner, which he opened. The display of velvet trousers, floral shirts, silk scarves, leather shoes and platform boots was astonishing and a drawer was filled with gold and silver bracelets, rings and watches.

'Well, isn't this paradise in a shithole,' Bradfield said as he threw O'Duncie a shirt and velvet trousers to put on.

'It's all paid for and legit – the receipts are in the bed-side-cabinet drawer. I know every piece of jewellery there so don't go nicking none,' he said with a smirk.

Gibbs opened the drawer, pulled out a handful of receipts and held them up for Bradfield to see.

'All thanks to drugs money, no doubt,' Bradfield remarked.

'No, the kids pay me rent.'

'Don't play games, your sister's dropped you right in it, so just get dressed and behave yourself,' Gibbs said.

'My sister's a mental case. We don't get on so she'd say anything to fuck me up.'

Bradfield continued going through the wardrobe and there was no sign of any drugs. He started to pick up the pairs of boots one by one and tip them upside down when suddenly a small bag of marijuana fell out. He grabbed it and waved it at O'Duncie.

'I don't know anything about that,' he said arrogantly.

Bradfield laughed, picked up another boot, shook it and this time two bags of marijuana and some heroin wraps fell out.

'That's not mine – you bastards brought it here to fit me up cos I'm black.'

'If I wanted to fit you up, Terry, I'd have brought more drugs and some LSD tabs with me.'

Bradfield threw the boot back in the wardrobe and as it hit the floor there was a strange-sounding thud. He bent down and rapped his knuckles on the plywood which produced the same sound, but when he knocked on the opposite side, by the drawers, the sound was hollow. He noticed that the wardrobe floor had a wooden slat divide held down by a screw at each end.

'Got a screwdriver anywhere?' he asked O'Duncie who said nothing but looked nervous for the first time as he pulled on the purple velvet trousers and zipped up the fly.

Bradfield lifted his right foot and slammed it down hard on the plywood causing it to splinter in half.

'Sorry, that was an accident,' he said as he ripped the broken pieces of wood away to discover a compartment filled with a pile of different-denomination banknotes. Some had elastic bands round them: there were ones, fives, tenners and some new twenties held together in a bank wrap. There was also a bag of coins and a medium-sized bag of what was obviously heroin.

Bradfield smiled. 'Well, sunshine, I'd say that lot equates to dealing and a long prison sentence with your previous drugs convictions.'

'Listen to me, cos I don't know nothin' about that lot; the last person who was here must have left it.'

'Well, you'd better hope we don't find your prints on the heroin bag or any of the notes then. You really have to wise up and start helping us, and I might just put a good word in for you with the judge.'

O'Duncie started to sweat as he buttoned up his shirt. Spencer Gibbs, using a clean handkerchief, began to carefully gather up the money and drugs, putting them into a pillowcase. He reckoned the notes amounted to roughly two and a half to three thousand pounds.

'Ain't you supposed to count it in front of me?' O'Duncie asked.

'So you're now saying this is your money, are you?' Gibbs remarked.

O'Duncie realized he'd messed up and knew his prints would be found so he admitted the money and drugs were his.

'We'll count it at the nick. You're being arrested for possession and supplying drugs as well as—'

O'Duncie interrupted Bradfield. 'You can have a cut of

the dough.' He turned to Gibbs. 'Split it between you both.'

Gibbs stared hard, which seemed to encourage O'Duncie.

'Come on, man, I know how to keep my mouth shut, like I never saw you find it, right? I dunno even how much is there, right, you with me? I mean help me out here, last time I got raided drug squad prick got away with a grand, so I know how it works.'

Gibbs reacted fast, his fist smacking into O'Duncie's face. O'Duncie howled as he fell backwards onto the bed and blood spurted from his nose.

'We're not drug squad or bent!' Gibbs shouted.

'Jesus Christ, man, you fuckin' busted my nose.' He looked at Bradfield. 'You saw what he did, he hit me.'

'I saw you trip up when you tried to escape arrest. Now shut up, wipe your nose and finish getting dressed.'

O'Duncie grabbed a corner of the sheet and wiped his nose before pulling on a pair of black Cuban-heeled boots and lastly an ankle-length brown-suede trench coat. Gibbs then put the handcuffs on and led him downstairs.

As O'Duncie was led out to the police car Jane could see how swollen and bloody his nose was, but she didn't dare ask what happened, she was just relieved that she wasn't in the bedroom when it did. Bradfield spoke with Jane who informed him that the young girl who'd been in bed with O'Duncie was adamant she was eighteen.

'I think she's lying, and she's given me a stupid name, Flower Summer, so do we take her in?'

'No grounds. She may be full of bullshit, not to mention drugs, but we can check her description and see if she's been reported missing by her parents. When we get back to the station inform Social Services about the squat and that there may be underage girls and runaways dossing down here.'

O'Duncie sat in subdued silence the entire way back to the station. Gibbs was handcuffed to him on one side and Bradfield sat on the other having told Jane to sit in the front of the patrol car. O'Duncie wore some kind of musk oil which permeated the car and Bradfield opened a window.

At the station Gibbs and Jane took O'Duncie to the custody area to be booked in. He was asked if he wanted to make a phone call but declined stating that it was pointless as he'd been 'done up like a kipper' and quipped that he couldn't afford a solicitor as they had all his money.

Just before they were to interrogate O'Duncie, DS Gibbs received a phone call that took the wind out of him. He caught Bradfield about to head into his office.

'Need a word, guv – it's urgent – before we have a go at him.'

'Listen, Spence, I don't want to waste any more time. What for Chrissake is so important?'

'I just got a call from Manchester CID – I'd sent a telex asking them to check all the aliases I had for the name Josh against drug dealers and anyone known as Big Daddy.'

There was an instant look of concern on Bradfield's face as he glared at Gibbs who licked his lips and continued.

'A Joshua Richards was arrested in Moss Side two weeks ago for GBH. He's six foot five, built like a stallion and well known locally as Big Daddy, not just because of his size: he has six kids all by different women. He's also a big-time drug dealer who runs between Manchester and London.'

'So Richards was probably supplying Julie Ann.'

'Yes, and probably Terry O'Duncie, but not for the last two weeks.'

'What?'

'Richards didn't get bail from the Manchester Court as they found a fuckin' Kalashnikov in the boot of his car along with LSD tabs. It means he's in the clear for Julie Ann's and Eddie's murders—'

'And Terry isn't Big Daddy.' Bradfield sighed shaking his head, and then shrugged before continuing.

'Richards is in the clear, and so by the looks of it is Dwayne Clark, so the positive side is Terry O'Duncie is now our strongest and most likely suspect for murder ... so let's go and put the pressure on him.'

The custody sergeant took O'Duncie up to Bradfield's office for an interview, but kept his hands cuffed just in case he played up, though he seemed reasonably relaxed and asked if he could have a coffee.

Bradfield was standing by his office window looking out onto Lower Clapton Road as Gibbs waited for the sergeant to leave the room. O'Duncie was sipping a beaker of coffee, his eyes flicking from one officer to the other.

'You gonna take these cuffs off me?' He raised his hand-cuffed wrists, and Gibbs got the nod from Bradfield to unlock them.

'You're bang to rights for the drugs, but I want you to tell me what you know about these two kids,' Bradfield said as he dropped Julie Ann's and Eddie Phillips' photographs in front of O'Duncie who looked at them briefly.

'Who are they?'

'Don't play games, we know your sister Anjali sent them to Dwayne Clark's address and he brought them to meet you at Primrose Hill.'

'My sister is a fuckin' nutter. If she has put me in trouble then I am not gonna take it. The bitch is just wanting money, she's a hypochondriac, sick in the head, so whatever she's told you will be a pack of lies cos I wouldn't give her any cash. I dunno a Dwayne or how many kids hang out at the house, they come and go all the time ... maybe I seen these two, but I dunno for sure. You should ask the others.'

'We did but it seems they have dodgy memories like you, so start thinking hard, Terry, because these two were murdered and I reckon you were involved.'

'On my life I dunno anything about any murders. I wasn't even at the squat when they were killed.'

Bradfield and Gibbs looked at each other with a wry smile and Gibbs leaned forward close to O'Duncie.

'For someone who wears all the flash gear and tries to look and act the part of a big man you're actually pretty dumb. Neither me nor the guv mentioned when the murders happened. With Dwayne Clark, were you?'

'I told ya I dunno him.'

'Dwayne's the sidekick of Joshua Richards, a drug dealer also known as Big Daddy,' Gibbs said.

O'Duncie looked nervous, especially at the mention of Richards.

'Never heard of a Joshua or Big Daddy, but I think the guy Dwayne might have stayed at the squat a while back. I helped him off drugs and I heard he'd turned his life round and started a legit window-cleaning business.'

Gibbs was going to press the matter but Bradfield raised his hand indicating not to bother. The fact O'Duncie knew Dwayne gave him a connection to Big Daddy and he decided to scare O'Duncie with a few lies.

'You didn't know we nicked Dwayne, did you? How

else do you think we knew about the Primrose Hill address and where the drugs and cash were hidden?'

O'Duncie didn't answer but Bradfield could see the look on his face was a mixture of anger and uncertainty.

'Dwayne reckoned you got Julie Ann up the duff and she tried to get money off you for an abortion but you told her to fuck off.'

'What? Eh? If he did say anything, which I doubt, then he's lying. So I knows both dem kids, no big deal as I didn't kill 'em and you got no evidence I did,' O'Duncie said arrogantly.

Bradfield knew he was still unsure about what was or was not the truth and trying to front out his predicament.

'Eddie Phillips told you we were asking about Julie Ann, and worried he'd grass you up, you had to kill him, didn't you?'

'No way. The kid may have been to the house but I never met or spoke to him,' O'Duncie said firmly.

Bradfield asked who did speak to Eddie and O'Duncie said he'd heard from one of the squatters that, while he was away, Eddie had turned up and nicked some of the squatters' gear. He said they also told him that Eddie had jacked up some heroin down by the Regent's Canal, fallen in and drowned. O'Duncie was adamant he didn't know any more. He fell silent before saying he would like to speak with a solicitor and have his money back, which he'd made from legitimate renting.

Bradfield knew he didn't have enough to charge him with any murders, but there was no way he was going to let a scumbag like O'Duncie back out on the streets.

'You're going nowhere tonight, Terry. You can have a night in the cells on the taxpayer. It will give you plenty of time to think about your situation, and how telling us the truth will be better for you. And remember, you're bang to rights for the drugs. Question is whether I charge you with straight possession or the more serious possession with intent to supply, but that depends on how helpful you are.'

'Come on, man, cut me some slack and give me bail. I'll turn up at court, I won't do a runner and I'll even put some of the cash in the police widows' and orphans' fund.'

'You're not getting bail or the money back at present. Julie Ann nicked a load of money before she was murdered and guess what, it wasn't on her when we found the body.'

'Jesus Christ, how many times I gotta say I ain't killed no one and I don't know anythin' about her money.'

'That's because she may not have told you she nicked it from her dad. Thing is though, sunshine, she didn't know the banknotes had sequential serial numbers on them, which means neither did you.' Bradfield paused to let O'Duncie take in what he'd just said and he could see he was becoming nervous.

'I've already got someone checking through the serial numbers of the notes we found in your bedroom, and I will have them all checked for Julie Ann's, her father's and Eddie Phillips' prints. If there is one dab on any one of them that matches yours, you're screwed.'

Bradfield could see O'Duncie was thinking hard to come up with a suitable answer.

'One of the squatters collects cash from the other residents for food and drink and gives it to me and I hid it in the wardrobe. We're a commune so we share things.'

'Just like you shared Julie Ann round for sex,' Gibbs remarked.

'I want that money back cos I got bills to pay.'

Bradfield leered. 'More like you've got *big* suppliers you owe money to?' he said, making a veiled connection to Big

Daddy, and paused, but O'Duncie just stared nervously as Bradfield continued. 'And they ain't gonna be happy with you if you stiff them, are they? In fact you might end up in the Regent's Canal as well, so you'd better start talking when we interview you tomorrow.'

Jane had called Social Services and was now sitting in the incident room with the stack of banknotes heaped on the desk. DC Edwards was typing up his report and looked over to her.

'What are you doing?'

Jane had taken a pair of tweezers from her handbag and was painstakingly lifting one note after another.

'I've got to count all this seized money and I'm worried about leaving my prints on the notes.'

'If you got bundles in the same denomination just list the serial numbers first.'

'But I've also got to count that big bag of coins.'

'Rather you than me.' He turned back to his report.

Kath popped her head round the door.

'I'm going off duty. Christ, it was a long day and really tedious in court. Two cases were called before mine and they were so drawn out I ended up last on.'

Jane stopped checking the notes. 'What did he get?'

Kath moved further into the room.

'Magistrate was impressed that the little shite admitted his guilt and asked for other offences to be taken into consideration. It was in his favour that none of the poor old pensioners whose life savings he stole, and who he scared the life out of, have to give evidence.'

Jane nodded and began to pick up the notes with her tweezers as Kath continued.

'Then the ponce solicitor asked for a lenient sentence

for the nasty thievin' git and went on about his remorse for what he'd done. My God, Jane, you should have seen how he reacted, blubbered and cried. He's remanded in custody to appear at the Crown Court for sentencing, but will probably get about two bloody years, and you know what makes me really sick?'

Jane lost concentration and had to start recounting a bundle.

'Worst thing is he'll probably be out in eight months and he's a nasty vicious little sod. Next time he'll probably kill someone, he's that twisted. Villains like Boyle are the scum of the earth, he even gave me this sick gloating smile as if to say he'd got away with it. You mark my words it's not the last time we'll hear of Kenneth Boyle.'

'At least you got him, Kath.'

Yet again Jane made a mistake and had to return to recounting the money.

'See you tomorrow,' Kath said and Jane told her she had a day off.

'Of course, it's the wedding.'

'Don't remind me, it's sort of crept up on me.'

Kath laughed and let Jane continue her counting whilst she wrote up the result of the Boyle case on a file for the collator PC Donaldson. Jane mentioned that he had gone home at 4 p.m. and Kath left the file on her desk saying she'd give it to Donaldson in the morning.

As Kath left the room Edwards finished his report and took it over to the files 'IN' tray.

'She never stops bloody yakking on – you'd think she was the only person ever to make an arrest. Right, that's me done and dusted.' He started to walk out, pausing by Jane's desk.

'At the speed you're going you'll be here all night. Tarra.'

Jane was really tired and finding it increasingly hard to concentrate, but with a day's leave coming up she had to finish recording all the serial numbers and then check her list to see if any were sequential, which she reckoned would take at least another couple of hours.

No sooner had Edwards left than DS Gibbs walked in.

'Guv wants to know if any of the notes run in sequential order.'

Jane sighed. 'Well, I'm sorry, but I'm on my own and it's taking a lot of time so . . .'

'Don't get your knickers in a twist, O'Duncie is being kept in custody overnight for further interviews.'

He took out a comb from his pocket and ran it front to back through his hair, making it stand up on end, and then ran his fingers either side of his head.

'I've got quite a way to go, but I'll finish checking all the notes before I go home.'

'Finish it tomorrow, but make sure the money is locked away in the property-store safe overnight.'

'I have the day off tomorrow as it's my sister's wedding.'

Gibbs replaced the comb in his pocket, and told her he'd get Kath to finish checking it all in the morning.

'Are you sure? Only I'm worried DCI Bradfield might disapprove if I go off duty just now.'

'I'll sort it out and tell him you got a big day tomorrow. I had to take a week off after my brother got married. Nothin' to do with the wedding, it was the stag night I had to recover from.'

'Thank you, I really appreciate it, not that I'm looking forward to the wedding: I'm chief bridesmaid.'

'Well, better a wedding than a funeral, eh, Jane?' He walked off playing air guitar and making the sound of the strings playing the wedding march. Jane was quite surprised as it was the first time he had called her by her Christian name.

The property office was closed. Jane knew that Duty Sergeant Harris had a key to the office and the safe, so she would have to get him to open it up for her.

'What do you want, Tennison?' Harris snapped as she approached.

Jane explained that she needed the property store opened, the seized money put in the safe and a property-deposit invoice signed.

'Well, one favour deserves another, so when I've done that you can take over on the front desk for an hour while I have my grub.'

She tried to explain that DS Gibbs had said she could go off duty. Harris said that it was busy out on the streets and there was no one to come in and relieve him so she'd better show some willing seeing as he'd allowed her to be attached to the murder team.

Jane knew it was pointless arguing and didn't want to interrupt Gibbs and Bradfield while they were busy so she did as she was told.

She dealt with two people who came in to report a couple of minor crimes and an elderly woman who'd lost her purse in the street. An hour and a half passed and Sergeant Harris hadn't returned. Jane suspected he was probably playing snooker, but she couldn't leave the front desk unmanned.

She'd just sat back down when a civilian courier arrived with the internal mail, which she signed for and then began to sort out into piles.

Jane noticed that an envelope was addressed to her. Opening it she read that there was a place available at the section house, but if she wanted the room she had to reply within forty-eight hours. She immediately started to fill out her personal details on the residents' form. Knowing that her parents would be upset she was moving out, Jane decided it would be best to tell them after the wedding. She completed the forms and put them in a return envelope addressed to the section house sergeant at Ede House.

As she sealed the envelope and popped it into the internal mail bag Sergeant Harris finally returned.

'Why's all that mail on the desk? You're supposed to put it in the relevant drawer trays.'

'I was about to but—'

'Then get on with it before you go off duty,' he sneered, deliberately trying to antagonize her.

She knew what he was trying to do but smiled. 'My pleasure, Sergeant. Sadly there's nothing for you.'

Having dealt with all the mail she returned to the incident room to get her handbag and personal belongings. As she passed Bradfield's office she could hear him and Gibbs chatting and wondered if there were any further developments, but she had no intention of hanging about to find out. As she picked up her handbag she noticed the open file Kath had left on the desk. She glanced at the mug shot of Kenneth Boyle and suppressed a shudder. There was something about his almost pretty-boy face, with its wide-apart dark hooded eyes and thin mouth that chilled her. No wonder Kath felt so angry about the short sentence: Boyle definitely deserved a lot longer for the stress and fear he'd inflicted. Flicking the file shut, Jane walked out of the office and headed to the bus stop, feeling depressed by the day's events.

David Bentley tuned the radio to another channel. David Cassidy's 'How Can I Be Sure' filled the van.

'Turn that Cassidy wanker off,' John said.

They were at the rented garage and had just finished attaching the advertising logos to the sides of the van: 'Home Decorating, Painting and Carpentry', 'Professionals at Reasonable Prices' – all of which could be easily peeled off at any time. The back windows were covered with pictures David had cut out from magazines: tins of paint, paper-pasting boards, paintbrushes and ladders. They had earlier purchased two smaller stolen Kango hammer drills for cash from a dealer in Essex and were now loading them into the van, along with the additional equipment needed for the job. John reversed the loaded van into the garage and locked the heavy metal garage door. David was using his walking stick and had not been very helpful due to his lameness, but John had tried to include him as much as possible.

'We'll unload the decorating gear in the back yard of the café tomorrow night when we start. Danny will be there to help carry it down to the basement,' John said, patting the garage door. They walked back towards their estate, and John put his arm around his brother.

'Don't look so worried.'

'It's gonna be all right isn't it, John?'

'Trust me, Dave, we been working on this for weeks, there'll be no problems.'

David's stomach tightened as he recalled his father using the same words when they went to the church to steal the lead and he fell off the roof. He was now terrified of heights, scared of ever going back to prison, knowing as a cripple he'd be vulnerable inside.

John started talking about a movie he wanted to see. *Theatre of Blood*, with Vincent Price and Diana Rigg, which had got rave reviews and was a real British horror movie, but David was not interested. He had a nagging fear in the pit of his stomach and knowing exactly what was going to begin the next night made it worse.

Sitting in her usual seat on the top deck of the bus, Jane put her earpiece in and turned on her pocket radio. By pure coincidence Jimi Hendrix was singing 'Voodoo Child'. She sighed, remembering the hideous squat they had been to that afternoon and the young kids living rough and taking drugs. She felt pretty certain that Julie Ann and Eddie Phillips had visited or lived there at some time. However, she was uncertain about Terry O'Duncie. For all that she loathed about his existence, he didn't appear to be a violent person; although he dressed like a pimp, he seemed to be playing at being a tough guy. She felt depressed and turning off the radio thought to herself, What do I know? It saddened her to think how young the girls had been at the squat; even some of the boys looked to be in their teens. She shuddered to think that they could end up like Julie Ann and Eddie, addicted to drugs, turning to prostitution and stealing to pay for their habit. They had nothing to look forward to but a wretched future, so different from her own; she had been raised within a caring family who were always there to love and protect her. Jane forced herself to think of something else. Her mind turned to her sister's wedding, but this annoyed her as she wasn't looking forward to it, didn't relish being a bridesmaid and feared the whole day would be a hideous experience. She turned her radio back on and ironically David Cassidy was singing his hit single 'How Can I Be Sure'.

CHAPTER SIXTEEN

Alone in her bedroom on Sunday morning Jane found it difficult to even look at herself in the mirror. The salmon-pink taffeta floor-length bridesmaid dress, now with the waistband and large bow in place, had been difficult to hook up as it was so tight. The corset was even tighter and it was hard to take a deep breath, and she was scared that if she did her bust would pop out as the neckline was so low, and the puffball sleeves kept slipping down her shoulder. The ensemble was topped with a coronet of fresh white tea roses, which was too large and slipped forward every time she moved. The dyed satin Cuban-heeled shoes matched the dress and all three bridesmaids were to carry a little posy of white roses and wear elbow-length white gloves.

'Dear God, I look ridiculous,' she muttered.

The entire family was gathered in the living area along with the other two bridesmaids, who were Pam's closest friends, although Jane had only ever met them at the church rehearsal.

Her mother shouted for Jane to get a move on as the car had arrived and the car for Pam and her dad was also due any minute. Jane gritted her teeth as she slowly left the bedroom and walked into the room where the other two

bridesmaids in identical outfits were shrieking and giggling with excitement.

Her mother was fussing, rushing here and there in a
worried state, wondering where she'd put the box of white
roses and freesias for the groom, best man and ushers to
pin to their morning-suit buttonholes. Her father was sitting nonchalantly reading the paper, his top hat between
his knees.

He glanced at Jane. 'Where's the bride?' he asked, fold-
ing the paper, then looked up at her.

'Good God, your dress is a bit low at the front, isn't it?'

Before Jane could answer Pam came out from her parents' bedroom, where she'd been for the last four hours
fixing her hair and make-up. Her floor-length white lace
gown, which had cost a fortune, was bunched up in her
arms and she suddenly wailed as the long white train
caught in the base of the door. It was panic as Mrs
Tennison shouted for her husband to find the buttonhole
flowers while she helped Pam. Mr Tennison remembered
they were in the hall and, annoyed with all the frantic
fuss, took charge of the situation, clapping his hands as he
instructed everyone to keep calm and get ready to leave.

'Bridesmaids go now, first car. Mother, you take the
flowers and get them to the groom and the boys, Pam and
I will follow at exactly eleven forty,' he said, checking his
watch.

'Pam, don't bunch up your dress, it'll crease.' Mrs
Tennison shook out the veil to straighten it and then
rushed back into the bedroom to fetch her hat.

Pam was in a panic. 'Where's my bouquet?'

'In the hall, sweetheart ... let the bridesmaids go to
their car now ... Where the hell is your mother?' Mr
Tennison sighed.

Jane had by now collected her posy of roses and held them tightly to her chest as she opened the front door and stood to one side as her mother scurried out with her hat on, stopped suddenly, turned and went back to the hall to get the box of buttonholes.

Pam looked at her father. 'Please don't get into a bad mood with Mummy – she's just excited like we all are. Can you get my bouquet, please?'

'For God's sake, Pam darling, you've got ten minutes before we need to leave. Jane, you keep an eye on your mother and help her hand out the buttonholes at the church – the chaps should all be there by now.'

The journey to the church took five minutes, the three bridesmaids squashed in the back seat and Mrs Tennison sitting nervously in the front. By the time they arrived the groom and best man were standing outside on the church steps looking anxious, and the ushers were showing the last few guests to their seats.

Mrs Tennison fussed round the girls, patting down their dresses, fluffing up their puff sleeves and straightening out their coronets.

'You all look absolutely gorgeous, and remember, Jane, as chief bridesmaid you take the bouquet from Pam when she says her vows.'

She gave Jane a tearful smile, patting her and leaning close.

'I hope one day it will be your turn, but you shouldn't have worn your hair down, I said put it up in a chignon. I've got a comb, just let me run it through.'

'Leave it alone, Mother, just go and sit in your pew.'

It was a waste of time: Mrs Tennison opened her small purse and took out a little comb and started tugging it through Jane's long blonde hair.

'That's better, now push the coronet up a bit as it's too low down.' As Jane used her right hand to push the coronet up her mother gasped.

'Good heavens, your bust is falling out. I don't know ... that woman made dresses for Alma Cogan – you'd think it would fit you better.'

Jane was appalled as her mother insisted on hitching up the front of the dress and pushing down her breasts.

Jane stepped back. 'Enough, Mother, and you need to straighten your hat!'

'I wasn't going to go with this one, but your father said the one I liked was too expensive.' She adjusted the hat. 'Is it all right now?'

'It looks lovely.'

Jane sighed with the relief as the groom and best man accompanied Mrs Tennison to her seat and then took up their positions at the front of the church while the bridesmaids went to wait in the small anteroom for Pam and her father to arrive.

The other two bridesmaids' constant nattering irritated Jane so she stepped outside to wait for her father and sister and saw the vicar at the foot of the steps looking at his watch.

'Is everything all right?' she asked him.

'Yes, we're just running a few minutes late. I've another wedding at one thirty, and then the usual evensong to prepare for as well, so we need to keep everything tickety-boo and on time.'

Jane, annoyed by all the fuss, politely said hello to a couple of guests who were late arriving, though she didn't have a clue as to who they were.

'How much older are you than Pam?' one of them stopped to ask.

Jane turned to face a flushed coiffured woman who she suspected was a friend of her sister from the hair salon, and said that she was four years older.

'Oh, must seem odd, Pam marrying before you.'

Jane stopped herself from making a sarcastic reply. Hearing the crunch of tyres on gravel, she turned to see the car carrying her father and sister pull into the church-yard. The vicar promptly paced up the steps and into the church and waved his hand at the organist who started playing the wedding march, which caused the other two bridesmaids to hurry out from the anteroom.

Mr Tennison helped Pam alight from the car and the two bridesmaids rushed down the steps to straighten her veil, and pull out the wedding gown's long beaded train.

'Right, we all set?' her father said quietly as they reached the church porch. Standing to Pam's right he linked arms with her and they proceeded to walk down the aisle followed by Jane and the other bridesmaids.

When they reached the chancel the groom stepped for-ward and shook hands with Mr Tennison who then gently lifted Pam's right hand and placed it on the groom's extended left hand before stepping back behind the bride.

Listening to their vows Jane was surprised to feel quite emotional. Her baby sister was so nervous, and stumbled over a few lines as she gazed at Tony, who had big raw hands and ruddy cheeks.

The ceremony was over within half an hour and after photographs outside the church there was another crushed journey to the Clarendon Hotel for the reception. The fur-ther photographs in the hotel grounds took ages, and the speeches, apart from her father's, dragged on and on. Jane was anxious to escape, but her father had hired a disco for the entertainment so she was obliged to stay. As more guests arrived the two other bridesmaids made a beeline for one of the ushers and the best man. Elderly relatives looked on and cheered as they watched Jane's parents attempting to do the twist to the Chubby Checker song.

It was an excruciating few hours before Jane decided to extricate herself and ask her father if she could get a taxi home.

'Don't be impatient – you can't leave until the bride and groom do ... She's changing into her honeymoon outfit soon and we have to wave them off.'

'I need to check in with the station in case I am needed.'

He gave a resigned sigh, and leaned close. 'Don't make excuses, you've had a face all day like you've been sucking a lemon, just try and show a bit of enthusiasm. It's Pam's big day, and who knows, maybe you could be the lucky one that catches her bouquet.'

Jane sighed and returned to her gilt-backed chair at the top table. She sipped at her champagne, which was now tepid. She had stuffed a paper napkin down the front of her cleavage to stop her mother constantly telling her to pull up the bodice. Out of the corner of her eye she noticed an overweight man accompanied by a small blonde woman approaching her table. There is always an embarrassing relative in a family and for the Tennisons it was Uncle Brian, their mother's older brother. Clinging to him like a limpet was his tiny wife Claire. They both appeared to have had too much to drink.

'Here she is, our own little Dixon of Dock Green ... Evening all.' Uncle Brian snorted as he laughed and gave a salute. 'Collared any big-time villains yet, or are you still directing traffic?' he asked.

Jane gave a small tight smile. 'Dixon's male and we're about to crack down on dodgy car dealers, Uncle Brian.'

He laughed loudly and his wife tittered.

'Well, when you want a nice reliable second-hand motor you know where to come. You know our Barbara's an air hostess with Dan Air now and travels the world on long-haul flights? She'd have been here today but she's in New York ... lovely uniform, wonderful job. It's the sort of work you should be thinking about.'

'She's lost loads of weight, you know,' Aunt Claire added.

'Good for her,' Jane said, recalling Barbara was at least thirteen stone plus and as haughty and objectionable as Uncle Brian. 'Mind you I've always thought an air hostess was a sort of glorified waitress,' Jane said sarcastically.

'She's dating a pilot and having a lovely time,' Aunt Claire said and gave Jane a sidelong glance.

'I'd never have let our Barbara go into the police. In fact I was surprised when your mother told us you'd joined, and those hats you have to wear, dear me, they're so ugly, but each to their own chosen path, I suppose.'

'I am finding it really fascinating, and I was at my first autopsy the other day. They make this Y-shaped incision that begins with cuts behind each ear and goes all the way down along the neck and chest to the pelvis so they can remove the intestines. The pathologist also peels the flap of skin off the face and over the skull.'

Aunt Claire's mouth was wide open in shock and disgust.

'Interesting, isn't it?' Jane said, smiling cynically.

Uncle Brian laughed and did another silly salute before whisking his wife onto the dance floor.

It was half an hour later when Pam returned wearing a smart suit and hat. She threw her bouquet over her shoulder, and the auburn-haired bridesmaid, who was by now very flushed and rather tipsy, caught it. With a sigh of relief Jane watched the 'happy couple' depart in a red MGB V8 Roadster, a 'Just Married' notice taped to the boot, along with old shoes and empty tin cans tied to the rear bumper, which bounced and rattled as the car pulled away backfiring. The MGB had been lent to them by Uncle Brian and was to be returned after the honeymoon was over, but Jane suspected it might not last out the trip to the Lake District and back.

By the time Jane returned home with her parents it was after nine and she felt drained. She couldn't wait to remove the salmon-pink nightmare dress and, after struggling out of the tight corset, she threw the dress on the floor and chucked her wilted coronet into the wicker bin. She lay on her bed in her underwear looking up at the ceiling. She realized that moving into the section house was definitely what she needed. She really didn't want to live at home any longer. Now that she'd completed and returned the forms for a room it was time to broach the subject with her parents.

She realized sadly that she had come to feel rather alienated from them. They had not approved of her joining the Metropolitan Police Force, although they had been proud at her passing-out parade at Hendon Police College. Her parents were always warm and loving and Jane knew she had nothing to complain about, certainly not when she thought of the squalor and neglect she had witnessed at the squat. She knew deep down her parents wanted her to be more like Pam, but the reality was that she and Pam were as different as chalk and cheese.

Jane smiled to herself. She was proud to be a police officer and determined to make a career of it, but as yet she was unsure exactly what she wanted to do after her probation.

Even though she was enjoying assisting the CID she knew there were many different branches of the force she could eventually apply for. Her sister had no ambition other than to get married and start a family. She had met Tony the carpenter only a year ago, started a whirlwind romance that led to engagement and, in Jane's opinion, too soon a marriage. She sighed, at least the day was over and done with. She could not for a moment contemplate ever wanting an elaborate ceremony like that for herself. That is, when and if she found her Mr Right, but she felt there was more chance of finding him if she wasn't living at home.

There was a tap on the door. 'Would you like some cheese on toast, dear?' she heard her mother ask.

'No thanks, I ate too much at the reception.'

'Daddy and I are going to have a sherry. Would you like to join us?'

'I'll come out in a minute, I'm just changing.'

Jane sighed and got off the single bed she had slept on since she was a child. She looked around her bedroom with its Laura Ashley wallpaper and felt proud of the silver-framed photographs of her in uniform and the Met Police plaque on the dressing table. She lifted her dressing gown from the hook on the bedroom door, and feeling guilty about the crumpled bridesmaid dress on the floor picked it up and placed it on a hanger in her wardrobe.

Her parents were sitting on high stools at the breakfast bar listening to soft jazz music on the radio. They were both eating cheese on toast and sipping sherry from small crystal schooner glasses.

'Hi, you must both be tired out,' Jane remarked.

Her mother gave a little shrug and sighed. 'We've been going over the entire day ... it was so wonderful and

273

everything went according to plan, didn't it, dear?' she said, looking at her husband for confirmation.

'Fabulous day, apart from your Uncle Brian and his munchkin wife going on and on about their precious Barbara being an air hostess. Even though she's allegedly lost weight I bet she still has to squeeze between the aisles.'

Jane laughed but her mother frowned and ignored his remark.

'Pam looked so beautiful, so happy and radiant. Tony's a very nice young man. At first I was worried they might have rushed things, but I think he will make a good husband and he's a carpenter so he's good with his hands – he'll work wonders on their lovely little flat, won't he, Daddy?'

Mr Tennison nodded, downed his sherry then slapped the base of the bottle of Lea & Perrins making sauce splash out over his toasted cheese. Jane noticed that her mother's cheeks were flushed and she wondered if after the champagne at the reception, and now the sherry, she was a little drunk.

'I've been thinking, the bridesmaid dresses cost so much that what you should do is get the dressmaker to cut down the neck, remove the puffs and shorten the length, then you'd have a beautiful cocktail frock. Pam was going to have her wedding gown made into one, but then she said she was going to keep it in the box so that when she has a baby it can be made into a lovely christening gown.'

Jane remembered Kath Morgan's remark. 'Oh my God, she's pregnant!' she exclaimed in surprise.

'Good heavens, no she is not. Whatever made you think that?' her shocked mother asked.

Jane shrugged and said nothing, though she wondered if it was true and Pam had kept quiet about it.

Her mother continued, 'She wants to start a family right away and I for one think it's a lovely idea. I never had a big white wedding.'

'What?' Jane interrupted, wondering what her mother was inferring.

'It's not what you think. My parents couldn't afford a big do, and don't forget the war wasn't long over. Daddy and I have always saved in a special account for your and Pam's weddings.'

'She'll have to get a boyfriend first, sweetheart. Am I right, Jane?' he said with a wink.

Jane hesitated and drew one of the stools out from beneath the breakfast counter.

'I need to discuss something with you,' she said quietly and was about to explain about moving out when her father pointed to the radio.

'Bloody hell, there's more on the news about that Lord Lambton scandal.'

'Dad, I really need to—' Jane started to say but he wasn't listening.

'He's a junior Defence minister. Apparently the *News of the World* somehow got hold of photographs of him in bed with *two* prostitutes whilst smoking marijuana,' he said.

'You'd think a Tory minister would behave better,' his wife added as she turned up the volume slightly.

'Blimey, he's admitted it was him in the compromising photographs,' Mr Tennison said as he moved closer to the radio.

Lord Lambton has admitted his indiscretions to the Prime Minister Edward Heath and stated he was not blackmailed – nor was there a threat to national security.

However, in light of the criminal charges brought against him by the police for possession of drugs Lord Lambton has tendered his resignation, which Mr Heath accepted with immediate effect. In other breaking news George Jellicoe, Lord Privy Seal and Leader of the House of Lords, has admitted 'some casual affairs' with call girls and also resigned. The Prime Minister has ordered an inquiry by the Security Commission into the activities of both Lord Lambton and Jellicoe, which will be chaired by Lord Diplock.

Mr Tennison clapped his hands, applauding the actions of the Prime Minister. 'Christ, it seems the only one in the government who wasn't paying for sex was Ted Heath himself.'

'What gets into those men: lovely wives, nice houses, and they go with prostitutes. It just beggars belief,' Jane's mother said, shaking her head. 'I worry myself sick about you, Jane. Every time you leave the house in your uniform I am on pins until you come home. It's all drugs nowadays, I mean if high society and our politicians are using drugs, whatever next? It's a terrible world.'

'I've applied for—'

'I don't care what you've applied for, Jane … What with you travelling on the Tube and bus every day, you only need one crazy person to see your uniform and you're an easy target for God knows what.'

Jane stood up and lingered beside her father as he turned the radio off. Her mother put her plate and glass on the draining board saying she would do the washing up in the morning. She kissed Jane goodnight and went to her bedroom.

Mr Tennison, a tall angular man with fine artistic hands

276

and a chiselled handsome face, put his arm around Jane. 'Pay no attention, sweetheart, your mum's just being over-protective. We're both proud of you and I am damn sure you'd never take foolhardy risks. All she really wants is for you to find a nice fella, settle down and have kids.'

'Dad, with the wedding preparations in full swing I didn't tell you something and I wanted to wait until I knew for sure I had a place.'

He looked somewhat confused. 'Are you leaving the police?'

'No.' She paused and took a deep breath. 'I'm leaving home. I have made a decision to move into the section house. It's Met accommodation for single officers. It's in Hackney so it will be more convenient for work.'

He looked surprised but remained calm. 'Well, you've always paid Mother a bit of rent, which she's really appreciated, but this is a very big move on your part, isn't it?'

'It's cost-effective, the rent's cheap, they have a canteen. Rooms are quite small and the bathrooms are communal, but there's a games room and two TV rooms. I think it will be good for me to mix more closely with other young single officers. The male and female residents are on different floors, there are strict rules and it's run by a no-nonsense sergeant.'

'You've thought it all out, haven't you?' he said bluntly, taking the last bite of his toasted cheese before dropping his plate in the sink.

'Of course I have, Dad, it's my life. I want to have a successful career and I need to stand on my own two feet.'

He turned on the hot-water tap and squirted washing-up liquid into the bowl.

'You are and always have been what I call the "quiet one", excelled at athletics, high-grade O and A levels, but I was surprised when you said you wanted to join the police force. Admittedly it's not something I would have encouraged, but when you don't get your own way you can be a right little madam. I want to show you something.'

He wiped his hands on a tea towel, went into the hall where his morning-suit jacket hung on the coat rack and took out his wallet.

He returned to the room, opened up the worn leather wallet and produced a small black-and-white photograph which he handed to Jane.

'I took that picture in the local park with my Brownie Box camera. Your sister would have been about three, you seven. Pam was on the swing and I wanted you to stand beside her, but you insisted on sitting on the swing and she stood beside you screaming blue murder but you wouldn't budge. Look at the expression on your face, that little satisfied smile because you got your own way.'

Jane looked at the little photo, which she'd never seen until now, and then passed it back, struck by how carefully he replaced it in his wallet.

'When are you moving out?'

'I'd like to go this week if possible. I don't want to upset Mum but—'

'Let me tell your mother and ease the way – you know what she's like, but you also know you have a room here with us whenever you want or need it.'

'Thanks, Dad. There are payphones at the section house and of course I'll visit on my days off.'

She would have liked to kiss him, but they had never been very tactile: he had always seemed to hold back from showing her and Pam too much affection. Deep down Jane understood why, but it was a subject no one in the family ever discussed.

'I'll wash the dishes – you get off to bed,' she said.

'All right then ... goodnight, love.'

Jane noticed he had left his wallet on the breakfast bar. She picked it up intending to return it to his jacket but opened it to have another look at the photograph of her and Pam. There was another black-and-white photo tucked behind it, creased and worn, not of her or Pam, but of Michael her brother who had had lovely blond hair and blue eyes. Jane was the firstborn, then Michael was born a year later, and the tiny photo showed the gorgeous little boy aged two laughing. Tragically, not long after the photograph was taken, he had fallen into a neighbour's back-garden pond and drowned. Shortly after his death they had moved to the flat they now lived in and then Pam was born.

Jane had been too young to have any tangible memories of Michael, but there were other pictures of him around the flat. The shadow left by his death was a sad, almost secretive pain her parents shared between themselves, but it was also the reason her mother was emotionally fragile and her dear father so guarded.

Jane finished washing the dishes, went to her bedroom and felt comfort in knowing that she would always have this safe protected place to return to if she ever needed it. She wondered how big the storage space in the section house would be and how many of her clothes and personal belongings she should take with her; pillows, blankets and clean bed sheets were provided. She'd just reached out to get her notebook and pen so she could make a list when the doorbell rang.

Jane was puzzled as to who it could be as it was now nearly midnight. The bell rang again and as she went into the hallway she saw her mother in her dressing gown, her hair in rollers and a flustered expression on her face.

'Oh my, I hope your sister's not had an argument with Tony already and come home.'

Jane tightened her old dressing-gown belt and didn't say anything, but knowing Pam, what her mother said did make sense. She unhooked the safety chain and opening the door was shocked to see DCI Bradfield.

'Sorry to get you up so late but I need to speak with you in private.'

Jane was nervous. 'Have I done something wrong?'

'No, no, not at all.'

She could see his eyes were slightly glazed and thought at first it was because he was so tired, but the smell of alcohol made it obvious he'd been drinking.

'Who is it, dear?' she heard her mother call.

'It's for me, Mum, someone from work and nothing for you to worry about.'

Bradfield stepped back from the door. 'Sorry, I thought you lived on your own. I didn't mean to wake the family ... It can wait till morning.'

Jane was intrigued and there was no way she could contain her curiosity until the following morning. She opened the door further.

'Please come in.'

Bradfield followed Jane into the living area. 'To be honest I hadn't noticed you were not at the station today until I asked where you were. I got the address from your file.'

She was a little annoyed that he had not even noticed she wasn't at work.

'I did tell DS Gibbs I had a day off for my sister's wedding and he said he'd inform you.'

'Oh right, well after the day he's had and under the circumstances it's understandable he forgot.'

Jane wondered what he meant, but didn't want to ask.

'Can I make you a coffee?'

'No, this won't take long.'

Mrs Tennison appeared and Jane introduced her to
Bradfield. Of the two her mother was the more embar-
rassed, touching her rollers and apologizing for her and
Jane's appearance.

'You'll have to excuse us but we've had a very big day
and my husband is snoring away already. Jane's sister got
married and she was a bridesmaid.'

'It's all right, Mother, DCI Bradfield wants to talk to me
about something important that's work-related so you can
go back to bed now.'

'Oh, if you'd like a sherry we have a very nice bottle
already open on the breakfast counter, or maybe you'd
prefer a whisky?'

Bradfield smiled politely. 'No thank you, Mrs Tennison,
this is just a quick call. You have no doubt had a wonderful but long and tiring day, so I apologize for the intrusion.'

Mrs Tennison smiled and touched her rollers again.
'Not at all, it's a pleasure to meet one of Jane's fellow-con-
stables ... in fact you're the first from her station.'

Jane blushed. 'A DCI is a very senior detective rank,
Mum, way above a uniform constable.'

'Really, you should have seen Jane today, she looked
beautiful in her bridesmaid dress with—'

'Goodnight, Mother,' Jane said firmly through gritted
teeth.

'I'm going, I'm going, but please do come for lunch one
Sunday ... I always do a roast with all the trimmings and
you would be most welcome.'

He gave a lovely shy smile and said he would be delighted to accept her invitation one weekend. Jane sighed with relief as her mother finally left the room.

Bradfield sat on the floral-covered sofa and Jane in the wing chair her father always used. He got out a pack of cigarettes, put one in his mouth, flicked open his silver Zippo lighter and was about to strike the flint wheel when he hesitated, gesturing to ask if it was all right to light up.

'Please do, I'll fetch an ashtray.'

She placed it on the arm of the sofa and he flicked his ash into it.

'There's something about you that's different: your teeth look really nice and shiny white.' He paused as he looked at her. She felt annoyed, closed her lips and wondered what he was inferring.

'It's make-up, you're wearing make-up, right?'

Jane nodded and then shrugged and swung her hair away from her face.

'Chief bridesmaid, so I had to look my best.'

'Right, right, I understand,' he said.

Jane could contain herself no longer. 'Can I ask why you are here, sir? Is it something to do with DS Gibbs?'

'Sadly it is, yes.'

'Is he OK?' Jane asked, worried that something bad had happened to him.

'Yeah, he's fine physically – I've just left him after we had a few beers. I wasn't going to speak with you until morning, but I thought it would be best to do it in private, away from all the prying eyes and ears at the station.'

As he dragged on his cigarette Jane couldn't think what was so important and curled her legs beneath her on the big chair.

Bradfield leaned forward.

'We grilled Terry O'Duncie yesterday and he started to open up a bit, then refused to say anything more until he'd spoken to a solicitor. We'd denied him any contact or a phone call on the grounds we thought he might tip off Dwayne Clark, who it seems has done a runner. He spent the night in the cells but the idiot late-shift duty sergeant forgot to mark up the sheet and tell the night shift he wasn't allowed any calls.'

'Sergeant Harris was late shift,' Jane said, trying hard not to sound pleased that Harris had messed up.

He nodded and told Jane that the 'cock-up' by Harris allowed O'Duncie to phone a bent solicitor called Cato Stonex who represented a lot of big drug dealers and got paid large sums of money to help them make up false defences. It transpired that O'Duncie told Stonex that he had been assaulted by DS Gibbs and also alleged that some of his money had been stolen.

'It's only his word against yours and DS Gibbs's though?'

'Not quite, Cato Stonex got a doctor in to see O'Duncie, and he diagnosed a recently broken nose. Stonex then went straight round the squat and took statements from a number of people who said that his ruddy nose was fine until we visited him and they heard us threatening him. Worse still is the young girl who was in bed with him says she saw Spence punch O'Duncie for no reason.'

'That can't be true – I was taking her downstairs,' Jane said guardedly.

'Exactly and that's very important. Spence did nothing more than accidentally trip O'Duncie up as he tried to escape, which caused him to stumble and break his nose on the edge of the bedroom door.'

Bradfield stubbed out the cigarette and looked towards the kitchen area. 'I wouldn't mind that whisky now, straight with ice, please.'

Jane got up and went to the cabinet, still unsure exactly why Bradfield had come to see her. She removed a cut-glass tumbler and poured a good measure of whisky before adding two ice cubes from the fridge.

'Spence and me wanted to interview O'Duncie again today,' Bradfield said as she handed him his whisky and curled up again in the chair. 'But his prick of a lawyer Stonex alleged his client had been seriously assaulted and some of his seized money stolen. The rubber heelers are now investigating and wouldn't let us interview O'Duncie until they spoke with him.'

'Sorry, who are the rubber heelers?'

'A10 department, set up by the Commissioner Sir Robert Mark. So-called because you can't hear them coming. They're a group of specially selected officers from uniform and detective branches brought together to investigate and stamp out corruption in the CID. They wanted to know how much money was in O'Duncie's wardrobe and who counted it, so obviously I had to tell them you did and they wanted to see your paperwork and property-store invoice for the amount.'

Jane looked worried. 'There wasn't any missing, was there?' she asked nervously.

'That's the problem: they couldn't find your list in the investigation files, or a property-store invoice, so I need to know where they are and how much money was there.'

Jane turned pale. 'I put the list in the bottom drawer of the desk I was using.'

He took a deep breath and sighed. 'OK, that's fine, but where's the bloody property-store receipt?'

'I don't know, sir.'

'What do you mean you don't know?'

'Sergeant Harris might have it as he put the money in the property-store safe . . .'

'I bloody well know it's in the safe because A10 checked and counted it today. They obviously think someone may have nicked some of it after we returned to the station, that's why they want your list, to check it against the money in the safe.'

'I hadn't finished counting all the money or checking the serial numbers against Mr Collins' list, sir. DS Gibbs said I could go home and then Sergeant Harris insisted I cover the front desk. He didn't come back for over an hour and I totally forgot to ask him for the receipt so he should have it.'

He took a long sip of the whisky. She was really nervous and could see he was annoyed, but was surprised he didn't shout at her. Truth was he knew he was partially to blame for not counting the money with Spencer Gibbs at the time or as soon as they returned to the station.

'Harris was off today as well so let's hope he counted the money and put the receipt somewhere safe, though knowing him I doubt it.'

Jane felt queasy and unsure what to say. She was worried that if any money was missing she'd be accused of theft and dishonesty.

'Well, it went from bad to worse. O'Duncie also told A10 that DS Gibbs slipped some money into his pocket during the search, which I know for a fact he didn't. No doubt they think I'm bent as well. What really pisses me off is that O'Duncie actually tried to blackmail us. Anyway, when they interviewed Spence they noticed he had bruised knuckles on his right hand and jumped to the conclusion it was because he thumped O'Duncie. With that and the money allegation they suspended him from duty pending further enquiries.' He sipped his drink and rattled the ice.

'I'm really sorry, sir. I didn't mean to cause all this trouble, especially for DS Gibbs and you,' Jane said, close to tears, fearing her career might be over before she'd even finished her probation.

He could see how upset she was and spoke softly. 'Hey, don't look so worried. A10 can think what they like, it doesn't scare me. They'll strut about and ruffle a few feathers, but believe me everything will be OK and Spence will be reinstated. In this job you sometimes learn the hard way; O'Duncie and his solicitor are just trying to muddy the waters and it was me that cut corners, not you.'

'Has he admitted that Julie Ann was at the squat for those missing two weeks?'

'Right now he's admitted fuck all, but I want the money thing sorted and you to check all the notes for sequential numbers first thing in the morning, then we can get them off to fingerprints branch. If by the luck of God a few match the serial numbers Mr Collins gave us, and we get his or Julie Ann's dabs on them, then we got Terry O'Duncie in the frame for her murder and A10 off our backs.'

'So is Terry O'Duncie the Big Daddy character?'

'Nope, we got a call from Manchester CID and it appears Joshua Richards is Big Daddy. He was arrested for assault and banged up without bail. He's a nightmare bastard apparently and probably why everyone is scared to death of him. He might be the guy that got Julie Ann pregnant, or it could be O'Duncie; truth is we will never know. Richards is out of the frame for her murder but I'd say he's Terry O'Duncie's supplier and that's how Julie Ann knew Big Daddy.'

'What about Dwayne Clark?'

'He's the sidekick runner for Richards and O'Duncie admits knowing him. He's gone into hiding and so far we can't break his alibi that he was in Coventry at the time of Julie Ann and Eddie's deaths.'

He finished his Scotch and placed the glass down on a small coffee table.

'We need something on O'Duncie to break him so he'll talk.'

'I hope it's the money.'

'Yes, but you have to understand that when you are asked to do something you must finish it, whether or not the duty sergeant wants you to cover the front desk. Any problems with Harris you come to me, do you understand?'

She couldn't believe he was still letting her stay on the investigation and was worried at one point he might tell her she was suspended.

'Yes, sir, I understand.'

'Good. A10 will want to take a statement from you, and are you clear about why I wanted to have a private chat with you?'

She nodded, but the truth was she wasn't exactly sure.

'You back me up and you back Spencer up about O'Duncie's aggressive attitude in the bedroom and the car.'

He held up his forefinger and thumb.

'I'm this close to nailing him, OK?'

She nodded, and he patted his pocket to check for his car keys then walked through the archway towards the front door. She followed and opened it; he towered above her and she was taken aback when he leaned close and kissed her cheek.

'We all sing from the same song sheet and everything will be fine, so be in early tomorrow.'

She closed the door after him. He smelt of whisky, cigarettes and faint lavender cologne. She replaced the chain lock, turned off the hall light and walked slowly back to her bedroom.

Bradfield got into his blue Ford Zephyr with Gibbs at the wheel.

'Christ, you took your time.'

'Yeah well, I had to be careful ... met her mother – lovely lady, invited me for Sunday lunch.'

'Come on, don't string me out.'

Bradfield patted Gibbs on the shoulder as he started up the engine.

'She was on her way downstairs with the young girl so didn't see you smack O'Duncie. I told her you tripped him up as he tried to escape and that's what she'll say when the rubber heelers interview her.'

'Thank Christ for that,' Gibbs said as they drove off.

Jane lay in her bed mulling over her discussion with Bradfield. Although he had reprimanded her about not finishing counting the money and about the receipt, she knew she had got off lightly because basically what he wanted was for her to lie.

CHAPTER SEVENTEEN

When it had just turned dark John dropped David off on the top level of the newish nine-storey car park in Great Eastern Street and got his wheelchair out the back of the van. He then handed David binoculars and a Shira-WT-106 walkie-talkie.

'This has been modified by Danny for a greater transmission distance. We already tested 'em and they work fine – we'll be able to hear each other. Don't have it up too loud, though, and I don't want to hear any idle chit-chat.'

'I know, John, I ain't stupid.'

'Yeah well, you only call us if there are any problems like—'

David sighed. 'The rozzers, passers-by, anyone reacting to any noise coming from the café ... you've told me loads of times.'

John patted his brother's cheek. 'Yeah well, I know what you're like for forgettin' things. See ya in the morning.'

No sooner had John left to go to the café than David felt how cold it was due to the wind being more intense at such a height. He was grateful that the car-park barrier walls were low enough for him to be able to sit in his wheelchair and still have a good view of the café, the bank and surrounding streets. Although he had a rug around him for warmth he was soon freezing cold, and he realized he'd best wear some thermal underwear, gloves and a woolly hat in future.

Silas had already opened the café back-yard gates and closed them as soon as John drove in and parked up the van. Danny opened the back doors and he and John started to unload all the equipment which was wrapped in decorators' sheets: the Acro poles, Kango drills, sledge-hammers, wire cutters and two large buckets filled with tins of paint and brushes.

'Come on, hurry up,' Silas said, worried that they may be seen.

'It'd save time if you bloody lifted a finger instead of just standing there watching us,' John snapped.

Silas cracked his knuckles, lifted a stack of wooden joists and muttered they were too long.

'For Chrissake, I've brought a fuckin' saw ... just get the gear inside.'

Danny glanced over to John. 'He's just nervous, John, so lay off him.'

'All right, all right. David's in position and I just want to get this stuff down the basement then get started with the job.'

Working through the night from 9 p.m. proved to be a lot tougher than John Bentley and the others had antici-pated: breaking through the brick wall was a depressing, arduous and time-consuming exercise. The wall was not one brick in depth but had four individual layers. Using masonry chisels and hammers they painstakingly removed a line of single bricks six feet long into which they inserted wooden joists, supported by Acro poles, to ensure the four-foot-high square hole they'd made through the brick-work wouldn't collapse in on them. Once this was done they were able to make a start on knocking through the next layer of bricks with heavy-duty hammers and chisels, taking their time so as to make as little noise as possible. As they moved through each layer of bricks they added more wooden supports. Silas had wanted to use the small electric Kango hammer drills, but John said it was safer for now to proceed slowly and use the hammers and chisels, but they would need the Kango to break through the concrete floor of the vault. Again Silas suggested using a small amount of explosive, but John, with Danny backing him up, was totally against it, fearing the shockwave would make too much sound, or worse still, cause the supports to give way.

Between them, Silas, Danny and John worked hard, with only a couple of breaks for tea or water to clear their lungs. As Silas had to open up in the morning, to make everything appear normal, he was allowed to have some sleep during the night in the flat above. John and Danny felt mentally and physically exhausted, and by 4 a.m. they had removed just three layers of bricks. Silas was sleeping when John suggested they stop and clear the bricks out of the café cellar as the sun would be up in just over an hour. Danny agreed, but chiselled out one brick in the fourth layer to see what was on the other side. He shone a torch through the small gap expecting to see the vault's concrete base, but was surprised to see two thick iron bars a few inches apart. He peered closer, using the torch to illuminate the dark void beyond the bars.

'Shit, there's iron security bars, and we've miscalculated the length of the fucking vault,' a disheartened-sounding Danny said.

'What? Let me see!' John exclaimed moving forward to look.

He put his hand into the brick hole to feel the thickness of the iron bars and Danny jerked it back almost spraining John's wrist.

'Christ, bloody watch it! If they're on a vibration alarm you could set it off by touching them.'

John took the torch from Danny and soon realized the room on the other side was a dusty basement storage room filled with old filing cabinets, broken furniture and assorted junk.

Danny became jumpy, worried that anyone going down to the bank basement in the day would see the hole. John peered through it and shone the torch to his right. From a distance of a couple of feet he could see the right angle of the wall and more iron bars, behind which was thick concrete with embedded mesh.

He turned to Danny. 'The concrete base of the vault is about two feet to the right.'

'So what are you saying ... we go through into the bank's basement and work on the vault base from there?'

'No, that's far too risky. We start digging a tunnel from here down under the bank's basement and then right so we can work upwards under the middle of the vault.'

Danny nodded in agreement. 'Those iron bars will run at least two further feet into the ground. I can rig an alarm bypass circuit between the bars so we can cut them away.'

'Do we use an angle grinder?'

'No, far too noisy. An oxyacetylene torch would melt through the iron bars like butter and with little sound.'

'I'll nip out and fucking buy one now, shall I?' John said sarcastically.

'I know where I can get my hands on one today. Might cost a few quid, but I'll have a few hours' kip, borrow a van and sort it out for tonight.'

Before leaving they concealed their handiwork by putting up partially prepainted plasterboards to hide the hole in the café basement wall. They also took out the bricks in large cloth sacks to the yard and covered them with an old tarpaulin, with the intention of dumping them later.

David had had to continually force himself to keep awake and the effort of staying alert had drained him. With a start he heard the walkie-talkie crackle into life and then heard John say it was 'time to get up', which meant that work was over for the night. The lift was broken so he started to walk down to the entrance of the car park, using the wheelchair as a support, but his bad leg was so cold and numb he was in agony. He decided to sit in the wheelchair, but even that had been an effort and caused friction burns on his hands as the slopes required him to slow the wheels so much. He did try using the brake but it was already well worn and not much use. He eventually made it to the ground floor where John was waiting in the van.

John told him Danny had made his own way home as he folded the chair and put it into the back of the van.

David got into the passenger seat. 'Christ, it was cold up there. I was freezing and me leg's killing me.'

John rammed the van into first gear. 'At least you were fucking sitting down all night,' he snapped. He didn't even mention the problems they had come across. He was so tired, he hardly said another word for the rest of the journey.

Arriving early at work, Jane was anxious about what had happened, and felt she'd let Bradfield and Gibbs down. She wanted to have all the money taken from O'Duncie's squat counted, recorded and checked against Mr Collins' list by the time DCI Bradfield arrived. She really hoped that some of the serial numbers would match against the money Julie Ann stole from her father.

Having grabbed herself a coffee she removed her coat, sat down at her desk and opened the drawer where she'd left her half-completed list. With mounting horror she realized it wasn't there and she frantically searched through every drawer, tray and file in the office but could find no sign of it.

'Oh my God, what am I going to do?' she said to herself, panic-stricken. She took some deep breaths to calm herself. Perhaps the A10 officers had searched the office and taken her list for their investigation. Maybe they'd even seized the money as evidence.

Jane ran down the stairs to the property office, only to find it wasn't open yet. Desperate to know if the money was still in the safe, so she could continue checking it, she went to ask the duty sergeant for his assistance in retrieving and booking it out from the store. To her dismay it was Sergeant Harris who was on a changeover to early shift after his day off. She found him in the cell area checking on the prisoners with a young PC who was handing O'Duncie his breakfast on a cardboard plate, along with a plastic knife and fork. Harris held out a cup of tea in a polystyrene cup.

O'Duncie saw her. 'Your boss an' his sidekick shouldn't a messed with me. My solicitor's gonna do 'em and get me outta here.'

Sergeant Harris deliberately dropped the tea. It hit the floor and splashed upwards. O'Duncie jumped up, dropping his breakfast of sausage, egg and fried bread. He started to shout abuse but Harris just slammed the cell door shut, pulled the metal wicket up and remarked that O'Duncie was a piece of shit.

Jane forced herself to be polite saying 'Good morning' and asking if, when he'd finished what he was doing, he'd be kind enough to open up the property store for her.

'I heard A10 were crawling all over the station yesterday giving Bradfield and Gibbs a hard time, thanks to that piece of garbage in there.'

'I don't know anything about it,' Jane replied rather unconvincingly as she always felt nervous in Harris's presence.

'Yeah right, well, I also heard they were looking for some paperwork of yours that seems to have mysteriously disappeared,' he said, holding his hands up and making sarcastic inverted-comma signs.

Jane remembered the last entry she'd written was 'Running total so far cash only £1,687', which she'd timed and dated, and wondered if Harris had seen it himself. She couldn't believe he'd be that spiteful, to stoop so low as to dispose of her paperwork just to get her in trouble, but the reality was she had no evidence as to who'd taken it.

'Sarge, did you make out a property-store receipt for the money?'

'Of course I did, I even counted it all for you, apart from the bag of coins, that is. There was nearly four grand, or was it nearer three, I can't quite remember,' he said with a cynical grin.

'Where's the receipt now?' she asked, wondering if he might actually have used the opportunity to steal some of the money when he counted it.

'I gave it to you, just before you went off duty. Don't tell me you've lost that as well?' he said in mock surprise.

Her anger rising, she stood her ground. 'No you didn't!'

He pointed to the three stripes on the side of his uniform jacket. 'A mere probationer's word against a supervising officer's? Sounds to me like you really screwed up.'

Jane had had enough of his arrogant attitude. 'Really, well, A10 are all over this because of you.'

He made out as if he was shaking. 'Oh I'm really scared, Tennison. I did my job by the book, there's nothing on me.'

'You forgot to tell the night-shift sergeant O'Duncie was not allowed to make phone calls. He rang a crooked solicitor and started making outrageous allegations, none of which are true, but it's got DCI Bradfield in trouble and Gibbs suspended so they are really furious. I'd say that's two senior officers who are gunning for you. Who do you think they'll believe about the missing paperwork and receipt, ME or you, Sergeant Harris?'

He glared at her and, lost for something to say, stormed off.

Jane was shaking with nerves but pleased that she'd finally stood her ground against Harris. Her good mood faded, though, when she realized she still didn't know if the money was currently in the property safe. She went to the canteen and there were a few uniform constables and detectives having their breakfast. Seeing Kath carrying a tray to a table she went over and sat opposite her.

Kath looked round to make sure no one was listening. 'Oh my God, Jane, it was all shit's hit the fan here yesterday. O'Duncie made some serious allegations, don't know exactly what about, but the rubber heelers were here nosing around asking questions. I heard poor Spence is suspended while they investigate the complaint.'

'He is and I feel partly responsible.'

'What's going on, Jane?'

'I'm in a bit of trouble. I didn't complete the list of all the banknote serial numbers or check exactly how much money was there. I left it in my desk drawer and now it's gone.'

'What? You left the money in a drawer and now it's been effing nicked!' Kath exclaimed in a whispered voice.

'No. Sergeant Harris put the money in the property-store safe. The list was in the drawer but …' She hesitated.

'Go on, but what?'

'I've no proof, but I think Harris took the list and kept the property receipt to get me in trouble.'

'God, that man's a prick. Don't get your knickers in a twist – just get the money out and I'll help you to count and check it all again.'

'I intended to but Harris won't open the store for me and it's closed at the moment,' Jane said, adding that it was possible A10 had seized the money, but she wasn't sure.

Kath ate fast, waving her fork around as she acknowledged a few officers. She told Jane that the large overweight PC in the corner having the 'Full English', with extra sausage, bacon and fried bread, was the property-store officer and he'd know if A10 had taken the money. If they hadn't she'd see if she could persuade him to open up a bit early, but there was no point asking until he'd finished everything on his plate.

Jane contemplated telling Kath about Bradfield coming to her home, but thought it best not to as she'd probably ask a load of questions or think there was some sort of conspiracy going on.

Kath scraped her plate clean and wiped her toast around it.

'There'll be a copy of the property-store receipt for the money in the store; the pages in the book are carbon so the amount Harris recorded will still be there.'

'Harris didn't tell me that!'

'Come on, Jane, he's trying to mess with your head, darlin'. Let's hope to God we do find all the money intact, cos if some of it's gone walkabout more hell will break loose. Oh! By the way, how was the wedding?'

'Pretty awful, I'm glad it's all over.'

'Ah, didn't get the leg-over the best man then? Never mind, eh?'

Kath spoke with the property-store officer, who obviously had a soft spot for her. He said he'd open up early, though it was nearly eight by the time he'd finished a second round of toast and marmalade. A10 had not taken the money and Jane signed out the same canvas bag that Harris had put in the safe; the copy receipt showed £2,780 cash in notes but not how much there was of each denomination.

As an afterthought, in case someone had been light-fingered, Kath booked out the money she'd seized from Kenneth Boyle's bedroom to recount it. Jane was glad Kath was with her; she knew the ropes and, as usual, was a calming influence. She confided in Jane that it always took a long time before stolen money could be returned as it took ages to determine who had the legal right to it. Jane asked what happened if there was more money left over than could be legally accounted for.

'Supposed to go to the Treasury and be used for good causes, but before that a few quid often goes missing as well. Some detectives manage to find owners for every penny ... well, more like they make up names and line their own pockets.'

'Do you think DCI Bradfield or DS Gibbs would do that?' Jane asked, beginning to wonder if she'd been used because of her inexperience.

'Shit, no way they're dodgy. They might give a suspect who deserves it a slap now and again, but thieving or taking a bung ain't their style.'

'What's a bung?'

'Boy, you've a lot to learn yet. It's taking money as a bribe. Once you're in the pocket of the bad guys there's no way out: they got you by the short and curlies for ever then. A smart detective won't risk prison, or throw away his career and pension for scum like O'Duncie.'

As they went upstairs to the incident room Jane felt more at ease with the whole situation, though ashamed that she'd doubted Bradfield and Gibbs's integrity. She hoped by meticulously checking through the money she'd find a connection to Julie Ann Collins and also that nothing dishonest had taken place, and she would therefore be able to help Bradfield and possibly get DS Gibbs reinstated.

Bradfield was waiting, eager to know how they were getting on, and see the list Jane had compiled so far. She didn't want to cause any more trouble so said that it wasn't in her drawer and A10 might have taken it, which he accepted. Kath explained that they'd had to wait for the property store to open and had just got the money out to check it. Bradfield told them to get another uniform PC to be present and use his office to count and check the serial numbers on the money.

A short while later Jane sat at Bradfield's desk with Kath and the collator PC Donaldson, who was known for his honesty and integrity. He was more than happy to monitor, assist and double-check the counting. Kath and

Donaldson laughed as Jane got out a pair of tweezers and explained she didn't want to leave her own fingerprints on any of the money. Kath produced three pairs of Marigold gloves and slapping them down on the table said that if they handled the notes carefully then the gloves would be fine and speed the process up.

Jane removed the pile of twenties first and started to list the serial numbers one by one.

'No wonder you were taking so long, darlin'. You don't have to write down every single serial number of the twenties: the bank has listed what they gave Mr Collins, which were ones, fives and tens, so just count and bag the twenties for now, OK? I'll start checking the fivers, you do the £1 notes and PC Donaldson can make a start on the tens. Let's get this show on the effing road.'

John Bentley was still in a deep sleep and snoring when his mother peeked in before quietly closing his bedroom door. She went to the kitchen and put the kettle on to make herself a cup of tea and could hear David in the bathroom – they'd had a recent invention called the 'electric shower' installed for him as he found it difficult to get in and out of the bath. He came into the kitchen in his dressing gown. His hair was wet and he looked exhausted.

'You want a cup of tea, son?'

'Ta. John still sleeping?'

'Out for the count. I dunno what time you two got home, but it was already light. What you been doing?'

'Oh, down the club, played a big game of billiards.'

'What, all night?'

'Yeah, it was a round robin.'

She poured a big mugful of tea and sugared it before sitting down opposite David.

'Your dad's about to be released.'

'I know,' he replied as he blew on his hot tea.

'I wish I could say I'm lookin' forward to it, son, but I'm not, what with John moving in and no sign of 'im leaving. I'll be worn out washing and cooking for all three of you.'

David slurped his tea, put two more sugars in and then sat stirring the mug.

'I need to get some groceries in,' Renee said.

David nodded and opened a packet of digestive biscuits.

'Price of bread has gone up, eleven pence a loaf. I was thinking I might make a big pot of stew, would you like that for your tea?'

'Yeah, sounds good. Do it for dinner, though.'

'I was thinking of having it ready for your tea at five. It needs a good few hours simmering so the meat will be tender.'

'Then put it on earlier – a late dinner will do.'

'I can do that … Are you out again this evening?'

'I'm meeting up with some friends to watch the latest "Carry On" film so I'll be out late.'

'Two nights out on the trot? John going with you, is he?'

'What's with all the questions, Ma? Just leave it out, will ya.'

She took a biscuit and nibbled at it.

'I see he's got a big van all done up.'

'What?'

'With painting-and-decorating signs on it. I saw you both in it last night when you left. I was going over to see poor Nancy Phillips, you know, the lady whose grandson got found dead. I thought she might like to go to bingo

301

but she didn't, been very poorly and the police won't release his body for a funeral yet.'

'Listen, John told you to keep your head down and not go out mixing with those gossips. You got to do what he tells you, Ma, or he'll get real angry.'

'Have I? Well, this is my flat and I like my bingo nights. I'm sick and tired of being cooped up and don't you think I'm stupid – I know when something is up, just like I do with your dad cos I been married to him so long.'

'John's just looking out for you.'

'Bollocks to that – he's never done nothing for me in years. He should get back with his wife, I mean God knows what she's up to whilst he's living here. Is he still paying the rent at his place?'

'I dunno, I'm gonna go back to bed for a kip.'

She leaned over and gripped his arm.

'He's not got you involved in something, has he? Don't you treat me like I got no eyes or ears, you both been skulking round for weeks, and if he's up to something you don't let him drag you into it.'

'He's just drummin' up work, Ma. He's openin' a new decorating company. He's good with his hands.'

'Like his dad was, but not for decorating. When did John ever lift so much as a brush? This whole flat needs a lick of paint; he should be gettin' it freshened up for when your dad gets out, you know how particular he is. Look at the washer and drier John got me – I was quite happy goin' to the launderette. I even got a fridge freezer and nothin' in it cos John says he don't want me shoppin' for 'im.'

'I go shoppin' with you, you know that.'

'All of a sudden you two are lookin' out for me when you never done it before. I was happy cleanin' offices, meetin' me friends and then John moves back in and takes over my friggin' life and I don't like it.'

'Leave it out, Ma.'

'I won't because I lived with your dad and I could tell when he was up to no good, I always knew, and I've thought for a few weeks you two were actin' like you were hidin' somethin' from me. Don't go tellin' me it's down to the slag your dad's kept payin' for cos I don't give a toss about her. I know she visits him in the nick and I don't care. I never have for years, not since you fell off that bloody roof. You are the only person I care about and I won't sit cooped up here whilst John drags you into some dirty business.'

She suddenly started to gasp, her face turning blue. She clutched her chest as she heaved for breath.

'You see what you done to yerself? Where's your inhaler?'

She fished into her apron pocket, found her inhaler and began to puff on it, her face now drained of colour as she gasped, her shoulders lifting up and down. David was helpless to do anything for her as the attack worsened and she sucked on the inhaler.

'Shit, Ma, go and lie down on the sofa. You need a doctor?'

She shook her head, the inhaler pressed to her mouth. She hissed and gasped as she got unsteadily to her feet. They slowly made their way to the lounge where she flopped down onto the sofa and closed her eyes. Gradually her breathing became steadier. David stood watching, and then limped to sit on the sofa arm.

'Are you feeling better now, Ma?'

She wafted a hand, but did not open her eyes.

'You want me to go get a doctor?'

'No, no, it's all right.'

'I can go to the phone box, ring for one.'

'Just leave me alone for a while,' she said, still gasping for air. Slowly she seemed to breathe more easily and relax and David watched as her eyes flickered and eventually closed. He waited until she fell asleep.

He felt exhausted after being out all night and needing to rest decided to go to his bedroom. As he passed John's room he looked in to see if he was awake, but he was still sound asleep snoring. John's hair was matted, and his skin looked chalky from the brick dust that permeated the café cellar as they knocked through the wall. His clothes were dust free as he had worn the white decorator's boiler suit over the top of them, even splashing the suit with paint by flicking a wet brush at it, so as to add to the illusion they were bona fide handymen if stopped by the police.

David lay down on his bed. He started to sneeze and scared he was coming down with a cold swore to himself. The thought of spending more freezing nights in the multi-storey car park was abhorrent, but as he began to drift off to sleep thinking about Florida, he knew it would be worth it.

It was almost 10 a.m. and Jane was double-checking the number of £20 notes when Kath suddenly slapped the table with the flat of her hand and excitedly held up a wedge of £5 notes.

'We got a match, darlin'! Look at this: the serial numbers on these fivers found at O'Duncie's match with the cash Mr Collins withdrew. We got five hundred quid's worth here.'

Jane's eyes lit up. 'Well, that much is definitely not the sort of money Julie Ann would have given O'Duncie for food and accommodation, and surely she wouldn't buy that much worth of heroin in one go.'

'Fuck me, this is going to brighten up DCI Bradfield's morning. There's other fivers here but they're not on the list so probably money O'Duncie made from selling drugs.'

PC Donaldson spoke up. 'I was going to wait until I'd finished double-checking all the tens to tell you, but I've got seventy that match the list.'

Kath counted on her fingers. 'That's a grand two hundred so far of nicked money O'Duncie's got.'

Jane grinned. 'There's only the £1 notes still to check but that shouldn't take long as Mr Collins only withdrew five hundred of them.'

'Well, that deserves a coffee and sandwich break,' Kath said as she picked up a £5 note from the table. 'What do ya fancy, Jane?'

Jane was stunned and didn't know what to say until she saw the sly grin come over Kath's face.

'Only jokin', but you can pay as we've helped you out here.'

Jane agreed and said there was money in her handbag. Kath snapped off her rubber gloves and asked Jane to carefully put the fives and tens that matched the list in the box to be sent to the fingerprint department.

PC Donaldson said he'd do the £1 notes with Jane while Kath went to the canteen.

She saw Bradfield there and he asked how it was going. She didn't want to steal Jane's thunder and simply said WPC Tennison had some good news for him. He was out of the canteen like a shot.

As Kath had anticipated Bradfield was jubilant, clapping his hands and full of praise for a job well done as he now had something concrete to put to O'Duncie, though he would have to wait until his solicitor Cato Stonex arrived to do a further interview, sadly without DS Gibbs. However, he was straight on the phone to tell A10 about the money and that WPC Tennison was available to make a statement that the young girl in the bedroom had lied about seeing DS Gibbs assault O'Duncie. The A10 DCI didn't sound happy, even though Bradfield and Gibbs were 'one of their own', and said they would attend the station to speak with Tennison in the afternoon.

After another half-hour Jane was also able to tell Bradfield that there was a total of £180 in £1 notes that matched the serial numbers on the list, making a recovered total of £1,380 in different banknotes stolen by Julie Ann Collins from her father. He asked Jane to put the box of money in a confidential dispatch bag, secure it well with a numbered ratchet seal and get two uniform PCs in a patrol car to take it to the lab for the attention of DS Lawrence asap. She was then to come to his office.

'Sit down, Jane. I just wanted to have a chat so that it's clear why I have not invited you to sit in on the interview with O'Duncie. I know you have the record of all the individual notes and amounts that matched, but A10 are coming in to talk to you.'

'Yes, sir.'

'So it's not possible for you to be in two places at once, right? So I've asked Kath instead.'

'I understand, sir, and I'm grateful you even considered having me present for the interview.'

'You've done a good job, Tennison, and learnt a valuable lesson about procedure, though I admit I should have advised you better after the search and seizure of the money.'

'You did, sir, but I was a bit confused and misunderstood you,' she said, revealing her loyalty and what she intended to tell A10.

'You're entitled to have your constables' federation rep present when they interview you.'

'Do I need to?' she asked nervously.

'No, but I would advise that you do. They play on inexperience, will try and twist what you say and can be threatening about a probationer's future career. It can be pretty daunting. PC Donaldson is the PCs' rep and he will stamp down on them if they try anything on with you.'

'Thank you, sir, I appreciate the advice and I won't let you down again.'

'I'm counting on that, Tennison, especially if you hope to join the CID as a detective someday.'

She blushed at his words and he cocked his head to one side, smiling.

'You look cute when you do that, you know. You get two pink spots on your cheeks.'

Jane returned to the incident room, followed by Bradfield. Kath thought she looked nervous and upset, unaware that she actually felt pleased. Kath turned to everyone and wafted her hand to get their attention.

'Listen up, we got a major link from WPC Tennison. She painstakingly matched serial numbers on the banknotes brought in from O'Duncie's drug squat.'

Everyone stopped what they were doing and listened to Kath as she continued.

'She discovered that nearly one and a half grand matched to the money withdrawn from the bank by Mr Collins, money subsequently stolen by his daughter Julie Ann.'

There was a round of applause, and Jane blushed again.

Bradfield looked at her, smiling. 'She's got us all out of a sticky patch and hopefully O'Duncie will now withdraw his allegations and DI Spencer Gibbs will be reinstated.'

The applause now turned to a cheer at the mention of the admired and well-respected Gibbs.

Sergeant Harris overheard the applause as he walked into the office carrying an envelope in one hand and a cup of tea in the other. It was rather eerie but more so for Harris, when on seeing him everyone went quiet, revealing their loathing of the man.

'What can we do for you, Sarge?' Kath asked.

'There's a Cato Stonex at the front counter, says he's—'

'Get that bastard O'Duncie brought up from the cells to my office, Sergeant Harris, but give me some time alone with Stonex first,' Bradfield said and slapped his thigh with Jane's report on the seized banknotes. He was really looking forward to the interview, especially with Cato present as well.

Jane wondered why Harris had come upstairs himself as normally he'd bark at the front-desk PC to pass on something to the CID. She looked questioningly at Kath who shrugged her shoulders.

Harris hesitated and Bradfield asked him if there was anything else. He nervously held up the envelope. 'Yes, sir, an officer found these papers left in the PCs' writing room and thought they might belong to Tennison.' He put the envelope on the table, turned swiftly and walked out, his nose very much out of joint.

Jane didn't really need to look in the envelope: she knew it was her lost list and the property-store receipt. She peeped inside, then looked at Kath and gave her a thumbs-up.

Bradfield leaned towards the two of them. 'What was that about?'

'Nothing, sir, it's just my application form for the section house,' Jane said, deciding it was over and done with where Harris was concerned and he probably wouldn't be on her back again.

As Bradfield walked out, Kath moved closer to Jane. 'That was good, you could have put that two-faced Harris bastard right in it, but you're learning fast, means you got one over that bugger and he'll know it.'

Cato Stonex wore a grey suit, blue shirt with a starched white stud collar, cufflinks and a dark navy tie. He was rather good-looking and very overconfident as he entered Bradfield's office carrying a large bulging briefcase.

'Good morning,' Bradfield said but did not get up. He simply gestured to the seat opposite him and introduced WPC Morgan.

'You need to know that your client has been using you for his own malicious ends.'

'Well, I would refute that, DCI Bradfield, especially as I have a witness who was present when DS Gibbs struck Mr O'Duncie in the bedroom.'

'She lied for him. WPC Tennison, who will be making a statement to A10, was already taking her downstairs when your client fell and broke his nose trying to escape arrest. I was also a witness to this and the fact O'Duncie tried to bribe me and DS Gibbs.'

'Well, the young lady seemed truthful enough to me when I interviewed her, and it's well known police officers protect, sorry, corroborate, each other like a "band of brothers".'

Bradfield smiled. 'She's fifteen years old, so that means

you took a statement from her illegally with no adult present to confirm it. O'Duncie was having unlawful sexual intercourse with her at the time we entered the room. It's a statutory offence as he's over twenty-four so it doesn't matter if he thought she was sixteen …'

Stonex was about to say something but Bradfield held up his hand. 'Please let me finish … then there's administering drugs, which he gave her before sex, to facilitate intercourse, which done to a fifteen-year-old is technically rape as I see it. That's what we're telling her poor parents as well.'

This was all news to Kath and something Bradfield had obviously kept to himself for the interview with good reason.

Stonex sat back in his chair, sniffed and rubbed his nose. He took a deep breath and sighed. 'You have been brushing up on your law, DCI Bradfield.'

'Well, I hate to see an upstanding solicitor like yourself had over by a lowlife drug dealer like O'Duncie, who won't even be able to pay your fees.'

There was a look of disbelief on Stonex's face as he asked what he meant. Bradfield went into detail about the money that had been stolen by Julie Ann from her father. He explained how £2,780 was found in Terry O'Duncie's room and the serial numbers on a total of £1,380 worth of different-denomination notes matched to the list provided by the bank. He added that the stolen banknotes were now all at the Yard being treated for fingerprints to be checked against those of their two victims, Mr Collins and O'Duncie himself.

'Nearly half the money seized is stolen and the rest believed to be the proceeds of drugs, so that leaves your client without a pot to piss in and facing a charge that he murdered Julie Ann Collins for the money.'

'So you're saying you won't be restoring the money?'

'Correct, and he will also be charged with possession with intent to supply heroin and marijuana, and with various other drugs offences. No doubt with his previous he will be sent to prison for a long stretch, but should it transpire that any of the money's legit then it could be restored to you as his solicitor.'

'On the assumption—'

'That we have ironed out the situation with your client's false accusations regarding his broken nose and DS Gibbs stealing any money,' Bradfield said and laid out the photographs of Julie Ann Collins' body.

'Your client has essentially denied knowing this victim as a close acquaintance, but as you've just heard we now have evidence to the contrary, not to mention her fingerprints in his bedroom at the squat. How you choose to break the good news to him is up to you.'

'Well, I certainly think it's time I had a serious conversation with him,' Stonex replied, annoyed that he'd been made a fool of, not only by O'Duncie but also by Bradfield who was one step ahead of the game.

'Good, WPC Morgan will escort you down to the cells.'

Cato Stonex hesitated but Bradfield pushed back his chair and stood up, checking his watch.

'We can reconvene in say twenty minutes or so.'

Kath returned to Bradfield's office a few minutes later and told him that Stonex was really pissed off with O'Duncie and the first thing he said was, 'I don't like being made to look like a clown, Terry.'

'Well, let's just hope he persuades O'Duncie to play ball. Otherwise we may still have unsolved murders on our hands.'

'That was a stroke, sir, holding back about the girl being fifteen and Julie Ann's fingerprints in the bedroom.'

'I've never met her parents and haven't a clue how old she is, but then neither's Stonex. As for Julie Ann's prints, well hopefully they might be there, but it wouldn't prove he killed her,' he said casually.

Kath knew he didn't always play by the rules, but she'd never realized how canny he was and he'd certainly put the wind up Cato Stonex.

'Do you think O'Duncie will confess now?' she asked.

'I fancy him more for killing Eddie Phillips, but to be frank there are some things that don't add up with him and Julie Ann. If he killed her in that shithole squat for the money then it would more likely have been just after she ran off from her dad's, but why bring her body all the way over to our patch? Why not dump or bury her somewhere out of town on the A40 or shove her in the canal like Eddie?' He checked his watch again and stood up stretching and began pacing the room.

'You want a cup of coffee?' Kath asked, not wanting to question his valid points.

'No thanks.' He lit a cigarette and continued pacing up and down.

It was another ten minutes before two PCs escorted the handcuffed O'Duncie and Cato Stonex to Bradfield's office. As they entered Stonex gave a discreet nod to Bradfield to indicate that his client was going to talk. The bruising from the broken nose had spread around O'Duncie's eyes and he had fresh pieces of cotton wool plugged up each nostril. He was very subdued and sat next to Stonex opposite Bradfield and WPC Morgan.

Stonex handed over a short statement signed by O'Duncie in which he retracted all the allegations he had made against DS Gibbs and Bradfield, confessing they were a malicious attempt to get out of trouble. Bradfield asked Kath to take it through to WPC Tennison to give to A10 when they turned up to interview her. He waited for her to return before commencing the interview. He didn't actually have to do so, but he liked watching the flash lawyer sweating and his client unable to keep his head up and look at him.

'You are now aware of the serious charges against you, and we know you were intimate with Julie Ann Collins, so I suggest—'

Before he could finish O'Duncie leaned forwards. 'She came to my place all on edge and looking a mess. She needed a place to doss down and told me her father had beaten the shit out of her with a golf club. I admit I'd slept with her a few times, but she was always up for it and there was nothing illegal, but this time she slept in one of the bedrooms downstairs.'

'How long was she at the squat on this occasion?' Bradfield asked.

'Four, five days, maybe a week tops. She just lay around all day smoking dope. I asked her if she was OK and she said she was in pain and being sick. I thought it was just her kidneys actin' up from the beating her dad give her. She became really strung out and started pestering me for heroin, so I gave her some for nothing an' then she wanted more. I said she'd have to pay and she said she wanted to, and she was all kind of crazy sayin' she'd been raped and was scared to say who it was as she reckoned he'd kill her. I wanted her to get out, but then she said she'd got a lot of cash. I swear before God I didn't believe her, but then she got all serious and showed me a big wedge of money saying we could do some dealing together as she knew junkies at the Hackney drug centre where she was on a rehab programme.'

'Was it the Homerton Hospital where your sister works?' Bradfield asked and he nodded.

'I said I needed to see a main dealer for supplies first and I was short on cash. She gave me one and a half thousand quid upfront to buy some good gear, and we'd agreed to cut the heroin down with powdered milk and then I would pay back what I owed her from the profit.'

'Wait, wait a minute, Terry. You expect me to believe she just handed over the cash? What, you think we are fucking dumb? No way would she trust you with that amount of money.'

'She did, listen to me, she knew the dealer so she was happy about it all. He'd been screwing her an' she said if I tried to fuck her over she'd get him to sort me out.'

'I need the name and address of your supplier.'

'Shit, man, I can't do that – it'll be like puttin' my head on the chopping block. I swear on my life I was gonna talk to Dwayne Clark to make the deal with a bloke in Manchester, but when I went round to his place he wasn't there and his missus said he was in Coventry.'

'You are walking right into it, sunshine. You said you were not at the squat when Julie Ann was murdered – that was a lie, you killed her and kept all the money, right, RIGHT?'

O'Duncie was sweating and twisting his body in his chair.

'No, honest, it's like I just told you. Dwayne wasn't at his place so I just went back to the squat with the cash, but she wasn't there and when I asked where she was one of the kids said she'd gone to Hackney for a few days. Then I heard she'd been murdered and I was scared to admit she had been dossing down at the squat because you'd think I killed her.'

Bradfield tapped the table with a pencil.

'So let me get this straight: you admit Julie Ann was living at the squat, and she gave you a large sum of cash to buy a job lot of heroin, is that right?'

'Yeah, that's right.'

'Why Manchester for the drug deal? I mean that's a good distance. Surely you know dealers closer to London?' Bradfield said, strongly suspecting Joshua Richards, aka Big Daddy, was the dealer.

'Listen, I'm telling you the fuckin' truth. Besides, heroin's much cheaper outside of London and we was asking for a big load of it.'

'I see … Why didn't Julie Ann go with you to see Dwayne?'

'Because she felt sick, throwing up all the time.'

'Did she tell you where she'd got the money from?'

'No and I didn't ask. Obviously I thought it was nicked, which I now know it was cos Mr Stonex told me it was her dad's.'

'You've got a fucking answer for everything, Terry.'

'It's the truth, man.'

Bradfield started jotting down some figures from the notes Jane had given him about the recovered money.

'We know she stole just under £2,000 from her dad, you had £1,380 that matched the serial numbers, so IF she gave you one and a half grand what you do with the other £120?'

O'Duncie looked anxiously at his solicitor who said nothing.

'I don't do maths,' he said nervously.

'Oh right, unless it involves heroin, that is?'

'I don't do hard stuff either – check my body, there's no needle marks. I just told you I never got to do the deal, that's why I still got the cash.'

Everyone was shocked when Cato Stonex suddenly banged his pen down on the table in anger.

'Enough, Terry, you're digging a big hole and guaranteeing yourself a long prison sentence, so I suggest you stop messing about and tell DCI Bradfield the truth.'

'OK, OK ... like I said I never done the deal cos Dwayne was already in fuckin' Coventry and I couldn't get hold of him. I lied to Julie Ann and told her I'd given the money to Dwayne who had to go out of town to get the gear and we'd have to wait until he got back.'

'So she was still at the squat waiting for the drugs?'

'Yeah, but I give her some Quaaludes and she said she was gonna go and shack up with Eddie over at Hackney and arrange some deals with the clinic junkies. She said she'd be back and threatened me again if I tried to stitch her up.'

By now he was sweating so much his face was dripping and he kept on wiping himself with the sleeve of his shirt.

'She only gave me £1,500 then left. I swear before God she left, man, and that was the last time I saw her. I never killed her, she left the squat a day or so before she was found dead. I can prove where I was: me and my girl went to the Chelsea Hotel, I even checked in under my real name.'

'The underage girl you were with when we arrested you?'

'Yes, but she told me she was eighteen ... we spent some of the money Julie Ann had given me on a few nights there, expensive meals, champagne, and bought a load of clothes and shoes in Carnaby Street. We were in the hotel room when it was on the news that she was dead, man. I got scared shitless so I just lied cos I honestly dunno what happened to her.'

Bradfield felt like it was two steps forward and a big hole-in-one going back.

O'Duncie's alibi had a ring of truth about it and could easily be checked out with the hotel and young girl. Feeling depressed Bradfield pulled out the photograph of Eddie Phillips from the envelope and pushed it towards O'Duncie.

'So what happened with you and Eddie?'

The room was stinking from the sweating O'Duncie as he looked at the photograph. He yet again glanced help-lessly to his solicitor.

'Just answer the question, Terry,' Stonex said.

'He'd been at the squat a few times with Julie Ann. They were on the same drug-rehab programme where my sister worked. After Julie Ann died he turned up saying he was scared because you lot wanted him to give the name of the dealer they used.'

'The dealer is the man known as Big Daddy? The man you planned to score off using Julie Ann's money?'

O'Duncie reacted, and slowly nodded his head.

'Yeah, all right, yeah, but I never met him, I swear on my life I dunno him and last I heard he got nicked in Manchester. I know he's a fuckin' nightmare if you cross him and Julie Ann was terrified of him. I only done busi-ness through his sidekick Dwayne, an' he can get crazy, kicking your head in.'

There was a pause as O'Duncie swallowed and coughed before he continued.

'Anyway, Eddie was fucked up when he come round to the squat, he was stinking of puke and crying. He said because Julie Ann had been murdered, he was being hounded by you lot, but he swore he'd never mentioned me.'

'Did he say anything about Julie Ann being pregnant?'

'Yes, but I knew it wasn't mine as I never shag junkies without protection because of hepatitis, and it couldn't be Eddie's as he was a right little nerd. I didn't know she was pregnant till Eddie said so, and Christ only knows whose it was as she was a right slag.'

'Do you know if Big Daddy raped her?'

'Not for certain, but it wouldn't surprise me, having heard what he's like.'

'And how did Eddie end up in the canal, Terry?'

By now O'Duncie's shirt was soaking wet with sweat, which ran in streams down the sides of his cheeks.

'Look, I admit he was a pest, but he'd done me a favour by not telling you lot she used to stay at my crash pad. He wanted to hang out away from the heat, so I said he could stay for a few days. Someone in the house gave him a pair of my old trousers and a shirt and he left. If they give him any gear it wasn't from me cos he had no cash.'

Bradfield sighed and drew back the photograph of Eddie and stacked it on top of Julie Ann's.

'We will check out your alibi. You will now be charged with drugs offences and be held in custody to appear at the Magistrates' Court where we will ask for you to be remanded in custody. Kath, go get someone to help you take him down to the charge room with Mr Stonex, but open the fucking windows in here first.'

A few minutes later Kath returned with a uniform PC to assist her with O'Duncie. As they left the room Cato Stonex remained behind and said he wanted to have a quick word with DCI Bradfield.

'You pulled a fast one and lied about speaking with the allegedly underage girl and her parents.'

Bradfield shook his head. 'You're long enough in the tooth to know how the game's played, Cato; besides you were only worried you'd fucked up by interviewing a juvenile alone.'

'We're not so different: all said and done we both have a job to do.'

'Maybe.' Bradfield paused. 'Where the hell did you get a name like yours from anyway?'

'It's a Saxon surname, Bradfield, and whether or not I like my Christian name is none of your bloody business.'

'Right Cato, mate-o, it's not my business but I don't take bent money from drug dealers for payment.'

'For what it's worth I don't think he killed Julie Ann and nor did Dwayne Clark.'

'What! You met up with Dwayne?'

'He called me. He has a cast-iron alibi. He was in Coventry to meet up with Joshua Richards, but as you know he got arrested. I've told Dwayne he's making a bigger hole for himself by hiding and advised him to come in voluntarily to be interviewed.'

'What about Eddie Phillips? Did O'Duncie or Dwayne kill him?'

'I don't know and that's not my problem to solve, but no doubt we will meet again soon,' Stonex said and left.

An angry Bradfield went to the incident room to speak with Jane about her interview with A10. She told him that once they saw the retraction statement by O'Duncie they only asked her a few questions and she confirmed his and DS Gibbs's version of events. They informed her that no further action would be taken and DS Gibbs would be returned to duty immediately. Bradfield said nothing, he didn't even smile, but returned stony-faced to his office slamming the door shut behind him, too preoccupied with the case to react to the good news.

It went from bad to worse later that afternoon as the knowledge that O'Duncie's alibi had been verified quickly spread round the incident room. The Chelsea Hotel manager confirmed that O'Duncie and his girlfriend, who they discovered was seventeen, had been staying there. The initial excitement over O'Duncie's arrest palled: their killer was still out there.

Bradfield ordered another search of the squat in Ashburn House on the Pembridge Estate by DCs Ashton and Edwards. He wanted to know if there was anyone else now staying there who had known Julie Ann, or had fresh information about her or Eddie Phillips. It was late afternoon when Bradfield and DS Lawrence, who were going over the forensics in Bradfield's office, were interrupted by a knock at the door and DCs Ashton and Edwards walked in.

'No one was at the squat, sir, but we found this.' A sheepish-looking Ashton held up a dirty black bin bag.

'It definitely wasn't there when we first searched the place,' Edwards nervously added and Ashton agreed.

Bradfield and Lawrence looked inside the bag. Amongst potato peelings and dirty used takeaway cartons there was a rucksack.

'It matches the description of the one Julie Ann Collins had,' Ashton said.

An angry-looking Bradfield grabbed the bin bag from Ashton and went to the incident room where Jane was sitting at a desk filling out some index cards. Bradfield told her to move and as she got up he cleared a space on the desk. Lawrence laid out some sheets of newspaper, put on some protective gloves and handed a pair to Bradfield who removed the rucksack from the bin bag and began to search through it. First he took out a worn-looking 'English History' exercise book, with 'Julie Ann Collins' written in large letters on the front, and placed it on the table. Lawrence picked the exercise book up and began to flick through it while Bradfield removed items of clothing from the rucksack and placed them in a pile on the table. Lawrence held the book open for Bradfield and Jane to see. 'She was a bright girl, and look at her neat and tidy handwriting. I wonder if she was maybe thinking about going back to finish her education.'

Bradfield retrieved a chopstick from the bin bag and used it to lift and separate the clothes. There was a white cotton bra, a few stained lace panties, two pairs of worn leather ballet shoes, the soles coming away from the stitching, and a frilled Biba blouse that was covered in food stains. Jane could still smell the strong patchouli perfume emanating from the clothing.

'Not much, but she was living rough for some time.' Lawrence sighed.

'Anything worth taking was probably nicked by the other kids at the squat.'

Jane just wanted to leave the room: she felt sad seeing all that was left of the dead girl. She pointed at the worn ballet slippers.

'Her father said she wanted to be a ballet dancer.'

'Well, she's never going to dance any more,' Bradfield remarked.

'No,' Jane replied and left him prodding at the clothing with his chopstick. It was obvious to them all there was nothing in the rucksack that would hasten the search for her killer.

Jane was in the ladies' locker room putting on her raincoat when Kath came in with a sly grin on her face.

'Spence is back in the office ... and I'm gonna pay him back for the Vicks prank. All DCs and detective sergeants, and that includes Gibbs, have to do a first-aid refresher test on resuscitation with the St John's Ambulance instructor ...'

'You mean mouth-to-mouth on a dummy?'

'Yeah, well, it's half a dummy they bring in, she's called Resusci Anne. The old battle-axe trainer is havin' a tea break in the canteen so I've only got a few minutes.'

Jane watched, rather confused, as Kath took out a lipstick from her make-up bag.

'This is called "Crimson Blush" and it's waterproof.'

'What are you going to do?' a curious Jane asked.

Kath was already on her way out of the locker room. 'Just wait – you'll find out soon enough.'

Jane buttoned up her raincoat, secured her locker, and then after giving her hair a brush went out into the corridor where she saw Kath come running down the stairs.

'Gibbs has just gone in for his test. You'd better not hang about or he'll think it was you.'

It was only a few minutes later when Gibbs, who had been irritated by being made to go through the mouth-to-mouth refresher training, stomped down the stairs. He went to the incident room to see if DS Lawrence and Bradfield had discovered anything of value from Julie Ann's rucksack.

'Anything of interest?' he asked.

Bradfield glanced up as Gibbs moved closer.

'Who've you been slobbering with?' Lawrence asked.

'He'll be wearing a matching blouse and earrings next,' Bradfield added with a grin.

'What are you two talking about? I've been doing mouth-to-mouth on Resusci Anne and I passed, thank you very much for asking.'

Bradfield laughed. 'I believe you, Spence, but the rest of the team won't.'

'I dunno what you're talking about ... I'm going to the canteen.'

'Bring me and Paul a coffee, sweetheart,' Bradfield said nonchalantly to the confused Gibbs as he walked out. He was totally unaware that he had bright red lipstick smudged around his lips. He found out soon enough as there were guffaws from officers in the canteen and Gladys the canteen lady told him she had the same colour lipstick.

CHAPTER EIGHTEEN

Jane's mother was in tears, her father close to it as they stood outside their Maida Vale flat waiting for the taxi to arrive.

'I'm perfectly happy to get public transport and it won't be busy this early in the morning, Dad.'

'No, you won't let us drive you there so I'll pay for the taxi. I'll not have you lugging that large case across London, especially Hackney.'

Mrs Tennison sobbed and wiped her nose on a hanky she kept tucked in her sleeve. 'I can't believe you are leaving Daddy and me all alone, Jane.'

Jane felt quite emotional herself and knew her mother was in some sort of denial, but she was not going to be made to feel guilty about moving out.

'For goodness' sake, Mum, the section house is only half an hour away in the car. Besides, you weren't like this when Pam moved out.'

'But that was different, Jane: she'd met someone, fallen in love and got married.'

'I'll visit on my days off and come home for Sunday roast, so ...'

Her mother wafted her hanky as she became more

upset. 'You only get one Sunday off a month ... it's deplorable and you must ask for more.'

'I don't make the rules, Mum, I just do as I'm told. I get days off in the week like today, and one of your roasts will taste just as good Monday to Friday. I'll even stay the night if possible.'

Her mother looked slightly calmer. 'You bring that nice detective that came to see you after the wedding.'

'He's a senior officer and my boss while I'm assisting the CID ... to him I'm just a minion.'

'Well, he seemed very nice, very polite.'

'If it makes you happy I'll ask,' Jane said, though she didn't intend to do so.

'That's the taxi coming,' her dad said.

To Jane's surprise he suddenly stepped forward and embraced her with a loving hug.

'Like I said you always get your own way,' he whispered in her ear. He squeezed tighter and kissed her on the cheek.

She whispered back, 'Thanks for telling her about me moving – you made it easier for me and I will miss you both.'

'I know, she just worries about you. We both do because we love you so much.'

Jane felt herself welling up and thinking of the loss of her brother Michael. For the first time she wondered if she was doing the right thing by moving out when it came to the effect on her mother.

As her dad put the suitcase in the back of the cab Jane embraced and squeezed her mother tightly before telling her she'd ring later that day to let them know she'd settled in.

*

Arriving at the section house reception Jane introduced herself to the duty warden, an elderly, grey-haired civilian man who sat behind a small desk drinking his morning cup of tea and enjoying a cigarette. He asked to see her warrant card and then asked her to sign in on the residents' register.

'Do you know your room number, luv?'

'Not yet, but I was told my room would be on the third floor.'

'Oh, slight problem there. The WPCs' floor is all full up so the only room available is on the men's floor.'

Jane was shocked and upset. 'But I was told that—'

'Got yer there, didn't I? I do it to all the new residents, even the blokes. Funny thing is none of them ever object to a room on the women's floor. You've been allocated room 308. There's a black disc on the key ring and you need to hang that on the board number whenever you're going out the building.'

Jane thanked him and he explained that if she was out and no black disc had been hung up she'd receive a 10p fine. The warden pointed to a row of six wooden cubby holes behind him stating that the residents' mail was placed in them and it was her responsibility to check for herself, likewise the message book.

'Right, you nip up to your room and unpack your case while I let Bob Turner know you're here.'

'Who's he?'

'Section house sergeant and that's his office just behind you. He likes to show the new ones round and tell them the rules and regs at the same time. He lives in a big room on the top floor so I'll go and let him know you're here.'

Jane's room was only slightly larger than the one she'd had at Hendon training college in the women's only tower block accommodation during her initial training, and not as comfortable-looking or big as the one at home. The single bed and side cabinet were on the left as you entered; to the right behind a sliding door was a small metal washbasin and mirror with a strip light, toiletry shelves to one side. Under the sink there was a white towel on a rail.

She put her case on the unmade bed and opened it. Not knowing how much storage space there would be she had not packed too many clothes. She looked in the far section of the wardrobe for some hangers. Inside there was a chest of drawers, the top of which she noticed had a pull-out section that could be used as a desk. Nifty, she thought to herself.

As she unpacked Jane realized she would have to get used to doing her own washing and ironing. She put her clothes in the wardrobe and placed her alarm clock on the bedside table, then put the empty case under the bed. She opened the window at the end of the room to let some fresh air in. Her room overlooked the rear courtyard of the building, which she was glad of as the rooms at the front of the building overlooked Mare Street, which was a main through-road and always noisy and busy. She was about to unfold the bottom sheet and start to make the bed when there was a knock at the door. She opened it and saw a balding, dark-haired and rather portly man in his early forties dressed in a white T-shirt, tracksuit bottoms and slippers.

'Tennison?' he asked bluntly without a smile and said he was Sergeant Turner.

She put out her hand. 'Pleased to meet you.'

'Likewise. Follow me, please,' he said with a limp hand-shake and gruff manner.

As they walked along the landing the first thing he told her was that men were not allowed on the women's floor and vice versa, unless there was a valid reason, and anyone wantonly caught breaking the rule would be asked to leave.

He pointed out where the ladies' toilets and bathroom were and opening a door opposite he showed her the small ironing room with two irons and boards.

'Is there a launderette nearby?'

'One downstairs in the basement next to the gym. Two front-load washers and a drying room with clothes racks next to it. We're hoping to get some tumbler-driers in the near future. There's a dry-cleaner's round the corner for your uniform. He accepts police chits and you can get them at work or from me. Canteen opening hours are marked up on the main noticeboard outside my office.'

Jane couldn't get over his abrupt, monotonous way of speaking: there was a total lack of emphasis to his words.

'My room is very comfortable and nicely decorated,' she said, trying to sound enthusiastic.

'Adequate, yes, nicely decorated, no. You can put posters up using that new Bostick stuff, no nails, and no pins.'

'Blu-tack?' Jane enquired.

'If it's blue and sticky then that's it.'

The tour of the section house was pretty straightfor-ward, and Sergeant Turner said little else other than to point out the TV rooms and canteen. Feeling rather pes-simistic, Jane returned to her room. She finished making her bed and neatly arranged all her toiletries before going to the canteen for lunch. It was very different from the police sta-tion's and actually looked like a proper restaurant. She was very impressed but couldn't help noticing that there were just six people dining and only two of them were sitting together and obviously about to go on late shift as they were in half-blues. She didn't recognize anyone from Hackney Police Station, but wasn't surprised as some of the hundred and twenty residents worked at other stations in East London.

She felt very shy sitting alone and no one appeared in any way interested in making her acquaintance. Jane perused the menu, which had a choice of starters, mains and desserts, all of which were appealing. Ten minutes had passed when she saw a large black lady dressed in a Met Police catering outfit come out of the kitchen swing door. Jane raised her hand and the woman, who looked to be West Indian and in her fifties, walked over with a big smile.

'Yes, dear, what can I do fer yer?' she asked in a friendly way.

'Could I order the shepherd's pie with mixed veg, please?'

The woman started to laugh loudly. The sound was so infectious and happy Jane felt herself grinning and wanting to laugh herself.

'I can tell you is new here, ain't ya, sweetheart?' the woman said. She picked up a pencil and small order pad on the side of the table that Jane hadn't noticed. Still smiling she explained you had to write down what you wanted, along with your shoulder number or name, and hand it in at the serving hatch next to the kitchen door. When it was ready they'd shout out.

'Tell yer what, dear, seein' as it's yer first day, I'll take yer order, but yer can fetch it yerself when it's ready.'

After a delicious lunch, much better than the food at the

station, Jane felt a bit more settled and cheerful. She returned to her room, where she stuck up her Janis Joplin poster and cleaned her teeth. She got out her police instruction manual to do some studying for her next continuation training exam and lay on her bed resting her head on her arm. She turned to the chapter on the Vagrancy Act of 1824 about 'street beggars', which she had to learn 'parrot fashion'.

It felt strange because other than Hendon she had never lived anywhere else but with her parents. Her old alarm clock's loud tick had never really bothered her until now, so she shoved it inside the bedside-cabinet drawer and turned on her little Zephyr radio. It wasn't long before she fell asleep.

She woke with a start to the sound of doors banging and loud voices coming from the corridor. She sat bolt upright and looking at her watch was surprised that she had slept for nearly four hours as it was 6 p.m.

Wondering what was happening she peeked out of her door and saw two women chatting. They had large rollers in their hair and were wearing dressing gowns and holding drawstring plastic cosmetic bags. She decided she'd have a relaxing hot bath, get changed and then go and see what was on TV.

The bathroom had four toilets, two bath cubicles and two showers with white plastic curtains. As Jane entered a very tall woman in a shower hat, a towel wrapped round her, emerged from a bath cubicle.

'Hi, if you're wanting a bath the water's not that hot at the moment, so I'd give it another half-hour or so to warm up. Or you could have a quick shower.'

'Thanks, but I'll wait and have a hot bath later.' Jane smiled.

'I'm Sarah Redhead and fairly new here myself – been here five months. I worked in Luton for four years before I transferred to the Met. I'm based at Leytonstone, what about you?' She had rather a cut-glass, high-pitched voice and a forceful personality.

Jane introduced herself and said she worked up the road at Hackney Station.

'My God, you'll be in the thick of it. I've heard this is a rough area with some pretty ghastly, nasty villains,' Sarah remarked loudly.

'I'm still a probationer so I haven't really come across them yet.'

Sarah started to walk off then stopped and turned back. 'There's a pub over the road we all use called the Warburton Arms. There's a few of us meeting up there at half eight and you're welcome to join us.'

'That would be nice – thanks,' Jane said, but she wasn't sure if she'd actually go.

'Good, I'll meet you downstairs by the warden's desk at half eight. Okey-dokey?'

By the time Jane returned both baths were being used and she had to wait for over fifteen minutes before a girl wearing looped earrings came out. Jane recognized her from the Harker lecture, but the girl hurried past whilst draping her bath towel around her.

'Hi, I was at the Dr Harker lecture. You were there, weren't you?' Jane said.

The girl stopped and looked at Jane. 'Oh, yes, sorry, yeah. I had a terrible hangover that day ... It went on for ever, didn't it?'

Jane gave a smile, not wanting to say that she had enjoyed it, but the door banged shut before she could say anything else.

The water was tepid and Jane suspected most of the hot had been used up by the other two girls. It reminded Jane of home and how her sister Pam would sometimes hog the bath and hot water. She found it a bit distasteful that the girl she had recognized had not wiped around the rim of the bath and from the occupied one came a loud voice singing Elvis Presley's 'Hound Dog', very badly and out of tune.

Jane washed her hair in case she decided to go to the pub. Having got out of the bath she wrapped a towel round her hair and waited for the bath to empty before using her soapy-water remains to carefully clean it. Wearing her towelling dressing gown, she returned to her room and realized she'd forgotten to pack her hairdryer. She sat on the bed and rubbed her hair vigorously to dry it off and then combed it out. Because it was long enough to reach just below her shoulders it would be a while before it was dry.

Still unsure whether or not to go out she picked up her instruction manual, but feeling fidgety she soon put it aside and decided she would meet Sarah after all. The thought of a lonely night in didn't appeal. When her hair was almost dry she put on a little make-up, jeans and a T-shirt, but reprimanded herself again as she had packed only her work shoes. She looked at herself: the shoes with the jeans were not suitable so she put on her old ballet-style velvet slippers and grabbed a small purse for her room keys and money.

Sarah was waiting by the warden's desk and wearing a patchwork coat with bright yellow flared trousers. As they walked over to the pub together Sarah told Jane that because the pub was a regular haunt for police officers the landlord Ron would often have a 'lock-in', closing all the curtains and continuing to serve well after hours because he knew he wouldn't get busted.

'He's a friendly old goat. Sometimes we stay that late he goes upstairs to bed and lets us help ourselves.'

'You drink for free?' Jane asked, thinking it was tantamount to stealing.

'Good God, no. We leave the money for our drinks on the till, along with a few pence extra for his hospitality. Last one out locks the door and shoves the key through the letterbox. You get a few bad 'uns in here, though mostly they've got form for petty crime, like a bit of thieving, handling nicked goods and the like, but they're no problem and use the separate public bar.'

Jane followed Sarah as they entered the saloon bar of the pub which was reasonably busy and a tad noisy for Jane's liking. A few people were sitting on stools at the bar chatting, some on the long velvet cushioned seating around small wooden tables, and a couple of young men were playing bar billiards in the corner.

Jane didn't have a clue which of them were police officers as everyone was dressed in plain clothes.

'Hard to tell who's police,' she remarked to Sarah.

'Blokes are easy – short hair and a bulge in their pants.'

'I beg your pardon?' Jane said, wondering what on earth she was inferring.

Sarah laughed as she walked up to the bar. 'Trousers ... back pocket ... it's where they keep their warrant cards, and the detectives have long hair and the bulge in the front,' she said and laughed at her own crude innuendo.

'What yer havin', Sarah?' Ron the landlord asked her in a strong Cockney accent. He had a large pot belly and thick dark hair in a quiff and his forehead was covered in beads of sweat. The top buttons of his shirt were undone revealing a chunky gold neck chain that bit into his flabby skin.

'G and T with ice and lemon. What'll you have, Joyce?'

'It's Jane actually and an orange juice is fine, thanks.'

'Do you like white wine?'

'Yes but—'

'She'll have a dry white, Ron,' Sarah told him and turned back to Jane. 'It might be a bit on the warm side but it's palatable.'

Sarah looked around the pub, and two women drinking in the far corner waved to her; they were with two men who both had long hair. Jane recognized one of them: he was the detective inspector at Hackney, but he wasn't on the murder team as he had to oversee the day to day crime investigations.

'Hey, how yer doing?' Sarah bellowed across the bar as she picked up her drink and went over to join them while Jane sat on a stool and waited for her wine.

'You want ice?' Ron asked, holding up her glass of wine.

She nodded and noticed how dirty his hands were as he plopped in two large ice cubes.

Jane looked over at Sarah, who was in deep conversation with her friends, and didn't know whether or not they'd mind her joining them. She felt uncomfortable as she sipped her wine and now wished she hadn't come to the pub.

'Well, well, well, if it isn't WPC Tennison.'

Recognizing the voice she turned sharply to see DCI Bradfield leaning on the bar beside her.

'Hey, Ron, give us a large one,' he said, holding up a £1 note.

'Can you not see I'm already serving someone, so get your own, Len, and there's ice under the counter.'

Bradfield lifted the counter flap, went behind the bar and helped himself to a double Scotch before picking up a bottle of white wine. From his slightly slurred speech, glazed eyes and cheesy grin Jane could tell he'd had a few already.

'Want a top-up?' he asked, tilting the bottle towards her glass.

'No, I'm fine, thanks.'

'Rubbish,' he replied and filled her glass to the brim.

She sat on a bar stool and watched as he slapped two £1 notes down next to the till and shouted to Ron that he was going to have another large one. He lifted his glass, said 'Cheers' and knocked it back in one before helping himself to the next.

'So, Tennison, tell me what you are doing in this dive.'

She sipped her wine. 'I've just moved in across the road and it's—'

The DI she'd recognized interrupted her as he asked Bradfield, who was still behind the bar, for a pint of bitter, one lager, two whisky chasers and three G and Ts. Ron said to serve him as he had to pop down the cellar to change the lager barrel. As Bradfield placed the gin and tonics on the bar the DI said to have one for himself, so he got another double Scotch.

'How's the murder inquiry going, guv?' the DI asked, handing him the money.

Bradfield leaned on the counter. 'Every time I think we're near to a result it's back to square one and the Chief Super's on my back. Right now it's depressing as well as time-consuming, in fact I wished I'd never copped the bloody job, and call me Len when we're off duty.'

Jane felt awkward as Bradfield had made no effort to

introduce her. She listened as the DI told Bradfield that a bloke from the local Horne Brothers men's clothing warehouse had been in earlier.

'He's got a new line of two- and three-piece pinstripes coming in, Italian made, top quality, and he's allowed to give a discount to Old Bill. You interested?'

'I don't know,' Bradfield slurred, now very unsteady on his feet.

'We're all getting one; as good as anything you'd pick up in Savile Row apparently.'

'How much are they?' Bradfield asked.

'They'd normally be thirty-five but eighteen cash to us.'

'Go on then, put me on the list.'

'Mannie Charles is doing the alterations so give me your exact measurements at work tomorrow,' he said and took the girls' drinks over to them.

The DI returned to the bar with his colleague who stood the other side of Jane.

'So who's your girlfriend, Len?' he said as he put his arm around her.

'WPC Jane Tennison, a probationer who's filling in as my squad indexer, and I've warned her to stay clear of reprobates like you two.'

'What you drinkin', darlin?' the DI asked.

Jane felt ill at ease as he still had his arm around her but before she could say anything Bradfield took the cork out of the bottle and topped her glass up again.

She felt even more awkward as the two men drew up stools to sit either side of her, and proceeded to flirt and pat her knees. Bradfield moved away from the bar to go and join the men playing bar billiards. The more uncomfortable she felt, the more they leered and made suggestions about how she could get satisfaction with either or both of them and asked if she had ever had a threesome. She wasn't sure if they were being serious or just teasing her for their own sordid gratification.

Sarah appeared at the bar. 'Get off her, you leery wankers. Just cos your stupid chat-up lines won't work with me and the girls there's no need to start on her.'

They laughed and Sarah took hold of Jane's arm pulling her from the stool. 'Come on over to our table, Janet, it's safer there. We're thinking about going for a curry – want to join us?'

'It's Jane, and thank you but I am going back to the—'

'Rubbish, come on, it's just down the road.'

'No really, I've work in the morning and I'm very tired.'

Sarah shrugged and went back to her girlfriends as both men followed her and said they would like to go for a curry as well.

Ron rang the last-orders bell to get everyone's attention. 'Right, that's it, you lot. I'm knackered so I'm off to me bed. If you want something help yourself and leave the money by the till, all tips gratefully accepted. Oh and if you're doing afters someone draw the curtains.'

Jane couldn't wait to get out and hesitated only to say goodnight to Bradfield, but he was no longer by the billiard table or anywhere in the pub.

Exiting the premises Jane heard the sound of retching from the side alley and saw Bradfield leaning forward, his hands on his knees, and being sick. He looked terrible, his shirt collar unbuttoned, his tie loose, and he was wiping his mouth with a handkerchief.

'Are you all right, sir?'

He peered at her.

'No I'm bloody not,' he said, straightening up, but he looked very unsteady.

'Do you need a hand?'

'No, just leave me be.'

She was embarrassed and had turned to walk away when she heard him retching again and being violently sick.

'Do you want me to get you some water?'

He rested a hand against the wall, sweating and dabbing at his face with the handkerchief.

He moved towards her. 'Just had too much to drink, that's all,' he slurred, and bumped into the wall. 'I need to get to bed.'

She moved closer, and he gave a boyish shake of his head.

'Be all right in a minute.'

'Here, lean on me and I'll help you walk over the road and get the warden to call a cab for you.'

'No need for the cab, I'm staying there,' he said and slowly lurched forward. She caught him, almost buckling under his weight.

She put her arm around his waist to help support him across the road. He was really very unsteady, and they zigzagged to the other side before he took a deep breath and tried to straighten up.

'Sorry about this, been knocking it back since lunchtime.'

They got to the entrance, and he made an attempt to stand without her assistance, but he almost fell over so she propped him up against the wall.

'Take a few more deep breaths.'

'What?'

He gasped and breathed heavily through his nose and then fumbled in his pocket for his cigarette pack. She had to help him take one out and put it in his mouth, then digging into his pocket he mumbled that he couldn't find his lighter and asked her for one.

'Sorry, I don't smoke.'

''S'OK, got it.'

His hand wavered as he tried to light the cigarette so she took the silver flip-top Zippo lighter from him, which after a few seconds she mastered and was able to hold the lit flame to his cigarette. He took deep drags, his hand shaking from the alcohol.

'God, the state of me ... you go on in and I'll make my own way ...'

He didn't finish the sentence and she was afraid he was going to slide down the wall. She took his arm and again helped him to stand upright, the strong smell of sick making her turn her head away.

'Sometimes, Tennison, it all gets to me ... People think it's just another dead junkie tart, so why give a shit what happened to her. Thing is she was just a kid who lost her way thanks to scum like O'Duncie and Big Daddy. Sometimes I think it's only the likes of us who really care, do you know what I mean?'

'Yes,' she replied, quietly touched by his words.

'Emotions never make sense – even her own father beat the shit out of her, yet he loved her. It's caused by pain, ter-rible, gut-wrenching pain.'

She nodded, and he took a few more drags of his ciga-rette before he tossed it aside. He didn't ask her to help him, she just slipped her arm around him as they headed into the section house. He was not as unsteady but she was afraid that if she didn't hold on to him he might fall over.

Bradfield somehow managed to walk straight as they went through the reception area into the lifts and he told her he was on the second floor. As they got out of the lift he insisted that he was perfectly capable of finding his own room, thanked her for helping him and gave her a hug.

Jane heard the sound of someone deliberately clearing their throat behind her and turned to see the section house sergeant.

'Dear God, Tennison, this is the men's floor. You've only been here a few hours and already you're breaking the rules.'

'I was just helping ...' She turned to indicate and say DCI Bradfield, but he had disappeared and whether he'd gone into his room or to the toilets she couldn't tell.

'Un-bloody believable, you're up to sexual antics and hopping into one of the men's beds before you've even slept a night in your own!'

'Excuse me, Sergeant, he had a severe stomach upset and—'

'Listen, my dear, I have heard every excuse under the sun and this is your first and last warning. Now get your backside onto your own landing sharpish, you should be ashamed of yourself.'

Jane saw no point in arguing and trudged up the stairs, the sergeant following behind shaking his head like an old grizzly bear as he made sure she went to her room on the third floor. Whether or not Bradfield had made it back to his room safely was not an issue for Jane: she was just angry that after only one day she had already made a very bad impression and no doubt the sergeant would take delight in telling the other residents.

CHAPTER NINETEEN

Clifford Bentley's surprise homecoming party had been arranged by his wife and sons for the afternoon of his release from prison. John had invited all his dad's old pals round to his mother's flat and the day before Renee had been to the hairdresser's for a set and perm. This was followed by a visit to the local butcher's for sliced ham, chicken legs, sausage rolls and pork pies. Next she went to the fishmonger's and got some jellied eels, whelks and cockles, while David went to the Co-op to buy bread, cheese slices and an assortment of spreads for the sandwiches, and chocolate finger biscuits.

The booze had been lugged home in the van by John – large tins of Watneys Party Seven Draught Bitter, a crate of Mackeson Stout, bottles of spirits, and mixers such as tonic water and orange juice. On seeing it all David said it must have cost a fortune. John laughed and said he'd got it at half-price, but David suspected it was nicked to order which is why his brother had got it so cheaply.

John took a suit and clean shirt for his dad to change into when he collected him from Pentonville. He picked him up in a Mercedes 280 Coupe, complete with chauffeur, supplied by one of his second-hand-car dealer friends, but neither of them spoke about the bank job. Arriving home late that afternoon Clifford was miffed to see that Renee had hung a big 'Welcome Home Cliffey' banner over the communal landing wall. David was by the front door to greet his dad.

'Silly bitch, she knows I don't want it publicized I'm out.'

'She means well, Dad,' David said.

'Means well? She might as well have put "from prison" in the middle of the bloody banner.'

The celebrations were in full swing and there was a rowdy crowd spilling out onto the landing outside their flat.

Renee was all dressed up with her hair in tight permed curls, and was standing in the hallway, but before she could even put her arms around her husband there was a 'Welcome home' bellow from his old pals. Clifford Bentley had always been a big cheese, and they treated him as if he was some kind of war hero rather than an old lag just out of prison. He walked right past Renee, without showing her the slightest affection, and joined his mates in the lounge.

After a few drinks and something to eat John led his father to the privacy of his bedroom to give him an update on the 'decoration job' at the café.

'We come across a problem beyond the first brick wall and we've ended up breaking through to the bank's basement, but—'

'Jesus Christ – did you not read my notes properly?'

'Yes of course I bloody did, but they were wrong. However, it's not a problem and we can work round it.'

'How long is it gonna take?'

'We can't work during the day – it makes too much racket. But we need to tunnel under the vault and cut through some iron bars—'

'Iron bars! How you gonna cut them?'

'Listen, I know what I'm doin', Dad. Danny's getting a knocked-off oxyacetylene torch to cut the bars. It's nice and quiet, as well as quick.'

'He's a fucking electrician, not a welder, and they're dangerous, ain't they?'

'Danny knows how to handle it – he used them when he was in the Army. We're goin' as fast as we can, but we can't foresee every problem.'

Clifford shook his head. 'Jesus Christ, you know I told you that we gotta get in there fast cos some of the fivers in amongst that cash will cease to be legal tender soon.'

'Yeah, yeah I know – but let's just forget about them and stick to the ones, tens and twenties.'

Clifford prodded his son in the chest. 'No bloody way! There could be fuckin' thousands worth of those fivers.'

'But how we gonna offload 'em all by the beginning of September? I can't just walk into a bank with a few thousand worth of fivers then open an account or ask for them to be changed for new ones in a shop.'

Clifford looked at his son knowing he'd made a good point. He screwed up his lips and frowned as he thought to himself.

'Listen, when you divvy up the money after the job, offload the hooky fivers on Silas and Danny. It'll be ages before they realize, and when they do you play dumb and lie about it, say you had a load as well and you had to burn 'em – yer with me?'

John nodded with a grin, realizing what a sly old dog his dad was.

Clifford patted him on the back. 'Don't waste any more time – the bloke in the nick who set the job up was a heavy for the Krays and still has some nasty contacts. I don't want them coming here with baseball bats to beat the shit out of us cos we ain't done a proper job.'

John sighed. They had only just begun the job and he knew it was going be at least another two or three nights before they could get to the concrete floor below the vault. Then they had the problem of cutting through that, but he didn't want to tell his dad yet.

'I'm gonna disappear for a couple of hours ... she's waitin' for me.'

'Christ, Dad! Can't you wait one night?'

'Listen to me, I been away eight years and I need a shag, so keep yer mother occupied.'

The drinking was in full swing. Elvis was crooning from the record player and most of the food had already been consumed. They had even sent out for more Watney Sevens, the empty ones stacked in a pyramid shape in the lounge for fun. Renee was in the kitchen clearing leftovers into a bin, plates and glasses stacked up on the sink waiting to be washed. David was leaning against the wall. He felt sorry for his mum. He knew his dad had skived off and she'd got herself all dolled up and spent a lot of time preparing the food for his homecoming, and he hadn't even bothered to talk to her or ask how she was.

'You don't have to do all the washing up, Ma. Put the stuff into the new dishwashing machine.'

'Not my good glasses, I don't trust it. They're all getting well pissed, and some dirty bugger was sick in the toilet.'

'I'll go and see if anyone wants any more food,' David said.

'Thanks, love. I'll stay put in here washing up. Yer dad's gone out, hasn't he?'

David said nothing.

Renee frowned. 'I know he's gone to that slag – he'll come back stinkin' of her. Well, all I can say is she's welcome to him.'

'I love you, Mum,' he said quietly and kissed her gently on the cheek.

She looked up at him and gave a weak smile.

'Yeah, I know you do, son, and a long time ago I suppose I loved your dad. Worn it out of me, he has, but he looks well, doesn't he?'

'Yeah, he's been workin' out at the gym in the nick. He always took good care of himself.'

'But he never took care o' you,' she said with a grimace.

'Leave it out, Ma. I'll bring you a sherry.'

'Get me a stout, it'll put some iron in me blood.'

John saw David in the lounge pouring stout into a glass. He leaned in close and said that he had been told by their father they couldn't waste any more time.

'He's sayin' we gotta get the fivers out before they get to be illegal, and he wants the job completed in the next few days.'

'For fuck's sake, John, he only got out this afternoon and already he's throwin' his weight around. Let's just forget about the bloody fivers, they're too much hassle. Besides, there'll be loads of deposit boxes with nice jewellery in them.'

'I know, I know, but it'll take time to fence and sell all the sparklers, and we need the fivers to pay off Silas and Danny.'

'I don't understand.'

'Dave, with all this new decimal currency shit the old fivers in the vault become worthless unless they're cashed in or used by September.'

He shook his head. 'It seems crazy to rush things, especially for pissin' five-quid notes that will be useless.'

'Yeah, well, Danny and Silas won't know what's in the bags until it's too late, will they?'

He paused as it sunk in. 'You crafty beggar, John.'

David limped into the kitchen. He'd poured the stout badly and spilt some of the overflowing creamy head down his fingers which he wiped on his trousers as he placed the glass down beside his mother who was washing the cutlery.

'Use the dishwasher, Mum.'

'Never gets between the forks, and there's a few silver ones from your grandmother. You can't put silver in the dishwasher.'

'You should sell them, get some money.'

'I might, but I've already got a little nest egg. Been saving all my earnings from cleaning for years – yer dad doesn't know. God forbid he finds it – he'd be straight down the betting shop. I always saved, even my pension. It was always me that bought you boys your Christmas presents, and every time he was banged up I was able to save even more.'

'Listen, I don't even want to know where you've got it, but do you understand all this new decimal currency yet?'

'A bit, but only cos I do the grocery shop. No more half-crowns, threepenny bits, or old pennies. Yer couldn't buy nothin' with a penny nowadays.'

'Well, if you've got any old fivers stashed you got to change them up or use them soon as they're gonna be withdrawn come September.'

'No more fivers? You gotta be jokin', gerraway with you. I got one in me purse right now. Who told you this, David?'

'When I got my benefits the other day the lady there mentioned it,' he lied.

She shrugged and began placing the cutlery in a drawer.

'It's a terrible world, and I think they're doin' all these changes to rob us blind. I mean eleven pence for a bloody loaf of bread.'

David smiled. The record player had stopped so he went to put another LP on. He contemplated putting on Des O'Connor hoping it would encourage the remaining few guests to leave, but he knew how much his mother disliked him so he just replayed the Elvis album.

Renee didn't want to go back into the lounge. The smell of cigarettes and cigar smoke always brought on her asthma. She cleared up most of the kitchen and downed her stout before she slipped along the hall to her bedroom. Clifford's plastic prison bag of belongings was on the floor. It was full of dirty socks and underwear, old denim shirts and jeans, and there were two pairs of old trainers that smelled terrible. She decided she'd do his washing in the morning, and was about to tie the top of the bag in a knot to stop the sweaty odour filling the room when she noticed a small cardboard box. She took it out and opened it to discover a bunch of letters with an elastic band round them. She cautiously looked to the door, and took the packet to the bed, pulling off the elastic band. There were a few letters from the boys, birthday and Christmas cards, and then a considerable amount of pale-blue envelopes. She had rarely, if ever, written to her husband. She never saw the point as she knew his 'bit on the side' visited him on a regular basis.

She opened one that smelt of violets and saw the unfamiliar looped handwriting and immediately knew who it was from. She sighed. To her the slut had always been a disgusting bitch, a woman who had been hanging on by her fingernails. Cloyingly sentimental, the letters were badly spelt outpourings of adoration for Clifford which sickened Renee. She had put up with her husband's infidelity for many years.

Before this woman there had been others; she suspected there had even been whores. But the most humiliating discovery had been that some of her friends had been having sex with Clifford. He could never keep his dick in his pants, but now she realized how much she had chosen to ignore his unfaithfulness. She had always told herself that it was because she put her two sons first, but now they were older and mostly taking care of themselves. She had accepted the abuse, anything for a quiet life, but holding the woman's letters made her feel wretched. She carefully replaced them in the box, then into the plastic bag. Whilst tying it tight she imagined it was Clifford's neck.

She stood, arms folded, looking out of the bedroom window and listening to the Elvis song coming from the living room:

Love me tender,
Love me true
All my dreams fulfilled.
For my darling I love you
And I always will ...

Renee carried the hard-backed chair by her bed over to the wardrobe, opened the door and got up on the chair. She had to stand on her tiptoes to reach for the hat box at the back of the shelf behind the shoeboxes. She eased it out and unsteadily got down before sitting on the chair and opening the lid. She lifted the soft tissue paper and removed the pristine white gloves, followed by the dark navy straw hat which had a yellow rose sewn onto the headband. She had worn it to a wedding twenty years ago, but not since. Now that the hat box was empty she pushed one side of the flat base up from the outside so she could remove the false interior bottom.

The notes were all ironed flat, and covered the entire secret compartment. She didn't touch them but stared at the thick neat rows. Some of the money she had discovered in the airing cupboard after Clifford's arrest. She had lied and intimated that the detectives searching the flat must have nicked it, which her husband and John had accepted. Now Clifford was home she wondered if the money would be safe in the hat box, but she could think of nowhere better to conceal it. She thought about what David had said about the £5 notes and began to sort them out, stacking them on the bedside table one by one.

Renee returned the other notes to the hat-box compartment, put back the false base, then carefully replaced the hat and gloves and the tissue paper before concealing the hat box once again behind the shoeboxes in the wardrobe. She began to count her £5 notes but stopped abruptly when she heard Clifford shouting for her.

'Eh, where are you at, Renee?'

She quickly stuffed the notes into her underwear drawer and covered them with stockings and panties.

'Renee, what yer doin'?' he shouted.

She stared at her reflection in the dressing-table mirror. 'Wishing I'd run away,' she said softly to herself.

She went to the lounge where Clifford was standing, legs apart, a large tumbler of Scotch in his hand, as he chatted to two friends who were sitting on the sofa drinking port and brandy mixers.

'We're starvin' – fry us up something.'

'Where are the boys?' she asked.

'Takin' some pals home and then goin' out to a club.'

'Bacon an' eggs, sausages and baked beans do?'

'Yeah, and do some of that fried bread, luv, and a pot of tea.'

Renee gave a smile and walked out. It was almost 9 p.m., and it surprised her that David had gone out clubbing – after all it wasn't as if he could dance.

CHAPTER TWENTY

It was almost 10 p.m. by the time John finished fixing the brake on David's wheelchair and dropped him off at the top of the multistorey car park, as the lift was still broken. David sat in the chair, put on some gloves, and wrapped the blanket he'd brought with him around his knees. John handed him the walkie-talkie and a small bottle of whisky.

'Don't go drinking it all and falling asleep on us. Just take a wee sip if you feel cold.'

'Cold? It gets bloody freezing up here! I've had to put on long johns, a vest, two jumpers and a thick coat to try and keep warm.'

'Good, then you won't need to drink too much of the whisky,' John said cynically as he closed the rear door of the van.

'God, it stinks of piss up here,' David said, pulling a face.

'Yeah, the tramps take a slash down on the first floor and the smell travels up the stairwell. You'll be OK now. Only make contact if you see someone or something suspicious. And don't use names, all right?'

'Yeah, don't worry 'bout me, I'm good.'

John drove down to the exit, turned right and passed the café and the bank before taking a small turning into a narrow lane behind the buildings. He pulled up by the café's yard, got out and opened a tall double wooden gate, then drove the van inside, parked up and closed the gates. Silas was waiting by the back door. The small yard was piled high with garbage and John noticed a few rats scuttling amongst the bags of waste food.

'Lookout's in place,' John said quietly, and went down to the basement followed by Silas.

Pots of paint, brushes and dust sheets were laid out and the fake painted plasterboard had been removed revealing the hole in the wall. John could see that Danny had dug a hole under the bank's basement to get access to the bits of the iron bars that were embedded underground, which he had now cut away with the oxyacetylene torch. He told John he had done an electric-circuit test on the bars and they were rigged up to an alarm, but he had managed to bypass it.

'I reckon our best bet is to dig the tunnel wide and deep enough for us to get in and out easily,' Danny said.

'What about the fat Greek?' John smiled.

Danny laughed. 'Yeah, maybe a bit bigger then, but we'll need more wood to shore the tunnel up, and we can dig under the other iron security bars on the right-angle wall of the bank's basement. Once we're a little way under the vault we drill through the concrete floor. It should be easy street from there on in.'

John was pleased, realizing the job might be completed sooner than he had initially thought. He said he had more wood in the lock-up garage. He pulled on his overalls as Danny handed the pieces of cut iron bar and bricks through the hole to Silas, who put them into a rubble sack.

*

David stared down at the dark street below. Once more he was glad that the height of the concrete wall of the car park was low enough to allow him to sit in his wheelchair, as he would have been in intense pain if he had had to stand throughout the night.

He raised the binoculars and began to scan the streets surrounding the café. He felt increasingly tired as the hours passed, and only a few cars, buses and black cabs moved up and down the otherwise empty roads. He figured it was so quiet because the location bordered on the City of London with its banking and financial offices, which were all closed at night, and there was little residential housing in the area.

It was 3 a.m. when he was suddenly woken by the sound of raised voices and glass breaking down below in the car park, directly opposite the café. Due to the angle he couldn't see who was making the noise, unless he leaned over the car-park wall.

He cursed himself for dozing off as he pressed the button on the walkie-talkie. He was about to say 'David to John' when he remembered they weren't supposed to use names, but John had not said anything about coded call signs so he improvised on the spot.

'Eagle to Brushstroke ... Eagle to Brushstroke, over,' he said, released the talk button and waited for a reply.

In the basement John and the others were taking turns digging, and filling sacks with soil. When they heard David on the radio they looked at each other with bemusement.

'What the fuck is he on about?' John exclaimed angrily as he grabbed his walkie-talkie and indicated for Danny and Silas to stop working so he could speak with David.

'I said no contact unless urgent.'

'It is, persons opposite you, over.'

'Who?'

'Don't know, can't see them.'

'Well, get in a position you can!'

David sighed as he hated heights and certainly didn't fancy leaning further over the wall, which was nearly fifty feet from the ground. He slowly raised himself out of the wheelchair. He felt dizzy as he bent over the wall and looked down to see a silver bulbous rose which he recognized straightaway as being the top of a policeman's helmet. The officer was remonstrating with a drunk vagrant who had obviously, from the wet stream on the pavement, been having a piss up against the car-park wall. David could see brown glass from a broken beer bottle glistening in the street light. He assumed the vagrant had dropped or thrown the bottle. He watched as the officer gave him a slap round the head and told him he was nicked.

David crouched down, pressed the talk switch and whispered, 'Stay quiet, it's a rozzer nicking a pissed-up tramp.'

There was a crackle and David was unsure if he'd got through.

'Do you read me? Keep the noise down – he's right opposite the front of the café, over.'

'Make contact when you have the all-clear, over,' John answered, knowing that a paddy wagon would probably be on the way to pick up the arrested vagrant.

He whispered to Silas and Danny that they would have to stop work and remain totally silent for as long as it took for the drunk to be carted off.

David stayed crouched down and a few minutes later heard the sound of the policeman's radio, but not what was being said. He peeked over the wall and saw the officer lift the vagrant by the scruff of the neck and drag him across the road towards the café. His heart began to beat rapidly and his mouth went dry as he wondered whether or not to make further contact with John. As the officer turned and looked up the street David ducked down and he could feel himself shaking with nerves, and although cold he began to sweat as he called John.

'Stay quiet, he's outside the café now.'

As John pressed the received button, Silas dropped the brick he had been holding straight onto a large tin of paint, sending a loud reverberating clang echoing around the room, which came through on David's radio.

Shit, shit, shit! David thought to himself as he watched the officer, who was now peering in through the café window. His mind was racing. He was panicking and wondered if he should scarper in his wheelchair, but he knew his brother would beat him black and blue if he did. He pressed the talk button.

'For Christ's sake what's going on in there? The copper's lookin' in the window now.'

Below in the basement the men froze and John glared at Silas for his blundering stupidity.

David sat on the ground, his knees squeezed tight to his chest, his arms and head buried between them. Hearing the ringing sound of a police-van bell he raised his head and saw the blue flashing light flickering in the sky around him. The van pulled up outside the café and the vagrant started to play up, shouting abuse and saying he wasn't getting into the van. The driver got out, opened the rear doors and the two officers picked the vagrant up by the arms and legs then unceremoniously flung him in the back, slamming the doors shut before the van drove off.

David breathed a sigh of relief. Saved by the bell, he thought to himself, and smiled as he radioed John.

'OK, rozzers and tramp gone, over.'

'Are you givin' the all-clear? Over.'

The incident had made David so nervous he now needed to take a leak. It got worse as he squeezed his legs together.

'Yeah, they've left in the paddy wagon. I'm freezin' cold and I really need to go to the lav, over.'

'Well, piss against the wall, or wait for me to collect you in ten minutes – I'm calling it a night now, over and out.'

Silas shook his head in disbelief. 'Why we stop? We have cut through bars, started to dig tunnel to vault so let's keep going.'

John prodded him in the chest. 'Cos I said so. That was a close call, thanks to your greasy fingers dropping that fucking brick. If the rozzer heard it he might get suspicious and come back, so we clean up, replace the plasterboard and call it a night right now.'

David was by now desperate and ended up partially wetting himself in his hurried effort to undo his fly and pull down his long johns. By the time John came to collect him he was shivering uncontrollably and was near to tears.

Renee was woken by the sound of the flat door closing and realized it was the boys returning home, but after looking at the bedside clock she was surprised to see it was half four in the morning. She turned over to go back to sleep but could see Clifford getting out of bed and pulling on his dressing gown.

'It's half four, Cliff – why you gettin' up now?' she asked.

'Need the toilet – besides, I'm used to rising early in the nick, you know that.'

After a few minutes Renee heard voices coming from the kitchen. She put on her dressing gown and walked in. John and Clifford both fell silent.

'Is everything all right?'

'Yes – go back to bed, woman,' Clifford said.

'Shall I make a cup of tea?' she asked.

Clifford glared at her. 'No, just bloody well go back to bed!'

She closed the door and went to the bathroom.

'David, are you all right in there?' she asked as she tapped gently on the door.

David was lying in the bath water. Every part of his body ached and he felt like he was on fire.

'I'm just having a nice soak, Mum.'

'Will you need me to help you get out?'

'No.'

Renee stood in the hallway feeling irritated that she couldn't even go into the kitchen and brew up a cup of tea. She already suspected John and David were up to something, but now her husband was home she was certain all of them were. The way John and Clifford had just looked at her was behaviour she'd seen from them many times before when something was going to go down. Then there would be the inevitable knock on the door from the rozzers. She worried her David was yet again being dragged into something. She decided she would find out what as soon as she was alone with him.

CHAPTER TWENTY-ONE

Jane arrived at work to find a note from Bradfield telling her she would have to return to normal duties. She wondered if she had upset him but, not wanting to question his decision, she reported to the duty sergeant. The Julie Ann case had gone cold.

They had also questioned Dwayne Clark, who had come in accompanied by Stonex. Detectives had not found any drugs at Clark's address, or at his friend's flat in Coventry, and as he had a strong alibi for the murder of Julie Ann he was released without charge pending further enquiries. The toxicology tests on the blood samples taken from the body of Eddie Phillips were under way and early indications were he had injected himself with pure heroin and in a drug-induced stupor fallen over and then collapsed into the canal where he drowned. The scientist concluded that the overdose alone would have killed him within a few minutes. It was believed that O'Duncie had deliberately supplied Eddie Phillips with the lethal heroin, intending to kill him as he feared he would tell the police about his drug dealing and abuse of Julie Anne. However, as much as it angered Bradfield, he knew he didn't have enough evidence to prove that it was O'Duncie who supplied Eddie and therefore couldn't charge him with his murder. Experience had taught him that 'some you win, some you lose', and no matter the result of a case you had to move on and not let it fester in your mind, but putting O'Duncie away for the rest of his life was something Bradfield would've loved to do.

The depression could be felt by everyone. Time was spent going over all their evidence to date, but they had no further suspects.

Jane hadn't yet seen Bradfield and wondered if he was sleeping off his hangover in his office. She was given a fifteen-minute break mid-morning and was on her way to the canteen when he walked into the corridor.

'Ah, I've been meaning to talk to you.' He was flushed, and she was unsure if he was about to tell her off or explain why he had put her back on normal uniform duties. He gave a cursory look around before he reached for her hand.

'Erm, listen, about last night ... I would have said something first thing but, well, you know we've been pretty caught up. I just wanted to apologize ... I hope I didn't make any untoward advances. I was well drunk but I remember you helped me back.'

'It was fine, sir, nothing happened.'

He grinned. 'Ah well, chance would be a fine thing, but thanks.'

He walked off, and Jane continued on her way to the canteen, when Kath hurtled up behind her.

'You ain't gonna believe what I might have dug up! It came at me like the proverbial brick in the head last night in bed, and this time, Jane darlin', if I'm right it really is my golden ticket into the CID.'

She hooked one arm around Jane's shoulders and waved

a single sheet of typed paper. 'But first I need your help to check something. You still got the list of serial numbers Julie Ann's father gave Bradfield?'

'The original is locked away with the exhibits, but I wrote them all down on some index cards as well.'

Kath's excitement was mounting as they hurried into the incident room. Jane pulled out the index cards from the carousel and handed them to her. Pushing her paperwork to one side Kath laid the cards in a row on the table, and then placed the piece of paper she had been carrying next to the cards.

'Right, I'll read out a number on my list and you check it against the Collins list,' Kath said.

'But we've already checked the serial numbers and matched the notes O'Duncie stole from Julie Ann.'

'We haven't checked my list,' she smiled, tapping her finger on the piece of paper she'd put on the table.

Jane could see it was a further list of banknote denominations and serial numbers. 'Did they find some more money at O'Duncie's squat?'

Kath shook her head. 'I woke up in the middle of the night and I just knew that I was missing something, but not what it was that I was missing, do you understand?'

'No I don't, other than you've lost something. I've been so bored and I had to cover the front desk yet again as I'm back on uniform duties. Did I upset Bradfield?'

'No he had no choice, Chief Super said to release you.' Kath looked back at the list, 'Shit, I know I am right.'

'Sorry, what you got?'

'OK, the money he'd hidden, some of it still had the currency wrapper round it, that's what I'd missed, well, until now.'

'Who'd hidden, Kath? I'm not following you.'

'Kenneth Boyle – remember that little scumbag? I nicked him turning over an old-age pensioner's place and we searched his flat.'

'The bloke you had up in court the other day, the one who got a soft sentence?'

Kath nodded and reminded Jane how Boyle had a load of money hidden in an old shoebox in his bedroom. He said he'd nicked it from other old people's flats, but having now checked the victims' original burglary reports, she realized the total amount of money stolen didn't add up to what was in the shoebox.

'Well, he'd probably spent some of it,' Jane replied.

'No, no, listen to me. That's what's been naggin' me. There was much more in the tin than he'd confessed to stealing. I thought at first he probably did more burglaries than he admitted, but then I remembered some of the notes in the tin had a currency wrapper round them like the ones Bradfield found at O'Duncie's.'

'My God, do you think some of the Boyle money may have been cash Julie Ann stole?' Jane asked excitedly.

Kath's eyes lit up. 'Yes. I've listed the serial numbers on what we found at Boyle's place so let's start checking them against Mr Collins' list – we'll do the ones in the bank wrappers first.'

Kath and Jane got to work. It was only a matter of seconds before Kath shouted, 'Bingo!' and started leaping up and down.

'Boyle was arrested a couple of days after Julie Ann's murder. Didn't I say he gave it up too easily about the burglaries? He looked like a cat that got the cream and will no doubt get a pitiful sentence. He thinks he's got away with it. I'm right, I'm right, I know it!'

It was Kath's turn to look like the cat with the cream as

one by one she ticked off further serial numbers that matched the money seized from Kenneth Boyle. She gave Jane a big hug and did a small sashay dance to DCI Bradfield's office and in her excitement forgot to knock before walking in.

'Get out, Morgan,' he bellowed and she saw that he was with DI Spencer Gibbs having a celebratory whisky over his reinstatement to normal duties.

'This is really important, sir. I think I may have found Julie Ann's killer.'

Jane finished the few bits she had left to do and was about to make her way down to the front office when she stopped to look at the photographs of Julie Ann pinned to the board on the wall. She stared at the beautiful face of the young girl before she had become addicted to heroin. The picture next to it, taken at the post-mortem, was covered by a piece of paper which Jane lifted back to reveal Julie Ann's drug-ravaged body. The marks on her neck were horrific, but her bulging eyes and swollen tongue caused by the strangulation were the most sickening sight. Jane hoped Kath was right about Boyle. Whoever had done this to Julie Ann deserved to be caught and put away for a very long time.

Jane shook herself and went downstairs. She found Sergeant Harris who, apologizing, said he needed her to continue covering the front desk. She knew he was deliberately making her do it, but was determined not to show any of the antagonism she felt towards him.

She simply smiled. 'Yes, of course, Sergeant Harris.'

He had never mentioned the recovered money and Jane's property-store lists; in fact since the incident he had been surprisingly polite when speaking to her, which made her feel even more suspicious. Jane wondered if he was just biding his time before doing something else to try to make her look bad.

An hour passed with no one attending the station counter and Jane was feeling quite bored. She sat down at the desk and remembering DS Gibbs's advice at the squat raid started to read the weekly published 'General Orders and Regulations'. She'd just become engrossed by a list giving details of which officers had been sacked or fined for misconduct when the front-desk phone rang. Jane picked it up, asking how she could help the caller. She listened as someone on the other end with a squeaky voice rambled on, not letting her get a word in.

She took the phone from her ear, held her hand over the mouthpiece and turned to Sergeant Harris who was sitting at the duty desk typing up a report.

'Sarge, I don't know if I should take this call seriously or not.'

'We take every call seriously, Tennison – what's it about?'

'Sounds weird ... he said something about picking up a conversation on his radio at home about a robbery.'

Sergeant Harris pursed his lips.

'Well, that's a new one on me, bloody time-waster – give it here.'

He got up from his desk and went over to Jane who handed over the phone.

'This is Duty Sergeant William Harris. Please slow down, son, if you'd just ...'

Jane smiled, realizing Harris was having the same difficulty understanding the caller.

He shook his head and raised his eyebrows. 'Just you listen up, son. Unfortunately we have had a serious incident that requires every officer's urgent attention. Please call back later.'

He put down the phone.

'I thought we took all calls seriously?' Jane said, wondering if she was chancing her luck with a flippant remark.

'Not with squeaky nutters, we don't.'

The door to the charge room opened. Gibbs walked out and crooked his finger to Jane.

'If I find out that lipstick joke is anything to do with you, you'll be sorry.'

'I don't know what you are talking about, Sarge,' Jane said.

'Yeah, neither did Kath, but I'll find out, I'll bloody find out.'

'What was he talking about?' Harris asked.

Jane shrugged. 'I don't know, Sergeant.'

DS Gibbs went to speak with Bradfield while Kath booked Boyle in at the station. Bradfield had moved fast after Kath had explained about the money and a paddy wagon had been sent to Brixton Prison to collect Boyle and bring him back to the station. Boyle had asked Gibbs, who was accompanying him, why he was being taken back to Hackney and Gibbs had replied that there were more break-ins they needed to speak to him about.

'He was really edgy and sweating. I made up a couple of addresses and he said he'd broken in and nicked money from them. Kath Morgan was spot on. He's definitely hiding something if he's confessing to crimes that don't exist.'

'Who's his brief?' Bradfield asked.

'Like last time, doesn't want one. Might change his mind when he finds out why he's really here.'

'Fuck him if he does. I'll get the files together, you bring Boyle up and tell Kath Morgan she can sit in on the interview with you and me.'

Ten minutes later Gibbs and Kath brought Boyle into Bradfield's office, sat him down and removed his handcuffs. He was unshaven, his face covered in acne, and nasty boils were visible on his neck above the prison-issue shirt. Bradfield got up and stood beside Boyle, placing a photograph of Julie Ann down on the table in front of him.

'Do you recognize this woman?' Bradfield asked quietly, leaning over so his face was close to Boyle's.

Boyle didn't answer.

'Kenneth Boyle, I am arresting you for the murder of Julie Ann Collins. You are not obliged to say anything, but what you say may be given in evidence.'

Boyle wiped his sweaty brow with his nicotine-stained fingers and was about to say something when Bradfield interrupted him.

'You refused a solicitor when DS Gibbs asked if you wanted one so don't even think about changing your mind or I'll write your confession myself.'

Bradfield opened his desk drawer and put a plastic property bag containing bundles of bank-wrapped £1, £5 and £10 notes on the table. When asked Boyle admitted they were some of the notes recovered from his home and said that he'd stolen them from a pensioner.

'Well, Kenny, I've had the notes checked for the murdered girl's fingerprints, and guess what – they're on some of them. One print is right next to yours. So if you know what's good for you I suggest you tell me exactly how they came to be in your possession?'

Boyle refused to look at Bradfield and shuffled his feet.

'Erm yeah, I did meet her and she give me the money,

365

right? She told me to get her some heroin, I mean what I said was I could score for her, right?'

'Right! So who's your dealer, Kenneth?'

'Er well, I dunno his name, but I seen him passing gear on the streets, right? I mean I dunno where he lives, that's the God's truth, sir.'

Kath crossed her legs as she watched the repellent Boyle attempt to lie his way out of anything to do with the murder. Bradfield concentrated on his notebook, tapping it with his pencil.

'I mean on my mother's life, the last time I saw her was after she give me the money. She said to meet up with her outside the hospital, well, I couldn't find this dealer so I went to tell her and she never showed up.'

Bradfield nodded his head and then picked up a pencil sharpener and began to twist his pencil round and round in it.

Kath was fascinated by how Bradfield deliberately changed his attitude towards Boyle, making it appear he believed him, encouraging him by accepting his story, and constantly nodding his head saying he understood how difficult it would be for Boyle to name his dealers.

'Right, that's right, but I swear before God that's what I intended doing, scoring drugs for her.'

'Yeah, I understand. I mean she was just a common little slag. She'd open her legs for drugs, right?'

'Yeah, she fucked anyone, even the blacks. She was a tart all right.'

Bradfield paused then spoke quietly. 'But she wouldn't screw you, would she?' he asked without any trace of emotion.

It was as if Bradfield had hit a raw nerve as Boyle pursed his lips.

'Yeah, I mean she was a slag, right? And she got this posh way of talkin', lookin' down on me.'

'That must have really pissed you off.'

Boyle nodded, and then Bradfield slowly pushed the photograph of Julie Ann closer.

'She deserved what she got.'

Kath watched as there was a glance between Bradfield and Gibbs, who had so far not spoken. Gibbs now leaned forwards, jabbing Boyle with his finger.

'She'd fuck anyone else but you, because you are a stinking little no-good thief. She told you to piss off, you got riled and decided you were gonna show this slag that nobody like her could refuse you and you made a grab for her ...'

Bradfield patted Gibbs's arm and he sat back. 'Easy, Spence, that wasn't how it happened, was it, Kenneth? Yes, you put your hands up for nicking from pensioners, and you owned up to the Magistrate. But this was different: she was lovely and you knew what she was, but that didn't matter, did it?'

'I don't go out with toms,' Boyle said, shaking his head.

'Oh come on, Kenneth, you liked her – and you'd got money now, all that cash you nicked. Did you offer to pay her?' Bradfield asked, and moved Julie Ann's photograph closer.

Gibbs leaned forwards again. 'Shit, you were gonna pay to screw her and she still turned you down? That must have fucked your head, cos you knew she was a slag, knew everyone else was getting it.'

'No.' Boyle's face twisted.

Bradfield slid in his next question. 'When did you know about the money she had? I don't believe she'd give you cash for drugs as she already had her own dealer.'

Boyle was so thick he couldn't see how Bradfield and Gibbs were playing with his head and there was a hideous pause as Boyle stared at the floor and constantly scratched his raw acne.

He wouldn't look up. 'She dropped her purse and—'

'Oh I see, she dropped her purse and you picked it up?'

Gibbs cut in. 'You ripped her blouse open and pulled off her bra so you could fondle her tits, but she resisted and you went ape and strangled her with her own bra.'

Still Boyle said nothing, but from the look of self-pity on his face Bradfield knew he and Spencer Gibbs had got it right about what happened in the kids' adventure playground. Gibbs replaced the picture of Julie Ann before she started taking drugs with the one of her body at the playground.

'That's what you did to her, you murdered her and then stole her money. Look at the photograph, see her eyes and tongue? Remember them bulging out as you squeezed the life out of her, can you? LOOK AT IT!' he shouted.

Boyle swiped at the table, and the photographs slid onto the floor as he started crying.

Bradfield leant over and patted Boyle's back. 'Come on, now, son, calm down. Take us through what happened, Kenneth. You'll feel better once you get it off your chest. Just tell us what happened because I know you never meant to hurt her.'

Bradfield waited as Gibbs collected the photographs and stacked them like a pack of cards.

'You got a tissue, WPC Morgan?'

Kath delved into her pocket and passed over a clean tissue. Bradfield handed it to Kenneth who blew his nose and then began to knead the sodden tissue.

'It was night-time and I saw her on a swing in the kids'

playground by the Kingsmead Estate. I went over to her, she stopped and looked me up and down and I told her I'd seen her around lots of times, even talked to her once, but she ignored me and said to go away. I tried to talk to her more and was being nice but then she told me to piss off as she was waiting for someone. But I guessed it was for a punter so I said I had money to pay her for sex and she laughed at me. She got off the swing and started to walk away so I touched her shoulder and asked her to stay. Next thing I knew she turned round and spat at me, she gobbed at me right in my face. She dropped her bag and bent over to pick it up and I dunno, I just went crazy – dragged her to the ground and got on top of her.' He started crying again.

'I know it must be horrible for you to recall it all, son, but you're doing well and it's almost over, so keep going,' Bradfield said, urging him to confess.

'Oh Christ, I dunno how it happened. I put one hand over her mouth then ripped her shirt open and pulled at her bra which came undone, then she bit my hand and when I pulled it away from her mouth she started to scream. I was scared someone would hear her and in a panic I put the bra round her neck and shit, I didn't mean it, but I kept on pulling it tighter and tighter ...'

He sobbed, using his hands to show how he had pulled the bra, crossing his wrists as it tightened round her neck, and then tightened it in a knot.

'I got scared and ran off with her bag. It wasn't for the money, I swear before God it wasn't for the money. I didn't know how much she had until I got home.'

Jane went to the ladies' locker room to hang up her uniform jacket before going off duty. She saw an upset-looking Kath sitting on a bench and hesitated before going over to ask if she was all right.

'Yeah, Kenneth Boyle just confessed to killing Julie Ann. It was so sickening listening to him go over it all. He's being charged now by DS Gibbs and will appear at the Magistrates' Court in the morning. It's weird, I just want to cry. But I tell you, Bradfield's a cool bastard. Just as I thought he was feeling sorry for the pathetic little shit, he laid it on him that he also killed the kid she was expecting. His voice was harsh and you could tell he loathed Boyle. Gibbs is the same, they kind of do a double act, but they got him to admit everything, no big drama it was just ...' She sighed. 'It wasn't making me feel good, which I honestly believed it would, you know, getting closure, but all I could really think of was what a waste of life. Anyway this time he won't get banged up for months, he'll be there for twenty-five years at least.'

Back in her room at the section house Jane couldn't stop thinking about what Kath had said about the waste of life. By the time she had got undressed and was ready to take a shower, she didn't feel like having anything to eat, or God forbid, going to the pub or sitting in one of the TV rooms.

Lying down on her bed, she found herself thinking of Bradfield and his remark 'Chance would be a fine thing'. Did he mean that he expected an approach by him to be rejected? She curled up and tucked her hands under her chin. At the beginning of the investigation she hadn't been impressed by his manner but now she knew she was infatuated and even in awe of him. Over and over again she had been surprised by him: the time she had seen him gently touch the dead girl's foot, his kindness at the

Collinses' house before he knew about their daughter's beating, how, drunk outside the pub, he'd told her that he felt as if they were the only ones who cared.

She remembered, too, all the odd things he had said to her, unsure if they were complimentary or not. She curled up tighter because now, lying alone in her room, she had to admit to herself that she hoped that he did like her.

Give me just a little bit of your heart now, baby …

CHAPTER TWENTY-TWO

Crossing the station yard to prepare for the early shift parade at 6 a.m., Jane was startled to see a disgruntled Sergeant Harris carrying a large black bin bag.

'Morning, Sergeant,' she said overbrightly.

'Bradfield's lot had a big booze-up in the CID office last night. The cleaner was refusing to deal with the mess until I offered to help, so I've had to schlep out these ruddy beer cans and bottles. Christ only knows how much they all put away, but I heard someone had to carry WPC Morgan to a taxi.'

'Can I help?'

'No, it's done. You can go out on foot patrol today, seven beat covering Shoreditch on the far end of the ground.'

'Can I get a panda car to drop me off?' Jane was surprised, yet pleased that Harris was letting her out on patrol for once.

'No, bloody well walk or get a bus. There's an outstanding call from last night on that beat so get the details from the control room.'

Jane spoke with the PC who was manning the phones and radios. It transpired the call had come in at midnight, but as it was very busy no one was available to attend and the disgruntled caller was told someone would visit him in the morning. The PC handed Jane a copy of the message and said the night-shift operator had told him the caller had some information about a possible robbery. Jane asked why the CID weren't dealing with it and the PC said the caller had a squeaky voice and sounded 'a sandwich short of a picnic'. Jane guessed it was the same person Harris had put the phone down on the day before. She looked at the caller's details. His name was Ashley Brennan and he lived in Hoxton Street. Gathering up her things, she booked out a Storno radio and put it in her handbag before heading off to catch the bus.

There was a faint drizzle and Jane was wearing her police-issue cape to keep herself dry. She laughed as she recalled the night shift on patrol when she and Kath had eaten fish and chips under their capes so no one could see.

She reached the terraced row of new, expensive-looking flats, and checked she had the correct address before pressing the buzzer for the Brennan flat. She waited a while and, when there was no answer, pressed again. A distorted female voice asked if she was delivering groceries. Jane gave her name and rank, then there was a crackle and whistling sound. Unsure if she had been heard she was about to repeat herself when the door clicked open.

Jane walked up the four flights of carpeted stairs and took a few moments to get her breath back before knocking on the door. She noticed there was a mezuzah screwed to the doorframe. The front door was opened by a small, overweight woman in her mid-forties wearing a floral blouse and grey pleated skirt with pink slippers.

'Mrs Brennan?' Jane asked, guessing she was Ashley's mother.

The woman gave her a quizzical, confused look. 'Thought you were our grocery boy. I was expecting an early delivery.'

'Mrs Brennan?' Jane asked again.

The woman pressed her finger to her right ear and Jane heard a high-pitched whistling sound.

'I'm very deaf, what do you want?'

Realizing that she was wearing a hearing aid, Jane spoke loudly and slowly.

'I am WPC Jane Tennison from Hackney Police Station and I'd like to speak to Ashley Brennan.'

Mrs Brennan called out Ashley's name and said that a policewoman was here to see him, but there was no reply. She let Jane into the comfortable-looking flat. She knocked on a closed door.

'Ashley, come out of your room – there's a policewoman here who wants to talk to you.'

'ABOUT TIME, LET HER IN.'

'She is in, dear.'

'I MEAN IN MY ROOM.'

Jane recognized the squeaky voice coming from the room as the one from the previous morning's phone call. Mrs Brennan opened the door and gestured for Jane to go in.

'Do you want me to come in with her?'

'No,' Ashley said.

Jane eased past Mrs Brennan, who was pressing her hearing aid and causing it to whistle again.

'I'm expecting some groceries.'

'Go away, Mother.'

'He doesn't have many visitors. Is it about my disabled parking?'

'GO AWAY, MOTHER.'

Ashley Brennan was sitting at a large wooden desk on a specially adapted swivel chair, which had a head rest, thick padded arms and an extra wide-cushioned seat. He was obese – at least twenty stone – and had a huge protruding stomach and thick fat arms, but tiny feminine hands. His size made him look much older than Jane suspected he actually was. He wore a cotton T-shirt and baggy tracksuit trousers, and as he swivelled round to face Jane she noticed he had small feet encased in embroidered slippers.

On the desk there was a telephone, filing tray, jeweller's-type magnifying glass, tweezers, soldering iron and bits and pieces of wire lying around next to an electrical circuit board of some sort. Behind him, on top of a long wooden cabinet, there were two reel-to-reel tape-recording machines and two large pieces of electrical equipment with numerous dials and yellow-coloured arrow meters. Jane suspected they were radios of some sort, but only because they were attached to a large aerial hanging out of the window.

'She's as deaf as a post,' he said.

Ashley had a yarmulke perched on the back of his head and his hair was thick and dark, parted to one side and oiled flat, but rather strangely he had a handsome face with dark eyes and a small nose.

'I'd like to see your identification, please.'

'But I'm in uniform.'

'You can never be too careful.'

Jane opened her shoulder bag and handed him her warrant card which he inspected and handed back. He invited her to pull over the chair that was next to his single bed and said she could use one of his pillows as a cushion.

She declined the offer of the pillow, picked up the chair, and sat opposite him.

'I have to say it's about time someone took me seriously. I have called so many times, and to all the local stations. I was thinking about calling Scotland Yard or writing an official complaint to the Commissioner about it.'

She sat poised with her notebook and pencil ready, assuring him that as a police officer and employee of the Commissioner she was there in an official capacity and would treat anything he told her seriously.

'Before we start can I just have your full name, age and date of birth for the record, please, Ashley?' Jane asked.

'Ashley, no middle names, and my surname is Brennan. Aged twenty and born 20.6.52.'

'You're nearly twenty-one then,' Jane remarked.

He opened his desk drawer and took out a large diary then swivelled round in his chair and pointed to the radio equipment.

'The one on the left is an RCA AR88, renowned for its performance and reliability as a surveillance and intercept radio during the Second World War. Works on six bands and uses fourteen tubes in a double preselection super-heterodyne circuit ... which I have modified to listen to the radio channels as well. The one next to it I'm very proud of as I built it myself. It's an SSB transceiver with silicon transistors and Plessey integrated circuits.'

The high-pitched voice she had recognized was even more obvious as Ashley needed to take short breaths between sentences.

Jane wished he'd get to the point of why he'd called the police, but she didn't want to offend him further by showing a lack of interest.

'And the bits on the desk, is that your latest creation?' she asked, hoping he wouldn't go into too much detail.

He looked at her as if she'd asked a silly question. 'No, it's the circuit board and bits for my mother's bedside radio that went on the blink. It's obvious I'm fixing it.'

Jane asked politely if he could move on to exactly why he wanted to speak with a police officer, and poised her pen ready to write in her notebook.

'I inadvertently picked up the transmission using the RCA when I was trying to tune into a station. At first I thought it was radio hams messing about, but the other night I became really concerned about their conversation. One was using the call sign Eagle and referred to the other as Brushstroke. Eagle said, "Stay quiet, it's a rozzer," which of course I knew was another name for one of you lot. Then there was a loud, metal-type banging sound and Eagle got quite panicky saying the rozzer was looking in the café window, but they seemed to relax when he'd gone. I've a list of dates and times for everything I recorded on my reel-to-reel.'

Jane stopped writing and looked up at him. 'Sorry, did you say recorded?'

'Yes, I like to record radio programmes and listen to the ones I enjoy again. This was different, very suspicious with no names used, and they were not trained in radio etiquette as sometimes after saying "over" they continued to speak instead of waiting for a reply.' He gasped and coughed.

Jane asked if he was able to determine the area that the transmission came from and he snapped impatiently that it could be a one- to two-mile radius, which in terms of London covered a lot of possible locations. He then detailed all the times he had overheard the conversations and said he had joined all the recordings together so the police could listen to the complete tape without changing reels.

Jane asked him to play back the last bit he had recorded about the rozzer looking in the café. It was difficult for her to hear clearly and make out exactly what was said as the voices were muffled and there was some interference, which Ashley explained was due to him moving the receiver dial to try and get a better signal.

Jane's concentration was interrupted by the front-door buzzer and Mrs Brennan shouting loudly on the intercom to ask if it was the grocery delivery.

The recording finished and Ashley swivelled round to face her.

'I am aware bits of the tape are not that clear, but I have listened to it over and over and have typed up what was said for you. Admittedly they never mention the word "bank", or for that matter "robbery", but look at the times these men are working – never in the day, always through the night, and then there's the banging sound which could be digging. "Eagle" I presume is surveying the place they are working from, and why so anxious when the policeman turned up outside the café? I am correct in my suspicions, aren't I?'

Jane closed her notebook and thought about how best to phrase her reply, as from what she'd heard she couldn't agree with him entirely.

'You may well be right, Mr Brennan, but I need to report this to the CID as it is something I as a WPC would not be allowed to investigate further. I'd like to take the tape and your notes of the conversation back to the station—'

He interrupted. 'I suggest, WPC Tennison, you do just that as I believe these men are committing a robbery, and you may already be too late to stop them.'

Ashley promptly placed the tape and notes in a large

envelope which already had his name and address on it. He licked and sealed the flap and then signed his name, the date and time across the seal. He heaved himself out of the chair, his balloon-shaped body wobbled and even the exertion of standing brought him out in a sweat. As he handed over the envelope Jane thanked him and shook his hand, apologizing if he felt they had not taken his initial phone call seriously. She assured him everything would now be passed on to a high-ranking CID officer.

'Good, I'll wait to hear of any developments and continue to monitor the situation on the AR88, but I lost contact last time so I may not be able to report any further conversations. My mother will show you out now.'

He tottered to stand beside his desk and pressed a buzzer, which made a shrill ringing sound, and then he eased himself back into his chair.

'Can I ask, Mr Brennan, are you a radio ham yourself?'

He glared at her. 'I most certainly am not. I only receive signals and never transmit. The microphone came with the equipment and is now purely for decoration purposes.'

Jane smiled. She knew he was lying and probably didn't have an operator's licence, but liked to listen to pirate radio just as she did. He had done the right thing by calling the police so she didn't press the matter any further.

Jane let herself out of his stiflingly hot room and saw Mrs Brennan standing in the hallway.

'I'm a bit deaf and my hearing aid's always playing up so he rings that bell when he needs me,' she said in a raised voice.

'Ashley could maybe fix it for you.'

'What did you say, my dear?'

'Never mind,' Jane said, and noticed the numerous boxes of groceries in the hallway. From one glance she knew the pancake mixes, cakes and buns were destined for the woman's son.

'He never leaves the flat. If we had a lift it might help. I have a little invalid car the NHS gave me to get about in, but it's only three wheels and one seat so I can't take him out in that. Our rabbi comes to see him when he can, but he's got a bad hip and can't manage all those stairs.'

Jane thanked her and skirting round the groceries left the flat. Walking back to the bus stop she wondered if Ashley could be right about a possible bank robbery, but doubted that the men would actually discuss it on the radio. Still, she'd have to report it to Bradfield now, although given the vagueness of the information, she didn't look forward to telling him.

The station was busy on her return at 10 a.m. as all the CID, desk officers and station clerical staff were in. It was time for her allocated refreshment break and during it Jane decided she would finish writing up her notes and then speak with DCI Bradfield. As chance would have it she'd just finished her porridge when he walked into the canteen looking the worse for wear after a heavy night celebrating.

As Bradfield approached Jane blushed slightly remembering her thoughts about him the night before.

'We got him! Kenneth Boyle made a full confession to Julie Ann Collins' murder and has been remanded in custody by the Magistrates' Court to await trial, which will probably be in at least eighteen months' time.' Bradfield was jubilant and Jane didn't tell him she'd already spoken with Kath.

'That's great, sir. How have Mr and Mrs Collins taken the news?'

'They're both distraught, but relieved they know what happened. The sad thing is that Mr Collins still blames himself for their daughter's death.'

Thinking she'd take advantage of Bradfield's good mood, Jane asked if she could have a word with him about another matter, which she was concerned about. He sighed and checked his watch.

She briefly recounted her conversation with Ashley Brennan and explained that, although he was a bit of an eccentric radio nerd, she felt there might be a robbery occurring, or about to happen.

He yawned. 'Where?'

'I don't know, sir, but it's possible the suspects are in a café that may be close to a bank and they could be attempting to break their way in.' Jane held up the envelope with the tape and notes.

'Ashley Brennan recorded the radio conversations and made a number of calls to the police which were ignored. I mean, what if he's right, we would—'

'All right, give it here and Spence and I will listen to it. There's a reel-to-reel player somewhere in the property store, so go and get that out while I look at the nerd's report.'

Jane tracked down the tape recorder. It was big and heavy so she asked DS Gibbs to help her carry it up the stairs to Bradfield's office.

'You missed a good celebration last night. I got so plastered the bastards locked me in an empty cell to sleep it off. Mind you, the state Kath Morgan was in was something else – singing and dancing on the tables.'

Having placed the tape machine on Bradfield's desk and plugged it in Bradfield asked Jane to get him and Gibbs a coffee and a ham sandwich each. Gibbs said he couldn't face food yet and a coffee would do, but Bradfield said to get Gibbs a ham sandwich as well. On her return to his office Bradfield was reading the notes Brennan had made.

'What's this Ashley bloke like?'

She described him as he sipped his coffee and ate his sandwich, whilst Spencer sat head down and unusually motionless in one of the hard-backed chairs.

'Sit down, Tennison. You want your sandwich, Spence?'

Gibbs frowned as he lit up a cigarette. 'I'll throw up if I eat anything.'

Jane sat down opposite Bradfield. He placed the transcription made by Ashley Brennan in front of him and said he wanted to follow the typed copy against the spoken words on the tape to see if they matched. Jane asked if he'd mind her reading over his shoulder and he said not at all. Standing beside him she lowered her head to read the transcript and noticed again how nice his cologne smelt. He switched on the tape machine. It was turned up very loud and although distorted in some places Jane listened more intently than before and something began to bother her. No one said a word or reacted in any way whilst they listened to the end of the tape.

Bradfield sat back in his chair and put his hands behind his head. 'What Brennan has typed up seems to fit with all the conversation on the tape. It's possible something is going down. Did Brennan have any idea of a location?' he asked Jane.

'He lives in Hoxton and reckons anywhere within a two-mile radius.'

Gibbs snorted. 'That's right next to the bloody City. There's loads of banks around there, not to mention soddin' cafés, so it'll be like looking for a needle in a haystack, Tennison.'

'Eagle could be a lookout and Brushstroke a decorator or something like that so ...' Jane said hesitantly.

'The information that it is a bank is not reliable. It could be a pedigree-pet shop for all we know!' Gibbs muttered.

'Right, you can go finish your early shift now, Tennison. Let me have a think about the tapes,' Bradfield said, and sat back to finish his sandwich.

Jane felt disheartened as he didn't seem that interested. She walked to the door, then hesitated.

'Should I type up a report?'

'Yes, you do that.'

As the door closed behind her, Gibbs got up to stretch and said he was still feeling hungover.

'Sit down, Spence, we need to take another look over this Brennan stuff.'

'You are joking? He's a weirdo and there's nothing in those tapes that rings real alarm bells for me.'

Bradfield lit a cigarette, and inhaled deeply before he continued.

'There are two possibilities here, Spence. One, Brennan's telling the truth, the tape is real and something big is going down.'

Gibbs laughed. 'I know you don't believe that.'

'Two, he could be trying it on, faking it to get his name in the papers and make a few quid, sort of like a—'

Gibbs butted in. 'Well, that sounds more like a nutter to me, Len.'

'Let me finish, will you? It could be a sort of copycat for the job that went down back in September '71. It was headline news for months and then some kind of government gagging order was made and it all went quiet.'

'What "job" you talkin' about?'

'You've a short memory, Spence. Big robbery – they got away with five hundred grand from a bank in Baker Street.'

'Shit, wait a minute, you're talkin' about that radio ham that heard the robbers and reported it. Yeah, it's comin' back now, the hangover was making me brain cells flat-line.'

Bradfield clicked his fingers. 'It was a Lloyds bank, and I'm thinking the ham guy was called, shit, lemme think, I know, Robert Rankin, Rawlins, no, Rowland – that was his name. The press headlined it as the "Walkie-talkie" bank robbery, you remember it now?'

Gibbs nodded. 'Yeah yeah, but it's obvious this kid Ashley Brennan is just trying it on, maybe even got his mates to help fake the tape?'

'Possible, but we are gonna have to check it all out, because if the tape is for real and we ignore it then we could all look like a bunch of pricks.'

'We'll also look like idiots if we waste time and energy trying to prove what we already know, that he's a lying geek.'

They both turned to the door as Jane tapped and popped her head in.

'I'm sorry, sir, but I was about to start work on the report and something kept worrying me. Would it be possible for me to hear the tape again?'

'Don't worry, we are going to check out its authenticity,' Bradfield said looking at Gibbs who rolled his eyes.

'I'm sorry, sir, but can you please play it again? It's very important,' Jane asked nervously.

Bradfield looked at Gibbs. 'She wants to hear it all again, Spence,' he said sarcastically and Gibbs shrugged his shoulders.

Bradfield fiddled with the rewind switch and swore as he failed to stop it before the tape flapped loose from one of the reels.

'Shit, hang on, lemme get it back on the bloody thing.'

'It's the bit where Brushstroke says something like "Get out, piss against the wall" and ends "I'm calling it a night now".'

Bradfield fumbled with the tape. 'Just let me fast-forward.'

He was so cack-handed that Gibbs took over and then, with the tape in place and fast-forwarded, he pressed play. Jane stood beside them listening then asked for it to be played again.

A bemused Bradfield looked at her. 'Why?'

'I could be wrong, but I really need to hear it again.'

As Bradfield rewound the tape and replayed it he and Gibbs looked at each other both shaking their heads wondering what on earth she had picked up on.

'I think I recognize the voice,' she said quietly, and both men turned to face her in unison.

'You are joking?' Spencer said.

'I may be wrong, but I think that Brushstroke is John Bentley. The reason I remember his voice is because of the way he shouted at me to get out of the flat the time I took his mother home.' She was trying to keep her voice steady.

Bradfield put his arm around her shoulders. 'OK, just calm down – listen to it again, but you need to be bloody sure about this.'

Gibbs looked annoyed. 'What were you doin' with John Bentley's mother? Are you friends with the family?'

Bradfield waved his hand for Gibbs to shut up.

'Take your time, Jane. We can play it over a few times if it will help.' He reached for Brennan's log and skimmed down the times listed before pointing out that all the conversations had taken place late at night through to the early hours of the morning.

'Seems like this Brennan kid never goes to sleep.'

'I doubt it. He's very overweight. Never goes out.'

'Play it one more time, Spence.'

The three listened as the last section was replayed, and then Bradfield rewound the tape. After a pause Jane bit her lips with nerves.

'I'm sure it is John Bentley. He scared me and that's why I remember his voice.'

'Well, seems this Ashley Brennan may be right about a bank job so I want a surveillance team on standby. If Bentley's involved we can tail him from his mum's home then see what he's up to, and who with.'

Jane was feeling very nervous as Bradfield yet again put his arm around her shoulders, trying to give her encouragement.

'Listen one more time: we'll play the whole tape again just to be a hundred per cent sure. If you're right we've got a good lead that we'd never have had without you recognizing his voice.'

'How old is this Ashley Brennan?' Gibbs asked.

'He's twenty, well, nearly twenty-one,' Jane replied.

'Jesus Christ, Len, are you taking this all seriously and ramping up a job on a few taped conversations made by a kid nutter? I mean it could be fuckin' anyone doing house renovations. Before we start organizing surveillance why not check the kid out to see if he's for real first?' a fed-up Gibbs said petulantly.

'He said that he had lost contact the last time – something about moving the aerial and he might not be able to make any further recordings.'

'Terrific, so there's no point going back to him, right?' Gibbs stubbed out his cigarette.

'Come on, Spence, loosen up. Since when do decorators use codenames and a lookout with a walkie-talkie? Yeah, I am taking this seriously, Spence. Years back I was on the arrest of the Bentleys. Clifford the dad, along with his sons John and David, were nicking lead off a church roof. David jumped Christ knows how far down off the roof and broke both legs. Clifford Bentley's a real hard case who worked with the Krays. He's in Pentonville nick for armed robbery. They're tough bastards, that family.'

'So if you nicked him don't you recognize his voice?'

'It was bloody years ago.'

Gibbs shrugged his shoulders as the tape was set up again. Jane was clenching her hands tightly as the tape was played from the beginning to the end. There was a pause as Bradfield switched off the tape and looked at her.

'Yes, I think it's him.'

'Need more than just "I think", Jane.'

'Too bloody right we do, because this kid Brennan could be a wanker just wanting to get his name in the papers,' Gibbs retorted.

'I don't think so. He seemed quite intelligent to me.'

Bradfield looked angry. 'I don't care about the kid ... Is it John Bentley's voice or not?'

She slowly nodded her head. 'All right, yes, I am certain that's John Bentley's voice.'

CHAPTER TWENTY-THREE

Renee guessed where her husband was going as the bathroom stank of his splashed-on aftershave and he'd put on a freshly ironed shirt, new trousers and well-polished shoes. She knew he wasn't going to the pub for a 'dinner time tipple' as he had claimed. He had to be going to see the slut, but Renee wasn't concerned and showed no interest or contempt, not even asking what time she could expect him home. If he was late for his dinner she'd just leave it on top of the kitchen table with a plate over it and he could then reheat it in the oven. But she was concerned about David as he was still in bed, and from the coughing and sneezing coming from his room she worried he was coming down with bronchitis.

John got up for some dinner at two o'clock and, still in his dressing gown, sat at the kitchen table eating his food and reading the paper. Renee asked why he didn't fancy joining his dad for a pint and John said lamely that dinner time boozing made him tired for the rest of the day.

She noticed his hair was dusty and brushed it lightly with her hand. 'Your hair needs a good wash. Is it cement?'

He flicked her hand away and she could see how dirty his fingernails were.

'Gerroff, Ma. I've been stripping plaster at mine and the dust gets everywhere.'

She shrugged her shoulders. God forbid he'd ever get a paintbrush out and do her flat up, she thought to herself.

'Doing your place up with the intention of moving back in, are yer?' she asked hopefully.

He sighed and although irritated made no reply, but she persisted.

'She movin' out or are the two of you getting back together?'

'Drop it, Ma.'

She could see she was riling him so stayed quiet and warmed up some soup, which she took through to David's bedroom with some bread and butter. She fluffed his pillow as he sat up and took the tray.

'You stay in bed. I think you're coming down with a bad cold. I'll get the thermometer and check your temperature.'

'I'm fine, Ma, and thanks for the soup. Are Dad and John in?'

'Your dad's gone out all done up to the nines, and John's in the kitchen eating dinner covered in dust. Says he's decorating his place, which means he's either going back with her or he's kicked her out and he's moving some new tart in.'

David was unsure what she was talking about as she started to pick up the clothes he'd worn that night from the floor.

'Leave it Ma, I'll tidy it later.'

'You're not well, son, so you rest and leave it to me.'

She put his T-shirt, jeans and underpants over her arm. Lifting his long johns she could see they were dry but urine-stained around the crotch. Knowing he often had accidents when he couldn't get to the toilet quickly enough she said nothing about it.

'What you wearin' long johns for? It's not that cold out.'

David ignored her and opened his bedside cabinet, took out his bottle of painkillers then tipped out four and swallowed them with a spoonful of his soup.

'You be careful, you'll get addicted to them, son.'

He winced as he rested against his pillow.

'I'll be all right, my back's just playing up. I wear me long johns for the warm, helps the pain. Thanks for the soup and bread, but I can't finish it all.'

'I notice your chair's not in the hall – is something wrong with it, cos you know if you walk too much it affects your back and leg, so where is it?'

'It's in John's van.'

'What van?'

'For goodness' sake, Ma, the one he uses for decorating,' he said, and closed his eyes.

With his dirty clothes over her arm Renee took the tray of half-finished soup and left him to sleep. Returning to the kitchen she put the tray on the counter by the sink and saw John had dumped his dirty dust-stained work overalls by the washing machine. She thought she would maybe take them to the launderette as she didn't want to use her pristine washer and tumbler-drier for workmen's clothes.

Renee went to watch TV in the lounge and with her feet up fell asleep. She woke with a start when she heard the front door slam shut. Dragging herself up, and a little disorientated, she called out to see who was either coming in or going out. There was no answer, and looking round the flat she was surprised that David and John had gone without saying anything, but not surprised that their beds were left unmade as usual. She checked the time: it was just after six thirty. With nothing else to do she went and got her wheelie cart and, having stripped the beds, gathered up the heap of washing left in the kitchen and put it all in the cart. She fetched her purse and left the flat to go to the launderette.

The white surveillance van was parked amongst vehicles on the road directly across from the Pembridge Estate. It was dirty and dented and one side had scrapes and rust. Barely visible were the spy holes on each side. The back windows were blacked out, but not suspicious as the tint had been made to look old and creased with the corners unstuck. The dashboard and interior front area was covered in old beer cans, newspapers and used takeaway cartons. The two officers in the back of the van had been there for almost fifteen minutes under orders from DCI Bradfield to monitor the Bentley men, but they had not seen them exit the flats before they parked up.

Outside the rented garage David was sitting in the passenger seat of the fake decorator's van while John changed into some paint-stained but dust-free overalls and some similarly stained working boots. John loaded the van with more wood to support the tunnel then closed the door of the garage. He got into the van, and as he drove off saw his mother in the distance leaving the estate with her wheelie cart.

'Where the fuck is she going?' he said in anger.

Instead of turning left John went right and, pulling up beside his mother, told David to open his window.

'Where the hell are you going?' he shouted.

Renee turned, startled at first, as she didn't recognize the voice.

'I'm goin' down the launderette wiv the bed sheets, David's clothes and your dirty overalls.'

David gave a small hand-wave to his mother. John pursed his lips.

'For Chrissake, you don't have to go to the launderette any more.'

'Yes I do. Are you off workin'? Cos David should be in bed as he's coming down with a cold.'

Leaning right over David, John wound up the window. He couldn't be bothered to argue with her and angrily crunched the gears as he did a U turn and drove off, not noticing the white surveillance van that was across the road from him.

As the Bentleys drove off, the two officers in the back of the van recognized John from the criminal-record photograph they had with them. One officer in the van, wearing workman's overalls, slid the concealed panel behind the front seats across and got into the driver's seat. Starting the engine he followed the Bentley brothers, keeping a good distance. He radioed to another unit, a male and female officer ready and waiting nearby in the back of a fake black cab.

'Bravo One eyeballed in white decorator's van, index, Juliet, Whisky, Bravo, One, Seven, Six Charlie. Heading North up Homerton High Street carrying white male passenger unknown.'

Seeing the surveillance cab in his wing mirror the officer driving the van held back.

'Two Four take over the tail,' he said over the radio and the cab moved in behind the van.

The surveillance vehicles constantly swapped position behind John Bentley's van, but always kept a car or two between them wherever possible so as not to be spotted.

In Shoreditch High Street the officer in the van radioed to his colleagues.

'Target right into Bateman's Row.' There was a short pause. 'Now left into Curtain Road … Two Five take over.'

'Two Five received,' the female officer in the cab replied and her colleague driving took up position behind the van.

The female officer continued. 'Target right into Great Eastern Street and moving slowly … Target now left, left, left into Charlie Papa.'

The other surveillance vehicles knew the code – the target van had gone into the multistorey car park. The surveillance cab parked up nearby. The male and female officer in the back of the cab got out and stood on a nearby corner holding hands, chatting and acting if they were a loving couple out for a stroll.

A few minutes later the target van drove out from the multistorey car park and turned left. From their position the two officers on foot could only see the rear of the van. The female officer got on the radio as she and her colleague dashed back to the cab.

'Target on move again left out of Charlie Papa, Two Four, you need to follow.'

The surveillance-van driver was parked up nearby and went to move into Great Eastern Street but got stuck behind a learner driver at the junction. By the time he was able to get back onto the main road Bentley's van was nowhere to be seen, and there were a number of roads he could have turned down.

'Two Five to Four, target lost,' he said dejectedly over the radio. Taking a chance he turned down a side road to look for the target vehicle but with no luck.

'Please tell me you're joking?' the now distraught female officer asked over the radio.

'I'm checking the back streets but no eyeball on target.'

'Well, you can explain to the boss you screwed up,' she replied.

'I knew we should have used more vehicles, and if you two hadn't got out on foot this wouldn't have happened.'

The two surveillance vehicles checked every nearby road and narrow lane, but all they found were high brick walls and gated yards that they were unable to see over. Getting out and looking over the walls was not an option. They decided to return to the Pembridge Estate and see if Bentley had driven back there. It never crossed their mind that John Bentley's passenger had been dropped off as they now assumed his turning into the car park was a deliberate ploy to see if any unmarked police vehicles were following him.

High up in his wheelchair David could see the white van going up and down the alleyways through his binoculars. He was in two minds about making contact with the café, but was worried about John getting mad with him for making unnecessary contact. He was relieved, and presumed the driver was lost, when he saw the van turn onto the main road and drive off up Kingsland Road towards Dalston.

As she waited for the drying cycle to finish, Renee read some of the discarded, out-of-date magazines that were lying around. When the drier stopped a woman offered to help her with the sheets, holding one end whilst she held the other, and together they folded all the bed linen. Renee had already put the other washing into her wheelie, and although the two women had hardly spoken to each other they smiled and both said 'Goodnight'. By the time Renee got back to Ashburn House her breath was rasping and the wheelie felt heavier than when she had started out. Climbing the stairs to the flat and heaving the wheelie up each floor tired her out, and she had to keep pausing to catch her breath. The flat was in darkness when she let herself in.

Feeling exhausted Renee made herself a cup of tea and had some biscuits, then decided to press on and make up the beds before the boys got back. Whatever time that would be.

She started on David's bed first. Noticing the mattress was slightly urine-stained in places she decided to turn it over. As she did so she saw newspaper and magazine cuttings hidden beneath it, some of which slid off the divan and onto the floor. Using both hands to balance the mattress on its side she shuffled the rest of the cuttings to the floor with her foot, and heaving some more she eventually succeeded in turning the mattress over. Renee found herself gasping for breath and had to sit down before she could gather the energy to pick up the cuttings. Some were from a travel brochure advertising hotels in Florida, and tucked inside the magazine was an envelope with David's name and address.

She looked inside the envelope and was surprised to find a passport. Opening it she saw that it was David's, and looking at his photograph she realized it was at least seven years old. Also in the envelope was a page from a medical journal, giving details about a hospital in New York City that specialized in orthopaedic surgery and treatment for rheumatological conditions. She was unsure what the medical terms meant but underlined was a reference to the hospital performing knee and joint replacements. It made her feel wretched as her poor son must have at one time hoped for an operation to cure his lameness. She sighed. In his dreams maybe, she thought to herself. She placed everything on the bedside cabinet, and set about making up the bed, tucking the cuttings and envelope back under the mattress after she laid the bottom sheet.

Renee noticed that it was almost eight o'clock and realized that she had not had anything substantial to eat since midday. She started to peel some potatoes for the mash and decided she'd cook the liver in gravy, and put on some frozen peas to go with it as well. She spread some newspaper over the table and got a small plastic bowl, tipped in a few potatoes and sat down to peel them. She always used the same small, sharp knife, cutting the skins off finely and methodically. As she did so she thought about David's cuttings and why he had hidden them. It made her feel depressed as he would never have enough money to get to places like New York, or anywhere in America. David was her favourite son, the handsome one, who had been the most caring and sweet-natured little boy. Now his life was ruined by his awful crippled leg, which was his father's fault. The tears started to trickle down her cheeks and drop into the dirty, potato-stained water as she thought of poor David's wasted life. Then she thought about her own life and wept for herself.

It was dark when Jane was woken by a knock on her door. She panicked, thinking she had slept in and was late for the 6 a.m. early shift. She looked at her bedside clock and was relieved to see it was actually only 9 p.m. Opening the door she saw Sarah in the corridor.

'Hey there, it's Sarah Redhead, and there's a DCI Bradfield in the quiet room who wants to speak to you.'

'Did he say what he wants?' Jane asked, pulling on a pair of jeans and a T-shirt.

'I'm only the messenger, sweetheart. He just said it was important. The old buzzard Sergeant is on the prowl so you'd better go down. God forbid a man's caught on our landing.'

Jane hurried down to the quiet room wondering what was so urgent.

'You wanted to see me?' she asked as she entered the room and saw Bradfield wearing a white raincoat with the collar turned up.

'Please, sit down. I need a quick chat with you about some developments regarding what you told us earlier today. I put a surveillance team on John Bentley. He was driving a white decorator's van that's not registered in his name, but that might be because he hasn't informed DVLC he now owns it so that he avoids paying any road tax or parking fines.'

'Where did he go?' Jane asked with excitement and relief.

'Don't know – they lost him up by a multistorey car park in Great Eastern Street. It's possible he sussed he was being tailed. Anyway, they're sitting on his mum's flat to see if and when he returns. The reason I'm here is because all this is happening as a result of you recognizing his voice on the tape and a lot of East Londoners sound the same so—'

'I am honestly sure it was him on the tape.' She licked her lips nervously.

'OK, he may be up to something, but he could also be working as a legit decorator. He had someone with him, but as yet we don't know who it was, other than a younger-looking white male. We also found out his dad Clifford has just been released from prison.'

'Do you want me to go into the station to type and index the reports?'

397

'Not much point at the moment. There's a shedload of banks in the area where we lost him, and Hatton Garden with all the jewellery shops is just up the road.'

'So do you think Ashley Brennan could be right?'

'Who knows, but we're going to try and find out. However, with the RCA equipment your report said he had, and bearing in mind some enquiries I made about it, he could actually be hearing someone talking in Brighton. We'll start from the point of his flat and work outwards, but even if we schlep all over London we may never pinpoint where the calls were coming in from.'

'Were there any banks near the car park?'

He sighed, irritated. 'Yeah, like I just said, there's loads of them in the area, but none have reported a robbery or anything suspicious.'

'Sorry, I just wondered,' she replied, feeling embarrassed.

He suddenly leaned towards her, staring into her eyes. She blinked rapidly with nerves, and as she swallowed he gently touched her cheek.

'If you are wrong about Bentley's voice then I'm wasting a lot of manpower, time and money.'

Before Jane could reply, the section house sergeant walked in, frowned and said there was an urgent call for Bradfield at the reception desk. Bradfield asked for the call to be transferred through to the sergeant's office so he could talk in private and told Jane to follow him.

Jane waited outside and a few minutes later he came out rubbing his hands together and looking pleased.

'OK, that was DS Gibbs. He's just visited the registered owner of the van Bentley was driving. It was in Kingston and he's a decorator, but surprise, surprise, the bloke's been working locally all day and his van was parked outside. So that means John Bentley's driving a ringer.'

'What's a ringer?' Jane asked.

'Bentley's using copied index plates, so he's probably no decorator.'

Bradfield started to walk away and Jane hesitated, not sure what to do, when he stopped and turned to face her.

'Thanks for your help. I just wanted to make sure I wasn't instigating a wild goose chase, but now with the added info from Spence I think we may be on to something. The lads checking out Great Eastern Street said there's a Trustee Savings Bank next to a café and a tailor's shop nearby that's had a light on all evening, so I'm going there now to check it out.'

'Do you need me with you?'

'No, sweetheart, I'm bringing Kath in as I've put her on acting detective duties. Besides, we gotta make further enquiries. Go and get some sleep as you've got uniform early shift in the morning.'

She felt insulted, as if he was treating her like a child, but he was gone before she had the opportunity to say anything.

Untroubled by events above ground, the frustrated and exhausted threesome in the basement of Silas's café were working harder than ever before. The tunnel was progressing well and was secured with wooden supports.

From his vantage point David could see with his binoculars there were lights on in the tailor's shop near the café. The main window had a curtain pulled across it, so it was impossible for him to see directly inside the shop. A small blue Morris Minor van pulled up outside the tailor's and a short, stumpy-looking bald man got out of the driver's side. He then opened the rear doors and lifted out two armloads of what appeared to be plastic-wrapped dry-cleaning. As he approached the front of the tailor's a woman opened the door and took some of the items from him. A few minutes later the man left in the Morris Minor van and returned half an hour later with another bundle of plastic-wrapped clothes, which he took inside the shop.

David was concerned and pressed the button on his walkie-talkie to make contact with his brother in the café. Silas answered and listened as David told him about the activity outside the tailor's shop, but as it was four shops down he was not unduly worried. John came on the radio and told David to keep contact to a minimum, unless it was something really important.

It was coming up to almost 10 p.m. when David saw a man wearing a baseball cap and raincoat walking arm in arm with a woman along the street. They stopped by the tailor's and the man pressed the bell. After a while he saw the blind on the entrance door lift and the short stumpy man let the couple in before closing the door behind them. It didn't appear suspicious, even at that late hour, and David just assumed it was someone who had arranged a fitting or was picking up some clothes.

However, Mannie Charles, the shop owner, was totally freaked out when DCI Bradfield and Kath Morgan showed their warrant cards and asked to have a chat with him.

Bradfield, in case of a lookout in the vicinity, had parked the unmarked CID car down a side street and walked to Mannie's shop. Bradfield knew who Mannie Charles was, but had never actually met him until now.

'Oy vey, you're giving me heart failure. I done nothing wrong, I swear on my son's life – it's all kosher,' Mannie pleaded nervously as Bradfield followed him in.

Bradfield calmed him down. 'Nothing to do with your business, Mannie. I just want to ask a few questions you might be able to help us with.' He looked around the dimly lit shop which was stacked with rolls of fabric on shelves lining the walls. On the counter there were more rolls of fabric and some swatches, along with two tailor's dummies draped in a pinstriped wool material.

'I've only just collected the suits from the Horne ware-house manager, but I should have all the alterations done by mid-week and ready for delivery,' he said, and pulled out a piece of paper from his pocket before continuing. 'Let's see. Ah, Mr Bradfield, I got you down for dark navy with silk lining, double-breasted and very good quality, a forty chest, thirty-four waist, thirty-six inside leg. Is that right, Mr Bradfield?'

Kath was puzzled, wondering exactly what Mannie was on about as Bradfield smiled and said he had ordered a new suit, but that was not what he had come about.

'My wife's out the back. She's working on the suits I've just brought in. I can fit yours now, make sure it's just right.'

Bradfield said he was sure the suit would be fine and his wife might be able to help with their enquiries, though this just seemed to worry Mannie even more and he said she was a bit of a klutz. The three of them headed through a door with mottled-glass panels which led into the sewing and fitting room. It was larger than the shop front, with a tall window at the back that had brown paper plastered across it and metal security bars. Next to it there was a heavy metal door that was padlocked, which obviously led to the back yard of the premises. Two big electric sewing machines dominated the room, and there were tables and more stacks of wool and linen samples. Mrs Charles, a diminutive woman with a curved back, was sitting by an old-fashioned pedal-operated sewing machine. She peered over the rim of her half-moon glasses as they entered.

'What do vey want?'

Mannie gestured for her to get on with her work. Using a small pair of scissors, she was removing labels from a heap of suit jackets and tossing them into a bin.

'Voz iz the matter, bubbee?' she asked her husband.

Bradfield reassured her. 'Nothing to concern or worry you, Mrs Charles. We're just here to have a chat with Mannie about some suits we want made up,' he said, deciding it was best not to involve her for the time being.

Mannie told his wife to go and make herself a cup of coffee. She took off her glasses and had to clutch the end of the table to stand. She was badly hunched and shuffled her way into a small kitchen area and closed the door.

'OK, Mannie, I'm wondering if you have seen anything suspicious happening around here recently.'

His eyes and mouth widened. 'Like what, Mr Bradfield?'

Bradfield asked if Mannie had seen anyone watching or asking about any of the nearby banks, or heard any sounds that were out of the ordinary, like heavy machinery or digging perhaps. Mannie shook his head.

'Have any of the other shop owners mentioned anything unusual?'

'I don't really have anything to do wiv 'em, Mr Bradfield. I just get on with my business and my customers are mostly regulars that book an appointment for fittings. Passing trade is very poor.'

'Who runs the store on the corner?'

'A bunch of Indian schmucks. They sell electric tools and machinery, but we never talk.'

Bradfield smiled. 'Do you get on with anyone in the street, Mannie?'

'The woman who owns the shoe shop is very nice and bought a coat and matching skirt from me.'

'What about the Greek guy who runs the café?'

'Silas, yes, he's always pleasant and friendly.'

'I take it he bought goods from you as well.'

'No. Why would he wear a suit in a café? He always gives me a little discount, which is kind considering he doesn't do much business apart from the bank staff next door to him. You should try his Greek coffee with a sweet honey and nut baklava. I love it, but the nuts always get stuck in my teeth.'

'Have you heard any noises coming from the café at night – drilling or stuff like that?'

'No, but I don't usually work here late at night. Me and the wife just wanted to get all the detectives' suits done.'

Bradfield asked about the back yards belonging to the shop owners in the street and Mannie told him he rented his out to a carpenter. He was unsure about the others, but as far as he knew most shop owners used them for their vans or storage.

Mrs Charles returned with her coffee in a chipped mug and sat at her sewing machine. She began altering the waist on a pair of suit trousers, and twisted the cloth expertly, working at unbelievable speed.

'Do you have a cellar, Mannie?' Bradfield asked.

Kath waited upstairs with Mrs Charles as Mannie led Bradfield down the narrow stone stairs to a large cellar the size of the entire space of the floor above. Racks of wrapped material were stored amongst cardboard boxes and old sewing machines. The walls were red brick and in many areas worn and in need of repointing. They could hear the sound of Mrs Charles on the sewing machine as it echoed through the floorboards.

Bradfield couldn't see any reason to remain there and asked Mannie to have a chat with his wife and let him know if she could add anything of interest. Walking back into the sewing and fitting room Bradfield saw Kath standing with her arms stretched out and Mrs Charles holding a measuring tape round her chest.

'What you doing, Morgan?'

'Well, now I'm working in the CID as an acting detective, sir, I thought I'd get a nice two-piece skirt suit for work.'

'Do it in your own time, not on the job. We're done here.'

Kath thought this was rather ironic as it was obvious he and a few other detectives were getting new tailored suits, but she said nothing.

Mannie unlocked the front door, and was ushering them out when he tapped Bradfield's arm.

'There is something a bit odd. I mean it might not mean anything, but we've all been given our marching orders by the council as they is going to knock this row of shops down. The leases are up in six months. Me and Mrs Charles can't work from home as the house is small and not big enough for all the materials and sewing stuff, so we looking for a new place to set up business.'

'What's odd about that?' Bradfield asked.

'Well, the Greek café, they got notices up that he's doing refurbishing, so to me it's a waste of good money if the place is gonna be pulled down, understand what I mean?'

Bradfield made no comment about the information, but asked Mannie for an empty suit-bag to be padded out with paper and old useless cut-offs. A puzzled Mannie did as he was asked and Bradfield thanked him for his time. 'We'd appreciate it if you kept quiet about our chat, Mr Charles.'

Mannie nodded. 'Mazel tov, Mr Bradfield – and, Miss Morgan, my wife will have the lady's suit ready for you in good time,' he said, and closed the door.

As Bradfield and Kath walked to the car she said, 'Do ya not want to take a look at the café?'

He put his arm around her shoulders. 'If they got a lookout positioned somewhere round here I don't want them getting suspicious. That's why I asked for an empty suit-bag that looks full – we just move on nice and casual.'

On the way back to the station Kath sat in the passenger seat as Bradfield drove. It was almost midnight: she was really tired and had been in bed suffering from an almighty hangover when they had called her in.

'There was something going on that I thought was rather odd,' she said, yawning.

He turned and frowned at her. 'I know, so that's why we'll check out with the council in the morning about the lease and see what we can get on this Silas geezer.'

'No, it wasn't about the lease, it was Mrs Charles cutting out labels from the suits and binning them. There was another stack of labels next to her with "Mannie Charles" on them.'

He said nothing as he was more concerned about the fact the café was next door to the bank. But he made a mental note to have a word with the detective who had been taking the orders for the suits. He had assumed it was just a few off-the-peg, cut-price Horne Brothers suits for some of the Hackney CID officers, and that Mannie was altering them to size, but judging by the amount of suits in the back room he suspected half of East London's CID were being kitted out and was curious as to why the labels needed to be changed. He sighed to himself as he realized the last thing he needed was A10 breathing down his neck again over a load of hooky suits.

David had watched the couple exit from the tailor's, confident he had been right and they were customers, as the tall man was now carrying a suit-bag. An hour later Mannie and his wife locked up their shop and drove off. David was shivering again with the cold, his back ached and his leg was throbbing. It was going to be yet another long freezing night.

CHAPTER TWENTY-FOUR

'I let you out on the streets and you go stirring up a hornet's nest, which results in Bradfield giving me another dressing down for not taking some nutter's call seriously,' Harris barked at her.

Jane had arrived for early turn the following morning only to find once again she was posted to the front desk by a furious Sergeant Harris who started shouting at her before she'd even removed her coat.

She didn't bother to say anything back to him, and when he asked what was going on she simply said DCI Bradfield had told her she wasn't to discuss it with anyone. This angered Harris more, but she was actually quite pleased that it did.

'I dunno what this place is coming to. She's not got either the experience or know-how and gets lucky with some banknotes, and the next minute she's been bloody promoted. I've thirty years' hard graft under my belt that seems to mean F-all to some people.'

'What are you talking about?'

'WPC Kathleen Morgan. She's like a Cheshire cat now she's been made acting detective. She's always put it about and used her equipment to get what she wants, and as for her stinking perfume . . .'

Jane let him rant on, and he didn't even seem to notice her walk off to deal with someone at the front counter. Just after ten o'clock, Jane went for her break and popped into the incident room to find Kath.

It was already a hive of activity and there were numerous officers she hadn't seen at the station before. From the way they appeared, some with long hair and scruffy clothes, others smart but casual, and a couple in workman's clothes, she guessed they were probably surveillance officers.

Jane noticed the index carousel was empty and Kath was boxing everything to do with the now-solved Julie Ann Collins case.

'Congratulations, Kath, on your well-deserved appointment as an acting detective.'

'I am over the bloody moon. I couldn't believe it when the boss said it was in recognition of the Kenneth Boyle arrest and my work matching the banknotes, which cracked the Julie Ann murder case.' She breathed on her nails and rubbed them on her jacket.

'Well, I am jealous. I mean it's going to be a long time for me to be even considered for the CID as I've got to complete my probation.'

Jane looked around at everyone. 'What's going on?'

Kath gestured to all the new officers.

'They're taking over the incident room for the John Bentley investigation and Bradfield has called for everyone to attend the briefing. I heard him tell Gibbs he wants you in on it as well.'

'Are you sure?' Jane asked excitedly

'Yeah, anyway, I hope they don't stick me in that stinking surveillance van. One time the buggers left me on my own while they went to the pub – I was in it for four hours sweating like a pig and bursting for a pee.'

DS Gibbs walked in wearing his long black worn leather coat and black ankle boots.

'Morgan, can you head up to the canteen and tell everyone on the team to come down in five minutes as Bradfield wants to get the meeting under way sooner rather than later.'

When Kath left he took Jane to one side.

'You may be right about Bentley being up to something.'

She blushed and admitted that at one point she had been terrified she might be wrong.

'You may still be, but fair dues, you stuck to your guns, even under pressure from me,' he said smiling.

She thanked him and leaving the room felt downhearted that he hadn't said anything about her being back on the team. Kath had obviously misheard.

She walked past Bradfield's office and paused.

'Where you off to, Tennison?' she heard Bradfield shout from behind her and stopped.

'The canteen for refs,' she said without turning, not wanting him to see the disappointment on her face.

'Get me a coffee and a pack of Bourbons while you're there.'

God, he's got a cheek, she thought to herself.

'You got three minutes so get a move on.'

Annoyed, she turned sharply and stood with her knuckles dug into her hips. 'Well, I'm very sorry but I'm busy on the front desk YET AGAIN, and only have one pair of hands, so for once you'll have to get your own coffee and Bourbons.'

He cocked his head to one side and knew instinctively why she was upset.

'Hold on, Tennison. Hurry up with the coffee because I

want you on the investigation and in the office for the meeting. Didn't DS Gibbs tell you?

She suddenly wished the ground would swallow her up and mumbled an apology for her petulant behaviour.

'It's all right, this time. Besides, you look kinda cute when you're angry,' he said, and looked at his watch. 'You got two minutes now.'

Jane was up the stairs like a shot.

Everyone was gathered. Jane stood at the back of the office as all the chairs were occupied. Bradfield had given Kath big sheets of paper to stick on the wall, with street and building diagrams drawn on them and notes neatly written in black felt tip. DS Gibbs had set up the reel-to-reel tape player in one corner of the room.

Bradfield looked refreshed and energized, even though he'd had only about three hours' sleep. He handed out copies of Jane's report detailing her visit to Ashley Brennan, and a transcription of the tape. He told DS Gibbs to start the tape and they all remained still and silent as they listened to the recording. The tape finished and Bradfield, perched on the edge of a desk, stood up and walked to the front of the room.

'Right, listen up. Anything you have read, heard or are told about this investigation stays within this team and these four walls. Do I make myself clear?' He looked round the room, staring everyone in the eye. 'If as much as a peep gets out, then believe me I will personally destroy the career of whoever's responsible.'

Jane had never seen him so serious, and by the expression on the faces of the others in the room neither had they.

'You've heard the tape and read Tennison's report so I

won't repeat what's in it. Clearly our suspects are using walkie-talkies and we believe the man referred to as Brushstroke is John Bentley. He's a hard nut who's done time for a very nasty GBH as well as other serious crimes,' he said, pinning up John's mug shot on a cork board.

'Word on the street is his old man's just come out the nick,' a detective said.

Bradfield nodded, pinned up another mug shot and tapped it with his finger. 'Clifford Bentley has just finished an eight stretch for armed robbery and was released from Pentonville a couple of days ago. But we don't know for certain yet if he's involved.'

'Pigs might fly if he isn't, guv,' an officer remarked, causing people to smile and nod in agreement.

A surveillance officer stepped closer to get a better look at Clifford's photograph.

'That's the guy we saw from the obo van staggering into the Pembridge Estate just after midnight. Pissed as a fart, he was.'

Bradfield asked if he was sure, and his partner in the obo van looked at the picture and confirmed it was Clifford Bentley. He realized that it might mean Clifford wasn't on 'the job' as he clearly wasn't working through the night.

'Any idea yet who was in the van with Bentley last night, guv?' the surveillance officer who followed the van asked.

'Not a hundred per cent, but it could be this man Daniel Mitcham, tough, nasty ex-squaddie and local boy,' Bradfield said, putting up a photo of the thuggish-looking Mitcham before continuing. 'He was arrested for the same GBH as John Bentley. They did porridge together and according to a snout are both close and drink in the Albion on Chatsworth Road.'

The two officers who had been in the surveillance van were whispering to each other.

'Something you would like to share with the rest of us?' Gibbs asked.

They looked at each other wondering who should tell him but Bradfield pre-empted them.

'It's not Mitcham, is it?'

'No, sir, very similar build and age, but the man we saw had shoulder-length blond hair, not dark like Mitcham.'

'Pity, but that still doesn't rule him out as we don't know exactly how many are involved.'

He continued, telling everyone that John Bentley was in possession of a decorator's van with copied index plates from the same type of van in Kingston. He then asked the surveillance officers who followed John Bentley yesterday evening to brief the team on what happened. The officer who had written the surveillance log went through every-thing in fine detail and said that they were not sure if Bentley had sussed he was being tailed, or they had simply lost him. They had returned to the Pembridge in the obo van and remained in situ to see if Bentley returned, but by 3 a.m. he hadn't and they were told to stand down by Bradfield.

Bradfield lit a cigarette. 'From now on the surveillance on John and Clifford Bentley will be round the clock, with three to four per vehicle and static points so you can take turns catching some kip during the night.'

He also informed them a team was already out watch-ing the Bentley flat and another out at Allard Street where Daniel Mitcham lived with his wife and two kids in a ter-raced council house. Even though they had as yet no sighting of Mitcham, he had a close relationship with Bentley so Bradfield was covering all possibilities.

An officer asked if it was known where John Bentley's van was now and Bradfield told him it was not in the vicinity of the Kingsmead or Pembridge and could be in a rented garage or lock-up somewhere, but it was hoped surveillance would resolve the problem.

'There is another man we believe to be involved, a Greek immigrant called Silas Manatos. Unfortunately he has no criminal record so we don't as yet have a picture of him, but we hope a surveillance team will soon.'

He walked over to the street drawing taped to the wall and indicated each building as he continued. 'Manatos runs this café in Great Eastern Street, which is right next door to the Trustee Savings Bank and may be the possible target for a break-in via the basement of the café and into the bank vault. Right now we have no firm evidence, witnesses or informants who have seen or heard anything suspicious. Reality is, ladies and gents, I'm acting on a gut feeling due to circumstantial evidence over Silas's lease of the café. He's having refurbishment work done, but the premises are due to be knocked down soon. I strongly believe that the target is the TSB; however, it could be any bank, or even a jeweller's, anywhere in London.'

Everybody looked at each other, surprised how vast an area they could be looking at, but Bradfield reassured them that if he was right about John Bentley then the surveillance teams should not only help to identify the other members of the gang, but lead them to the premises to be robbed.

DS Gibbs, sitting near to Bradfield, was uneasy. 'We're going on a lot of "assumption". We could have the wrong location,' he said.

'Yeah, I know I have to consider that, but these guys are obviously up to something and we just have to step up the surveillance. I am going to talk to the manager of our suspected target today. Morgan, you can come with me, but I don't want anything that gives away that we are on to them as it will make them back off and then we'll have nothing.'

He then asked Jane to get back to Ashley Brennan and ask if he had picked up any further conversations overnight. She said she would call him straight after the meeting.

Kath saw a mug shot of David Bentley in amongst the papers Bradfield had placed on the desk and picked it up. He looked very young and from the arrest date on the photo she could see it was taken many years ago, but it was interesting that he had fair hair.

'Excuse me, sir, but the bloke in the van with John Bentley, could it have been his younger brother David?' she suggested, handing him the picture.

'I thought about that, Kath, in fact I nicked him years ago and this photo of him was taken in a hospital. He fell off a roof nicking lead and the doctors said he'd be a cripple for life and only be able to get around in a wheelchair so I doubt he'd be able to serve any useful role in a bank job.'

Jane raised her hand and Bradfield asked what she wanted.

'I'm pretty sure I saw David a week or so ago. He was walking behind the wheelchair, sort of using it as a support. Some young lad upset him and he reacted pretty quickly.'

'Is there anyone in that family you don't know, Tennison?' DS Gibbs remarked.

Bradfield frowned at him and then looked at Jane. 'Come on, pretty sure or sure?'

'Well, he was with a woman who I know to be Renee Bentley and he looks like an older version of his mug shot, his hair is much longer.'

Bradfield asked the surveillance officers if he looked similar to the man who was with John Bentley in the van and they both said he did.

'So if he can stand up he could act as a lookout,' Bradfield said and paused to think for a second before looking at the surveillance officers. 'I don't think Bentley sussed you tailing him. Where exactly was the car park he drove into?'

'The multistorey one in Great Eastern Street,' the officer replied.

'The one opposite the café and bank?' Bradfield asked.

'Yes, sir.'

'You'd get a 360 view from the very top so I'd say it's the perfect spot for a lookout to see what's coming from every direction. John Bentley could have dropped his brother off on the top floor. You most likely couldn't find his van because it would only take him thirty seconds or so to park up in the yard behind the café and close the gates.'

There was a buzz in the room as everyone realized Bradfield could be right. Kath mentioned that from the tape it sounded like a patrolling uniform officer had been spotted by the lookout when arresting a drunk.

'Maybe it's worth trying to find out who it was, guv.'

'Good thinking, Kath. Spence, check with uniform downstairs and with City of London Police as their patch borders the area. If the officer's actions fit with the information "Eagle" relayed over the walkie-talkie then there's even stronger evidence it's the right location.'

'We hope. There are other banks in that area with cafés nearby or next to them,' Gibbs remarked.

Bradfield gave him a disapproving look and one of the detectives suggested a night-time raid on the café to catch them in the act.

Bradfield shook his head. 'No, not at the moment. I want to keep up the surveillance and identify John Bentley's team. We don't know if they only go into the café on certain nights, so we need to sit, wait and watch first. By rushing it we risk blowing the whole operation and the Bentleys walking away scot-free.'

Gibbs sighed. 'But if Bentley sussed the surveillance team then they're already on to us, so a hit now might result in finding digging equipment, maps, the walkie-talkies or other incriminating evidence before they get a chance to dispose of it.'

Bradfield ignored him and took out some papers from his file and pinned them to the cork board.

'This is a list of the teams I want you to work in and it also details the street position each obo van and vehicle should take up. Obviously I need to find surveillance premises in Great Eastern Street, but that's not going to be easy if the car park is Bentley's lookout point. Now let's get out there, gather the evidence and build a watertight case to get these bastards put away for a long time. Are there any questions?'

The officers in the room looked at each other. He knew that there would be some that disagreed with his decisions and others who agreed with DS Gibbs, but as he expected no one argued with him. Everyone gathered round the list to see who they were working with. Bradfield leant over to Gibbs.

'I'd like a word with you in my office.'

'I'll just contact City of London Police first and—'

'Now, Spence,' Bradfield said firmly and picked up his folder.

Gibbs followed Bradfield into his office where he slammed the file down on the desk and turned sharply.

'Why are you being so negative and challenging my authority, Spence?'

'I'm not ...'

'You were questioning my decisions and pulling faces in the meeting and I won't have it, especially not in front of junior officers,' he shouted and paced up and down the room.

Gibbs could see he was really pissed off.

'If it looked or sounded like that then I apologize, but all I'm trying to do is point out that you're working on assumptions and no hard evidence. I'm worried you're making things fit because it suits your thoughts on the investigation.'

'Oh do you really! Well, thank you for that, but I know what I'm doing. And one other thing: lay off Jane Tennison about the Bentleys. You know as well as I do she's not in with any criminals or taking backhanders like some I could name in that CID office. If she hadn't met the mother by chance then we wouldn't have had anything to go on.'

'You're being a bit overprotective.'

'What?'

'Well, seems to me that maybe your judgement's a bit off because you have the hots for her. I mean no offence.'

'I do take fuckin' offence, Spence. She's got the makings of a good copper – and don't forget she was prepared to back your corner when you smacked the shit out of Terry O'Duncie.

'I fucking lied for you, so you owe me and I expect you

417

to back me up over this Bentley thing from now on. Find that PC their lookout saw with the drunk, and see if we can get a light aircraft or military 'copter to fly over the café today to get some aerial snaps of the rear yard.'

Jane changed into plain clothes before an officer drove her to the Pembridge Estate. Having never been on surveillance before she was quite excited, and knew she could learn a lot from the other officer, who was a surveillance specialist. She was dropped off around the corner from the obo van, which had been painted to look as though it was a wholesale fruit and veg delivery van. She approached it, remembering what she had been told to do. She scanned the vicinity to make sure it was all clear before standing by the rear offside wheel and knocking on the side of the van: two short taps, three, then another two. The officer inside opened one rear door and she darted into the back.

The sudden impact of the smell nearly made her sick. It was a mixture of stale sweat, beer, cigarettes and urine. The interior of the old transit van was dimly lit by the square-light inlet in the roof. Jane could see it was pretty basic – two rickety wooden benches with storage space under them ran along either side, and on top were the same thin, tatty stained mattresses and blankets that prisoners used. At the far end was a little stool beside a small desk with a newspaper on it, a torch hanging on a nail from the side. Above it was a police radio, microphone and headset which he held to one ear as he leaned forward and peered through one of the spy holes.

'Welcome to the Hackney Hilton, luv, and next time don't come with your job handbag – sticks out like a sore thumb that you're a plonk,' he said, using the derogatory term she detested. He then rolled the newspaper into a ball and tossed it towards a cardboard box holding rubbish. Next to it were two old beer bottles and he pointed to them, grinning. 'Men's piss bottles. We got an empty milk carton somewhere for the ladies, though.'

Jane was mortified.

'I'm DC Stanley, and believe me I've been cooped up in a lot worse. I was jokin' about the milk carton. We nip out if there's no one about, or lift the flap in the floor there and pee on the road. As you can smell, some officers' aim isn't too good.'

'I couldn't see the spy holes from the outside.'

'Well, that's the idea, luv. This one I'm at is part of an apple stalk, other side is a pear, back door's potatoes and the air vent on the frame lets you see out the front.'

'I thought it would all be a lot more high tech.'

'This is the Old Bill, luv, not James Bond or MI5. I came straight here from a different overnight job so I'm knackered and me neck's killing me. You can take over and eyeball the estate. If you see any of the targets, let me know and I'll nip in the front and drive,' he said, showing her the small sliding door to the front of the van.

She sat on the stool and peered through the hole; it was very uncomfortable as she had to crane her neck and keep her head up to see properly. Stanley lay down on the bench, dragged a blanket over himself, and closed his eyes. Jane knew there was no way she would be able to sit monitoring the estate in the same position for hours. She reached for her shoulder bag, took out her powder compact mirror, opened it and held it by the spy hole.

'If that worked do you think I would sit on that stool in the same position for hours?' Stanley said and pulled the blanket over his head.

Jane felt embarrassed and dropped the compact back in her bag.

Clifford Bentley was nursing a hangover whilst having a bath and John and David were still asleep. He hadn't returned home until after midnight and had been very drunk. Renee knew from experience that he could be volatile and violent when he had been drinking, so she had pretended to be asleep as he fell into the bed beside her.

No one, apart from her, had eaten any of the liver, peas and mash she had cooked the previous evening and left out in a tin-foil-covered serving dish. 'What a waste,' she said to herself as she tipped it into the rubbish bin.

She heard David coughing loudly and went to listen outside his bedroom door, where it sounded even worse. She inched the door open. The curtains were closed and he was gasping for breath, his chest rattling as he coughed.

'You want me to bring you a cup of tea or hot toddy, dear?'

'No, I'm OK,' he said, sounding terrible.

She could see he was sweating profusely and went over to feel his head. He was very hot and she realized he was running a high temperature. He didn't seem to have the strength to argue, so she fetched a bowl of cold water, rinsed out a cloth and sat down on his bed, gently dabbing his forehead. She opened his bedside cabinet and took out a jar of Vicks VapoRub. After unbuttoning his pyjama top she rubbed some into his chest.

'You got a terrible cold and chest infection. I've been warning you to rest because I know you take after me. My asthma is shocking and if I get a cold as well then it always goes straight to me chest.'

David kept his eyes closed. He felt really ill and didn't

have the strength to ask her to leave him alone. She kept on rinsing the cloth in the water and placing it across his brow. She jumped up when she heard Clifford's voice.

'I didn't like the look of that congealed mess you left out last night, and I'm starving now. I'll have some bacon and eggs with fried bread and a mug of tea.'

'Can't you see David's sick? Listen to him trying to get his breath – he's got a temperature and I think we need to call the doctor out. God only knows what time he and John came home this morning.'

Clifford stepped forward and nudged the bed with his foot.

'David, are you all right, son? What's the matter with you? Is she fussing over you too much?'

David barely managed to nod, he felt so weak, then Clifford grabbed Renee's arm tightly, ushering her out the room.

'Just leave him be and get me some breakfast,' he said, pushing her into the kitchen and shutting the door before going to John's room. John was snoring and in a deep sleep so Clifford shook the bed and waited for him to wake up.

'Listen, our David's sick.'

John yawned. 'I know, he was in a really bad way this morning when we got back.'

'Are you workin' tonight?'

John moaned and sat up. 'We've hit a couple of obstacles and it's taking longer than I thought. Me, Danny and Silas are knackered. We've worked our bollocks off and need a night's break. Besides, there's no way David will be up to it this evening.'

'What obstacles?'

'We reached more embedded iron bars. There was a

brick wall behind them which we thought would take us into the vault area. Danny cut the bars with the oxyacetylene and when we removed the bricks we'd reached the vault's concrete base.'

'Sounds like it's all goin' well to me.'

'It was, until we discovered the concrete was reinforced with thick wire mesh.'

'So what you're tellin' me is the fuckin' job is going to take longer than planned.'

'Yeah, we now gotta focus on making the hole wide and deep enough to crawl through with the Kango drills and large wire cutters so we can cut through the concrete and mesh.'

Clifford kept his voice low. 'You should keep pressing on, John, but I can see you're knackered. I'll stand in for David tomorrow night if he's not better, you go get some more sleep.'

Clifford shut the door and went to get his breakfast. Passing David's room he could hear the rasping cough. He'd be a liability as a lookout, and it felt good to Clifford that he'd be taking over.

Bradfield and Kath had a midday meeting with the portly and pompous bank manager of the TSB, Mr Adrian Dunbar, who wore a pinstriped suit, red-silk bow tie and matching handkerchief sticking out of his breast pocket. He had a slight lisp and was shocked when given the reason for the detectives' visit. He said that no one who had come to the bank had been acting suspiciously and there had been no reports of suspicious sounds of any kind, be it machinery or hammering. He was very confident and was not in any way overly concerned.

'The vault is on a timer and can only be opened during

banking hours. Just the assistant manager and I know the code, and if you get it wrong twice it triggers the alarms. In addition, any attempt to cut through the steel vault will cause an inner vibration which will set the alarm off and cause an iron shutter to come down between the outer entry door and the vault itself, making it impossible to exit.'

Bradfield and Kath were shown the vault area. The massive steel door with the big locking wheel in its centre was certainly impressive.

'As you can see it is impenetrable. The vault is fireproof and airtight, and the air conditioning is turned on automatically when the door is correctly opened.'

'Well, someone managed to break into the bank in Baker Street a couple of years ago and it was a similar set-up.'

'I am aware of that, Detective, and so were the people who built the vault and installed the security for this bank and I can assure you it is not a similar set-up. Our vault is, as I said, impenetrable. This steel wall is twelve inches thick.' Dunbar slapped the palm of his hand against it.

'Well, I hear you loud and clear, Mr Dunbar, but isn't there a possibility that even with all this high-level security the robbers could be intending to come up beneath the vault?'

Mr Dunbar laughed and dismissed the possibility, saying that when the rebuilding was commissioned they had laid thick wire-meshed concrete and the steel floor was inches thick. Kath glanced at the disappointed Bradfield as it really did appear they had the wrong bank. Even when asked about the contents secured in the vault Mr Dunbar was less than forthcoming and said that over four hundred customers used the facility due to the impressive security measures. His pomposity hardly flagged when he said that the bank took every precaution with regard to their customers' property and the whole point of the vault was privacy. Each client had a key to their personal secure box and the bank held a second key – both keys were required to open the box. A log book had to be signed and dated by the customer before permission was granted for them to remove and view the contents of their box in private. They would then take it out of the vault and into a small secure room where they could view their valuables, or if they wished to simply place an item in a box there was a table inside the vault to use. A member of staff was always present outside the room, and as the bank manager Dunbar would try and deal with the customers personally.

'Can you tell us what the deposit boxes contain?' Kath asked.

'I don't know, they are private, but I imagine it more than likely money, jewellery, antiques, private letters and wills.'

'Could you show us inside the vault, please, Mr Dunbar?' she asked.

'I suppose so, but this is all very irregular. Would you both please turn your backs while I press the code to disable the alarm.'

Bradfield glanced at Kath tight-lipped: it was as if the odious little man didn't trust them.

Dunbar pressed in his entry code to the vault and began to turn the wheel. There were sounds of heavy-duty clicking and beeping before he was able to ease the massive iron door open with the assistance of Bradfield. Kath was transfixed as she looked around the inside of the pristine shiny vault. She'd never seen anything like it before and could understand why Dunbar was rather arrogant about the security. In the enclosed vault his voice echoed and the shiny steel floor made their footsteps resound. There was row upon row of deposit boxes, whose locks and handles glinted in the bright overhead lights. Dunbar assumed a superior attitude, holding both arms aloft as he pointed to the array of precious locked items. There was a large steel safe built into the side almost two feet in height and width, with a locking number dial on it.

'Excuse me, sir, there appears to be another safe within the vault. What does that contain?'

Dunbar explained the contents belonged to a member of the Saudi Arabian royal family who had paid for it to be built in for his personal belongings.

Bradfield shook Mr Dunbar's hand, thanking him for his time and patience. It seemed that they were mistaken about the TSB being the target and he apologized for troubling him.

Bradfield looked at Kath as they got in the car.

'You reckon he's a woofter?'

'Who?' Kath asked.

'Dunbar. It's the red bow tie and hanky. They say woofters use hankies as a gay code and he spoke like he had something stuck up his arse.'

'I wouldn't know,' Kath replied, shaking her head.

Jane ached all over. No one had entered or left the Bentleys' flat, and sitting hunched up looking through a small hole for hours had given her a cricked neck and terrible headache.

She sat back and stretched as Stanley, who had snored for nearly three hours, stirred himself. She physically jumped when the rear door of the van was knocked on in the standard coded manner.

Stanley scuttled to the double doors to look in a gap of the blacked-out window, then opened one door for Bradfield to jump inside.

'Jesus Christ, Stanley, it stinks in here! Dear God, don't you ever toss out your rotting food?'

'Listen, I was in a static op last night and collected the van from the drug squad this morning, so it ain't all my mess. Nothing has moved all day, so we don't even know if the targets are in their flat – and I need a leak,' he said, leaning over to lift up the hatch for the pee hole.

Bradfield put his foot on the hatch. 'Not in here, it stinks enough. You can go and stretch your legs and get a bite to eat, Stanley, discreetly – as only an officer so highly trained and skilled as yourself can do!'

'Very funny, guv,' Stanley said, and pulled on a donkey jacket. 'You and Tennison want anything?' he asked.

Bradfield said he was only paying a flying visit and Jane asked if she could have a cheese sandwich and a bottle of water.

Stanley crouched at the back doors and waited for Jane and Bradfield to give the all-clear before jumping out.

Bradfield sat on the bench close to Jane who was still keeping observation on the Bentleys' flat, unsure what to say or why he had come. He sat with his raincoat buttoned up and lit a cigarette.

'How long have you been here?' he asked.

'Nearly three hours.'

'I'd say punishment enough.'

'I'm sorry?'

'Time spent in this dilapidated stink-hole van is punishment. And in case you're wondering, fuck all has happened at any of the observation points and it's looking like we got the wrong bank.'

'You make it sound as if it's my fault.'

'We wouldn't be here if you hadn't put John Bentley in the frame. Ashley Brennan's heard nothing further on his poxy radio, and we have nothing suspicious occurring at Silas's café.'

'Maybe Bentley realized he was being tailed and called it off.'

'Even if he hadn't they'd need a fucking atomic bomb to blast open the bank vault. According to the pompous prat of a bank manager it is completely impenetrable with a massive concrete and steel base and James Bond shutters to lock in any intruder.'

She stared out from the peephole, trying hard not to show how distressed she was that he appeared to be blaming her.

'I only met him once, but I still believe it was John Bentley's voice on the tape. If you want me to change my mind, or suggest it has been my fault then—'

'Fault?' he snapped, interrupting her. 'I'm here because I don't want you to take any flack. If we have the wrong bank then that's down to me, but we both know something is going down and I have a gut feeling—'

'That I'm right?'

'Not about that – my gut tells me that we're close but time is running out, and if they are planning to rob a bank we may have screwed up because we've concentrated on Silas's café.'

Jane turned to face him, watching as he sighed, rubbed his hair and shrugged his shoulders.

'You must be exhausted,' she said.

'Yeah, but I just wanted you to know that you might

have to stand up for yourself when the Chief Super gets the update. They always want someone to blame and this has cost more than a few quid getting in all the extra officers – but the reality is it's down to me, and my decision. You acted in good faith, I've acted on impulse.'

She turned back to the peephole, trying to think of the right thing to say.

'When Stanley gets back tell him to give it until 6 p.m. and get another team to take over from you.'

He moved along the bench so he was behind her and placed his hand on her shoulder. It was not in any way premeditated, but she felt her body lean back against him. He gently moved his hand to stroke her hair.

'You've got a lovely-shaped head.'

She laughed, turned and looked at him. 'Thank you.'

'What's so funny?'

'Well, you sort of pay the oddest compliments and sometimes I am not sure how to take them. You said I have nice teeth, but you always seem to be critical of me, snapping that elastic band for me to tie my hair back, "Take your hat off", "Put it back on", you confuse me.'

'Ah well, all you need to know is that …' He hesitated.

'Know what?'

'That I have wanted to do this.' He tilted her chin up, leaned forward and kissed her. It was such a sweet, gentle kiss and Jane was completely taken aback.

'So now you know that my compliments were heartfelt. I have no notion how you feel, and I may be making a total arse of myself, so you don't have to say anything.'

She wanted to put her arms around him. She had an overwhelming desire to hold him tightly and tilt her head up for him to kiss her again, but she felt nervous. So she covered her embarrassment by peering through her peephole pressing her flushed face against the cold sides of the van.

'Wait – Renee Bentley is coming out of her flat.'

Bradfield leaned closer to her and Jane moved her head to one side so that he could look.

'She's a wily old lady, and reared a nasty son of a bitch in John, never mind being married to one as well. But I doubt she's going to be handling a sledgehammer and helping break into a bank.'

Her face almost touched his as she suggested that she should get out and follow.

'You can do, but keep your distance as she might recognize you. I'll wait for Stanley to return.'

Jane snatched her coat, grabbed her bag and Bradfield eased open the van doors to let her out. As she stepped out into the fresh air she had to catch her breath. She felt nervous and her heart was pounding. She could hardly believe what had just happened. She calmed herself down but couldn't keep the smile off her face.

CHAPTER TWENTY-FIVE

Renee walked slowly as she made her way along Chatsworth Road, which was lined with shops and market stalls displaying a colourful array of fresh fruit, vegetables, bread and cakes. The sound of traders shouting out the price of their wares in Cockney accents filled the busy street. Jane was able to follow Renee at a safe distance and used some stall-browsing as cover whenever Renee stopped to look at something. Eventually Renee went into an Indian shop. Hesitant, Jane looked through the window from the street. She could see Renee walking between tall aisles of tinned food towards the post office counter at the far end of the shop. Jane decided to go in, and seeing the stack of baskets by the door she picked one up. She moved quickly to stand behind one of the shelves and was able to watch Renee from a round convex mirror placed high in the corner of the shop. Working behind the post office grille was an Indian man wearing a black turban. Renee waited while he served another woman. Jane moved a bit closer.

'Good afternoon, Mrs Bentley,' the Indian man said as Renee approached the counter.

'Can I ask you somethin', Mr Singh?' Renee spoke

loudly, bending towards the grille and sliding him her pension book.

'You certainly can.'

'Me son said some £5 notes won't be legal come September and I can't use 'em. Is that right?'

Jane saw Mr Singh smile, but was unable to hear his response as a woman and two noisy children demanding sweets were now standing beside her. She moved closer to listen, but Mr Singh was counting out Renee's pension money which he then handed over and she placed it in her handbag.

'Do you have any travel magazines for Florida, that's in America?' Renee asked Mr Singh.

He said he wasn't sure as his wife dealt with all the magazines, but there might be something on the racks by the door. If not, a travel agent's would be the best place. Jane had to turn her back as Renee walked towards her. Renee then went to the magazine rack and spent five minutes looking through it before going to the till where she asked Mrs Singh for some cough medicine and aspirins as well as some cigarettes and a packet of Maltesers. Renee paid then left the shop. Jane could see Mrs Singh looking at her suspiciously as if she was a shoplifter, so she bought a large bar of chocolate before hurrying out.

Renee went back to the estate, and as Jane returned to the surveillance van she saw Stanley and approached him.

'What's happening? Are you following someone?'

'No, but if I was you'd probably have just blown my cover by carrying your police bag.'

'I'm sorry, I forgot what we were doing,' an embarrassed Jane replied.

'Think of it as a lesson learned. We've been relieved for the day, two other officers have taken over for the next shift. Sorry, but I left your cheese sandwich and drink in the van.'

Jane smiled. 'It's OK, I'm not hungry.'

'How'd the tail on Renee Bentley go?'

'Nothing unusual. She just did a bit of shopping,' Jane replied, but inwardly she was puzzled by what she had overheard. She wondered if there was any connection regarding the £5 notes and the request for a travel magazine for Florida.

Having got the bus back to the station Jane was finishing typing up her surveillance report when Kath walked in.

'Well, there's nothing going on at any of the surveillance points. Chief Super's just been in and according to Gibbs he gave Bradfield a real pastin' about the cost of the operation. Between you and me, cos I saw the TSB vault, there is a big possibility we've been focusing on the wrong effing bank.'

'But it doesn't make sense. It is right next to a café' – she gestured to the pinned-up mug shots – 'and the Bentleys are obviously up to something.'

'Bradfield's got a couple of guys checking out other banks and jewellers' in close proximity to cafés, but it might not even be connected to the Bentleys. The taped calls could be coming from God knows who or where.'

Jane sighed. 'I'm sure it was John Bentley's voice.' But in reality she was now beginning to doubt herself.

'Well, I believe you, but don't get your knickers in a twist about it. As it is we can nick him for ringing a van with false plates, no insurance and probably a forged tax disc.'

'But we don't even know where he keeps the van yet, and they're just minor offences really.'

'All part of the game, Jane – you win some, you lose some.'

Jane sighed and went back to typing her report as Kath leaned over her shoulder to read it.

'That's interesting – Ma Bentley enquiring about illegal fivers and travel to the States. I wouldn't mind getting some sun in Florida, but chance'd be a fine thing.'

Jane was about to add that travel to the US was expensive and not something she thought any of the Bentleys could afford, when suddenly Kath burst out laughing.

DS Gibbs was there in full uniform, his police helmet under his arm.

'Evenin' all,' Kath said, squatting down then standing up with her hands behind her back. Jane wondered if he had been sent back to uniform due to the O'Duncie assault incident.

Gibbs shook his finger. 'Haw haw, very funny, Morgan. Bradfield wants me to visit Silas's café dressed like a plod on the pretext that Mannie Charles' shop got broken into and I'm makin' local enquiries. This bloody helmet's too small,' he said, and put it on.

Kath laughed again. 'You might get a free moussaka and sticky cake, Spence. Do you want someone to go with you? Cos my uniform's downstairs.'

'Bradfield's already lined up Sergeant "Happy" Harris to go with me. You two completed your reports yet?' he asked, and they both said yes.

He told them to book off duty and turned to leave the room causing the helmet to fall from his head. 'Bloody thing.' As he bent down to pick it up Kath goosed him and he shot up.

'Very funny, Morgan, keep yer hands to yourself.'

'You should tell some of the blokes at the station to do the same. I've been touched up more times than you've had hot dinners.'

Returning to the section house Jane was eager to have a bath after being hunched up for hours in the stinking surveillance van. She hadn't seen Bradfield at the station and was concerned about his dressing down by the Chief. She also wondered how she was going to react when she saw him after what had occurred between them. Just thinking about it made her smile.

As she passed the sergeant's office she noticed the door was open. He got up and approached her with a stern look on his face. She was beginning to wonder if he and Sergeant Harris came from the same mould.

'Your mother has rung three times this afternoon. She's upset you haven't made contact to let her know how you've settled in. I was in two minds whether to tell her about your indiscretion on the men's floor—'

'You didn't, did you?' Jane asked.

'No, she sounded worried enough as it was. Neither I nor the wardens are an answer service. We only take urgent family calls to residents, so kindly inform your mother of the rules,' he said, returning to his office and closing the door.

Deciding she'd better call home straightaway, Jane went to the payphone at the end of the corridor opposite the lifts. She dialled her parents' number and hearing the answer beeps pushed in a few 2p coins.

'About time, Jane – Daddy and I have been worried sick. We appreciate you must be busy but you promised to call and you haven't, so we've been really anxious.'

'How did you get this number?'

'I called the station and they put me through to the incident room. That lovely Mr Bradfield answered the phone and said you'd been in an oboe van all day and had gone off duty. What were you doing in a van?'

Jane felt embarrassed wondering what Bradfield must have made of the call. 'It's an obo van, Mum, short for "observation". And they don't appreciate personal calls to the station or here.'

'Are you coming home for Sunday lunch?'

'I'm not sure if I'm clear this weekend as I'm still on attachment to the CID.'

'Well, surely you're allowed a weekend off? Pam will be here – they had a terrible time in the Lake District. It poured with rain and that MGB broke down so they had to hire another car.'

'Oh I'm sorry. Uncle Brian should cover their costs.'

'Well, they weren't paying for the car – turns out it was his wedding present to them. But he had to get a truck to go and pick it up – the rear suspension thingy went.'

'Mum, I'm going to have to go as I've got a lot of studying to do for CTC.'

'Will you try and come for lunch on Sunday? We miss you.'

'I miss you too, and I'll let you know. Is Dad OK?'

'Oh he's fine. He worries about you, and we haven't seen you for so long.'

'It's only been a few days, Mum, and I've been really busy.'

'What have you been doing?'

Jane sighed. There was no way she could go into any kind of description of what she'd been involved in, and was thankful when the 'pip, pip, pip' started.

'Got to go now – I'll call about lunch.'

'Bye bye, and make sure you do or I'll have to phone you again.'

The call was cut off and as Jane replaced the receiver she felt a tap on her shoulder.

'Hi! It's me, Sarah Redhead. Can I borrow some 10ps from you? I'm totally out of change and have to call my brother urgently.'

Jane gave her five 10ps and eight 2ps from her purse.

'Thanks, June, probably won't need all this and I'll pay you back as soon as. Maybe have a drink in the pub later?'

'Yes, maybe,' Jane replied, but had no intention of going.

She looked at her watch: it was 8 p.m., and last orders in the canteen were at half past seven. She was so tired she couldn't even be bothered to pop out to get a takeaway and replacing her purse in her bag saw the bar of chocolate she'd purchased when following Renee Bentley. Opening it she broke off a large chunk and began to eat it as she got the lift to the women's floor. What had started out as a positive day had now become a worrying one. She knew that if she was wrong about John Bentley there could be repercussions for Bradfield. It mattered to Jane that she was right. Not just for her sake but Bradfield's as well as she realized how much she cared for him.

Gibbs got into 'plod' mode; he was almost in step as he walked side by side with the much taller and wider Harris. They were heading along Great Eastern Street just before 8 p.m. and the area was quiet with few pedestrians or vehicles.

'Can't wait to hear what Silas has to say for himself,' Gibbs said.

'Do you know what he looks like as there may be a few

bubbles in there,' Harris asked as they reached the café. Spencer smiled, knowing 'bubble and squeak' was Cockney rhyming slang for 'Greek'. He said he had a full description of Silas from Mannie Charles and shaded his eyes to peer into the darkened café between the posters.

'There's a light on at the back so somebody's probably in,' he remarked, and banged on the door.

It was a minute or two before the interior light came on. Silas slowly inched open the door. He'd seen them from an upstairs window and his heart was pounding.

'Yes, officers, how can I help you? You wanna a tea or coffee perhaps?'

'No thanks. Can we come in, Mr ...?' Gibbs started to ask and deliberately paused to let him answer.

'Manatos, Silas Manatos,' he replied nervously as he stepped back to let them through.

Gibbs noticed the serving counter was covered in dust yet the coffee machine was clean, as were the cups and saucers stacked beside it.

'How's business?' he asked.

'Not so good ever since council tore down the old housing across road to build that multistorey car park. I lose much trade, but I get by and have some regulars still, early morning, but afternoons quiet.'

Spencer nodded and jerked his hand towards the door.

'Saw the refurbishing notice on the window – you hoping a new look might help bring a few more punters in?'

'I was gonna make area to eat downstairs, then open evenings as well to serve nice real Greek meze food. I start work and someone tell council. They tell me stop, cos I have no right to do dat even though I lease the place.'

'Sorry to hear that,' Gibbs said.

'The builder I hire to do work not happy. I say stop and he keep pesterin' me for money for all materials he bought. I think he is, how you say, cowboy, right?'

Harris stood looking around, and then removed his helmet. 'You live here, Mr Manatos?'

'Yes, upstairs.'

'Alone?'

'My wife an' kids already return to Greece as business poor. I gonna go over permanent soon as the council agrees how much I'm gonna get for what's left on my lease. Did they send you to tell me I gotta leave?'

Gibbs gave him a reassuring smile. 'No, we're here because there was a break-in at the tailor's shop. They tried the hardware store as well, but ran off when we arrived.'

'This happen tonight?' Silas asked, looking surprised.

'Yeah, looks like kids nicking petty cash from the till. They got in and out via the back way. Did you hear anything?'

'No, I hear nothing.'

'It looks like they climbed over the adjoining walls. You mind if we check your yard?' Harris asked.

'Sure, lemme get the keys. But I telling you I don't hear or see nothing.'

Sweating, Silas made a show of searching around the counter and then brought out a set of keys on a large ring.

'Door is at back, I show you.'

Harris and Gibbs followed him.

'Mind if I use your toilet?' Gibbs asked, and Silas told him it was in the corner of the eating area.

Gibbs stepped out of view. Hearing them go into the yard, he nipped behind the serving counter and opened the door which, as he'd guessed, led down to a basement.

438

He pulled out the torch he'd brought with him, shone it on the steep stairs and slowly made his way down. The cellar smelt damp, and as he shone the torch round he could see the far wall was lined with freshly painted plasterboard. In one corner there were two ladders, some stacked tables and chairs and on the floor were pots of paint, paintbrushes and a couple of old buckets. A white dust sheet caught Gibbs's attention. Lifting it back slowly he saw two differently sized gas tanks on a metal trolley with pressure gauges and rubber tubes attached to them.

In the yard Harris flicked on his police-issue torch. Shining it at Silas's face he noticed the Greek man was sweating more profusely than before. Looking around Harris saw there were stacks of bricks piled up on one side of the yard, and several sacks filled with soil were propped up against the wall.

'That lot belong to the builders, do they?' he asked Silas.

'Uh, yes, I also ask them to build raised areas with small brick wall and fill with soil so I can grow my own herbs and spices for meze. Now that all a waste of time as well,' he said, wiping his forehead with his shirtsleeve.

'I doubt they would have come over your wall,' Spencer said, joining them. He then pointed to the building to the left of the café and shone his torch on it.

'I see next door have built an extension in their yard; they competition for you?'

'Na, is part of new bank that open a few years ago. They build reinforced extension for vault area, terrible noise and filth for months.'

Gibbs grinned. 'The kids will be having a crack at that next.'

Silas let out what was clearly a nervous and fake laugh as he led them back into the café serving area.

Gibbs and Harris thanked Silas for his time as he let them out and locked the door behind them. They walked back to the panda car parked round the corner and got in. As he drove them back to the station Harris told Gibbs about the bricks and soil in the yard and the spice and herb story Silas came out with.

Gibbs smiled. 'They ain't painting and decorating down there. All the brushes are dry and I saw remnants of soil in the buckets, also there were two gas tanks down there.'

'What sort of gas?'

'One was an oxygen tank and the other something called acetylene ... whatever that is.'

Harris whistled. 'You mix the two together in a blow torch so you can cut through metal.'

'As all painters need to!' Gibbs exclaimed cynically and did a drum roll on the dashboard.

'What do you reckon to Silas then?' Harris asked.

Spencer loosened his tie, unbuttoned the uniform jacket and sat back. 'The Greek's a detective's delight. He had a rehearsed answer for everything, sweated like a pig and was shitting himself.'

It was almost 9 p.m. and Jane was in her pyjamas, about to go to bed after a long hot bath. She was just brushing her teeth when there was a knock on her door.

'Hey there, it's Sarah again. I've got the money I owe you.'

Jane was surprised Sarah hadn't said her surname as usual. She held out her hand as Sarah plonked a bag full of 1p and 2p pieces into it, apologizing and saying she'd had to raid her penny jar.

'Also, your DCI is in the quiet room and needs to speak to you again, but the old buzzard is patrolling as usual, so if you do go down I'd put some clothes on.'

Jane dressed quickly and gave herself a quick spray of Miss Dior perfume before hurrying downstairs, but Bradfield was not in the quiet room, so she tried the TV lounges and the snooker room, with no luck. She was just heading along the ground-floor corridor to walk over to the pub when she heard him call 'Jane' from behind her.

'Sarah Redhead said you were in the quiet room – has something happened?'

'I was, but I popped to the gents. There's nothing new to tell you about the case. I just wanted your company, and to talk.'

There was an embarrassing silence as neither of them seemed to know what to say. Bradfield had obviously showered and changed and was now wearing jeans and a T-shirt.

'Would you like a drink in the pub?'

She hesitated, and then he leaned towards her and took her hand.

'This was a bad idea, sorry. You go back to your room and I'll see you in the morning.'

She gripped his hand tightly. He lifted it to his lips and kissed her fingers.

'Do you want to risk coming to my room?'

She nodded. He released her hand and looked up and down the corridor.

'I'm on floor two, number 20. Use the stairs, I'll go up in the lift and check the coast is clear.'

She watched him get in the lift, waited a minute and then with her heart thudding in her chest hurried up the first flight of stairs. Turning to head up the next flight she panicked as she heard a flurry of footsteps. The petite blonde girl she had seen at the Harker lecture, and in the bathroom, walked through the swing doors from the men's landing, put a comical finger to her lips and giggled.

Jane looked down the landing and saw Bradfield at the far end waving for her to come forward, so she ran the entire way and followed him to his room. He opened the door quickly, ushered her inside and as she turned to face him he embraced her in his arms and kissed her passionately. He lifted her up, gently laid her down on his single bed and positioned himself beside her, gently brushing her hair from her face.

'I didn't think you would come ... you smell lovely.'

She gave a soft laugh. 'I'm scared stiff, especially as the crabby section-house sergeant is on the prowl.'

Bradfield was very gentle, kissing her tenderly before he pulled off his T-shirt, and then unbuttoned her blouse. She had been in such a hurry to get dressed she hadn't put a bra on and he sighed staring at her breasts before he bent down to kiss each nipple. Aroused, she pulled his head closer, moaning with pleasure. He looked up and grinned.

'Shushhh!' He put his hand over her lips. 'You are so lovely ... have you any idea how much I've wanted to hold you?'

He kept on kissing her and Jane felt as if she was flying. Then he took off her jeans, undressed himself and lay naked next to her. He remained so quiet and so loving that she gave herself to him, whispering that she loved kissing his cheeks, his eyes and his mouth. Jane was not completely sexually naive. She had been involved with a boy from college and had had a short relationship with one of the class instructors at training college. But she had never felt this way, or been so adored and cared for so tenderly.

It had just been plain sex before, but this was different. After making love to her once he became rougher and more sexually explicit, whispering what he wanted her to do and how he wanted her to touch him. She found his sexual confidence encouraging and it made her lose all her inhibitions so that she enjoyed the sex and was satisfied in a way she had never believed possible.

Two hours later Jane watched as Bradfield opened the door and took a look up and down the corridor.

'OK, it's all clear. Goodnight …'

He tilted her chin up and kissed her as she eased past him and hurried towards the stairs to go to her room. She had just passed through the double doors when Gibbs stepped out of the lift and headed along the corridor and rapped on Bradfield's door. Bradfield opened it fast with a beaming smile thinking it was Jane, but seeing Gibbs he reacted quickly to cover himself.

'Christ, you woke me up.' He yawned.

'I just finished typing up my report – you want to go for a drink? The pub's still open and I want to give you an update.'

'Yeah sure, let me get my trousers on.' Bradfield closed the door. He didn't want to let Gibbs in in case he smelt Jane's perfume.

Unaware of how close she had been to being discovered by Gibbs, Jane flung herself onto her bed. She felt happier and more contented than she could remember.

As they sat at a table drinking their pints, Gibbs explained to Bradfield what had taken place at the Greek café.

'Although no one was working in the basement and no van was there I'm dead certain we've got the right café and bank, Len. The guy Silas was sweating and talking non-stop, making this and that excuse about having builders in, then having to give up on a rebuild in the cellar. The vault of the fucking bank is literally adjacent to his back-yard wall, he's that close. There were loose bricks and soil bags in the yard – I reckon the bricks are from a hole they've made through a wall in the cellar and the plasterboard is used to conceal it when they ain't working. The soil must have come from digging a hole under the vault. I'm bloody sure of it.'

Bradfield could feel his guts churning.

'What about tools in the basement?'

Gibbs shrugged and said he didn't see any spades or pickaxes, but they could be in the tunnel or hidden upstairs: he hadn't wanted to spook Silas by asking to look up there. However, he was excited about what he had seen in the basement.

'Although it looked like it was being done up, there was a gas cutting rig hidden under a dust sheet. It's an extreme heat-cutting torch, and no way does a basic renovation need something like that. I checked it out – it can cut through metal and steel and it is real dangerous equipment if you don't know what you're doing.'

'Fuck me,' Bradfield said, draining his pint.

Gibbs picked up their empty glasses to get a refill but Bradfield stood up.

'No, I want to get some shut-eye as it's gonna be all systems go tomorrow. They're definitely not through into the vault yet, and for some reason they've been having a rest day.'

'Do you think they sussed the surveillance and called it off?'

'No, otherwise Silas would have got rid of the gas tanks. Was he suspicious of you and Harris?'

'Nervous, yes, but I reckon he believed me about the break-in. Besides, you primed Mannie Charles to say it was true if he was asked. Silas hasn't got a pot to piss in and needs the money so I don't even think he'll tell Bentley we paid a visit as he was shitting himself.'

Bradfield patted Gibbs's shoulder. 'Good work, Spence. You get off home for some shut-eye. We beef up the surveillance from tomorrow, twenty-four hours non-stop for as long as it takes, if necessary.'

'It was a good night, boss, huh?' Gibbs said.

Bradfield smiled. 'You have no idea just how good it was.'

CHAPTER TWENTY-SIX

Detective Chief Superintendent Shaun Metcalf arrived at Hackney at 8 a.m. in a dour mood. Bradfield was in his office going over the reports and surveillance logs and the entire team was on tenterhooks. The DCS wanted a full update of the situation before agreeing to any further course of action.

Bradfield went over everything calmly and succinctly, detailing all the new information and evidence. The DCS remained tight-lipped and listened with his head slightly lowered, making it difficult to gauge whether or not he was going to sanction 'Operation Hawk'. Metcalf looked over all the reports himself to make sure Bradfield was not exaggerating his case. Eventually he pulled at his nose, sniffed and slowly laid down the papers before getting up and pacing around the room deep in thought, leaving Bradfield still wondering what his decision would be. He stood by the window looking down onto the street below and eventually turned to face Bradfield.

'You've got a green light, Len, but on one condition – I don't want individual arrests made for a conspiracy to rob the bank. I don't want a cock-up like that Lloyds Bank job where they never got the ringleader ... I want those bastards caught on the job, inside, shovels in hand, while their lookout is in position as well. You nick them all together and the case is strong. Plus one or two of them might turn Queen's Evidence against each other, especially the Greek as he seems likely to talk.'

'Thank you, sir. It was always my intention to get them all bang to rights on the plot, and I'm very grateful you agree,' Bradfield said as he stood up and shook Metcalf's hand.

'You haul in whatever extra manpower you need. Do whatever is necessary, but don't jump the gun as this will be a big press plus for the Met if you succeed.'

Bradfield had to take deep breaths to control his excitement. This could be a major step forward in his career and he was not about to mess it up.

'I've still got surveillance on all the suspected team, so if there is any movement to or from their individual addresses we'll be on it right away.'

'Good. I know your station CID people are helping out with the surveillance, but wherever possible get it done by the unit from the Yard. They're much more experienced and blend in with the surroundings more easily.'

As soon as Metcalf had left the station Bradfield was eager to sort out suitable observation points in Great Eastern Street, and then hold a briefing for Operation Hawk. The incident room was buzzing, and Jane was disappointed when Sergeant Harris came in and said that due to abstractions he was now two officers short on early turn and he needed Jane to go out in uniform and direct traffic by the Eastway underpass tunnel, where a major RTA had occurred and a driver had been killed, then come back and man the front desk.

Kath, overhearing and seeing Jane's crestfallen face, went up to Harris and asked to have a word.

'Sarge, if it wasn't for WPC Tennison we would never have identified the targets for this operation. It's the biggest robbery case we've ever worked on at this station so she deserves to be part of Operation Hawk. Besides, why can't you ask for an officer from another nick to assist?'

'I make the decisions about staffing, not you, Morgan.'

'Actually, DCI Bradfield does when it comes to a CID operation, so maybe you should ask him,' Kath said, gesturing to the door as she saw him enter the room.

'Ask me what?' Bradfield said, putting the reports back in the desk tray.

Harris started to explain his position but Bradfield didn't even let him finish.

'DCS Metcalf has authorized Operation Hawk and stated I can have whoever I want on MY team.'

Harris was annoyed. 'I assisted DS Gibbs at the café last night. Tennison is a uniform officer, not a detective, and as such I need her to cover the front desk.'

Bradfield glared at him. 'WPC Tennison is part of my investigation whether you like it or not! I signed off your overtime last night out of the CID budget, and gave you four hours extra as compensation, but if you like I can soon put a pen through it.'

A disgruntled Harris had no option but to back off. Bradfield gave a smile and wink to Jane before returning to his office.

'Thank you, Kath,' Jane said quietly.

'Forget it. Harris obviously helped out last night not just for the overtime. I reckon he thought he could use it to get you off the team and back in uniform to spite you. He's a sly bastard who plays Mr Nice with ulterior motives so watch him like a hawk.'

They both laughed at the pun. Kath said she had to go to a meeting with the lady who owned the shoe shop next to Silas's café.

'Isn't that a bit risky? Silas might see you and suspect you're police.'

'No flies on me, darlin' – I arranged to meet her at her flat above her other shop in St John's Wood. Catch ya later.'

Hebe Ide's flat was above her boutique shoe shop in St John's Wood High Street. It was small but elegant with very expensively priced shoes – way out of Kath's price range – in the window display. The shop's exterior and interior were very different from those of Hebe's other shop next to Silas's café in Shoreditch.

Hebe Ide was a very well-endowed woman in her forties, with heavy make-up and bleached blonde hair worn in a chignon. She was smoking and wearing a floral satin padded housecoat when she opened the door. Kath showed her warrant card, introduced herself, and was led up a narrow staircase. Following behind Hebe she couldn't help but notice her very shapely legs, but didn't much like the gold mule slippers she wore.

The hall was lined with model-like pictures of Hebe, and Kath thought she looked rather like a cross between Diana Dors and the 1960s songstress Yana. As they passed the photographs Hebe stopped and tapped one with her red-varnished fingernail.

'I used to be in show business. In fact I was named after a character in an opera. Do you know Gilbert and Sullivan's *H.M.S. Pinafore*?'

'Yes,' Kath replied. She'd heard of it, but never been to the opera in her life.

'In the opera Hebe is the first cousin of Sir Joseph Porter, First Lord of the Admiralty, and my surname Ide originates from a village of the same name in Devonshire.'

'How interesting. They're lovely pictures. I was just thinking how much you remind me of Yana,' Kath said, trying to get the subject onto something she knew.

'I met her a few times. She did the lot, modelling, acting and singing. "Climb Up The Wall" was her best song for me. She was so sexy and wore fantastic gowns that floated out at the back like a mermaid's tail, all sequinned and so tight it was a wonder she could breathe, let alone sing.'

Hebe led Kath into a chic drawing room with thick piled carpet and a velvet settee with matching chairs. More photographs of Hebe adorned the walls. The fireplace was art deco with a mantelpiece above laden with silver-framed pictures of Hebe.

'I gave up show business when I got married, but I still miss it, especially since my Arnie passed away. The shoe shops were his, been in his family for years, and now I run the business, no children, other than my little Poochie Poo,' Hebe said, stubbing out her cigarette before picking up a tiny white fluffy poodle from the settee and kissing it.

At first Kath hadn't noticed the dog, which was now licking Hebe's face repeatedly. It hadn't moved an inch or made a sound when they'd entered the room and Kath, thinking it was a cushion, had almost sat on it.

'So how can Poochie and I help you?' Hebe asked, once again kissing the dog who responded with more licks to her face.

'I'm here concerning your shop in Great Eastern Street and—'

'Bloody council have decided to demolish the whole row for development. I use it mostly for storage now as I have a Sunday stall at Petticoat Lane Market. The cheaper shoes sell like hot cakes there, but I don't know where I'm going to store all the stock when Hackney Council kicks me out. I've got a small green van I park up in the yard there, but I can't keep the shoes in it because some little buggers will only break in and steal the lot.' She put the dog down, got up, pulled a cigarette from a small silver case and lit it.

Kath was about to speak but Hebe was off again.

'I'm not doing good business ... there's no real passing trade since they demolished the houses and built that monstrosity of a car park. It's so bloody tall it blocks the sunlight into the shop and now the place smells damp and looks dowdy. Who knows, maybe it'll be a blessing in disguise when they close me down.' She sighed and took a long drag of her cigarette.

Kath had been briefed by Gibbs about what she should say, but it was almost impossible to get a word in edgeways.

'The car park is part of the reason I'm here,' she said.

'Have the other shopkeepers complained to you about it as well? I rarely see or speak to them now. I only open up on odd days and pop in early Sunday morning to get stock. Arnie and me lived in the flat above the Shoreditch shop when we first got married. Horrible place – the smell of the curries from next door used to come through and stink our shop out.'

'I thought it was a hardware shop next door?' Kath remarked.

'It is, but the home cooking of the Pakis stank, not to mention the smell from the fat Greek's café as well. Anyway, after Arnie passed away I rented the flat out until recently. The tenants were more trouble than they were worth, always complaining that this or that didn't work. We bought this place and opened the shop downstairs. It's much more upmarket round here. I shouldn't say it, but the truth is I sell the same shoes for a much higher price and no one who buys a pair bats an eyelid.'

Kath leaned forwards. 'Please, Mrs Ide, I don't wish to appear rude but I have to get back to the station soon.'

'You should have said ... anyway, how can I help you?'

'Well, a high number of quality cars have been stolen from the multistorey car park recently and we think it's a professional gang who steal to order, change the plates and sell the vehicles on.'

'I thought there was an attendant in a kiosk during the day?'

Kath had to think quickly and lied. 'We think he's part of the gang. If you are agreeable we'd like to put a sur-veillance team in the upstairs of your shop for a few days as it's directly opposite the car park. Hopefully that way we can catch them all.'

'Oh I see. Will you need me there?'

'No, not at all. Your property will be treated with respect and securely locked when the officers leave.'

Hebe inhaled, and then, deep in thought, perched on the arm of the chair by her poodle.

'Yes I'm agreeable. I'm hardly there and the shop is not worth opening really, and I guess my van will be safe while your lot are there,' she said, removing a set of keys from her handbag and handing them to Kath who thanked her.

'Can I ask you something?'

'Of course you can,' Kath replied.

'Well, obviously with the police using the shop I can't open, so I wondered if there will be any form of compen-sation for loss of my earnings?'

Kath was flummoxed and didn't know what to say, but she replied that she'd ask her DCI.

Whilst Kath was visiting Hebe Ide, DS Gibbs and another detective were at the multistorey car park hoping to find out what sort of view it gave and if there were any signs that someone had been camping out up there at night.

During the day there was a so-called security guard manning the exit. He wasn't very helpful and said that as it was a Saturday hardly anyone used the car park, so it was only open 9 a.m. to 4 p.m. He grumbled that it was a waste of time him being there but as he got time-and-a-half pay it was worth it.

Once the guard had stopped complaining, Gibbs and DC Hudson, posing as business executives, asked if company cars could be left overnight. He said that it was up to them, but as there was no security on duty anyone could come and go from the car park during the night. He moaned about winos and junkies using the ground-floor stairwell to sleep in and told them the stench of urine was overpowering. He didn't bother showing the officers around, claiming he had arthritis and couldn't walk up the slopes or stairwell and the lift was out of action. Hudson drove the unmarked police car from floor to floor. When they reached the top they were in two minds about getting out as the wind was howling, and it was freezing cold. Gibbs pulled rank so young DC Hudson begrudgingly got out of the car and had a good look round before returning.

'You find anything interesting?' Gibbs asked as Hudson got back in the car.

'You get a fantastic view of all the surrounding streets and shops, right across Shoreditch and the City as well.

I could even see St Paul's and the Post Office Tower – wish I'd brought me camera.'

'I meant anything interesting to the investigation, you dope, Hudson.'

Hudson opened his hand. 'Over there, the bit where you can see the café clearly, I found these discarded cannabis roaches and the faintest trace òf what look like wheelchair marks in the grit. There's some discarded chocolate-bar wrappers and an empty tin of Shandy Bass as well.'

Gibbs sighed. 'Bloody well go and get 'em then, they may give us some fingerprints.'

Hudson pulled up his duffle-coat collar, climbed out of the car again and did as he was asked.

Leaving their vehicle in the car park while they went to look for a suitable observation point to monitor the front of the café, Gibbs and Hudson walked casually along the road on the opposite side, and stopped by an old two-storey block of terraced flats. They were council-owned, run-down and the lower floor was boarded up with a notice stating that the building was soon to be demolished. They went round the back via an alleyway and headed up the rear concrete staircase that led to the top-floor corridor. The top-floor flats were all boarded up, except one which was still obviously occupied as outside there were a couple of well-cared-for pot plants and a small washing line with some cotton knee-length lady's knickers hanging from them. The net curtains were clean, and even the front door looked freshly painted.

Ignoring Hudson's suggestion that they remove the boarding from an empty flat, Gibbs shook his head and knocked on the door. 'You've a lot to learn, son. They're old lady's knickers on the line. Using her place will be warm, with plenty of tea, coffee and biscuits, while we watch the café.'

The door was inched open and, as Gibbs had guessed, an elderly lady in her eighties was standing in front of them holding a mop.

'I been livin' here thirty years and I've told ya a hundred times I ain't bloody leavin' – now piss off,' she shouted, and pushed the wet mop into Gibbs's chest.

'She obviously thinks we're council officials,' Hudson said with a smile.

Gibbs produced his warrant card and introduced himself. The old lady put down the mop, apologized and invited them in asking if they'd like a cup of tea and a biscuit. Gibbs smiled smugly at Hudson.

Jane was taking the names, warrant numbers, ranks and departments of all the new officers arriving in the incident room when a tall gaunt man in a black raincoat walked in carrying a large black box with a handle. Jane thought he looked rather lost and asked for his details for the team list. He told her he was clerical staff from Hounslow and had come for a meeting with his brother-in-law DS Spencer Gibbs.

As Jane wrote down his details she explained that DS Gibbs was out on enquiries but should be back soon, and told him that he could wait in the office or the canteen. He said the office would be fine, plonked his large box on the floor and sat down as DS Gibbs walked in carrying a tape recorder from the property store.

'Frank! How ya doin? Thanks for coming over,' Gibbs said.

Frank stood up, said hello and they shook hands.

'Have you got the equipment?'

Frank nodded and pointed to the black box. 'Yeah, it's heavy and I'm still an amateur when it comes to using it. But I'll see what I can do for you.'

'The guvnor's in his office and looking forward to meeting you,' Gibbs said and Frank followed him to Bradfield's office with his equipment.

After being introduced to Frank, Bradfield cleared a space on his desk for Frank to set up his Citizens Band radio. Gibbs put the tape recorder down next to the radio and also handed Frank a copy of Ashley Brennan's notes which listed the times and frequencies of the suspect conversations. Frank was twiddling with a dial when he looked up nervously at Bradfield.

'I know it's illegal, but I only bought it for a bit of fun off a Yank I know, to listen to airport control at Heathrow as I'm into planes.'

'Don't worry about it, Frank. No one's going to prosecute you as you're doing us a favour,' Bradfield said, in an effort to reassure him.

Frank nervously twiddled away with the frequency control, but all he was picking up was hissing static. He kept on repeating that he was just an amateur and would do his best, but it might take a while for him to link the wavelengths.

'You might have been better getting that Ashley chap to help you,' Frank said.

'He's too much of a geek and he said he'd lost contact. He rambles on in radio jargon, but if you need to call him for some advice then—'

Suddenly the radio began to whistle and the sound of a voice saying 'Over' could be heard.

'Oh, hang on, looks like I've got something,' Frank said excitedly.

'Bloody hell, don't tell me Bentley's in the café right now?' Gibbs remarked.

Bradfield waved his hand indicating for them to be quiet and leant over Frank to get closer to the CB so that he could listen.

Two Eighty-four from Golf Hotel receiving, over, they heard over the CB.

'Is that their call sign?' Frank asked, and Gibbs said the voice sounded familiar.

They then heard another voice reply. *Yes, Two Eighty-four receiving, over.*

Can you return to the station to man the front desk as bloody Bradfield won't release Tennison ... over.

'That's fucking Harris talking to a PC!' Bradfield exclaimed.

'You've tuned into the station-radio frequency, Frank,' a deflated Gibbs told him.

Bradfield was not pleased and took Gibbs to one side.

'We should get the bloke who picked up the radio transmissions on the Lloyds job – he seemed to know what he was doing.'

'Give him time, he's just nervous.'

'We haven't got it, Spence. If he doesn't get a result in the next few hours we'll have to bring in someone else.'

'Where you gonna get 'em from? This equipment is illegal. Pull your finger out,' Gibbs said as he patted Frank's shoulder.

Bradfield straightened his tie, and ran his fingers through his hair. Spencer, taking care of the guv, asked if he had his fags and matches, and he nodded as they left for the office meeting.

Bradfield, followed by Gibbs, walked into the room, where the haze of cigarette smoke now hung like a blue cloud. Those who were sitting stood up, and as one officer started to applaud everyone joined in.

Jane watched in awe as Bradfield laughed and said the applause was a bit premeditated and they would all get a lot more than a few hand-claps if they got the result they were after. He stood at the front of the room with Gibbs and placed a notebook and file down on the table in front of him then pointed to the mug shots of the Bentleys and Daniel Mitcham.

'You'll all be pleased to know that DCS Metcalf fully supports Operation Hawk and has given me the green light to proceed.'

There was a cheer and Jane could see the excitement on people's faces, as well as feel the buzz of anticipation as Bradfield paused briefly before continuing.

'Sadly there has been no movement today, to or from any of the suspects' premises. However, that doesn't mean they're on to us. On the contrary, after DS Gibbs's uniform stint last night, I'm certain that the TSB is the target bank to be robbed via a tunnel from Silas Manatos' café.'

He asked Gibbs to give them a run-down on what he had uncovered when visiting the café under the guise of a decoy burglary at Mannie Charles' tailor shop.

'Are we still on for the cut-price suits?' an officer asked jokingly, causing a ripple of laughter around the room.

Gibbs smiled. 'I'll pay for the lot if we get a result on this job.'

Bradfield held his hand up to indicate that he wanted to get back to the serious matters.

'We know the suspects weren't at the café last night, but there could be all kinds of reasons for that. It's unlikely they'll work during daylight hours, or try to break into the bank vault while it's open, so fingers crossed there'll be some action tonight. We now have two good observation points in Great Eastern Street which give us an excellent view of the café and the bank, and the cream of the crop from Scotland Yard's surveillance unit.' He nodded at the scruffily dressed officers in jeans and tatty coats leaning against the back wall. He continued, 'They will be doing the tails and manning those points along with myself, DS Gibbs and a selected few of you. As soon as this meeting is over the new observation points will be manned.'

Jane listened, impressed by Bradfield's calmness and clarity as he outlined exactly which teams were to be in place, and where.

'Will we be taking them out tonight, guv?' a detective asked.

'Only if we can be sure the targets are actually inside the bank and that is a decision the DCS supports. I appreciate we won't know for sure from the ops, but we can see the back yard of the café from the rear of the shoe shop, so once they start loading the van with bags or sacks of their spoils we take 'em out then if need be. Given the amount of safety-deposit boxes in the vault it will take more than one run to load the spoils into their van. When that goes down the arrest team need to be on their guard. Make no bones about it, John Bentley and Danny Mitcham are nasty pieces of work and would take great delight in giving a copper a good kicking. Clifford Bentley may be old but I can assure you he'll still know how to take care of himself in a stand-up fight.'

'Truncheons won't be much use to us then, guv,' an officer said.

Bradfield gave a cynical smile. 'Off the record, should any of you come by a spare pickaxe handle that just happened to be lying nearby then defend yourself as you see fit.'

'The handles are already sorted,' Gibbs leant over and whispered to him.

Bradfield told them that the DI in charge of the Yard surveillance unit had already given him the teams his officers were to work in, and which observation point or vehicle they would be in.

'We will work on the Yard's team radio frequency and I don't want to hear anyone else but them or me making communication. They'll be using coded communication, so if our suspects are monitoring police radios they won't have a clue what's being spoken about.'

DC Hudson asked how he would know what was being said and Bradfield explained that his CID officers would be paired up to work with the surveillance officers who would explain things, and when it came to making arrests the surveillance officers would not be involved in order to protect their identities.

He told his Hackney, and other local CID officers, that after the meeting DS Gibbs would read out who was working with who and at which location.

'Any questions so far?' Bradfield asked.

They came thick and fast and he had to keep instructing them to ask their questions in an orderly fashion.

A surveillance officer raised his hand and Bradfield pointed to him.

'Do we have any intel that suggests the suspects might be armed?'

There was a sudden hush and there were a few worried looks. It was something that no one had as yet considered, even Bradfield, but he wasn't going to admit it.

'Good question – there is no intel about that, but my

gut feeling is that they won't be armed. This appears to be a tunnelling job as opposed to a "by the front door" armed bank robbery, and real guns aren't the Bentleys' style. I know that may not reassure all of you so I will instruct Duty Sergeant Harris to issue firearms from the safe to those of you who are authorized to use them. Let me be straight that using firearms is a last resort and they are only to be used if any of the suspects pulls a gun. The last thing I want is a gun fight at the corral, bullets flying around and an own goal where one of us gets shot by a colleague.'

A scruffily dressed undercover officer, who had long greasy hair and facial stubble, stuck up his hand. He was wearing woollen gloves with the fingers cut off, the wool in places unravelling as he had been pulling off strands throughout the meeting.

'How we going about monitoring the suspects' walkie-talkie communications?'

'We have an expert on board, provided by DS Gibbs, who has equipment to monitor other radios in the vicinity.'

'How does it work, guv?' he asked.

Bradfield turned to Gibbs with a cheeky grin. 'I think you're best placed to answer any questions.'

'Uh, well, it's to do with amps, frequencies, megahertz, etc. All a bit complicated really so I won't bore you with the details,' Gibbs said, and looked at Bradfield as if to say, 'Don't you dare ask me to elaborate further.'

Another officer put his hand up. 'I assume the bank must have an alarm? Surely if they try to get into the vault it will go off?'

'If they attempt to open the vault door from the outside out of banking hours all hell will break loose with more bells ringing than a monastery. However, my bet is they have a good bell man on their team. The TSB manager thinks the bank is impenetrable but the thing is, if the alarms are down, it's not. For any of you not familiar with the term "bell man", it's a villain's term for someone who's an expert electrician, especially when it comes to alarm systems. They know how to cut, bypass and disarm them without triggering the system. That's why I think the former Army engineer and electrician Danny Mitcham is on the Bentleys' team. He also trained with a bomb-disposal unit for two years.'

Bradfield gestured towards the mug shot of Mitcham, adding that he had been discharged from the Army for stealing electrical equipment and seriously assaulting the military policeman who tried to arrest him. He did not add that as yet they had no clarification that he was actually connected and it was simply his gut feeling.

'You think they'll be using explosives?'

'I doubt it. It's a very confined space and too dangerous. Explosives were used by the gang that did the bank robbery two years ago, and the dust nearly choked them all.'

There were murmurs and nods of agreement about Mitcham as the same undercover officer asked the next question.

'Did the DCS give any indication of how long Operation Hawk's to run?'

'It's going to be for as long as it takes.'

'Shit, that could be weeks, months even? Me granny's knitted gloves'll be shredded.'

'We stay on this, and we wait. But my bet is they'll be in the vault any day now.'

Again murmurs erupted and Bradfield had to quieten them down. This time Kath put her hand up.

'It might be nothing, but WPC Tennison's report from yesterday afternoon says she heard Renee Bentley ask the postmaster when some old £5 notes would no longer be legal tender.'

Gibbs shrugged. 'It's September this year and it's the ones issued between 1963 and 1971 – they were the first issue with Queen Elizabeth's head on. What's strange about that?'

'I don't see Renee as someone who'd have a lot of old fivers stashed away for a rainy day. But a bank would, and she might just be asking about the fivers on behalf of her old man and sons. I mean, you don't want to turn a bank over and have a few grand of fivers that will soon be worthless.'

Bradfield hadn't read Jane's report and he knew Kath had raised a valid point. He gave a cold glance towards Jane wondering why she hadn't told him. She blushed and looked away.

'Thank you, Kath, good point. But it can only be resolved by interviewing Renee and I can't very well do that before arresting the rest of her family, can I?'

'She also wanted to know about travel brochures for the US – strange when you think she's probably never been further than Southend.'

Yet again Bradfield was caught off guard.

'Yes, Kath, as I said it will all be noted down for the interviews. Right, let's move on. DS Gibbs will read out your teams and surveillance positions, as well as call signs and vehicle allocations. Take note of who's with who and their call signs. Don't try and be smart by putting it to memory because when the action starts you'll forget. I want you out there on the plot by half four at the latest. Do your job well and don't let me down.'

*

It was a further half-hour before the meeting finished. Everyone filed out to go up to the canteen for takeaway refreshments before Operation Hawk got into full stride. Jane was about to leave with Kath when Bradfield gestured towards her.

'Tennison, see me in my office.'

She started to put her chair back against the wall.

'Leave the fucking chair,' he growled, and stormed off.

She followed him into his office wondering if he was worked up over her surveillance report. Entering the room she saw DS Gibbs's brother-in-law Frank, wearing headphones and twiddling the CB radio knobs. Bradfield was blunt and told him to take himself and his equipment to the incident room to play with. As soon as Frank closed the door Bradfield turned to face Jane and stood right in front of her.

'Why the fuck didn't you tell me Bentley's mother was asking about soon-to-be illegal fivers?'

'I did a full report for you yesterday, before I went back to the section house.'

'If they know there's a load of worthless fivers in the bank then someone with inside knowledge must have tipped the Bentleys off. I doubt it's the bank manager, but it could be an employee. So if Dunbar goes spouting off to the rest of the staff about my visit and the Bentleys get to hear about it, then Operation Hawk is fucked.'

'I'm sorry, I didn't think ...'

'No, you didn't. My career's on the line here and you don't seem to care.'

'I'd left my report in the filing tray and you took them all this morning to read, so I—'

'You think I had time to check everything before the DCS arrived? Anyone with an ounce of common sense would have told me personally. Why didn't you tell me last night when we were together in my room?'

She was so shocked by what he had just said that she didn't know what to say, other than mutter that she was sorry as she fought hard to hold back the tears.

'You're off surveillance so stay in the incident room, man the radio and make sure everything is indexed and filed correctly. Now, get out of my office,' he snapped furiously. As she turned to open the door he reached out and caught her arm.

'Sorry I sounded off at you. I sometimes forget you're still a probationer with a lot to learn. Just forget about it this time, but don't ever let it happen again.'

She walked out, closing the door quietly behind her and feeling devastated. Not so much about being grounded, but by the way in which he had spoken to her. It hurt, and she felt as if she had let him down.

Jane was physically shaking and felt faint as she went downstairs to the ladies' locker room. It was hard to understand Bradfield's outburst after what had happened between them in his room the previous night. She chastised herself for being so oversensitive and crying. She knew she had made a big mistake and one that she would never forget, but she had learned a lesson – albeit the hard way.

Leaning over the metal sink she turned on the tap and splashed cold water over her face. As she patted it dry with a paper towel Kath banged in and flung her arms around her.

'Oh listen, I am so sorry if I landed you in it with Bradfield at the meeting. I didn't mean to, and if he gave you a bollocking I'll have a chat with him. Are you all right?' she said, seeing the sad look on Jane's face.

'I'm fine … he was actually quite good about it.'

'Oh Christ, that's a relief, because he's working under such pressure I thought he might have torn a strip off you about Renee Bentley.'

'I'll get over it, Kath, don't worry about me.'

Kath smiled. 'Good for you, girl, but you're my friend so I do worry. If anything's ever bothering or upsetting you then I'm here for you, OK?'

Jane smiled and nodded.

Kath looked in the mirror, fluffed up her hair and then turned to Jane.

'I've not been attached to anything so big and it's more exciting than a murder inquiry for me. How about all those undercover guys? I've got the hots for one of them. It's a massive operation and the guv will get a big promotion if we pull it off. Mind you, if it all goes tits up, he could be back in uniform directing traffic.' She gave Jane a hug and sashayed to the door with her hands on her hips.

'*I'm like a lonely little rose waiting in the shade, I need your sunny smile,*' Kath sang, and saw that Jane looked confused. '"Climb Up The Wall" – it's a song by Yana. I have to say, that Hebe Ide was a piece of work. But I reckon she'll give me a good discount on a lovely pair of sling-backs.' She started singing again as she walked out of the locker room.

Jane was at a loss as to who Yana was, but Kath's excitement and enthusiasm were contagious. She hesitated briefly before taking a deep breath and heading back up to the incident room. It was strangely quiet as by now everyone on the team had left the station to take up their observation positions. Frank was hunched over a desk at the far end of the room still wearing headphones and twiddling knobs, and it almost made her laugh. He suddenly sat bolt upright and asked her to get Gibbs and Bradfield. She didn't want to go anywhere near the DCI at present, so said that they had probably left the station. He frantically began turning various knobs and dials and Jane asked if there was anything she could do to help. He took off his headphones and threw them down on the table.

'Thought I had something there for a second, but it was just static, I think. God, I wish I knew more about how these things work. I really need to use the bathroom – would you mind just keeping a listening ear for a minute or two?'

'Oh fine, I don't mind at all,' Jane replied, and he left the room.

She sat in his very warm seat and put the headphones on. All she could hear was static crackles. Curiously twisting one of the dials, she was stunned as Janis Joplin began to sing her favourite song.

Take another little piece of my heart now, baby ...

Wanting to get rid of the music she turned the dial a bit more and heard the sound of a rasping cough and a male voice trying to say something in between coughs. But she couldn't make out what he was saying. Jane looked at the tape-recording deck that was connected to the machine but didn't know how to turn it on.

She listened as the man coughing cleared his throat of phlegm and spoke in a croaky voice.

You hold this (cough cough) *button down to talk like this, then* (cough cough) *when you finished say 'over' and release it to listen to the reply.*

The coughing became worse and then there was a click and nothing but radio static. She turned in a panic as

Frank reappeared and lifted one side of the headphones from her ear.

'I've just heard a man's voice. Sounded like he had a bad cold, and it was hard to make out what he was saying but I think he was telling someone how to use a two-way radio.'

'Did you record it?' Frank asked.

'I didn't know how to work the thing,' she replied in a worried voice and passed back the headphones.

Frank twisted the dials back and forth and one of the sound-indicator arrows began to swing from left to right.

'Nope, I just got static. Maybe something or nothing, so best we keep it between us as I left my post and it wasn't recorded.'

Uneasily Jane agreed.

To appease David, who was acting like a petulant child, John had told him to show their dad how to work the walkie-talkie, little realizing they'd been overheard. With a temperature of 102 and a fever so bad he couldn't get out of bed there was no way David could be lookout that night. Clifford joined John in the kitchen and they sat down to enjoy a saveloy-and-chip tea.

'You gonna be OK? Did he show you how to use it?' John asked.

'Yeah, it's not a brain teaser, and to be honest the way he is tonight he'd be a liability up on the car-park roof. He can hardly sit up, let alone stand. He's that fucking sick you'd hear him coughing a mile away.'

John put his arm around his father and hugged him tightly.

'Well, he is, and always was, a liability. I gotta be honest, I'm glad you're looking after our backs. So eat up and we'll get moving in half an hour.'

The doorbell rang and both men froze, wondering who it was. It rang again and they heard Renee saying she was coming followed by the sound of the front door opening.

John inched the kitchen door open and saw Renee ushering in the local GP. He turned to his dad with gritted teeth.

'Jesus Christ, she's only got the fuckin' doctor in,' he whispered, and closed the door before continuing. 'I'm tellin' you, Dad, she's a bigger liability than bloody David. I done a drawing, workin' out how deep and at what angle we hadda dig the tunnel and slung it in me bedroom bin when I'd finished with it. She must have taken it out to have a look as I found it on the kitchen table.'

'Don't worry, son. She's that thick she won't have a clue what your drawing means.'

Clifford then opened the door and went to David's room.

'Is he all right, Doc?' he asked.

John could hear the doctor saying that it wasn't pneumonia, but a severe bronchial infection, and David should stay in bed for a couple of days. He wrote out a prescription for some antibiotics and Renee thanked him for coming, before showing him out.

'I'm going out to get David's prescription,' she said, taking her coat down from the hall stand. Clifford shrugged, indifferent, as she picked up her purse.

'Do you want me to get somethin' in for your tea?'

'No, we've had ours. And we're goin' out to a club,' Clifford said.

'But David's in no fit state to go drinking. You heard what the doc said; didn't ya?'

'I meant me and John, you dozy mare. So don't wait up.'

Renee buttoned up her coat and stared at him accusingly before leaving.

David lay in bed feeling as if his body was on fire. His chest was hurting, as well as his leg and his back, and the headache he had was unbearable. He was annoyed that he wasn't taking any further part in the robbery for at least two days. But the reality was he knew he was too ill to sit in the cold car park for another night.

John walked in and took the walkie-talkie from David's bedside drawer. He looked at the profusely sweating face of his brother.

'We're off now. You get plenty of rest and take them antibiotics when Mum's back. We told her we're off to a club, OK?'

'I'm sorry, John, but will I lose any of my cut because I can't go wiv ya?'

'Course not, you stupid bugger. Family always share, right?'

It was six thirty when Clifford and John left the flat and headed out of the estate to get the van from the lock-up, unaware that their movements were being monitored, and a fleet of surveillance vehicles would be on their tail.

CHAPTER TWENTY-SEVEN

Everything was going smoothly as the surveillance vehicles followed at a distance behind John and Clifford Bentley, who were now in the 'rung' van travelling in the direction of Great Eastern Street. Undercover officers were on the number 55 bus tailing Danny Mitcham, who, like the Bentleys, clearly hadn't got a clue what was going on around him. Bradfield's hunch about the bell man had been spot on.

Op Three at the shoe shop relayed in code that John and Clifford had just pulled up at the rear of the café and Silas had come out to open the gates, which he had unlocked earlier in anticipation of their arrival.

Five minutes later Danny Mitcham was seen by officers from Op Four, which was the flat belonging to the elderly woman in the derelict building opposite. Mitcham was strolling casually down Great Eastern Street and, stopping in front of the café, he had a quick look around before knocking on the door. As soon as Silas opened it he slipped inside.

Bradfield was still in his office catching up on paperwork, but finding it hard to concentrate as the anticipation of the night ahead ran through his body like adrenalin. He was able to monitor the situation by listening to one of the surveillance radios he had with him, and DS Gibbs was keeping in contact from Op Three by telephone. It was his intention to go to one of the observation points in Great Eastern Street later in the evening.

Gibbs was concerned that the multistorey car park might not be the lookout point for the gang, as John Bentley hadn't driven in to drop anyone off. Nor had they seen anyone enter with a vehicle to drive up to the top floor, or for that matter even go up on foot. He was about to phone DCI Bradfield when Clifford Bentley was seen exiting the café from the rear. He walked up the alley, across the main road and towards the car park.

'Fuck off, you stinking bastard,' Clifford said as he kicked the legs of the drunken tramp lying on some cardboard boxes by the stairwell to the upper floors.

Groaning, the tramp watched Clifford climb up the stairs out of sight before putting his mittened left hand up to his mouth and pressing the transmit button concealed on his wrist, which operated the hidden radio sewn into his coat.

All units from Foxtrot One, Target Two on foot travelling up Charlie Papa with comms device.

OK, received by Silver, DS Gibbs replied, as he watched from the front window of the shoe shop. He could see Clifford climbing up the stairwell, and looking through the binoculars that he was carrying a walkie-talkie. A couple of minutes later Clifford had reached the top floor and was surveying the area.

Gibbs breathed a sigh of relief. He rang Bradfield from the secure line they'd installed in the shoe shop, and updated him.

'Good job, Spence – I heard it on the surveillance radio but didn't have a code book in front of me so was having to guess some of what was said. What's it like in the shoe shop?'

'Bit of a shithole compared to the old lady's flat, but of course that's where you decided you'd like to watch from for some reason,' Spence said cynically.

'My rank comes with privileges, Spence, so I get first pickings. Any sounds coming from the café basement yet?'

'No. An officer's down there with a listening device, well, a big stethoscope really, so if and when there is any sound we should pick it up. What's happening about the bank manager? You still gonna speak with him at his home tonight?'

'No, he might become overanxious and start shooting his mouth off to the staff, or worse, make an appearance at the bank late at night to check it over. How's your brother-in-law getting on?'

'I put Frank in the old lady's place, so he'll be with you. He's got the CB and everything else set up.'

'Still twiddling with his knob, is he?' Bradfield asked, and laughed.

'He made out he was like the radio genius Marconi to me at a family get-together. Be handy if he did pick up some chatter between the Bentleys, but either way we've got everything in hand down here. Backup vehicles with armed officers are parked up well away to cut off every possible escape route, and someone at each op is carrying a revolver as well. Strange that David Bentley isn't with them though.'

'I think I might have cracked that one. Tennison's report said Renee bought aspirin and cough mixture, then there was the doctor visiting the flat earlier, and it must be bloody cold up on that roof all night. I reckon David's on a sickie and had to drop out, so the old man has stepped in – which is great for us. He'll never see the light of day again as his sentence will ensure he dies in prison.'

'You're a heartless soul at times, Len.'

'Thank you, Spence. I'll be down there a bit later hopefully, but I need to catch up on this paperwork so that I won't be too snowed under when we nick 'em all.'

Jane had finished the indexing and was sitting alone in the office. She was unsure how long she was supposed to work for, or even if someone was going to relieve her so she could at least get some refreshments. Having listened to all the radio interaction between the surveillance officers she was really upset that she was cooped up inside. Even being in a tatty, stinking obo van would be more exciting than this.

She heard someone enter the room.

'Are you here to relieve me?' she asked. As she turned round she realized it was Bradfield.

'Why? You bored?' he asked, dropping a bunch of files on her desk. 'This lot needs indexing as well,' he said bluntly.

'I thought you might have been Kath, I haven't had a meal break all day.'

'Go on then, take half an hour. I've got a radio in my office as well so I'll keep a listening ear on things. I'll ring Gibbs and tell him to send an officer back to relieve you for the night at ten.'

Jane thanked him, and as she left the room he asked her to bring him a coffee and a ham sandwich when she'd finished her refs break.

When she returned he was sitting at his desk with his feet up and his raincoat bundled up to act as a cushion for his head. She placed the mug down on his desk and said that she was more than willing to stay on if he felt she would be useful. He lowered his legs and twisted his head from side to side.

'To be honest I think they're at least two nights short of getting into the vault. But the good thing is we're all in position and up and rolling. Tomorrow night will be more interesting, but right now we need to play the waiting game. If you think it'll be an experience then by all means stay on. If not, I'd go and get some shut-eye so you're fresh for tomorrow.'

She nodded, and then hesitated. 'So you think they'll go into the bank tomorrow, or the next night?'

He sighed, leaning back in his chair. 'Well, only because it's the weekend and with the TSB closed they can work both day and night. The overtime bill for this operation is astronomical, so the sooner they break in and we get them nicked, the easier it will be on the Commissioner's pocket.'

He grabbed the mug of coffee and grinned, raising it up as a thank-you. Jane hesitated.

'My mother – remember you met her when you came to my parents' flat? She wondered if one Sunday you might like to come over for lunch.'

He cocked his head to one side.

'Well, that's very kind of her, and maybe at some time that could be on the cards. Right now it's a bit difficult but pass on my thanks for the invitation.'

She nodded, feeling foolish. 'Well, I'll stay on for a while, and if you need another cup of coffee or anything just shout.'

He sipped his coffee and she hovered for a moment.

'Jane, about what happened between us – you still all right about it?'

She blushed and nodded.

He held out his hand. 'Come here, come on.'

His desk phone began to ring, but he ignored it. Jane took his hand and he drew her closer. Her heart pounded as he reached up and touched her face and she leaned close for him to kiss her.

Gold from Silver, pick up phone, urgent, Gibbs said over the radio.

Bradfield released her, grabbed the phone and with a look of dread on his face gestured for her to leave as he took the call from the shoe shop.

'Don't tell me they're into the vault already, Spence?'

'No, it's still all quiet. But there is a slight problem. Hebe Ide, the woman who owns the shoe shop, has turned up and is filling up her van in the yard with shoes.'

'Well, let her get on with it. In fact help her if need be, so you can get rid of her quicker.'

'We can see Silas in his yard looking up and down the alleyway. He must have heard something and be wondering what's going on. Thing is Kath Morgan asked her if we could use the shoe shop to watch the car park for a team nicking classy motors.'

'Sort it, Spence, and quick. If Silas speaks to her then it could be game and career over for us. I'm on my way down there now. I'll use the back-street entrance and go to Op Four at the old lady's'.

Hebe tottered back and forth into the shop, carrying out shoeboxes and piling them into the back of her green Morris Marina van. She was wearing a gold lamé miniskirt, high wedge sandals and a lacy blouse showing off her cleavage. She had gone in through the front door and then unlocked the back to load the van. Gibbs went down to speak with her in the hall.

'I'm sorry about this, love, but I got a last-minute offer for a Sunday market stall in Kensal Green. Normally I do Petticoat Lane, but there's more money to be made at Kensal Green. It's an early start in the morning so I thought I'd just pack up the van and drive it home tonight.'

To get rid of her as fast as possible Gibbs told Hudson who was working alongside him to stack the boxes by the back door for her to load them, but not to go into the yard in case Silas saw him. Surprisingly, Hebe was quite professional, checking the sizes before piling them in a neat and orderly way into the back of the van.

Silas had by now gone upstairs to his flat and was looking out of the back-bedroom window. He could see Hebe loading her van, and thinking that John and Danny were about to start work with the electric drill, he rushed down to the cellar and told them to stay quiet and not move. John said his dad had already been on the walkie-talkie and told them there was a woman entering the shoe shop.

'Is that bloodies Hebe woman. She owns it and thinks she's a Yana lookalike – always singing her song "Climb Up The Wall". She makes me go up the wall sometimes. Anyway I just check out what she doing.'

Silas peered round the shoe-shop rear gate, which Hebe had already unlocked because she'd be leaving, once she had loaded the shoes. She was bending into the van, her skirt riding up her bottom and revealing her lacy knickers. DC Hudson was about to put some more boxes by the back door when he heard Silas's voice and ducked out of sight.

'Hello there, Hebe darlin', how you keepin'? I hear

sound in your yard so thought it best I check it out as
there been some break-ins lately.'

'Hey, Silas love, long time no see. The shop's OK, I'm
just loading up for market day tomorrow, and then I've
got a hot date at a club with a nice young man.'

'You no change, Hebe. How's business? Mine not so
good.'

'Same for me, darling – to be honest I'll be glad to see
the back end of this shithole, and some of these shoes I'm
gonna be sellin' at less than cost. Eh, you don't need a nice
pair of loafers, do you? They're real suede and nice stitching.'

'No ta – you need any help packing?'

Gibbs was upstairs and could hear everything. His heart
was pounding as he prayed that she didn't say she already
had some help.

'Na, I'm virtually done and these cork-soled sandals
don't weigh nothin'. Thanks for askin', though.'

'OK, you have good night, Hebe.'

She lit a cigarette, laughed and said she was intending to
do just that as Silas returned to his café.

Gibbs watched from upstairs as Silas closed his yard
gates and went inside. It had been a narrow escape. He
went downstairs and told Hudson it was all clear.

'Excuse me,' she whispered to Gibbs as she stepped
inside the shop. 'You wanna tell me who you're really
watching out for, a gang of car thieves or the fat Greek?'

'What makes you ask that?'

'It's just I noticed you got people at the front and back
of the upstairs, and Silas was being nosy, not friendly.
That's why I didn't say someone was already helping me
load the van.'

Gibbs told her she was right, but he couldn't go into

details and asked her to keep it to herself. She said that she was the soul of discretion, and besides she hated the fat leery Greek.

Gibbs went upstairs. It was a further ten minutes before Hebe finished her cigarette and loaded the rest of the shoes into the van, assisted by Hudson who was still stacking them by the door.

'I'm goin' now,' she said, and gave him a come-hither glance.

She winked at him. 'Maybe we can have a drink sometime.'

'I'm always very busy,' Hudson said nervously.

'What size shoes are you?' she asked, looking down.

He gulped, unsure what she was actually looking at. 'I got big feet.'

She ran her hand through her bleached blonde hair, gave him a sensual smile and looked down again.

'So I see, well, you know what they say, big feet, big—'

'Hands,' he replied quickly, knowing what she actually meant.

'Big hands are useful as well, sweetheart. Anyway, best I get off. You go and help yourself to a pair of shoes in the basement as a thanks for helping me load up the van.'

It was a relief when she left and he was able to go back upstairs.

'Sounded and looked like the blonde bombshell had the hots for you,' Gibbs said, taking the mickey.

'She scared me, Sarge. I wouldn't know how to handle a woman like her.'

'She'd eat you up and spit you out, son, but you'd learn a lesson or two at the same time.'

One of the officers who had been listening in the shoe-shop cellar suddenly came running upstairs.

'Sounds like they've started drilling – you can hear it through the walls, even without the listening device.'

As Gibbs reached the shop floor he could hear a dull rumbling sound, which increased in intensity and volume as he ran down the basement stairs. The drilling noise echoed around the room as bits of sand and stones on the floor bounced up and down like ping-pong balls under the heavy vibration. Gibbs felt something landing in his hair and looking up saw that loose plaster was crumbling off the ceiling. The officer with the listening device looked anxiously at DS Gibbs.

'I hope this place doesn't collapse on my bloody head!'

'Course it won't, son, but if it does be sure and let me know.'

Gibbs hot-footed it back upstairs.

Renee had given David a large dose of medicine and he was feeling a little better. His temperature had gone down, and he managed to eat a slice of toast and some chicken soup. She had left him to sleep while she watched *Coronation Street* then checked again to see how he was. Edging quietly into the room Renee stood by his bed and looked down at his handsome face. She felt such overwhelming love for her youngest son, and she couldn't bear the thought of ever being parted from him. She fetched a hard-backed chair and placed it beside the bed. He had lovely soft hands with slender fingers and she wanted to reach out and hold them like she'd done when he was a little boy afraid of the dark. He opened his eyes and blinked.

'What you doing?' he asked quietly.

'Checkin' you're OK, son. I need to talk to you about something and with your dad and brother out this is my best opportunity.'

'What do you want to talk about?'

'They think I'm like wallpaper, with no thoughts or feelings. But after years of what they've put me through they've wrung the life out of me – well, your dad has more than John, but he scares me as well sometimes. Cliff's knocked me around for years, but you get sort of used to being abused, because fighting back or arguing only makes it worse. Eventually you learn to keep out the way and say nothing, especially if you want a quiet life. I used to tell myself I stayed because of you two boys, but the truth was I never had the guts to get out. The only time I ever felt really safe was when he was in prison.'

'Why are you telling me this, Mum?'

She sighed, patted her knees and straightened her apron.

'Oh David, I ain't stupid, love. The years of turning a blind eye and pretending not to know what's going on made for an easy life. But truth is I always knew ...'

'I don't know what you're talking about.'

'Yes you do, David, and I know you and John have been up to something illegal. And your dad's involved too, now he's out. I don't know what it is, but I'm begging you to stay out of it. Don't get involved, son, for your own good.'

David said nothing, but couldn't look his mother in the eye.

She shook her head. 'There's no point in denying it, because I know. I've seen all the signs, seen them too many times not to know. And now I'm too old to walk away, but you can.'

He turned his back to her. 'That's a joke, me walking away.'

She got up and leaned over him.

'I got money saved, David, money I've kept hidden for

481

years. I'm giving it all to you because I want you out of here. I want you free of them, once and for all.'

'Thanks, Ma, but a few quid won't help me. And you got it wrong, we're not doing anything, I swear to you.'

Her face twisted. 'DON'T LIE TO ME!' she shouted, and kicked the chair over. He had never seen this side of her and he watched with alarm as she took deep breaths, afraid she was bringing on another asthma attack.

'It's not a few quid, David, it's my life's savings.'

She walked out of his room to her bedroom, got her hat box from the top shelf of the wardrobe and threw it down onto the bed. Removing the lid she tossed out the tissue paper, the gloves and her precious hat she'd only worn once. As she stuffed the money into a brown paper bag the doorbell rang. She froze. It rang again and she started to gasp for breath as her chest tightened in fear that it was the police. She took some puffs of her inhaler and, using the wall to keep steady, moved slowly from the bedroom to the front door, clutching the bag of money.

'Renee lovey, are you in? RENEE?' Nancy Phillips shouted.

Recognizing Nancy's voice Renee felt slightly less anxious, but she was still breathing heavily. She opened the door.

'Hello, love, sorry to knock so late but I'm burying my grandson tomorrow.'

'Tomorrow? But it's Sunday, isn't it?'

'Yes, but the coroner released Eddie's body yesterday and then it's a bank holiday on Monday and I was worried about keeping his body in the lounge for viewing for nearly five days, you know, what with the smell. Anyway the vicar's been very kind and said he'd hold the funeral service on Sunday for me. I'm havin' a few drinks after.

I'm askin' all the people I know from off the estate, cos poor Eddie didn't know nobody but junkies and no-good louts. Everyone's chippin' in and I thought you might like to, what with havin' two boys yourself.'

'Just gimme a minute, Nancy,' she panted, and eased the door half shut. Opening the paper bag she took out a £5 note, drew a few deep breaths to keep steady and opened the door again.

'Here you are, luv. I'll be there to pay my respects.'

'That's ever so generous of you, Renee – everyone's been so kind.'

She shut the door as David appeared in the hall. He looked worried.

She glared at him. 'You look like you're about to wet yourself, David. You still sayin' you're up to nothing? Poor Nancy's burying her grandson. He was just nineteen years old and there's lots more poor kids like him on this estate. I should have given her this money, at least she'd make good use of it.'

She gasped for breath, held up the bag and waved it at David who was holding onto the doorframe to stand upright.

'You need to lie down, Ma.'

'Makes two of us.'

She shoved the paper bag into his chest. 'You take this, go to Florida, get away before it's too late and the coppers come knockin' for real.'

He opened the bag and looked inside, then stared at his mother as she gasped and heaved for breath.

'Jesus Christ, Ma, where did you get all this cash from?'

'Cleaning fuckin' offices, washing down floors, taking in ironing and saving from my pension, take it, take it all, David.'

She went to lie down on her bed and began to cry.

He came into the room using his stick, and seeing her weeping made him feel close to tears.

'Florida's just a dream, Mum. I didn't really mean it.'

She plucked a tissue out of the box on her bedside table and blew her nose.

'Yes you did, son. I could tell by yer voice when you told me that's where you wanted to go … there's enough there for more than a plane ticket.' She never mentioned what she had found under his mattress and that she knew he had a passport.

He slowly edged to her bedside and sat beside her. He gently stroked her lined pale face and then bent to kiss her soft worn cheek. She gave him a warm smile, followed by a lovely girlish cheeky grin, and leaned closer.

'There was some cash your dad hid in the airing cupboard behind the boiler. I told him the cops took it when they came to arrest him the last time, so he thinks they nicked it and shared it amongst themselves. But I've been hiding it in me hat box for all the years he was banged up.'

She asked David to get her hat, which was lying on the floor. She sat up and he gently put it on her head and adjusted it. He stood back and smiled, as the wide brim and the flower in the headband made her look ridiculous.

'I'll wear this for the funeral tomorrow,' she said, finally smiling back.

'I love you, Ma, love you with all my broken heart.'

CHAPTER TWENTY-EIGHT

Beneath the café Danny, John and Silas were taking it in turns to use the Kango model G electric hammer drill to dig through the thick clay soil. They were now under the vault and starting work on the concrete base. It was hard, and progress had been slow, as only one person at a time could use a shovel in the claustrophobic tunnel. They were all exhausted and covered in dirt and dust. Although they had tied handkerchiefs over their mouths and noses, the dust from the concrete still got through and made them cough and sneeze. By now they had made a wider, deeper space under the vault and could just about kneel down, or lie on their backs, to drill the concrete and cut the embedded wire mesh with a bolt cutter. Although the Kango only weighed fourteen pounds the awkward angles they were forced to hold it at made it feel much heavier. After filling a rubble bag with concrete they had no choice but to wriggle backwards, dragging the heavy bag as they went. The oxyacetylene torch would have cut through the mesh quickly, but it was awkward to pull through the tunnel and the heat from the flames would make it feel like a sauna.

John and Danny were doing the brunt of the work as Silas was so unfit and overweight he couldn't keep up with them, and kept moaning that he didn't feel well and needed to lie down for a bit. John had commented to Danny, out of Silas's earshot, that the fat git would be doing them all a favour if he dropped dead from a heart attack and then they'd each get a bigger cut of the money and goods in the deposit boxes. John was having a break for some water when he thought he heard something coming from the radio. It had been difficult to hear due to the racket of the machinery.

Danny emerged from the tunnel and pulled the hand-kerchief from his face as John pressed the speak button on the walkie-talkie.

'Are you callin' us, Dad? Is everything OK?'

'No it's not, I'm fuckin' freezin' up here. How much longer before you're in?' Clifford asked, finishing the hip flask of brandy he'd brought with him.

'We're working hard, but it won't be tonight.'

'Then down tools and come and get me,' Clifford said.

'We're taking a break, but we're not ready to leave yet. Give us another hour or so.'

'Shit, don't do anything, don't make an effin' sound. Someone's just pulled up in a van outside the tailor's shop,' Clifford said tensely, at the same time annoyed that he was stuck out in the cold.

Bradfield, stationed at Op Four, was asleep in the armchair and the old lady had gone to bed when Frank picked up some conversation on his CB radio. He gently shook Bradfield's shoulder and he woke with a start. 'What you got?'

'Bit crackly in places, but I heard the tail end clearly and it's on tape.'

Frank was about to rewind the tape and play it but Bradfield told him not to in case they started a conversation on the walkie-talkie again and he missed recording it. 'It's OK, I've written it down in shorthand,' said Frank.

'John Bentley, Target One, said "It won't be tonight", so I assume he was talking to Clifford, Target Two. They still aren't into the vault.'

'Was that it?' Bradfield asked, alert now.

'No. Target Two said there's someone in a van pulling up outside the tailor's shop.'

'It'll be fucking Mannie!' Bradfield exclaimed, and hurried over to the front window.

He could see Mannie under the street light unloading suits from the van and taking them into the shop. 'Shit, how long's he been there?' He turned to the surveillance officer who had earlier played the part of the tramp and was now watching what was happening from the window.

'Just arrived, sir. I was waiting to see what he did before I disturbed you, but Frank got to you first.'

Frank had removed the headphones so the CB was now on loudspeaker for Bradfield to hear what the suspects were saying. He recognized John Bentley's voice.

Tell us what's happening, Dad.

The driver's alone and gone into the shop.

Is it the shoe-shop woman? Is she back again? John was wondering if Hebe had returned because she was suspicious.

No, it's a little geezer gone into the tailor's shop.

Bradfield was pulling his hair out wondering what the hell Mannie was doing there so late at night. He watched him return to the van for a third time and carry another armful of plastic-covered garments into the shop. When he closed the van's back doors Bradfield thought he was going to leave, but he went into the shop shutting the door behind him. Bradfield phoned Gibbs.

Seeing the light flashing on the silent phone they had installed in the shoe shop Gibbs answered it and Bradfield updated him on Mannie Charles's movements.

'What you going to do?' Gibbs asked.

'There's nothing I can do. If I send anyone over to the front of the shop then Clifford will see them from the rooftop and get suspicious. We'll just have to sit it out like our targets are. So make sure you don't make a sound in your op.'

Bradfield sat down in the armchair again and shut his eyes, but he couldn't sleep. It was the frustration and the underlying fear that the whole job would go wrong and they'd have no result for all their efforts.

It was nearly 2 a.m. by the time Mannie Charles eventually turned off the lights and locked up his premises.

'The tailor has come out the shop, guv,' Frank said, and Bradfield got up and went over to the window.

As Bradfield stood back and watched Mannie drive off in his van he heard Clifford and John's voices over the radio.

The coast is clear now, but can we pack up soon as my bollocks are almost frozen?

OK, I'll pick you up in thirty.

Bradfield knew it would still be at least half an hour before John and Danny were on the move as they would have to replace the plasterboard to conceal the hole in the wall and tidy up.

Unaware he was being watched Silas stood in the yard hosing his and Danny's boots down. John drove out from the alley and then across the main road to the car park where he pulled up outside and Clifford, who was already waiting, jumped in.

Bradfield told the mobile surveillance units to keep well

back as there would be little traffic on the road. He reckoned the targets would be returning to their home
addresses anyway, where the other officers waiting in
observation vans would pick them up again. It seemed
that Danny Mitcham was still at the café, and as there was
no drilling sound Bradfield assumed he was sleeping there.

Once John Bentley was well away from the area, and all
the lights were out in the café, Bradfield gave the coded
signal over the radio that everyone in Ops Three and Four
could stand down. He instructed them to meet him in half
an hour in the canteen at City Road, the nearest local
police station, for a quick debrief. Those watching the suspects' home addresses were to remain in situ and take it in
turns to get some sleep.

Returned to Hackney Station after the debrief, Bradfield
and Spencer went to the incident room.

'At least we know they're coming back later. They must
be close to getting into the vault and when they do we
pounce,' Gibbs said, yawning.

'I hope so because these all-nighters do my head in.'

Bradfield went over to the board with the array of mug
shots and tapped the photograph of David Bentley.

'I hope we get him as well. Maybe they'll use him
tomorrow. Be nice to bang up all the Bentleys at the same
time.'

'What about Renee their mother?'

'Arrest her as well if she's involved,' he said. Tapping the
mug shot of Clifford Bentley he continued, 'He didn't wait
long, only out the nick a few minutes and gonna be back
for the rest of his natural any time soon.'

'Let's hope it doesn't all turn to rat shit,' Gibbs said,
yawning again.

Bradfield glared at him. 'Why are you being negative again? If everyone does their job properly nothing will go wrong and we'll catch them red-handed on the plot. That's what the DCS wants and that's what he's gonna get, right?'

'Right, but I was just playing devil's advocate because what if they come back and it doesn't go down for some reason?'

Bradfield lit a cigarette, took a long drag and inhaled deeply.

'We just wait. Besides, it's a bank holiday weekend so it gives them an extra day to work. I bet they're planning to get it done before everything opens again on Tuesday.'

'Come on, Len, how long can Operation Hawk go on for? I mean, we don't actually know how close they are to the vault. What if it's another week? You then run a greater risk of them sussing out a surveillance unit, and if that happens they'll fuck off out the country, leaving us with egg on our faces. Why not take them out when they go back tomorrow night, while they're in the tunnel?'

Bradfield inhaled again, letting the smoke drift from his nose.

'No, I want them with the goods in their greedy little mitts. It's my career on the line here, Spence, not yours. And if this goes belly up I won't have one.'

They were interrupted by a deep groggy voice. Kath's head popped up from behind a desk in the far corner where she had been trying to sleep, using her coat as a makeshift blanket.

'Good to hear you both sounding so confident. You got a cracking team working for you, guv, and every single one of us are behind you one hundred per cent.'

Gibbs laughed. 'You've only been in the CID two

minutes so what do you know about how everyone feels?'

'The guv's right, Spence, you are negative. But I'm not. I got you Julie Ann Collins' killer so I deserve to be at the bank when you open the vault to nick Bentley's gang. And if you try and move me aside, I swear I won't go away quietly.'

Gibbs ignored her, and said he was going to see if there was an empty cell so he could try to get a few hours' kip.

Bradfield smiled at Kath. 'I like your positive attitude,' he said as he stubbed out his cigarette.

'You mind if I say something personal, guv?'

'When have you ever held back, Kath?'

'Well, you can go off like a rocket sometimes if anyone gets too personal.'

He cocked his head to one side. 'Come on, spit it out.'

'OK, here goes ... it's about Jane Tennison and the stuff in her report about Renee and the fivers she forgot to tell you about. She's been working long hours, feeling tired and it was a genuine mistake.'

'We're all tired, Kath.' He was starting to sound irritable.

'Yes I know, but she's really keen and hates to let anyone down. It's not bollockings she needs but encouragement. She's young, eager to learn, and yes, sometimes a bit overenthusiastic ...'

'Thank you, Kath, point taken. Now if you don't mind, I'm knackered.'

'I'm sorry, but I've known you for a long time and I know you can be a charmer when you want to be. It's pretty obvious she's got the hots for you.' Kath paused.

Bradfield shrugged and avoided making eye contact with her.

'You can tell from the way she looks at you. You've

always been a heart-breaker and I doubt she's ever met anyone like you. So please just behave, because I like her.'

He gave her his lopsided smile and stuck another cigarette in his mouth.

'You also smoke too much.'

'Mind your business, Kath, and don't push your luck, not if you want to be present when we make the arrests. Now get out, go and get some kip.'

Kath said goodnight and made a zipping motion across her mouth before leaving the room.

Bradfield sighed. He did smoke too much and knew he'd already crossed the line with Jane, but he'd been unable to stop himself. He decided once the arrests had been made he'd send Jane back to uniform shifts and make it clear there would be no Sunday lunches at her mother's.

Jane arrived at the station just before 6 a.m. and went to the ladies' locker room to get changed. She'd found it hard to sleep during the night: every time she closed her eyes she couldn't help picturing Bradfield's handsome face with his unruly curly hair and brilliant blue eyes. She kept wondering what would have happened in his office if they hadn't been interrupted by the call from Gibbs on the radio.

Putting on her jacket she looked at herself in the mirror. The murder inquiry had been fascinating, and often emotionally draining, but the adrenalin rush she felt being privy to Operation Hawk was even stronger. Before working with Bradfield, Jane hadn't considered becoming a detective but for her Bradfield epitomized what being a good detective was all about: compassion where needed and the ability to instantly change approach where necessary; always keeping in mind the forensics and fine details of an investigation, no matter what it might be. Being a detective and dealing with serious crime was more stressful than uniform work but Jane thought it beat working with Harris on the front desk any day.

Jane looked in the mirror and adjusted her bow tie. She touched her face recalling the way Bradfield had pulled her close and touched her cheek as he was about to kiss her. She was suddenly awoken from her thoughts by the sound of Kath's voice.

'That's the last time I sleep with Spencer Gibbs – I hardly got any kip at all.'

'You slept with DS Gibbs?' Jane asked, looking rather stunned.

'He didn't even have the decency to let me use the bed ... I had to kip on a mattress with a blanket on the floor. At first he started singing rock songs and keeping a drum beat on his thighs, then when he did fall asleep like a log he snored like a foghorn!'

'Was it your place or his?' Jane asked, somewhat confused.

'We shared an empty cell to grab a few hours' kip before going back on duty,' Kath explained as she started to undress to have a shower.

'I'm so excited about Operation Hawk I couldn't sleep, so I decided to come in early. Is Bradfield back?'

Kath hesitated and nodded her head. 'Yeah, he's crashed out in his office, you know how obsessive he is.'

'I'll see if he wants a coffee and some breakfast,' Jane said with a smile.

Kath saw through Jane's smile but felt apprehensive. 'Don't go disturbing him – he was so tired and moody earlier he'll bite your head off.'

'Oh right, I won't,' Jane said, looking rather dejected.

Kath knew she'd promised Bradfield to keep her mouth zipped, but out of concern she felt she had to say something. 'Listen, Jane, don't think I'm poking my nose in, but is there anything going on between you two?'

Jane flushed, leaned closer and whispered, 'Please don't tell anyone, but we spent the night together.'

Although she didn't show it Kath was stunned and needed time to think about what she should say to Jane. 'Don't worry, I won't. Right now I need a shower to freshen up so I'll see you later, darlin',' she said as she wrapped a towel round her and walked across the room to the showers, muttering to herself, 'Shit, shit, shit.' She stopped as she heard Jane singing.

'Have another little piece of my heart now, baby ... You know you got it, if it makes you feel good.'

CHAPTER TWENTY-NINE

Renee had pretended to be asleep when she'd heard Clifford enter the bedroom. He got into bed beside her and was snoring loudly as soon as his head hit the pillow. She had heard the bath water running and then the banging of John's bedroom door closing. She turned over onto her side and clasped her hands beneath her chin. Hanging on the wardrobe door was her best dress, and on the dressing table was the hat that she had only ever worn once.

It was a Sunday morning and she'd usually have a lie-in, but she just couldn't get back to sleep so she decided to make herself a cup of tea. Slowly easing herself out of bed so as not to wake Clifford, she put on her old dressing gown, picked up her slippers and crept out, closing the door silently behind her.

She put the kettle on the stove and popped two slices of bread into the toaster. There was no margarine left so she took out a bowl of dripping from the fridge and spread it onto her toast. She sat down and started to write out a shopping list, licking the lead of the pencil as she decided what she needed. She'd still got some leftover stew so they could have that for their dinner, but she was out of potatoes. The kettle boiled and she looked at the filthy clothes left by the washing machine. John's jeans and T-shirts were covered in grey powdery dust and his boots were caked in soil beside them. She put the clothes in a plastic bag, picked up the boots and placed them back down on an old newspaper. She decided to take them to the launderette later, but it would have to wait until after the funeral of Nancy Phillips' grandson. She went into the bathroom to wash her hair.

Half an hour later Renee went into the kitchen where a bleary-eyed John was sitting in his dressing gown reading an old paper. He was exhausted, and every muscle in his body ached from being cooped up in the cramped tunnel lifting the Kango drill. He'd poured himself a mug of tea from the teapot, but it was tepid and he piled in the sugar stirring it hard. He looked up and saw his mum with her hair still wrapped in a towel. She hardly spoke to John as she fried bacon and eggs, made a fresh pot of tea and set the table around him as he slurped the dregs from his mug.

'How's David?' he asked.

'Not well. He's still got bronchitis and by the looks of it a high temperature. I'm worried stiff about him and in two minds to call the doc again. '

'Just keep givin' him the medicine,' John grunted, and poured a fresh mug of tea. She finished the fry-up and put two platefuls of food with thick wedges of fried bread on the kitchen table along with a bottle of HP sauce.

Clifford walked in and sat opposite his son. Picking up the HP sauce he slapped the bottom twice and a large splodge fell onto his plate. He ate with his mouth open, making a terrible chewing sound. Some egg yolk dribbled down the side of his mouth which he wiped away with the back of his hand.

'Nothin' beats a fry-up.' Clifford spluttered, his mouth full.

'Go dry yer hair, Ma,' John said, and as Renee left the kitchen he got up and kicked the door closed behind her.

Despite being pleased when Clifford had said he'd take over from David, John felt his father hadn't done a very good job as lookout. His dad had stunk of brandy when he picked him up, and John was afraid of him falling asleep on the job because of the booze.

'Mum says David's still pretty bad so I can't risk takin' him as lookout. You'll just have to fill in again, Dad, but lay off the brandy this time.'

'Bollocks to that, it's freezing up there at night and the brandy is the only way to keep warm. In fact get Danny or Silas to be lookout and I'll help out in the café.'

It was something John had considered, but the last thing he wanted was his father looking over his shoulder all the time and nagging him.

'Your guts are too big for the hole we dug and Silas has to be at the café as owner in case anyone comes calling. Danny's younger and fitter, plus he's kosher with the electrics and will check for any alarm system we might have overlooked. If we start earlier today I reckon we'll be in the vault by late evening.'

'Are you sure of that? Seems a bit quick after where you left off this morning.'

John was certain they would break through into the vault, and because the area was quiet at the weekend they would have more opportunity to use the Kango drill without being overheard. He knew that once the job was done the break-in would not be discovered by the manager until the bank opened for business on Tuesday morning, after the Monday bank holiday.

'I told Silas and Danny I wanna work during the day as it's a Sunday. All the shops round there are closed and there's very little foot or vehicle traffic.'

Clifford looked surprised as he gulped down a mouthful without chewing it properly. 'I'll stand out like a spare prick at a wedding in daylight.'

'No you won't, only if you stand up all the time. Did you not notice the gaps in the wall for the rainwater to drain away? Just look through them till it gets dark.'

'Fuckin' brilliant and what about daytime security, or anyone who comes up to the top floor to park?'

'Don't worry about it. According to Silas, because that patch borders the City, all the local businesses are closed at weekends so it means there's nobody to use the car park and no attendant on duty in the pay kiosk. If anyone did drive in there's loads of room on the ground floor so why go all the way to the top.'

'I was thinking that now I'm the lookout, as well as one of the persons who put the job up, I deserve a slightly bigger cut than I'm getting, don't I?'

'You're a greedy old sod, Dad. OK, I'll slip a bit extra on the side for you.'

'Shake on that, son,' he said, putting out his hand.

'But don't say anything to the others or they'll start kicking off,' John said, shaking his father's hand.

Clifford laughed, coughed up some phlegm and, pulling a dirty handkerchief from his pocket, spat into it.

'If we finish the job by early Monday morning there'll be plenty of time to stash the stolen goods. I've already rented another lock-up nearby in Dalston to count out the proceeds.'

'Good thinkin', son, the filth will be crawling all over the place.'

'I know, and Silas is likely to be the first person the police will be looking for. I'll give him his cut of the cash so he can make his getaway and fly out to Greece.'

Clifford smiled. 'Make sure he's loaded with the dodgy fivers.'

John laughed. 'There's a secluded area in nearby woodland where I'll bury our cut of the money for a few days while the heat dies down, but I'm not sure yet what to do with any jewellery we find.'

'Don't worry, I know a good fence who can take it off our hands. What you gonna do with the van, son?'

'Take it to some wasteland and set light to it, along with anything else that might lead the police to any of us.'

Clifford patted John's back. 'Good lad, looks like you thought of everything.'

'Well, I was taught well, wasn't I, Dad?' John pushed his chair back and checked the time.

'OK, we go in half an hour at just after eleven.'

Clifford nodded and poured himself another mug of tea.

'I'll be ready, son, just finish me breakfast and then put some long johns on under me jeans and shirt and a couple of jumpers on top as well.'

John left the room to speak with his mum. Clifford took the opportunity to quietly fill his hip flask with the remains of the bottle of brandy, sticking the flask into the inside pocket of his donkey jacket which was hanging in the hallway.

Renee had changed into her dress and was in the lounge drying and brushing her hair in front of the electric fire when John walked in. He told her that he and his dad were off down the bookie's for a flutter and then the pub. She asked when they'd be back and he said he didn't know and she wasn't to wait up.

'What you want for tea? There's some stew left over,' she said, as she sprayed lacquer on her hair, making it stiff.

John replied that they'd get something from the chippie and as he turned to leave he stopped and looked at his mother.

'What you all dolled up for?'

She pulled on her white gloves and put on her hat, looking at John in the mirror as she adjusted it.

'Ma Phillips is burying her grandson today. Half the estate is going and everyone's given money for flowers and beverages.'

'On a Sunday? You are fuckin' havin' me on. Besides he was a pitiful waste of space, and what have I told you about not going out the flat?' John shouted.

Clifford heard them talking and walked in with his donkey jacket slung over his shoulder.

'Leave it out, son. It's always good to show respect.' Clifford turned to Renee. 'But don't you go on the lash or blabbering with your bingo mates, you come straight back home, right?'

'I heard you the first time, Clifford. It's sunny out, so what you want your big heavy coat for?'

'Because, you nosy cow, we might be doing some night fishing for carp on the Lea tonight. Me mate Chaz has invited me and John along.'

She laughed and took another look at herself in the mirror. She'd even put a bit of lipstick on. She wanted to see how David was doing before she left for the funeral, so she went out across the hallway and popped her head around his bedroom door.

'How are you feelin, son?'

'Not so good, Ma. I'll try and get up later.'

'I won't be gone long, love.'

'You look real nice, Ma. That's a very pretty dress and hat you're wearing.'

He gave a sad smile and blew her a kiss as she said she'd see him later and closed the bedroom door.

After a minute John looked in on David who was lying with the eiderdown pulled up to his chin.

John spoke quietly and told him their dad was going to be filling in for him again.

'I'm sorry to let you down, John, but I'm still feelin' really rough.'

'Yeah, well, it's sorted. But he's gonna take your cut of the wedge for the two nights,' he said, and moved a little closer before continuing. 'I reckon we'll get through to the vault by midnight and have the divvy-out done by morning. Come Tuesday the whole of the Met will be turning over London lookin' for who done the bank so I'm gonna torch the van and bury our cut in the woods till things die down.'

David looked worried. 'They won't catch us, will they, John?'

'No bloody way. They haven't got a clue what's going on or they'd have nicked us by now. By this time tomorrow we'll be fuckin' rich.'

As David smiled and coughed he saw his dad standing behind John.

'Froze me bollocks off last night. It's the wind that whistles round the effing place. It's no wonder yer come down with a bad cold, son.'

'Sorry, Dad, and thanks for taking over from me.'

Hearing the front door close and realizing they had all gone David eased himself to a sitting position on the bed and tried to get to his feet. He had to sit back down again as he felt so sick, but it was his nerves more than still feeling ill.

DC Stanley had switched from Op One and was now down at the far end of the estate with a colleague watching the garage where John Bentley's van was parked. He was distracted by a call over the radio.

Oscar Pappa Five from One receiving, over.

'Yeah, go ahead, over,' Stanley replied.

Eyeball on Targets One and Two leaving premises with female occupant, all on foot towards you.

Stanley looked up the road and in the distance could see John, Clifford and Renee coming from the estate and heading in his direction.

He turned to his colleague. 'It looks like they're taking Renee with them now!'

'Maybe she's going to be lookout,' his colleague said.

'Well, she doesn't look dressed for it,' Stanley replied, and heard the sound of a number of vehicles passing the observation van.

'Holy shit, I don't believe this!' He turned to his mate and gestured for him to look through the peephole.

His colleague crouched down and peered through. 'It's a funeral cortège and they're parking up in front of the garages. If the Bentleys are going to a funeral they can't be working on the bank job during the day.'

'Or tonight – round here there's usually a big piss-up afterwards.'

'Clifford and John don't looked dressed for a funeral,' his colleague remarked.

'Shit, I don't know whether to inform Bradfield or wait and see what happens,' Stanley added, rubbing his head.

Floral tributes adorned the sides and front of the old

gleaming hearse. Written in carnations almost ten inches high were the words 'Grandson Eddie', and more flowers were lying on top of the coffin. There were two more Daimler funeral cars parked behind the hearse. The drivers, wearing black suits and ties, stepped out of the vehicles for a quick smoke and to stretch their legs whilst they chatted with the funeral director, who was wearing a black top hat and carrying a long black traditional undertaker's stick.

John and Clifford followed behind Renee thinking she was going to Nancy Phillips' flat, which was near the garages, and therefore wouldn't see them getting in the van. They both froze on the spot when they reached the point where they could see clearly along the row of garages.

'Jesus Christ, this is a fuckin' joke, how the hell are we gonna get the van out?' John whispered in disbelief through gritted teeth.

'Can't we get them to move?' Clifford whispered back, sweating profusely as he had so many clothes on.

'Oh yeah, that's very bright, Dad. They all watch us drivin' out in a van with false logos and copied number plates – that's just what we need. We got no option but to bloody wait.'

Renee turned and saw them both whispering. 'I thought you two were going fishing?'

'We were, darlin', but Dad thought we should pay our respects to Ma Phillips and her grandson,' John said lamely, unable to think of a better excuse.

'You've changed your tune – the lad was a waste of space not five minutes ago,' Renee said, knowing they were up to something.

John and Clifford had no way of contacting Silas as he

didn't have a phone in the café and it was too far for a walkie-talkie to work. All they could do was stand and watch impatiently as mourners began to gather around the waiting funeral cars. Nancy Phillips, dressed in a black-lace dress with matching black hat, directed who should go into which car. It all suddenly became too much for her and she broke down in floods of tears. Renee put an arm round Nancy to comfort her and she asked if Renee would accompany her in the Daimler behind the hearse. It was something of a relief for John and Clifford when Renee agreed and said she'd see them at the church.

Jane was in the incident room with Kath, who had decided to say nothing to her about Bradfield until Operation Hawk was over. Bradfield was in his office, but had lifted the mood by supplying bacon-and-egg rolls as well as teas and coffees. DS Gibbs was briefing the detectives who formed the outside arrest teams. He told them that for now it was a waiting game, but it was more than likely that the arrests would be made tonight and they would be called into position when the time was right.

'DCI Bradfield will be making the arrests inside the vault with a couple of you as backup. Team One will take out Clifford Bentley on the car-park rooftop. It's likely he'll try and sling the walkie-talkie over the top, so if anyone has a good pair of hands stand down at the bottom and try and catch it before it breaks into hundreds of pieces.'

They all smiled. One of the officers said he played a bit of cricket and would be the catcher.

'Teams Two and Three will cover the back alley in case any of the suspects try and do a runner. The Greek's a fat bastard so he should be easy to nab, but Danny Mitcham

is likely to be quick on his toes and so is John Bentley. You
have Bradfield's authority to use any force required to
take them out should they resist arrest, but do not draw a
firearm unless absolutely necessary,' Gibbs said, and
placed a map on the wall before continuing.

'These are the positions you will take up when DCI
Bradfield tells you to, and you will only move from them
as and when he gives the order. Is that clear?'

They all nodded and Jane could see the excitement on
their faces. Even though she was not part of the arrest
team she could feel the buzz.

Kath had a forlorn look on her face as she raised her
hand in the air and Gibbs nodded at her.

'I assumed I'd be on the arrest team.'

'Why's that, Morgan?'

'Well, I did a good job on the Collins murder and ...'

Gibbs smiled, 'Course you did, Kath, and that's why
DCI Bradfield's taking you with him as part of his arrest
team.'

Kath's face lit up. Others in the room were happy for
her, but one or two had envious looks on their faces.

Gibbs had just finished when DC Stanley radioed in
about the funeral. Two detectives laughed and made
derogatory comments about Eddie and his gran which
upset Kath.

'Grandma Phillips must have spent all her savings on
her Eddie's funeral. It's always the way round here: live a
rotten life but get buried in style. I've seen processions
with horse-drawn hearses and bands, all for a two-bit
criminal. Maybe its cathartic tears for a wretched existence, but that kid didn't deserve to die so young and he
was all she had to live for.'

Gibbs went to Bradfield's office and he could see from

the look on Spence's face that it wasn't good news. He explained to him that it seemed the Bentleys, apart from David, were going to Eddie Phillips' funeral, which meant they wouldn't be going near the bank, especially if there was the usual piss-up afterwards.

'Christ, that's all I need! I've got a team of officers costing a fortune in overtime and tomorrow the bank holiday will be double pay for them all. A shedload of money and they could end sitting with their thumbs up their backsides watching nothing for God knows how long.'

'There's still Silas and Danny at the café. They might start work on their own and then the Bentleys join them later.'

'You don't know that for certain, and if they do start work and get in the vault without the Bentleys, what then!' Bradfield snapped, infuriated by the situation.

'Do you want a surveillance unit to tail the Bentleys to the funeral?'

'Yes, but tell them to keep their distance behind the procession.'

The funeral procession turned left out of the garages onto the street and moved off slowly, led by the funeral director who was walking in front of the hearse. The two Daimlers and the mourners in their own cars followed on behind. Stanley and his colleague watched as the cortège travelled along the side of the estate.

Bradfield went to the incident room and listened to the radio with Gibbs. They heard Stanley telling the surveillance vehicles that the procession was on the move and the targets had got into someone's car to accompany it. On hearing this Bradfield contacted the two ops down at the bank and asked if there was any movement in the café or any walkie-talkie transmissions, but they both responded with a negative causing him to slam the phone down.

'Listen, guv, should we maybe save a few quid in over-time and stand everyone down for today?' Gibbs asked.

Bradfield, deep in thought, said nothing.

'What are you going to tell DCS Metcalf?' Gibbs asked.

'Nothing. He'll be that livid over the waste of man-power and money he might pull the plug on us and I'm not going to let that happen, not when I'm this close,' he said, holding his thumb and index finger an inch apart.

'So what's the next step?' Gibbs asked.

Jane and Kath could see Bradfield's increasing frustration and the two male detectives present left the room fearing he was about to go ballistic.

'If I knew I'd be taking it, Spence, so stop asking stupid questions! Get down to the op at the old lady's and await my orders.'

'Are you not going there?'

Bradfield glared at him, but before he could answer DC Stanley's voice came over the radio again.

Victor One to Gold, over.

'Yeah, go ahead,' Bradfield said.

There was silence in the room as they waited for an update.

Stanley sounded subdued. 'We can't see the two male targets anywhere, looks like we've lost them.'

Bradfield was fuming and slammed his hand down on the table. 'How can you bloody well lose them in a funeral procession that's travelling at a snail's pace?'

'I don't know, guv ... but somehow we did.'

The office phone rang and Bradfield nodded to Gibbs to answer it as he spoke with Stanley on the radio.

'Well, you'd better find them again and fast.' He threw

the radio mike onto the desk and noticed Gibbs waving a hand trying to get his attention.

'What now?' he asked in a raised voice.

'It's the officers at the old lady's. John Bentley just dropped his dad off at the multistorey.'

Bradfield slumped down in a chair, shook his head and looked at Gibbs wondering what the hell was going on.

'I don't know whether to laugh or cry, Spence. This bloody case will be the death of me.'

'You referring to your health or career, guv?'

'Piss off.'

The officers in the shoe shop confirmed that an angry-looking Silas and Danny had opened the yard gates and let the van in. Knowing all three targets were inside the café, Bradfield actually managed a smile. 'Looks like it's game on again, Spence. I can feel it in my gut that we're going to nail those bastards tonight, so let's get down there.'

'I take it I'm back in the shitty shoe shop?' Gibbs asked.

'It's too risky for you to go in with Clifford watching from the car park. You're in the old lady's with me as we can use the back staircase.'

'Should I come with you, guv?' Kath asked.

'Not just now. Stay here with the arrest teams and you can help Tennison with the indexing. I've got to pop back here later this afternoon to deal with something so I'll take you with me when I go back down to the op.'

Jane loved watching Bradfield smile and laugh. She was glad to see he was once again on a high, but at the same time she felt sad that he hadn't even said a word or really looked at her since she came on duty. However, she knew how busy and distracted he was and tried not to let it bother her.

Kath noticed the way Jane was looking at Bradfield

with smitten eyes, but said nothing. She decided to have another word with Bradfield when he picked her up later.

Silas was in a real temper, prodding John in the chest with his stubby finger.

'Me an' Danny are pissed off, you are fuckin' late and we been workin' our bollocks off.'

'Listen, we come out of the flats, and there's only a bloody hearse parked right in front of the garage, we couldn't believe it, cars lined up for the mourners. We just had to wait until it all moved off before we could get into the van.'

Silas's mood changed and he laughed. 'We'd better get down to work.'

John crawled into the tunnel and took over from Danny. He'd just started the drilling when Clifford made contact.

'Eh, stop work everyone. He says there's some kids out the front kicking an effing can around.'

'Shit,' John snapped.

Silas waved his hand for them to keep quiet as he went up to the ground floor.

He opened the café door and stepped out.

'Oi! You two will get a thrashin' if yer don't move off! You're disturbing the peace and quiet – move it ... PISS OFF.'

They didn't need a second warning and were off up the road like a pair of whippets. Silas then went upstairs to his flat to use the toilet and was sitting reading an old newspaper when he thought he heard the toilet from the shoe-shop flat flushing. He finished his business, did up his trousers and stood leaning against the wall listening.

Hudson who had just used the toilet was heading down

the stairs when his concerned partner looked at him and whispered,

'What in the hell were you doing? Bradfield said not to flush the toilets when the targets were in the café! I could bloody hear it in the basement!'

'Well, what you want me to do, leave a floater, for Chrissake?'

Silas went back down to the cellar. John and Danny were sitting with dust-caked handkerchiefs round their mouths and John was wearing swimming goggles pushed up over his eyebrows.

'Listen, I'm worried as I think I hear a toilet flush next door when I was on de crapper.'

'Shit, that Hebe woman's not come back, has she?' Danny wondered.

'Me dad ain't seen nothing or he'd have said,' John remarked.

'Her Morris is not in her yard as I check already. Hold off everythin' while I go take look and see what happening.'

'See if that bloody tailor's van's still there as well,' John said.

'He pain in arse. He honest, hard-working Jew, but sometimes don't take a day of rest – not even the Jewish Sabbath,' Silas remarked, raising his hands in the air.

'Get some fish and chips, will ya, Silas, I'm starving,' Danny said, but John said they couldn't afford to waste time eating.

Danny turned angrily to John. 'Listen, you were late because of that fuckin' funeral and I've been down here an' I'm starvin' and I ain't gonna eat any of that sweet shit Silas got ... never mind his stinking cans of tuna.'

Silas cracked his knuckles. 'Don't you go callin' my food shit, them tins are good quality.'

John sighed. 'Eh, the pair of you, just calm down and go get us some fish and chips, Silas.'

No sooner had a tense Bradfield arrived at the surveillance flat when yet again Mannie Charles turned up at the tailor's shop in his Austin van, this time accompanied by his wife. The couple began to bring out plastic-covered clothing items to stack inside the parked van. Two women were walking together and stopped to look through the shoe-shop window, and it seemed an age before they moved off. All these incidents were relayed by Clifford, each time causing work to cease in the café basement.

Bradfield was pacing up and down the old lady's living room, cursing under his breath as she shuffled behind, desperately trying to hand him two buttered scones on a plate. Gibbs took the plate from her and said Mr Bradfield wasn't hungry but he was and wouldn't let them go to waste.

Bradfield watched Silas leave the café, worried that he might have seen or heard Mannie Charles arrive and was going over to speak to him. If Mannie mentioned anything about his and Kath Morgan's visit the other night it could result in everything going wrong. If they did a runner he didn't even have arrest teams in place yet. He thought about calling them at the station to take up positions nearby but decided to wait. The officers in the shoe shop were warned Silas was on the move.

Bradfield watched anxiously as Silas went to the shoe-shop window and pausing briefly looked in whilst shading his eyes with his hands. Silas moved on and Bradfield could feel his blood pressure rising as he got nearer the tailor's shop. It nearly exploded when Mannie and his wife walked out and stopped to have a chat with Silas.

Thankfully it appeared to be a brief hello before they got into the van and drove off.

The sound of Clifford's voice came over the radio asking where Silas was going and Danny told him it was to check out the shoe shop and get fish and chips. Clifford said that the tailor had pissed off and he hadn't seen anything at the shoe shop and told them there was no time for food.

Silas went into a phone box, picked up the phone book and started to flick through the pages. He then dialled a number and held the door open with his other hand as it was so hot inside. In the shoe shop the officers heard Hebe's phone ringing. It wasn't the one they had installed for the observation so they knew not to pick it up and simply let it ring, which it did for almost a minute.

Silas left the phone box, content that Hebe was not there and he must have been mistaken about the toilet flushing. He continued down the street and turned left entering a fish-and-chip cum kebab shop. The undercover officer tailing him went in behind him and pretended to be looking up at the prices on the illuminated menu positioned above the fryers. Silas ordered a large doner with chilli sauce and two portions of fish and chips. He chatted with his fellow countryman in Greek as he prepared the order. Silas was so engrossed that he didn't even glance towards the undercover officer. He asked for salt and vinegar on the fish and chips and watched the food being wrapped in paper and placed into a plastic bag. He paid at a till at the end of the counter whilst the undercover officer ordered sausage and chips.

It was coming up to five thirty when Frank, who was twiddling the dials on the CB radio, indicated that he had picked up something. Bradfield rushed over and pulled the headphone jack out so he could listen on the loudspeaker. Clifford said a woman walking a dog was passing and asked how much longer they would be. John said that due to the number of stoppages they had been forced to make it would be an hour or two after midnight, at the earliest.

Bradfield was no longer frustrated at having to play the waiting game, and he was glad to hear from the shoe shop that Silas had returned and the drilling had started again. He took Gibbs to one side and spoke quietly.

'I'm popping out for a bit and will be back a little later with Kath Morgan ...'

'What's the secrecy for?'

'If you let me finish I'll tell you ... I'm going to get the bank manager, Dunbar, and bring him to the op so he can hear what's going on for himself.'

'Is that a wise move?' Gibbs frowned.

'I need him to open the vault when they get in. I'm also concerned there may be someone at the bank giving the Bentleys inside information and if it's Dunbar the look on his face and reactions on the plot here may well give him away.'

Unseen by Clifford, Bradfield left the op via the staircase at the rear of the building and got into an unmarked car waiting in a side street. Gibbs, Frank and the other officers positioned in the flat remained, monitoring the radio action and the café.

Bradfield returned to the station and bumped into Kath on the landing as she was returning from the canteen.

'Tell Tennison I want to see her in my office,' he said bluntly.

'Why, what's she done wrong now?'

'Nothing, just go and tell her,' he said and walked off, but a suspicious Kath followed.

'She's my friend, not to mention an innocent naive probationer, and some of the team are beginning to notice the
infatuated way she looks at you. She doesn't take her eyes
off you, and I've seen your little flirty glances to her.
They'll start makin' jokes about it, the smutty bastards.'

'Leave it out, Morgan. It's my problem to resolve, not
yours. Now do as I asked and tell Tennison to come to my
office.'

Kath wished she could have said that she knew more,
but not wanting to betray Jane's trust she kept her mouth
shut and went to find her.

Jane knocked on Bradfield's door before going in, anxiously wondering if she was going to be on the arrest
team.

'Kath said you wanted to see me.'

He drew her by her hand into the room and closed the
door.

'Listen, I want to have a chat with you. Right now I
have to be really on the ball and I need to iron a few
things out with you.'

She smiled and kept hold of his hand.

'You know what went down the other night – it
shouldn't have happened. And I think you should know
that as much as I would like it to continue, it has to stop,'
he said, and released her hand.

'Like I said, I have to be totally focused right now and
you are a distraction. So I have made a decision. We agree
that it was something that shouldn't have happened and as
you've done more than eight hours today you can book
off duty and have a few days off.'

'I don't understand. I thought you liked me, and I want
to stay on and see this case through.'

'I do like you, Jane, but you really need to get some rest,

you look exhausted. Why not get away from the section house? Maybe pop home and spend some time with your family?'

'I would like to remain at the station, at least for tonight, please,' she said quietly, hardly able to take on board what he was saying.

'I have just given you an order. You're officially off duty, so go home, and no arguments, all right?'

Her deep breaths made him feel really guilty and he couldn't resist gently touching her cheek.

'Come on, it's for your own good. I'm sorry, but it's not going to go any further between us. I should never have allowed it to get this far.'

She pursed her lips, trying desperately not to burst into tears. She swallowed and waited as he opened the door to usher her out.

No one but Kath noticed a forlorn-looking Jane picking up her handbag and leaving the incident room. Her heart went out to her and she followed Jane down to the ladies' locker room.

'Are you all right, Jane love?'

'I'm fine, thank you ... I've been told I'm off the investigation and to take some time out.'

Kath couldn't help herself as she put her arms around Jane and hugged her. She suspected this was Bradfield's way of stopping Jane getting too infatuated with him.

'He's only looking out for you as a probationer, Jane. The long hours are taking their toll on the experienced guys, so God knows what effect they must be having on you.'

Jane nodded, but was close to tears. She just couldn't understand how he could have been so dismissive about their night together. She couldn't look Kath in the eye for fear she could tell that it was not about being sent home but how hurt and humiliated she felt by Bradfield's rejection. Kath lifted Jane's head up, looked at her and sighed.

'Come on now, sweetheart, don't let him get to you.'

'Has it been that obvious, Kath?'

Kath cocked her head to one side.

'That you're tired, hurt or infatuated with him? Listen, darlin', this case is a big deal for Bradfield. He can't afford to lose concentration or do anything wrong as his career's on the line and maybe I should have warned you this morning when you told me ...'

Jane didn't want to hear any more and hurried out through the station yard. She didn't want anyone to see she was so close to crying. She couldn't even bear to get on the bus so decided to walk back to the section house feeling flushed with embarrassment. Had everyone known? Did they all realize how she felt about Bradfield? She walked fast feeling even more humiliated, fearing she'd been the brunt of jokes or snide remarks. The more she thought about it the faster she walked until she was almost running flat out.

CHAPTER THIRTY

It had been a lovely service, thought Renee as she walked out of the church and saw Nancy talking with two women she recognized, but hadn't seen or spoken to for many years.

Renee smiled and nodded. 'That was a right good send-off for your Eddie. The vicar said some kind words and the hymns were a lovely choice.' Renee leaned forward, kissed Nancy on the cheek and then hugged her.

'You ain't going, is ya?' Nancy asked.

'I'd best get back home as my David's not well. His leg's been playing up badly of late and—'

'I'm havin' no excuses, Renee Bentley. David's a big boy now and can look after himself so you're comin' to the wake and that's that. Besides the Crane sisters are here, come up from Southend for the day. They was just sayin' they ain't seen ya in years, so we all need a good chin-wag and knees-up.'

Before Renee could say no the Crane sisters linked arms with her and pulled her along, asking how she was doing.

The Star and Garter in Cambridge Heath Road had a large rear yard with tables and was decorated with a beautiful array of late-spring flowers in pots and hanging baskets, but the snug where the upright piano was positioned was where they all congregated. The landlord greeted them with a sherry on the house. Laid out on tables were sausage rolls, sandwiches and bowls of jellied eels, prawns and cockles. On the bar counter there was a pint glass with a bit of paper stuck to it saying 'Eddie RIP'. Nancy shoved the remainder of the money she had collected into it to pay for the booze, and others who hadn't seen her before the funeral dropped in £1 notes.

Renee spotted the piano. It had been too long, longer than she could remember, since she had last played one. She couldn't read a note of music but was always able to play any tune by ear and had been popular on Sundays at their local when she and Clifford were younger. Sunday was the only day they'd get out as a family for a booze-up. She'd sit and play a medley of songs while everyone sang along, and her two young boys were content with a bag of crisps and a bottle of pop whilst playing tag or hide-and-seek outside with the other kids. They were days when Renee wasn't browbeaten and the drudgery of her life didn't wear her to the bone. Back then she, Clifford and the boys were a happy family. Renee knew that Clifford and John would be upset that she'd gone to the pub having told her to go straight home after the burial, but stuff 'em, she thought, looking forward to a sing-along and a knees-up.

Back at the section house Jane couldn't shrug off her feelings of bewilderment and humiliation. She began to chide herself for being so unprofessional and knew if she hadn't been so besotted with Bradfield she'd still be at the station working in the incident room. Just thinking about it made her feel worse; she didn't want to sit in her room moping about and feeling sorry for herself. She put on some make-up and brushed her hair, then decided to go over to the Warburton Arms to see who was about for a drink.

To her surprise the pub was not that crowded for a Sunday night before a bank holiday, although it was only just after seven o'clock. She made her way to the bar and sat on one of the stools.

'White wine and couple of ice cubes, please, Ron.'

She nearly fell off her stool when someone gave her a hug from behind.

'Hi! It's me, Sarah Redhead. I'm only here for a quick G and T as I'm on night shift at ten. Tonight will no doubt be like a Saturday as it's a public holiday tomorrow. Saturdays are always busy, what with all the punch-ups, and you can guarantee there'll be some drunks falling over and cracking their skulls open.'

Sarah perched on the stool next to Jane, who for the first time was actually pleased to have her as company. She was incredibly loud-voiced and launched into a bizarre story about a corpse with a glass eye, which had fallen out and dropped down the drain in the mortuary.

'You won't believe what they popped into his eye socket as a temporary replacement.'

Jane shrugged. 'A marble?'

'No, that's too small. It was a table-tennis ball they cut in half, and they used some felt tips to draw an eye in the middle.' She shrieked with laughter.

Jane cringed. 'Did it work?'

'Well, yes and no. It was OK until the grieving widow turned up to identify the body and couldn't understand why the false eye had changed colour. She had a closer look and fainted. Well, the upshot was ...' She looked over Jane's shoulder, spun around on her stool and shouted, 'Julian! JULIAN!'

Jane recognized Dr Harker immediately as the forensic scientist whose lecture she'd attended. She blushed, remembering Lawrence teasing her about how she'd known about fibre transfer.

'Hello, it's Sarah Redhead, and this is Janet Tennison. Janet, this is Julian Harker.'

'We've met. How are you, *Jane*?' he said intentionally to embarrass Sarah, but Sarah didn't flinch.

'Let me get you a drink, Julian. Is that a pint of lager?'

'Yes, thanks.'

'And another white plonk for JANE and G and T for me, but I would appreciate a slice of lemon this time. On my slate, if you would be so kind, Ron.'

Ron told her to help herself to the lemon while he poured the pint. Julian gave Jane a small smile and raised an eyebrow as Sarah leaned over the bar to pick up a small saucer of lemon slices. He drew up a stool to sit beside her as Ron placed their drinks on the counter.

'You have been such a stranger, Julian, and sadly I'm on night duty so I can't stay too long,' Sarah told him.

'That's a shame,' he said limply.

Jane listened as Sarah talked to Julian as if she wasn't there. Sarah told him how impressed she'd been by his lecture and couldn't wait to get details of when and where he was next speaking so that she could attend. He was rather quiet and said he was due to go to the United States to lecture and attend forensic seminars on research and future technology. He was very polite as Sarah rambled on about a television documentary she had seen featuring new forensic tests to detect gunshot residue. It could link a suspect to a crime scene, and even show how close the suspect was to the gun. Harker obviously found it as tedious as Jane as he kept looking at her with an apologetic smile on his face.

At last Sarah finished her second G and T and got off her stool. Putting an arm around each of them she said she would have to love them and leave them as she was off to shower and change into her uniform. There was rather an awkward pause and then Julian tapped Jane's arm.

'I remember you were going to be a bridesmaid, isn't that right?'

'Yes, at my sister's wedding.'

'Well, being so young and attractive, I doubt you will be always the bridesmaid, as the saying goes.' He gave a soft laugh.

She suddenly wanted to leave and slipped off her stool.

'It was nice to see you again, Dr Harker.'

'Ah, leaving me already? Why not stay and have another drink?'

'I'm on nights as well,' she lied.

'Perhaps we could have dinner one evening on your day off? I'm still in London for a couple of weeks yet.' He peeled away some of the top layer of a beer mat and wrote his contact number on the white bit.

'Call me when you have a free night.'

She said nothing as he handed her the beer mat. She did not intend to go out with him since she knew he was married, but she smiled and slipped the number into her pocket.

Jane hurried across the road back to the section house, suddenly deciding to ring her parents. Her mother answered in a timid but posh voice.

'Mrs Tennison speaking, how can I help you?'

'Mummy, it's me, Jane.'

'Oh my good heavens, I was just thinking of you. Your father and I thought you might have come home for Sunday lunch, but we didn't hear from you and I wanted to ring–'

'I've been really busy, Mum.'

'You sound a bit down, darling,' she commented, her voice reverting to its normal tone.

'I'm fine. I've got a couple of days off so I was thinking about coming home.'

The joy in her mother's voice made her feel tearful.

'I'm so excited! Pam and her husband will be here for lunch tomorrow as it's a bank holiday; it'll be just lovely with all the family together. I miss you, Daddy misses you.'

'I'll see you later tonight then. I'll get the bus and Tube home so should be with you in a couple of hours.'

'Oh that is good news. I'll make up your bed right now.'

'Thanks, Mum, see you later.'

Jane went to her room to get her light denim jacket. She had clothes and nightwear at home so didn't need to carry anything but her handbag.

She waited at the bus stop outside the section house. It was by now seven forty-five and she realized she had not even thought about what was happening at the station. She gritted her teeth trying not to think about Bradfield, but couldn't help wondering how the observation on the café and bank were going. The red double-decker bus clattered to a halt at the stop and Jane showed the conductor her warrant card as she climbed on and made her way up the stairs to sit at the back, as usual.

It was very warm. A few windows were open but there were only two passengers on the top deck. Jane felt depressed, staring through the window as the bus stopped and collected a few more passengers whilst some got off.

They were just pulling in at the next stop when there was a resounding clash of gears and looking down from the window Jane saw an elderly woman picking up some groceries that had fallen out of her bag. She closed her eyes remembering how she had helped Renee Bentley pick up her groceries, and then assisted her back to the flat on the Pembridge Estate where she had the confrontation with her son John. Jane took a deep breath and felt hurt again, thinking that if she hadn't recognized John Bentley's voice Operation Hawk might never have taken place.

She was startled from her thoughts and almost fell from her seat when the bus suddenly jolted forwards and stopped. She pressed her hands hard on the back of the seat in front of her as the gears shuddered and the bus lurched forwards and stopped again. Jane looked down from the window as the bus conductor got off and went to speak to the driver. There were a few shouts and yells from passengers below and one man was swearing profusely.

The conductor got back on the bus and spoke in a loud voice so people upstairs could hear.

'We got engine trouble so you're all gonna have to wait for the next bus. Can you come down from upstairs and EVERYBODY OFF, PLEASE.'

Jane made her way downstairs and onto the pavement, where the rest of the passengers were complaining loudly. The conductor remained on the bus and lit a cigarette while the driver went to find the nearest call box to ring for a replacement. Jane heard an upset passenger ask when the next 253 bus would be along and the conductor said about half an hour or more as they were short of drivers.

They were almost directly across the road from the Star and Garter pub, and Jane could see that it had a nice railed rear yard and quite a few people were sitting at the outdoor tables drinking and chatting, kids running around playing games. The double doors to the pub were open and from the noise filtering out to the street it sounded quite lively, with a piano playing and people singing 'Roll Out The Barrel'.

Jane thought her mother would start to worry if she didn't arrive within two hours so decided she'd check and see if the pub had a payphone that she could use.

The old-fashioned pub had a big circular counter and was filled with drinkers leaning up against it. The partition leading to the snug bar was crowded and the bellow of 'Knees Up, Mother Brown' now began to ring out with the occasional wrong note played on the piano.

Jane found a payphone and put in a quick call to her mother who wondered what all the noise was. Jane explained where she was and what had happened with the bus and her mum thanked her for the call. She then had to edge along the bar before she could find a gap between drinkers to signal to a sweating barman that she wanted to order a drink. She began to feel embarrassed, and out of place, as the mostly male drinkers were overweight, pot-bellied men. Some of them were in short-sleeved shirts and a few wore vests, exposing their hairy chests gleaming with sweat. There was a round of applause and cheers as the song ended and then thudding out from the piano came a few chords before they started to sing 'The Lambeth Walk'.

Jane was eventually served and ordered a glass of lemonade. After paying for it she thought she'd have a quick look in the snug where people were still singing at the tops of their voices. Jane was surprised to see the pianist was Irene Bentley, but didn't recognize the woman standing next to her conducting everyone in the sing-along. It was obvious they had both had a good drink and Renee's straw hat was lopsided and the flower in the band was flopping up and down as she banged the piano keys. The woman next to her had one hand on the piano top to steady herself and her words were slurred; in fact almost everyone in the snug appeared to be rather drunk as they leaned against each other and swayed to the thumping keys on the old piano. Jane noticed the pint glass on the bar counter with 'Eddie RIP' and with a jolt of recognition realized it was the wake for Eddie Phillips. She wondered if the woman with Renee at the piano was his grandmother Nancy. She had not intended moving further into the snug bar, but found herself pushed forwards by two men singing loudly and trying to get through the crowd with a round of drinks. The song ended to loud shouts of 'A big hand for Nancy and Renee' and applause filled the room as Renee staggered to her feet, took a bow and Nancy hugged her. She saw Renee look in her direction so gave a nod hello but Renee didn't respond and instead whispered to Nancy.

A young, thuggish-looking man replaced Renee at the piano and began to sing the popular song:

'A *white sports coat and a pink carnation*
I'm all dressed up for the dance
A white sports coat and a pink carnation
I'm all alone in romance ...'

Jane thought Renee hadn't recognized her and had just turned to leave when she heard a scream and the singing and piano-playing came to an abrupt halt. Turning round Jane saw Nancy pointing towards her. Her face was sweating and red as she elbowed her way towards Jane, and before she knew it the irate woman had made a grab for her shirt and knocked the lemonade glass out of her hand.

'You got a fuckin' nerve coming here and spyin' on us. My grandson's dead cos you bastards give him a beating.'

The room was silent and people looked at each other wondering what was going on.

'SHE'S A BLOODY COPPER!' Nancy hollered as loud as she could.

Jane could see everyone was looking at her and, terrified, she tried to push her way through the men behind her and out of the snug, but they didn't move. Ma Phillips made another lunge, grabbed Jane's shoulder, spun her round and spat in her face. Everyone began crowing and screaming and even though the pianist started playing and singing another verse they all began herding around Jane. It was Renee who grabbed Nancy and pulled her away from Jane.

'That's enough, the lot o' ya! Leave 'er alone, Nancy. She's uniform, not CID filth, and nuffin' to do with Eddie's death.'

Unsteady as she was on her feet Renee stepped forward and positioned herself between Nancy and Jane.

'I know this girl and she's all right. Leave it to me and I'll see her out. Go on, get back to yer singing.'

Nancy glared at Jane.

Renee raised her arm to hold Nancy back and spoke calmly. 'We're here to show respect to your grandson Eddie. He'd be turning in his grave if you got nicked for belting a copper at his wake.'

'A *white sports coat and a pink carnation*
I'm in a blue blue mood …'

Renee waved her hands for everyone to back off, hooked her arm through Jane's and moved towards the exit to the back yard of the pub. Jane helped her keep her balance.

Once in the rear yard Jane helped Renee sit down by a bench table covered in dirty glasses. She took a tissue out from her bag and wiped Nancy's spit off her face.

Renee looked at her and shrugged. 'It was my fault Nancy kicked off. I recognized you first and said you were a copper. I didn't get a chance to finish telling her you'd helped me out before she erupted. But to be honest, luv, you shouldn't have come here.'

'I'm sorry, but my bus broke down and—'

'Whatever the reason I don't wanna hear it. You did me a good turn and I figured I owed you one.'

'I really appreciate what you did in there.'

Renee started to stand up but stumbled back onto the seat.

Jane hesitated but couldn't stop herself. 'So how's your family? I heard your husband was released recently.'

Renee looked up with a squinting half-smile on her face.

'If John and Clifford could see me now they'd not be best pleased, but family is family, no matter what I got notions about, but …' She tried to straighten her hat. 'My David's the only decent one. I take care of him cos the other two are no-good bastards.'

Holding on to the table she pulled herself to her feet and started to return to the snug, but stopped and glared at a woman at an adjacent table. She had long dyed blonde hair and was wearing a silver lamé dress.

'You slag!' Renee shouted.

Jane couldn't believe it: one minute Renee was fine and the next she was screeching in a rage. Unbeknownst to Jane this was the woman Clifford had been having an affair with for years. Renee lurched across the table, picked up a half-finished pint and threw it over the woman, who jumped up and started screaming whilst clutching her soaking-wet hair. Jane watched aghast as Renee threw a punch that missed before toppling forward knocking the woman to the ground. Shouts and cat-calls erupted as the pair of them struggled and punched at each other, and people came out from the snug wondering what on earth the ruckus was about.

Jane was trembling; she had never seen two women fight in her entire life. She took the opportunity to get out fast and headed across the road to the bus stop. She took deep breaths to calm herself, and looking back across the road saw two men pulling Renee and 'the slag' apart.

The conductor was sitting on the platform smoking as another 253 bus pulled up behind the broken-down one.

'Right now, everyone all aboard! If you've kept your tickets you can still use 'em,' he said as he tossed his cigarette butt into the gutter.

Jane didn't bother to go upstairs this time as it was only a few more stops before Bethnal Green Tube station. She was still shaken and only then realized she'd left her denim jacket in the pub, but there was no way she was going to go back to look for it.

When the conductor approached she showed her warrant card again and he looked at her.

'Sorry about the delay, officer. I'm surprised you went in the Star and Garter – it's a real notorious hang-out for

East End villains. Lucky you weren't in uniform or they'd have tossed you out head first.'

He wasn't to know what had happened, but what he said made Jane feel even more upset. She wanted to be at home with her mum and dad more than she could ever remember.

Bradfield and Kath went to the bank manager's house in Islington to tell him about what was happening and to ask him to accompany them to the observation point in the old lady's house. En route Kath had tried to broach the subject of Jane and how distressed she was after her meeting with him. Bradfield had frowned disapprovingly and made it quite clear there was nothing going on and she should keep her nose out of his business. As far as he was concerned the matter was over and done with. Tennison was on a few days' leave and would return to normal uniform duties on her return.

'Fine, whatever you say.'

'Didn't mean to sound off at you, Kath, but I got a lot on my plate. She's a sweetheart and I maybe need to make it clear I'm no good for her.'

As hard as it was to bite her tongue and say nothing, Kath valued being present at the arrests in the bank vault too much to say anything further on the matter.

Adrian Dunbar was perplexed and anxious as Bradfield told him that he was to accompany him to an observation address where a team of officers were monitoring an ongoing break-in at the bank.

He paced up and down his living room, shaking his head and refused to accept what he was being told. Bradfield gave him a quick rundown on the events of the last couple of nights.

Dunbar shook his head. 'It is simply not possible to gain access to the vault like that. The security system is of the highest calibre and if they have got as far as you say the alarm would have gone off by now. I think you are mistaken and overreacting, Chief Inspector.'

'I'm not prepared to go into all the details here and now, but we believe the suspects have what is known as a "bell man" who is an expert in bypassing even the most sophisticated alarm systems,' Bradfield said, trying to keep his temper in check.

'Not the ones in my bank. Since the Baker Street robbery it was designed to be impenetrable, thick metal bars, concrete, steel mesh—'

Bradfield was really impatient. 'It's not YOUR bank and neither is what is stored in there. If you want the suspects to get away with it then fine, stay here and don't help us. But you might find yourself looking for a new job.'

Dunbar walked over to his phone and picked it up, but a suspicious Bradfield put his finger on the button to cut off the dial tone.

'I need to contact my head of security,' Dunbar said aggressively.

'No, Mr Dunbar, there may be someone in your bank who has given inside information to the suspects, so at present only you can know what we are doing.'

He watched Dunbar's reaction closely. He did look nervous but it was impossible to tell if he was involved or worried about his career. However, there was no way Bradfield was leaving the house without him, or letting him out of his sight, and within the next hour they were at the op with a very subdued Dunbar listening in disbelief to the suspects' walkie-talkie conversation on Frank's CB radio.

*

John Bentley pulled up his goggles and backed out of the tunnel section which they had now widened to make it easier and quicker to remove the debris from the vault's thick concrete base.

He was covered in cement dust and sweating heavily. Danny and Silas could see he was livid as he grabbed the walkie-talkie from Silas, pressed the transmit button and started to shout at his father.

'Yet again you and your man inside got the fuckin' layout wrong! The floor also has a bloody thick sheet of steel plating, not just concrete, so I dunno what the hell we are gonna do now. Are you hearin' me?'

'You wouldn't be in there on the verge of Aladdin's cave if it weren't for me, so shut the fuck up and get on with it.'

Danny told John to calm down as he dragged forwards the oxyacetylene cutting equipment which was strapped to a two-wheeled heavy-duty upright trolley.

'Listen, there's plenty of gas left in this thing and it will cut through steel just like it did the iron bars.'

John was sceptical, plus it was a very confined space to haul the connecting hoses and two tanks into as they were bigger than a deep-sea diver's oxygen equipment. Danny said they could take turns in doing the cutting as it would get very hot and would be physically draining.

'You done all the cutting so far, Danny, and know how to use it. I don't wanna risk it – you said that stuff is dangerous if you don't know what you're doing.'

'Jesus Christ, all right, just bloody calm down, I'll do it.'

Danny tested the pressure gauges on the two tanks as it would be hard to do so once in the tunnel. He then put on a welding mask and thick leather gloves to protect him from the sparks and molten steel when he began the cutting. Danny sat in the tunnel facing John and Silas as they slowly lowered the trolley with the heavy cutting equipment onto the ground by the tunnel entrance. Danny gripped hold of the trolley handles and dug the heels of his boots into the soil ready to heave it backwards and towards him.

'Right, when I say go you push like mad, John, and I'll pull. Stand by ... ready ... GO.'

John pushed the trolley and Danny pulled with all his strength. It took ten minutes of hard, exhausting effort to eventually get it into position to work on the steel. Danny turned on the oxyacetylene gas, held his lighter to the end of the cutting torch and there was a loud WOOMF as it ignited and the flame burst out of the end, lighting up the tunnel. The flame startled John who scuttled out backwards as quickly as he could.

'Jesus Christ, you hear that fuckin' thing go off?' he asked Silas nervously.

At an angle away from his face Danny held the lit torch to the steel and watched as the metal slowly turned cherry red. Then, as he pressed the oxygen-blast trigger, the reaction produced even greater heat and the flame began to cut through the steel.

'Is like a bloody big volcano eruption,' Silas said as he heard the rumbling sound from inside the tunnel and watched the smoke filter out from the entrance hole.

Ten minutes later the noise from inside the tunnel abated and they heard Danny call out.

'Go see what he wants,' John said to Silas, as he didn't want to go inside the tunnel again while Danny was using the cutting torch.

After a few seconds Silas reappeared from the tunnel and gestured with his finger and thumb.

'He reckon is no that thick, maybe few inches, and couple of hours to cut through. He also wants a big bottle of water as like inferno in there.'

John excitedly slapped Silas on the back and picked up the walkie-talkie.

'We're back in business! The torch is slicing through the steel like butter and will take about two hours, then we're in.'

'Good,' Clifford replied bluntly.

Bradfield had an excited grin and a 'told you so' look on his face as he checked his watch and looked at Dunbar who, having heard what John Bentley said to his father, was sitting with his head in his hands feeling sorry for himself. If the suspects were breaking through into the vault that night it would only be a matter of hours now before Operation Hawk went into overdrive. Bradfield called the incident room and the arrest teams were relieved and excited by the news. He told them to go the station yard at City Road Police Station and wait there until further instructions.

'Not long now, Mr Dunbar,' Bradfield said.

Dunbar looked up at him. 'I'm sorry I doubted you, but I just can't believe this is happening. I'll do whatever you need me to, and if anyone in the bank is involved rest assured I will help you find them.'

'I'm sure you will, Mr Dunbar,' Bradfield replied, uncertain if his loyalty was to him or the suspects.

Bradfield turned to DS Gibbs who was standing beside him and reiterated that it was imperative, as DCS Shaun Metcalf had ordered, that the targets had to be inside the vault before he gave the go-ahead to move in and make the arrests.

Gibbs was shaking, more than ever aware that it was going to be one hell of a night.

When Jane arrived home her mother was elated and fussed around her, saying she was sure she'd lost weight. Jane asked where her father was and was told that he'd nipped to the off-licence to buy a few bottles of wine, a sparkling one for tonight to celebrate Jane's homecoming and a couple for lunch the following day. Her mother leaned forward and looked closely at her daughter's head.

'What have you got in your hair?' she asked as she touched her fingers to it and looked at them.

Jane stepped away from her and rubbed her fingers through the right side of her hair. She hadn't realized some of Nancy Phillips' spit had landed there and made her hair sticky.

'It's nothing, I didn't wash the shampoo out properly.'

It was a lie, but there was no way she was going to tell her mother about the incident at the pub. Instead she said she would like to have a bath and change.

In her bedroom Jane kicked off her shoes and pulled off her jeans before sitting down on the freshly made bed. She felt exhausted and close to tears as the depression over Bradfield suddenly hit her again, but she forced herself to undress and put on her dressing gown. As she went into the hall her father appeared and held his arms open to embrace her.

'How's my little girl? Your mother just told me you were home, come here.'

He had so rarely been physically affectionate and she loved the feel of his arms around her.

'So how are you?' he asked and stepped back to look at her.

'I'm fine, Dad, just very tired.'

'Well, you go and have a nice bath and then you can tell us all about work.'

Lying in the foamy bath water, she closed her eyes. How could she tell them about work, about being spat at by a woman full of hatred of the police? How could she explain about Operation Hawk and John Bentley, or least of all her infatuation with DCI Bradfield?

The tears that had been close to the surface since she left the section house now streamed down her cheeks. She slowly slid her body further and further down into the hot water until her hair floated around her head and it felt as if she was drowning.

The tap on the bathroom door followed by her mother's voice made her surface and she was glad she had locked it.

'We had sausages and mash for supper. Would you like me to heat a couple for you, with some baked beans or a bit of salad maybe?'

'Sausage and salad, thanks, Mum. I've nearly finished washing my hair.'

'Well, don't be too long, dear, it's after ten and we'll want to be up early to get everything ready for lunch tomorrow.'

Jane raised the wet flannel to her face and pressed it to her skin. She wondered again what was happening at the bank and felt annoyed that she couldn't be there as part of the team. She sat up and pulled the bath plug out before wrapping a hand towel around her wet hair and drying her body with another. Then, wearing her dressing gown, she went into the living area where her father was sitting at the breakfast bar eating some cheese and biscuits. He looked up at her with a gentle smile.

'You should have called us, you know how worried your mother gets. What's this nonsense about you not being allowed to take personal calls at the police station or at the section house?'

'I don't make the rules, Dad, but it was thoughtless of me. I promise I will call more often from now on and keep you both updated, but sometimes I'm on late shifts until 10 p.m. or later if it's busy.'

'So, tell me how everything is.'

She went to the worktop where her mother had left a plate of two sausages, a side salad and slice of bread and butter. She spooned some mayonnaise onto the salad, and poured a glass of water, before sitting down beside him.

'Well you know, Dad, being on probation I am not really involved in very much. There's a lot of typing up reports, indexing and filing at the moment.'

She ate hungrily as he finished his biscuits and cheese. He washed his plate, tea cup and knife in the sink and pointed at the pan of peeled potatoes and vegetables.

'Your mum had me prepare them for tomorrow. It's your favourite, roast lamb, mint sauce and an apple turnover with custard for pudding.'

She smiled and said it sounded delicious.

'I'm thinking of trading in my old Rover for something smaller. Uncle Brian is looking for a good second-hand Mini for me. What do you think of them?'

'Well, I would say a Mini would be ideal, less petrol, but are you sure about using Uncle Brian?'

He gave a soft laugh and said that he was a trifle uneasy about it, but if he could get a good trade-in price he would have a friend check it over. And if he didn't go for a Mini he might get a Volkswagen Beetle. It felt good to be sitting at home at the breakfast bar she had known for years, and having a conversation that took her mind off work.

'It's good to be home, Dad.'

He finished drying his dishes and put them away with a smile.

'She's got me well trained. Mind you, I hate cleaning greasy trays after a roast dinner. I'm glad you and Pam will be here tomorrow. It's nice to sit down together for a nice family lunch and you and your sister can help clear and wash up,' he said with a cheeky smile.

Jane laughed and he patted her shoulder before he left the room and she finished her sausage and salad.

Mrs Tennison appeared with her hair in rollers, and wearing her familiar quilted dressing gown.

'I'm going to have an early night to be ready and fresh for the morning. Pam will be over by midday with her husband. It would have been nice if that good-looking inspector was coming. Did you ask him about Sunday lunch sometime?'

'Yes, but he's a Detective Chief Inspector, and is much more senior than me. They don't tend to socialize with junior ranks outside of work.'

'Well, that's a pity. Is there anyone else you like or are seeing? You can always invite them instead.'

'I'm not seeing anyone, Mum, I've been really busy. Shift work makes me restless and it's difficult to get into the right sleep pattern. In fact I was going to ask if you could give me one of your sleeping tablets.'

Mrs Tennison hesitated, and moved closer. 'You know Daddy doesn't like me taking them. I only have half, just enough to get me off into a sound sleep, otherwise I toss and turn all night. He thinks Mogadon is addictive, but I don't take it every night.'

Jane smiled and said she doubted her mother would become a junkie overnight, but then seeing her reaction to the term tried to make light of it.

'It's a police word for a drug addict.'

'I know that. I do worry about you and hope you don't get involved in any of those drug-related horror stories we read about every day.'

Jane took her mother's hand. 'I've promised Dad that from now on I'll make a point of calling you more often.'

'Every night, if you can, dear.'

Jane had just returned to her bedroom when her mother tapped on the door and passed her a tissue containing one of her sleeping tablets. She whispered to her not to tell her father, and then blew a kiss from the door.

'Night night, darling, see you in the morning.'

Jane took the sleeping tablet with a sip of water from the glass on her bedside table.

She turned off the small lamp and lay in the darkness, wanting and waiting for sleep. For a while she thought about Operation Hawk and how everyone at the ops and arrest teams must be waiting anxiously for Bradfield's command to make the arrests. Although she had felt that he had misjudged her professionally, and she'd been humiliated and hurt, she now felt calmer and more positive. She was determined that when she returned to the station she wouldn't show her feelings, especially towards Bradfield.

CHAPTER THIRTY-ONE

It was 2.30 a.m. and Bradfield was on tenterhooks listening to the suspects' conversation on Frank's CB. By now they were all clued in as to which of the men were talking.

'He's cut through, we're finally going in!' John Bentley said excitedly to his dad over the walkie-talkie as he sat next to Silas in the cellar.

'It's about bloody time! Still all clear out here. Don't take longer than necessary or get greedy as we need to be well away before sunrise,' Clifford's gravelly voice replied.

'I'll call back when we're nearly done and pick you up on the corner, OK?'

'OK. Yeah, received.'

Clifford felt good, although there was something that was worrying him, but he said nothing to John as they were almost home and dry.

Danny was first through the hole in the vault floor, which was just wide enough for him and John, but not Silas. Taking the gas tanks back out of the tunnel would have been tiring and time-consuming, so John pushed while Danny lifted the heavy tanks up into the vault out of the way. Once John was in the vault he stood next to Danny and, using the light from one of the Eveready bicycle lights he'd rigged up to a sports headband, they looked round in awe at the large twenty-four-foot-square room lined with rows and rows of locked numbered drawers held in wall-to-ceiling cabinets.

'We need to find box 320 and open it first,' John said.

'Why, is it your lucky number or something?' Danny asked suspiciously, which angered John who snapped back.

'Yeah, cos there's at least a hundred thousand of used notes in it from a previous bank robbery. That's what kick-started this job in the first place.'

Danny scanned the drawers then pointed to his right.

'It's over there.'

Silas was in the tunnel and John called out to him.

'Hand me up a load of pillowcases and the holdall containing the gear we need.'

Silas did as he was asked and John unzipped the holdall, removing the contents and placing them on the small table in the room: two club hammers, crowbars, flat-head chisels and four bike torches to help light up the vault.

'Help yourself, Danny. Let's get to cracking this lot open.'

John slammed the forked end of a crowbar into the small gap at the top of deposit drawer 320 and whacked it hard twice with a club hammer to force it in. He then pushed the bar forwards and upwards, causing the drawer to make a popping sound as it broke away from the lock. He pulled it out, placed it on the table, then prised open the lid and saw that it was packed with £20, £10, £5 and £1 notes. Danny was looking over his shoulder, which annoyed him.

'What are you waiting for? Get on with it and start down the far end. Get the drawers out, open them up, take out what's valuable and shove it in a pillowcase.'

Danny went to the far end of the vault as John started to put the money into a pillowcase, making sure that the soon-to-be-worthless fivers were in a separate one. It was his intention to pass them off to Silas on the grounds they were more common than tens and twenties and therefore easier to use or pass on. His dad had wanted him to give them to Danny as well, but he'd been a long-time friend, and John knew he was not a man to cross, or you'd pay the price.

They forced open one drawer after another and the hammering sound of metal against metal echoed round the vault like a chorus of musical chime bells. John and Danny were screaming and shouting with delight as the contents spilled out of the drawers. Some were filled with valuable jewellery, others with silver cutlery and Georgian tea services, along with more trays filled with cash. They were working at a frenzied pace as they stuffed the pillowcases full with a treasure trove of looted goods. They then handed them to Silas who looked inside and rubbed his hands together in delight.

Danny raised his arm and John stopped.

'I got a tray filled with bags of what looks like heroin and cocaine,' Danny said.

'Leave it,' John replied.

'Why? It'll be worth a fortune on the streets, probably more than the cash we got so far.'

'I don't deal in shit like that. It ruins lives and kills young kids, so do as I say and leave it,' John said, making it clear he meant every word.

Bradfield was on a high. He remained calm as he told the arrest teams to move out of City Road, but to stay in the backstreets away from the bank and café until he gave

the order for them to take up position to block off the possible escape routes. He also called the officers watching the
Bentleys' place and Danny Mitcham's flat and told them
to come over and support the arrest teams. His mind was
racing as he wondered if he had covered every eventuality,
but he could think of nothing that could go wrong. He
knew that Operation Hawk was on its way to being a
huge success and was now eager to arrest John Bentley
and his team.

'Are you OK, Mr Dunbar? It'll soon be over.'

'I'm very nervous, Mr Bradfield, and somewhat worried
as they'll obviously have hammers in their hands.'

'Don't worry – all I need you to do is open the vault as
quietly as possible and then step to one side and let me
and my arrest team do our job.'

Bradfield phoned the shoe shop to tell the officers there
that the suspects were now in the bank vault. He spoke
with DC Stanley who said the officer in the shoe-shop
basement using a listening device could hear the sound of
metal being hammered.

Bradfield turned to Spencer Gibbs. 'We're going over to
the bank in fifteen minutes, Spence ...'

'Why not go now if they're in the vault?'

'I don't want to burst their bubble of joy quite yet.
When I give the order you get your team in the shoe shop
to go out and cover the back alleyway in case any of 'em
try to escape from the rear of the café. I've also got backup
teams in unmarked cars at each end of the alleyway to
block the route off in case they try to get out in the van.'

'How are you getting into the bank?'

'We're going in by the front door with Dunbar.'

'We?' Gibbs asked, having thought he was to cover the
rear alleyway.

'I want you with me on the arrests, Spence. Kath and four other officers will be with us as backup, and if the suspects kick off I'm carrying,' he said, making reference to the revolver he had in a shoulder holster under his jacket.

'What about Cliff Bentley? He'll see us going in.'

'He'll be taken care of. The two officers dressed like tramps will go to the top of the car park and take him out as we move in.'

'What if he raises the alarm before they get to him?'

'Chance I have to take, but even then where are the bastards going to run to? They won't try and escape empty-handed. We've got them, Spence, we fuckin' got 'em like rats in a barrel!' Bradfield said and patted Spencer's back.

Clifford felt his teeth chattering with the cold as he looked down on the street below from his vantage point. Everything was quiet and there was an eeriness about the stillness of the night that troubled him. He knew via the walkie-talkie that they had broken into the vault and soon they'd all be rich beyond their wildest dreams. He sat back against the wall and began to think about what had been worrying him earlier. It seemed strange that he'd not seen one single police patrol car or a uniform officer pounding the beat all night. He'd seen a few patrol cars the previous night and knew that when David had been lookout a tramp had been arrested by a uniform officer and a paddy wagon had turned up. Clifford began to wonder if uniform patrols had been told to stay away from the area, or was it just pure coincidence?

Inside the vault John and Danny were still breaking open the deposit boxes. Silas was sweating heavily as he crawled to the café cellar with pillowcases of money and valuables. He then took these upstairs and placed them by the back door to be loaded into the van when they were all ready to leave. Although they were exhausted the euphoria and exhilaration at what they were about to get away with was pumping the blood through their veins and keeping them going.

Silas went back into the tunnel to collect more loot and stood up so that his head was sticking up through the hole in the vault floor.

'Is nearly 4 a.m. and sun will rise in hour or so.'

Danny looked at John. 'We must have amassed a fortune so far. Maybe we should call it a night.'

John bent down to look at the heavy combination-dial safe that was embedded into the wall and floor between the rows of deposit drawers.

'We open this – it's gotta have somethin' of big value inside. I'd reckon a load of cash, or really expensive jewellery.'

Silas shook his head. 'Come on, John, is not good idea. I agree with Danny, we have plenty and need to load up the van.'

'Use the torch to cut it open,' John barked at Danny.

'I'm happy with what we got so let's just get out of here,' Danny said impatiently.

John was livid. 'What's your fucking problem? I brought you in on this job and I'm running the show, so do as I say.'

'You want what's in it then you do it,' Danny shouted.

'I fuckin' will,' John said and hauled the oxyacetylene rig over to the safe. He asked Danny to turn it on and light it for him, which against his better judgement he did.

'You help Silas load the van and come back for the last

few sacks and whatever I find in here,' John said.

Still troubled by the lack of police patrols Clifford started to walk round the car park. It was a near full moon so he had a good view. He looked at all the buildings and windows overlooking the bank and café to see if there were any lights on and noticed the derelict flats that were to one side and slightly set back from the car park. He could see that all except one flat, on the second floor, were boarded up but there were no lights on in the premises. Using his binoculars he looked closely at the net curtain and suddenly saw it move slightly but there was no sign of anyone peering. It crossed his mind that it may just have been the draught, but the night was still with little or no breeze. Through the binoculars he saw two tramps come from the rear alleyway of the flats. He recognized one as the man he'd kicked and knew from the way they moved at speed towards the car park they were not drunks. Fearing the worst he pressed the walkie-talkie communication switch.

'Get the fuck out of there now! The rozzers are on to us,' he whispered frantically.

Clifford moved around the wall of the car park and looked over to see one tramp hurriedly enter the building's stairwell and the other run up the car ramp.

'They're in the car park, John, I gotta try and get outta here,' he said quickly and waited. 'John, John, can you hear me? Get out now!' But still there was no reply.

In the flat Bradfield swore when he heard the transmission over the CB loudspeaker and realized that Clifford had somehow discovered that the police were watching. He was worried all hell would break loose now that he had lost the element of surprise.

Bradfield radioed the officers in the car park. 'Target on

rooftop making escape, cut him off and arrest now. Be warned he is extremely dangerous and violent!'

'We've got to move in now, Spence. Are you ready to go?'

'I just spoke with Stanley at the shoe shop and I don't think the suspects in the bank heard Clifford,' Gibbs said.

'How could they not hear them when we all did here?'

'Stanley said the Greek and Danny loaded some bags in the van a couple of minutes ago and went back inside. If they'd heard Clifford they'd all be well on their toes by now,' Gibbs replied.

Frank raised his hand and waved it to attract Bradfield's attention.

'Not now, Frank, I'm trying to think.'

For once Frank wasn't prepared to shy away from speaking up. 'I believe Spence is right.'

'How would you bloody well know?'

'Well, I don't know for certain, but it can only be one of two things.'

'What are you talking about?' Bradfield asked in an angry tone.

'The batteries on the walkie-talkie have gone flat, or they've taken it into the vault where it won't work.'

'Of course it will, we just heard Clifford on it.'

'His works and sends transmissions. Problem is they won't hear it in the vault because the signal can't penetrate the steel surrounds.'

Bradfield's anger abated in an instant and he smiled realizing that in all their euphoria it had never crossed the suspects' minds that a walkie-talkie would be useless inside the vault. He was now almost certain that John, Silas and Danny were still totally unaware of what was happening outside the bank.

Clifford ran down the ramps of three floors and finally found a parked car that he could hide behind in the hope the officers would run straight up to the top floor. His heart was pounding as he lay flat on his belly in the small gap between the front bumper of the car and the wall, so he could see the feet of anyone passing or looking around. He thought about the others and assumed they had heard him and were now frantically trying to get away with the stolen goods and money. Hearing the sound of someone running up the ramp Clifford held his breath as best he could. From under the car he saw feet and heard a voice.

'We're nearly at the top, guv. No one's passed us so he's still up there and his only way to escape is to jump.'

Clifford waited until he could no longer hear the officer's footsteps. He got up and took off his jacket. Holding it up against the driver's-side window he used his elbow to dampen the sound as he smashed it open. Once inside he felt under the ignition barrel and ripped out the cables. Hotwiring a car was second nature to him.

As Bradfield crossed the road with his team he walked with a determined and confident stride. He radioed the officers sent to arrest Clifford and asked if they'd got him. One of them said they'd reached the top floor but Bentley wasn't there and must have somehow got away.

DC Stanley was listening and responded to the conversation.

'Impossible, I've got an officer still monitoring the ramp exit and stairwell. They saw your two go up but no one, I repeat no one, has left the car park.'

Bradfield's adrenalin was pumping as he radioed the officers in the car park. 'He's hiding somewhere, so find him. I'm going into the bank with my team now ... All arrest units take up positions now. GO, GO, GO!'

He watched impatiently as a nervous Dunbar fumbled through various keys to open the front doors of the bank. He lit a cigarette to keep himself calm and told Dunbar to get a grip of himself.

Once inside the bank Dunbar deactivated the windows, doors and entry-alarm system and they all headed to the vault room at the back of the premises. Before they could get through to the vault there was a set of iron-grilled doors and Dunbar deactivated the alarm before opening them.

Bradfield, Gibbs, Kath and two detectives stood at the vault door. Dunbar was shaking like a leaf as he whispered to Bradfield.

'It's on a time lock so the usual multi-digit code will be useless. I'll have to use the "duress" code, which will set off a secret alarm signal to Scotland Yard alerting them to a forced-entry condition.'

'That's not a problem, just fucking OPEN IT,' he whispered harshly.

Dunbar began to press in the code but he was shaking and worried about pressing the wrong buttons more than once, which would lock the whole system down, and then no one would be able to get into the vault until it was reset by an expert. Bradfield pushed him aside.

'Give me the numbers,' he said impatiently. Dunbar told him the digits and Bradfield entered them into the electronic key pad. Two seconds later they could hear the sound of clicks and whirs as the bolts began to slowly retract.

Inside the vault John was still using the cutting torch on the safe and had one locking bolt to burn through before he could open it. Silas popped his head up and grabbed two more bulging pillowcases on the vault floor next to the hole.

'We loaded van, John. This is last lot so we need to radio your dad and get de fuck out of here.'

'Where's Danny?'

'In tunnel behind me, getting annoyed waiting,' Silas said, and handed Danny the pillowcases which he stuffed into a sports bag.

'I've nearly cut through so stay there and help me carry out what's in the safe and then I'll call me dad.'

Silas handed Danny another full pillowcase. As John leant over and turned the pressure up on the oxyacetylene tank he noticed the vault door start to open. He knew in an instant what was happening and looking at Silas shouted, 'Someone's opening the fucking door! Get out now!'

Dunbar and Gibbs gripped the vault wheel tightly and started to walk backwards, heaving and pulling open the heavy door. Bradfield turned and looked at Kath who was shaking from the adrenalin rush brought on by what they were about to do. He put his hand on her shoulder to reassure her. 'Best feeling in the world being a detective and nicking a villain on the plot.'

Looking into the vault Bradfield and Kath saw John Bentley. The next few seconds seemed to occur in slow motion as Bentley's eyes widened in panic and the torch flame gave off an eerie blue light that illuminated his stricken face.

The explosion that followed was like a massive bomb going off. Terrifying screams could be heard as fractured bits of metal and steel became lethal projectiles. The vast fireball had only two ways to go, out of the vault, into the bank and down the tunnel, engulfing and burning everything in its path. The giant fireball travelled across the bank like a massive wave, and as it blew out the front windows the explosion lit up the night sky. Bits of glass and metal debris glistened in the flames as they rained down onto the street.

The officer listening in the basement of the shoe shop felt the building tremble as if there were an earthquake. As he ran to escape bits of the basement ceiling began to crumble and collapse around him.

The officers on the outside arrest teams and in the ops ran instinctively to the front of the bank, fearing for the safety of DCI Bradfield and the officers who were with him.

Clifford had just pulled out from the car park in the stolen car. As he drove past the bank the explosion and flying debris terrified him. He swerved across the road, mounted the pavement and narrowly missed a lamp-post. Some of the glass from the bank windows flew in through the smashed window of the car and caused minor cuts to the right side of his face. As he drove off at speed he didn't have a clue what had happened, and hoped and prayed that John had escaped. Even if he'd been arrested he knew his son wasn't a grass. Clifford reached into his jacket pocket and removed the walkie-talkie, thinking briefly about using it to try and make contact with his son. However, now suspecting the police had been listening in, he threw it out of the window and watched in the mirror as it broke into pieces on the street.

Seconds before the explosion Danny Mitcham had managed to get out of the tunnel. He was in the basement when the blast hit him from behind and knocked him flying across the room. He ended up on the floor at the foot of the basement stairs, dazed and wondering what had happened. He knew that the police were on to them and they would have surrounded the back of the café.

Looking round at the tunnel he could see the brick wall and wooden supports they'd inserted had collapsed and wondered if Silas and John were trapped under the soil and debris. He didn't have time to try and help them: self-preservation and escape were his priority now.

Seeing the holdall of money and jewellery at the top of the basement stairs he grabbed it, as well as his donkey jacket which was hanging on the door. Then he ran to the top floor of the building. He looked into the bedrooms and found a chair which he used to stand on. After pushing the loft hatch open he threw the holdall up and pulled himself into the loft. Using his bare hands and feet he ripped and kicked away some of the roof tiles and squeezed through the hole onto the roof of the café. He looked around and could see smoke billowing up from the bank. He couldn't believe the amount of glass and brick debris that covered the street below. Unseen he ran across the rooftops to the end of the terraced buildings where he shimmied down a cast-iron drainpipe to the ground. He could hear the distant scream of approaching sirens.

Clifford dumped the car a mile from home behind some garages. He set light to it, so as to ensure no trace of his fingerprints could be found. He was in a state of hysteria as he wandered the streets, gasping and trying to calm down, whilst wondering what to do. He had considered going on the run, but had no money, clothes or other means to survive and was too old and heavy now to break into houses. He thought about John and wished he was with him. He knew the police had rumbled them, but wondered if they already knew who was involved, or if they'd been watching the flat as well. Clifford made his mind up: he was going to go home and front it out. If the police started calling he'd say he was at a funeral wake with his wife, or shacked up with his mistress. He knew both of them would back him up for fear of a slap.

It was almost 6 a.m. and daylight when an exhausted Clifford returned to his flat on the Pembridge. He went straight to John's room to see if he was there, but the reality was he knew he wouldn't be. He went into the bathroom, undressed and splashed cold water over his face. The small jagged cuts were bleeding and he kept on splashing cold water over them before dabbing them with a white styptic pencil. The aluminium sulphate stung, but he knew it would cause the blood vessels to contract which would help to stop the bleeding.

He then went to his bedroom where Renee was asleep but lying fully clothed across the bed. The smell of alcohol coming from her permeated the room. He nudged her, but she just moaned, so he lifted her feet and repositioned her body to one side before getting into bed. As he lay next to her he stared at the ceiling and for the first time it entered his mind that John might still have been in the bank at the time of the explosion. His heart was pounding as he looked at Renee and wondered what on earth he was going to tell her and David.

Danny Mitcham had the spare key for the lock-up garage John Bentley had rented. When he got there he was shaking from the agonizing pain in his back. He thought maybe he had damaged some vertebrae when the blast from the explosion hit him. It wasn't until he tried to remove his T-shirt, and it stuck to his back, that he realized he had been badly burned by the fireball, which had also singed the hair on the back of his head. He winced in agony as he eased off his T-shirt and his burnt skin peeled away. Looking over his shoulder Danny could see the bright red weeping blisters on his skin. He knew he needed the wound tended at a hospital, but he couldn't risk going to one. He decided he would go out late at night and break into a chemist's for what he needed to treat himself. He would also nick some clothes and food, then after a couple of days of lying low in the garage he'd make his way to Spain.

Danny looked inside the sports holdall and opened the pillowcases. In one there was a large amount of cash, which was all in fivers. In the others there was a little cash but mostly jewellery, items of gold and other valuables. He reckoned he'd done well for himself and smiled even more when he removed the large bags of heroin and cocaine from his trouser pockets. Now these really will make me rich, he thought to himself as he opened a bag of cocaine, put some on his fingers and sniffed it up his nose. He'd never taken any hard drugs, but needs must and he was glad when the cocaine kicked in, numbing the painful burns on his back.

CHAPTER THIRTY-TWO

Jane slept until after 9 a.m. The first decent sleep she'd had for weeks. She felt refreshed and no longer anxious about having been told by Bradfield to go home and take a few days off work. She helped her mother prepare the lunch and found doing the ordinary small things, like laying the table and putting out the wine glasses, made her glad she was at home. By the time Pam and her husband arrived it was almost twelve. Jane was truly pleased to see her sister and hear all about the honeymoon in the Lake District, laughing as she spoke about the dreadful weather and how the MGB car had broken down and had to be towed back to London. Jane could see that her sister was blissfully happy, and Tony hardly got a word in edgeways as Pam began detailing all the gifts they had received.

Mr Tennison was in the open-plan room watching television and reading the newspaper. Mrs Tennison put the leg of lamb on the dining table and asked her husband to carve the meat. He turned the sound down on the TV and joined them at the table. Whilst he cut some slices from the lamb joint his wife fussed around putting vegetables and roast potatoes on everyone's plates and telling them to help themselves to gravy.

Jane complimented her mum on her cooking. When everyone had finished Jane and Pam helped to clear the table and washed the dirty plates and cutlery while their mother made the hot custard to go with the lovely apple turnover. Jane and Pam took the bowls of dessert to the table, then Jane fetched the jug of hot custard. Her father was uncorking another bottle of wine when he pointed at the silent TV.

'My God, the IRA must have exploded another car bomb in the City,' he exclaimed, then went over and turned up the volume to hear what the newscaster was saying:

As you can see from the carnage around me here in Great Eastern Street a large explosion occurred in the early hours of this morning. A number of people were injured during the blast, some we believe fatally. At present the police have not released any names or further details about the incident.

Jane was about to pour custard on her father's dessert. She looked at the screen and saw the ambulances and police cars and a fire engine still dousing down what was left of the Trustee Savings Bank. The instantaneous shock, and the thought of possible fatalities, caused her to drop the jug of custard. It broke into pieces as it crashed against the dessert bowl, causing hot custard to splash onto the table, the floor and Jane's T-shirt and jeans.

She gasped, staring back at the TV screen.

The reporter continued:

It is not yet clear what caused the massive explosion, and the IRA has not as yet claimed responsibility. There were no coded warnings sent to any news agencies as was the case with the car bombs in March this year outside the Old Bailey and the Army recruitment office in Whitehall, where one person was killed and two hundred and fifteen people injured.

Jane grabbed her father's arm.

'Daddy, please ... I need your car keys ... please! I have to go the station! Don't try and stop me, just let me have your car keys.'

She wasn't aware that she was screaming and pulling at his arm. 'Gimme the keys, for Chrissake!'

Her father was taken aback by her outburst and went to the kitchen area where he got the car keys from a drawer. He didn't try and stop her when she snatched them from his hand.

'I'm sorry, I have to go ... I am so sorry,' she said as she hurriedly left the room.

They all heard the front door slam and Mrs Tennison looked confused and frightened as she turned to her husband.

'She's only just passed her driving test! Go after her and stop her!'

He went to follow but slipped on the spilt custard, knocking over a dining-table chair.

Jane hurried down the stairs and out of the flats. She ran down the path and turned to look up and down the small backstreet where her father usually parked his car. Seeing it midway down the road she ran towards it, fumbling for the right key to unlock the driver's door. She got into the car and was gasping for breath as she started the engine. The gears crunched as she pulled out and drove to the end of the road, turning into Edgware Road and then straight through a set of red lights into Marylebone Road.

Jane realized she'd forgotten her handbag and therefore didn't have her warrant card with her to prove she was a police officer if she was stopped for dangerous driving. She forced herself to slow down and drive more carefully, and thankfully it being a bank holiday the roads were very quiet. She breathed heavily and told herself to try to remain calm. The news report about an IRA car bomb made no sense. It seemed to her that something had gone terribly wrong with Operation Hawk.

As she drove past the front of the station Jane saw reporters and television news crews being held back by uniformed officers. A senior civilian from the Met's press bureau was standing on the top steps of the station trying to address the throng who were firing questions at him from all angles. Jane drove round to the rear of the station only to discover it was the same, with a line of uniform officers keeping the press back and refusing entry without police identification.

A PC she didn't recognize raised his arm to stop Jane, so she pulled up and wound down the window to speak to him.

'I am WPC Jane Tennison, please ... I work here.'

'I need to see your warrant card, otherwise I can't let—'

'I saw the news and in the rush to get here I forgot my ID. The officer over there knows me, ask him.'

The PC spoke with the officer and she was let into the station yard. Manoeuvring the car into a parking bay she was distracted when she saw Detective Chief Superintendent Metcalf by the back door talking to two officers. They looked pale and drained.

She winced as she scraped the side of her father's car along one of the metal pole dividers for the motorbike parking area. She didn't even bother to look at the damage as she ran towards the entrance.

Inside the station it was mayhem. Every phone was ringing and a large number of officers, who had clearly been drafted in from other stations to assist, were wandering the corridor asking where the parade room was.

Jane saw an agitated Sergeant Harris appear waving his hands and shouting for people to get out of the front desk area and keep the corridors clear. He raised his voice even higher.

'The parade room is on the left of the rear yard as you exit the building. DCS Metcalf will be addressing you all there in ten minutes' time and will give further instructions.'

Jane tugged his shirtsleeve. 'Sarge, what's happened?'

'Not now, Tennison. If you wanna help then assist the officer on the front desk while I get this lot to the parade room. I'll tell you all about it when I get back.'

Jane pushed and shoved her way through the throng towards the front desk, but there were still a lot of uniform officers milling around, and the front doors to the station were closed. At the top of her voice she yelled out the directions to the parade room and gradually the front desk area cleared. She could hear the frustrated reporters and news teams outside shouting out questions and saw a PC she knew on the duty-desk phone. When he'd finished she asked what was going on, but he said he didn't really know as he'd come on for late shift and had been told by Harris to man the front desk.

Jane decided to go to the incident room hoping she might get some proper answers. As she ran up the stairs she saw Sally, the pregnant civilian indexer she had replaced on the Julie Ann Collins case. Sally was leaning against the wall in floods of tears and Jane knew that worry for the safety of her friends and colleagues must have brought her to the station.

'Can you tell me what's happened, Sally?'

'It's Kath, no one's seen Kath … Oh my God …'

'Is Kath hurt?' Jane asked anxiously.

'Dead … some of them are dead,' Sally wailed.

'What? Who exactly is dead?'

'I don't know, no one will say and some are in hospital.'

Sally looked faint as she slid down the wall and sat on the floor. Confused, Jane tried to help up the inconsolable woman, but she just wanted to stay where she was and be left alone. Jane still had no idea of exactly what had happened. She knew that if anyone had died in the explosion they would have been taken to Hackney Mortuary. Asking a passing PC to look after Sally, she ran as fast as she could out through the back of the station and across the churchyard towards the mortuary.

Pushing open the door to the reception area Jane saw some of the surveillance officers and detectives from Operation Hawk standing looking at each other, lost for words. She knew that something terrible had happened, but she couldn't bring herself to ask exactly what. She dreaded having her own worst fears confirmed.

A mortuary assistant in his green gown and white wellington boots opened the door from the corridor to say that the undertaker's van was on its way from the scene of the explosion. They would be bringing in body bags via the back entrance and he needed some assistance. Jane felt helpless as she and the others followed the head mortician down the corridor to the van bay, where he pulled open the double-door metal shutters to let the first black van reverse in.

Jane was surprised, yet in some ways relieved, to see Sarah Redhead get out of the passenger side of the van as the mortician opened the rear to remove the body bags onto a trolley.

'Thank God, Sarah. Can you tell me if a WPC Kathleen Morgan is here or at the hospital as ... ?'

Sarah, normally so loud-spoken, took Jane by her arm and whispered, 'I haven't a clue who's in the bags. We got called to go to the bank to control the cordons and keep the press and public out. When they got the bodies out we were told to accompany them here and then go off duty. I've been on for sixteen hours now.'

'Has nobody said anything about who has died?'

'I'm a uniform WPC like you, Jane. I don't ask, I just do. Unless you're on duty you really shouldn't be in here. All I can tell you is the scene at the bank was horrendous. Glass, metal and bricks were all over the streets.'

They had to stand back as another undertaker's van reversed in. At the same time the head mortician told a couple of officers to take the first body through to the fridge area for storage.

The undertaker driving the latest arrival got out and spoke with the mortician.

'Bit of a jigsaw in this bag – it's full of bits and pieces the forensic guys found in the vault. God only knows which bits are the police and which bits the bad guys.'

Jane felt as if she had been punched in her heart by what she'd just heard.

'Body parts?' she repeated breathlessly.

The head mortician looked at Jane. 'You're that probationer who was in here the other week to watch the post-mortem on the murdered girl. What's this case got to do with you?'

'It's OK, she's working on it as well,' a voice said.

Jane looked and saw a dazed DS Spencer Gibbs getting out of the passenger seat of the undertaker's van. He looked terrible. He had a dressing over the left side of his face and both his hands were bandaged. His jacket was blackened and singed and he was obviously in considerable pain.

'My God, what happened to you?'

'I was in the bank and got hurt during the explosion.'

Jane was still in shock. He glanced at her.

'Have you been sick over yourself?'

'No, it's custard. Was Kath with you?'

Gibbs took a deep trembling breath and nodded.

'Bradfield as well.' His voice quivered and he started to walk off.

'What happened, Spence?'

'I need to get back to the station as I've got things to do.'

Jane felt more optimistic. Although Gibbs was injured he had survived. She followed him out of the mortuary and could see he was wincing and gritting his teeth as he walked. She stepped closer.

'I'm confused, Spence, and really need to know what's happened.'

He stopped and looked at her. His voice was sad.

'Kath and Len didn't make it—'

A shocked Jane shook her head as she interrupted him. 'But you were with them, how did you ...?'

'I was behind the thick vault door with the bank manager when the explosion occurred so our bodies were protected from the fireball and flying debris. Our injuries are just heat-blast burns.'

Jane felt her legs begin to shake as she feared the worst.

'They were standing by the entrance to the vault and took the full blast. They didn't stand a chance, Jane,' he said, welling up.

'They're dead?' she asked disbelievingly.

'Yes. I'm really sorry as I know how close you were to Kath.'

Jane felt as if her legs were going to buckle under her. Gibbs took hold of her arm to support her as they walked slowly back to the station.

'For what it's worth some of the suspects died. We don't know exactly who yet due to the injuries, but from what's left I think it could be John Bentley and the Greek. It seems Danny Mitcham escaped over the roofs and I'm going out to look for Clifford Bentley later.'

As they walked across the station yard Sergeant Harris approached them and told Gibbs that DCS Metcalf had been asking the surveillance officers and other team detectives awkward questions, wanting to know the ins and outs of Operation Hawk and why, once the suspects were in the vault, it was so long before they went in to make arrests.

'Bastard's looking for a scapegoat to blame already. I ain't gonna let him blacken Len Bradfield's name so I'll take the rap.'

Harris took him to one side. 'Are you sure that's wise, Spencer? Metcalf hasn't the bottle to blame a dead man who everyone respected and who had an unblemished career. If you say it was in any way your fault he'll blame you publicly for Len's death and that's your career screwed. Do you really think Bradfield would want it to end that way?'

Gibbs shook his head and realized Harris, for all his many irritating faults, spoke with experience and sense.

'You should go home, Spence, you look awful.'

'I'm all right and I want to make the NOK call before Metcalf does.'

'Are you sure that's a good idea? He is the senior officer investigating this now.'

'I was his friend so I'll make the call, and if Metcalf doesn't like it then tough.'

'Don't lose your head, you got to stay in control,' Harris said.

Jane heard bits of what they were talking about but didn't know what a NOK was and didn't want to appear nosy or irritating by asking. She interrupted with a light tap to Gibbs's arm.

'Can I do anything to help?'

'No, I got to do this myself,' he said and walked off into Bradfield's office.

Harris turned to Jane. 'Canteen's closed as it's a bank holiday so make him a nice cup of tea,' he said, and looked her up and down before continuing. 'What's that yellow stuff on your clothes? You look a mess.'

She apologized explaining that she had been off duty, but had come in after seeing the news. She asked him if she could stay on and work.

'Yes, but put your uniform on as this station is going to be the focus of press and top-brass attention for a long while yet.'

She said she would make Gibbs a tea and then return to the section house to change.

Jane went into the small kitchen and put the kettle on before unthinkingly washing the usual array of dirty mugs that had been left in the sink.

When she took DS Gibbs a cup of tea he was sitting behind Bradfield's desk, leaning forward with his arms on the table, his head resting between them. At first she thought he was asleep. He looked up and took out a hand-kerchief to wipe his nose.

'Two sugars, right?' Jane asked with a smile.

'Thanks,' Gibbs said.

'Did your NOK call go OK?' she asked out of polite-ness, still unsure what it meant.

'I don't think she could really take it all in, but I'll go over to be with her later.'

'I'm sorry, who do you mean by "she"?'

Spencer sighed. 'Len's wife. It was awful as I could hear their two small kids playing in the background, and now I gotta do Kath's NOK call.'

Jane suddenly realized that 'NOK' was short for 'next of kin' and couldn't believe what Gibbs had just said. Was Bradfield married? It wasn't possible, it couldn't be true, she thought to herself before speaking as calmly as possi-ble under the circumstances.

'Married. I didn't know married officers could live at the section house.'

Gibbs sipped his tea, and gave a small shrug of his shoulders.

'His wife was finding it hard to cope with all the late hours he worked. She'd get anxious, wondering if maybe he'd been hurt as he hadn't come home when expected. Len told me she would often sit up waiting for him. He spoke with the section house sergeant who said he, and a few others, could use a spare room when things got busy. Len reckoned it would help stop all the anxiety at home and then a rumour goes round that they were splitting up. It didn't bother him as he always felt that his private life was his own personal business and nothing to do with anyone else and ...' He bowed his head trying to stifle a sob. 'God help me, I loved and respected that man so much and now I gotta tell poor Kath's mum and dad she's dead.'

Jane had to take deep breaths to steady herself. She gently patted his shoulder.

'Sorry, Spence, so sorry.'

She turned away, knowing she was going to break down. She clenched her fists, digging her nails into her palms. She hurried out of the office, down the stairs and out to the rear entrance of the station in a state of denial.

With no handbag, warrant card or money she walked to the section house and had to ask the 'old buzzard' to let her into her room. She gasped for breath as she shut the door behind her. She stared at the big poster of Janis Joplin with her wild hair and the silly feather boa, her arms lined with bracelets and rings on her fingers. The scream came from the pit of her stomach.

'No, no, no, no!'

She tore the poster down and began ripping it to shreds as the song that had constantly been running through her mind seemed to drill into her heart:

> *Didn't I make you feel like you were the only man –*
> *yeah!*
> *An' didn't I give you nearly everything that a*
> *woman possibly can?*
> *Honey, you know I did!*
> *And each time I tell myself that I, well I think I've*
> *had enough,*
> *But I'm gonna show you, baby, that a woman can*
> *be tough.*
> *I want you to come on, come on, come on, and take*
> *it,*

Take it!
Take another little piece of my heart now, baby!
Oh, oh, break it!
Break another little bit of my heart now, baby ...

Still crying Jane took off her stained clothes, changed into a clean pressed shirt and skirt, then brushed her hair and tied it back with an elastic band. Hard as she tried she couldn't stop the floodgates opening as she remembered Bradfield tossing the elastic band onto her desk and calling her Veronica Lake.

She splashed cold water over her face and held the towel against her eyes until her sobs quietened.

'Take control, take control, do it.'

Jane picked up her hat, put it on and stared at her reflection in the mirror. Her uniform suddenly felt like a protective armour. As she returned to the station she gritted her teeth and knew that, whatever anguish she was feeling or had to face in the future, she would now be able to contain it inside her.

Sergeant Harris saw her sitting at the front counter desk looking pristine and calm.

He paused briefly and spoke softly. 'Good girl.'

'Thank you, Sarge.'

CHAPTER THIRTY-THREE

A team led by Metcalf had raided Clifford Bentley's flat that afternoon. He was asleep in bed and the officers had to wake him. When asked where their son John was Renee said she hadn't seen him since the previous afternoon when she had left to go to a funeral and Clifford said it was the same for him. He maintained that he paid his respects to the passing funeral procession, and then returned to the flat without John to spend the afternoon and night caring for his very sick son David. He didn't know what time his wife got home from the funeral as he had already gone to bed and was in such a deep sleep he didn't hear her come in.

Whilst Metcalf spoke with Clifford and Renee two officers searched David's room only to discover he was not there and there were signs that he had taken clothes and a number of personal belongings with him. This was news to Clifford, who was now totally dependent on Renee to confirm his alibi and back him up. He then said John had taken David away for a few days as a surprise break to help him get better.

When Metcalf said that it was a trip that John would not be coming back from there was a look of horror in Clifford's eyes and Renee demanded to know what he meant. She listened wide-eyed and motionless as Metcalf explained about the explosion, and the certainty that John had died in it whilst Clifford had done a runner.

The fact that John was dead, as a result of a plan probably hatched by Clifford, was too much for Renee to comprehend. She could not, as she had done so often in the past, protect her husband again. With her hands clenched in an attempt to control herself Renee told Metcalf that Clifford had not been at home on the Sunday afternoon or evening, and had definitely not been there when she got back from the wake sometime after midnight. She added that David was at home when she left for the funeral. When questioned about the whereabouts of her youngest son Renee claimed that she had no idea where he was, but he had left home on the afternoon of the funeral to get away from his brother and his father who had always manipulated, bullied and controlled him. She gave Metcalf details of a taxi firm David had used to book a taxi to take him to Heathrow Airport, but she was adamant that she had no idea where he was going from there as he hadn't wanted her to be put in a position where Clifford or John could force it out of her.

Clifford was enraged when he was arrested, and demanded to know why Renee didn't tell him about David. Renee had just smiled cynically, asking why he was suddenly worried about a son he'd never cared for or shown any real love to. She told him she hoped that David would at last find a decent and happy life.

It was early evening when a live press and TV news conference was held at Hackney Police Station in the main CID office. The packed room fell silent as DCS Metcalf entered and Sergeant Harris closed the doors behind him to stop anyone else entering the already crammed room.

Metcalf stood firm and upright next to a large projector screen. Harris turned on the projector and a picture of the Metropolitan Police Force Crest and the two fallen officers came up on the screen.

Metcalf cleared his throat. 'It is with deep sadness that I have to inform you of the tragic loss of Detective Chief Inspector Leonard Bradfield and Detective Constable Kathleen Morgan during the explosion at the Trustee Savings Bank in Shoreditch. Our thoughts and sympathies are with their families at this time of loss. I have only the highest praise for DCI Bradfield: his professionalism and leadership were beyond reproach, as was the devotion to duty of all the officers who took part in Operation Hawk, some of whom were badly injured. They are all examples of police officers who, on a daily basis, display outstanding courage in the face of danger.'

The flash of cameras was relentless. As Metcalf paused to take a breath he was met with a flurry of questions from the journalists, who wanted to know more about the case and the suspects.

He held his hand up. 'The incident is under investigation, so as I'm sure you all appreciate I am restricted in what I can say. However, I can tell you that two suspects were killed in the explosion, but their identities have yet to be confirmed.'

Yet again there were further interruptions from the journalists, who wanted to know if there were only two bank raiders, and if more why and how had they escaped.

Again Metcalf held his hand up. 'We believe that at least two suspects escaped during the aftermath of the unexpected explosion. One man, who was a lookout, has since been arrested and is being interviewed as we speak.'

Metcalf nodded to Sergeant Harris who put up a slide

of the last arrest photograph of Daniel Mitcham. Metcalf said that Mitcham was still at large, gave a full description and warned the public not to approach him if they saw him, but to dial 999 immediately. Lastly he told them that another suspect by the name of David Bentley was also on the run, and though not believed to have been present at the scene of the crime during the explosion he was wanted for conspiracy to commit robbery. He apologized that there was no current photograph of David Bentley, but gave a full description of him and emphasized that he was disabled, walked with a limp and used a walking stick or wheelchair.

Jane was working at the front desk during the press conference and knew it had finished when she saw Sergeant Harris escorting journalists and camera crews out of the station.

He joined her at the desk and said she could take a break.

'I don't mind staying on here, Sarge.'

'No, love, you take your break. I'll look after things here.'

She went to the canteen. Usually it would have been alive with chatter and officers clattering around with their trays. Tonight, though, there was an almost eerie silence, and when the officers did talk to each other it was in whispers.

Through the evening more details of what the teams had uncovered circulated round the station. Jane was told what was left of John Bentley's burnt and dismembered body had been recovered from inside the vault and identified by matching the teeth of the deceased against dental records. Silas Manatos had to be dug out from the tunnel underneath the vault. Although intact his body was burnt beyond facial recognition by the fireball that engulfed the tunnel between the café and bank. No dental records could be traced locally for Silas, but his owl pendant had in effect welded to his body. His medical records showed that he had broken his right leg three years ago and the post-mortem examination found evidence of an old break and subsequent healing. Combined with the police evidence that Silas was part of the gang, and in the café at the time of the explosion, this was enough for the coroner to confirm and publicly release the identifications to the press.

With the assistance of Scotland Yard's Special Branch it was quickly discovered that a David Bentley had flown on a Boeing 747 flight from Heathrow to Miami Airport on the Sunday evening. The British Overseas Airways Corporation ticket was one way and had cost him £150. The FBI were informed and said the chances of finding him now were slim as he had not stayed at the hotel he had shown on his landing card and could now be anywhere in Florida or the East Coast of America. DCS Metcalf considered sending a team to the States to look for him, but decided against it. He knew that where families like the Bentleys were concerned blood was thicker than water and David had spent many years being cared for by his mother Renee. One day he would return to Hackney, and when he did they'd arrest and charge him with conspiracy to rob the TSB.

In the days that followed, Jane felt Kath's presence daily, often hearing her voice and laugh, and was grateful Kath had taught her how to handle discrimination and have the strength to stand up for herself. Jane had even put a couple of dents in the roller towel herself at times of frustration, but she had come to learn that the nature of a police officer's work was often to remember but move on, so no one really talked much about Kath or Bradfield's deaths, or how much they were missed. Any reference to Bradfield was quietly dealt with, but she knew she was not the only one to feel a dark sadness that he was gone and no longer storming out of his office, barking orders. A new DCI was sent to Hackney to take over the day-to-day running of the CID and Kath Morgan was replaced by another officer waiting to be made detective.

There was some light relief after all the tragedy. It was discovered that the officers who had already paid for and received their suits from Mannie Charles were all wearing hot property. They weren't in fact 'off the rail', but classy suits that had been stolen from Aquascutum in Regent Street by the Horne Brothers warehouse manager and Mannie's wife had removed the labels and substituted them with their own. DS Gibbs had been tipped off by a mate who worked in the CID office at West End Central and arrested the Horne manager and Mannie whilst investigating the break-in. It had everyone laughing and wondering if they should return the suits or keep quiet, until Gibbs brought in the suit ordered by Bradfield that was still hanging in his office in a plastic wrapper. As Bradfield had been six foot four there were few men it would fit, or who would want it. With gallows humour one detective lightened the gloom by suggesting he might like to be buried in it, but many couldn't hide just how much Bradfield was missed.

Jane found that sinking herself into her daily work helped keep her emotions in check. It was only at night, in the privacy of her room at the section house, that she found the horror overwhelming. She would constantly remember Kath, and sometimes break down in tears. Other times she would fall into an exhausted sleep and wake with the nightmare of the explosion, and then it was Bradfield who dominated her every thought. Had he tried to protect Kath? She was certain that he would have, but then the thought of him left her bereft and unable even to cry.

Daniel Mitcham was finally arrested when he tried to use a false passport when boarding a P & O Ferry at Dover destined for Boulogne in France, from where he intended to make his way to Spain. Although he had changed his appearance by cutting his hair and wearing glasses and a cap, it was the burn to the nape of his neck that made one of the Customs officers suspicious. When the holdall he was carrying was searched it was found to contain a false bottom. Hidden inside was £10,000, mostly in soon to be unusable £5 notes, a quantity of valuable jewellery and a large stash of drugs.

The police had been intercepting and checking any mail to his home address. As a result they had discovered the cash and jewellery he had sent to his wife to enable her to join him in Spain when he found a place to live. The police had let the mail through and his wife hadn't declared she'd received stolen goods so they had arrested her. Mitcham was promised that the charges against his wife would be dropped, his kids wouldn't end up in care, and he would get a reduced sentence if he co-operated. It was an offer he was in no position to refuse.

Danny told them the full story, and also agreed to give Queen's Evidence against Clifford Bentley, who had so far refused to say anything.

After the bodies and body parts had been removed from

the bank, DS Lawrence and his forensic team had spent days at the location trying to ascertain exactly what had caused the explosion. They knew from the hole in the steel vault floor that the suspects must have been using an oxyacetylene torch, but as it was not in the café it was likely that it had been blown to pieces and become mixed up with all the other debris from the vault. Every piece of metal was eventually gathered up in dustbins and it was a painstaking task at the lab sifting through it all and putting the oxygen and acetylene tanks back together. The answer came after Paul Lawrence had meticulously rebuilt the remains of the acetylene tank pressure gauge and discovered the dial was stuck on 30psi. He knew that the gauge must have been on 30psi at the moment of explosion, and that acetylene, being an extremely unstable gas, was dangerously explosive at pressures above 15psi. Lawrence concluded that John Bentley naively thought that turning up the pressure would increase the heat intensity and speed up cutting the safe open. The explosion was inevitable and unavoidable, and tragically happened at exactly the wrong moment for the officers who, as a result, were killed or injured.

Due to the intense political and press interest concerning the deaths of two police officers, and the severe injuries to others including the bank manager, the rubber heelers from A10 were called in as a matter of course to carry out an internal investigation. They had been told to look at all the information DCI Bradfield had acted on, and decide whether it was reliable and correct. The big question was whether he could have reasonably foreseen that dangerous and volatile cutting equipment needed to be used to get into the vault, in which case the suspects should have been arrested as soon as they broke into the vault.

For once it was an investigation that the A10 officers did not relish and they deliberately cut corners, especially as there was not one officer on the team who did not stand by the decisions made by the deceased DCI Leonard Bradfield, whose actions had also been given the green light and were supported by DCS Metcalf. Everyone knew that it would be wrong to tarnish the good name of a highly respected and much admired man like Bradfield, who had acted in good faith and done what he believed to be right at the time. Even the Commissioner himself recognized this fact by later recommending both DCI Bradfield and WPC Morgan for a posthumously awarded Queen's Police Medal for an 'exhibition of conspicuous devotion to duty'.

Jane was working on the front desk when Harris came in and told her that Metcalf wanted to see her.

'Why? What does he want?' she asked, worried she was going to be reprimanded, or worse made a scapegoat.

'Search me, but get a move on – he doesn't like to be left waiting.'

The bank robbery investigation was being led by DCS Metcalf who had to compile an in-depth report detailing the full extent of the tragedy that surrounded Operation Hawk. Jane had escaped being questioned by A10, but an interview with Metcalf was worse. She headed to the office that Bradfield had previously occupied, refusing to remember the last time she'd seen him behind that very desk.

Metcalf was flicking through a thick file as she sat down opposite him, waiting nervously and wondering why he had called her in.

'Now, I have it formally noted by the late DCI Bradfield that you recognized the deceased John Bentley's voice from a recording made by a young boy called Ashley Brennan. Is that correct?'

'Yes, sir, I went to Brennan's home address and—'

'I am aware of how you came to be in possession of the tape,' he interrupted, and continued to read through the file.

'Initially you had been helping Bentley's mother after an asthma attack, correct?'

'Yes, sir,' Jane said, realizing it was best to keep her answers brief.

'That was very commendable and thoughtful of you, and somewhat fortunate for DCI Bradfield and the commencement of Operation Hawk,' he said, and smiled.

'I hadn't thought of it like that as I was just doing my job.'

'Nevertheless you apparently stuck to your guns when it was suggested that you may have been mistaken about it being John Bentley's voice.'

'Yes, sir.'

'Good. I like to see WPCs on probation proving to be confident, and being able to recall someone's voice after only a few brief moments is quite exceptional.'

'Thank you, sir,' Jane said, feeling he was being overindulgent and wondering why.

He flicked to another page in the file and looked her in the eye before continuing.

'DCI Bradfield quite rightly set up surveillance on the Bentley family and your observation about the voice on the tape proved to be correct. As the team indexer you were also responsible for typing up all the officers' reports, including those made by DCI Bradfield and DS Gibbs?'

'Yes, sir.'

'I was wondering, were you ever aware of, or privy to,

a report that was allegedly made by DS Gibbs concerning dangerous-gas tanks used for cutting metal, which he saw in the basement of the café?'

Jane realized he was asking her a leading question and hoped she was about to give the answer he wanted to hear.

'No, sir,' she lied without a flinch or blink.

He gave her a satisfied smile. 'Good, I was obviously misinformed. I'm not keen to take this matter further as I suspected it was a malicious rumour. Thankfully you have confirmed that for me, but please keep it between us.'

He glanced up and closed the file, then gave a short nod as he stood up to shake her hand.

'I am confident that you have a good career ahead of you, WPC Tennison. I have taken note of your professionalism and will happily give you a personal recommendation should you wish to apply for CID at the end of your probation.'

As she left the room Jane now knew for certain that an internal cover-up had been going on. She did recall writing up a report regarding the concerns raised about the gas tanks by DS Gibbs, and knew that it would now have been removed from the case file and destroyed. Metcalf was obviously worried that Bradfield's failure to contemplate the risks in Operation Hawk had resulted in the carnage and loss of life that followed the explosion, but that would have been an embarrassment for him and the police force as a whole.

Metcalf had obviously seen her as a weak link, but her meeting with him was yet another learning curve. Whether or not she approved didn't matter, she was in no position to question the outcome Metcalf and the top brass desired, not if she valued her future career. She smiled to herself and thought Kath would also have kept silent.

It was somehow a relief that when she returned to the front desk, Sergeant Harris was his usual blunt self. Pointedly he looked at his wristwatch.

'I'll excuse you for not being back here on time, but then of course you were with the top brass. Everything go well with Metcalf?'

'Yes, Sarge, he mentioned ...'

He stood straight and wagged his finger.

'Don't want to know. Life goes on, Tennison, that's all you've got to know.'

There seemed to be no way anyone would ever talk about what had happened on that terrible day. No one wanted to show their feelings. Jane found it impossible to share her deep pain, and that was the way it would remain.

THE AFTERMATH

Kath's parents had requested a small personal funeral which was attended by some of the officers she had worked with at the station. They all wore their best uniforms and white gloves, with the detectives in smart suits, white shirts and black ties. It had been a quiet, simple, but moving service and many present had openly cried as Kath had been such a well-liked officer. Jane had forced herself to remain in control of her emotions, but when the organist played 'Nights In White Satin' as the service ended, she nearly broke down. She remembered laughing with Kath as she joined in singing the song with Gibbs outside the men's shower room. She also recalled how Kath had joked with Spencer about playing the same song at her funeral. Seeing Gibbs standing straight-backed, his face etched with pain, Jane knew he was remembering her too. Kath would be hard to forget. Jane had learned so much from her and knew she would always remember her warmth and compassion.

After the service, DS Gibbs introduced Jane to a tall, attractive woman who had been very distressed throughout the funeral service, openly weeping. Gibbs confused Jane as he had referred to the woman as Kath's partner.

'She spoke very warmly of you, Jane. It's nice to meet you.'

'She was a good friend, I will miss her.'

'Yes, she was a very special woman.'

Kath had never mentioned her partner and it was some time before Jane realized what their relationship had been. It dawned on her just how little she had really known about Kath's private life. She now realized Kath's jovial remarks about good-looking men had been a necessary front to hide her sexuality, from an all too often sexist and homophobic police force.

Gibbs picked up Jane's puzzled expression although she had covered it quickly.

'So now you know. I loved that woman, and if she wanted her private life kept that way, that was her business, but there's one thing I want sorted. The lipstick on the dummy's gob, when I had to do the first-aid crap, it was bloody Kath, wasn't it?'

Jane felt the tears welling up and she nodded.

'I knew it ... Christ, I am going to miss her.'

'Me too, she was getting you back for the Vicks-up-the-nose joke at the post-mortem.'

He turned away, because like Jane, he was near to tears.

Bradfield's funeral was organized by his widow and Spencer Gibbs. She had chosen the hymns and readings and he had spent hours preparing the eulogy he had been asked, and was honoured, to give. Sergeant Harris and other uniform officers of all ranks lined the streets and as the funeral cortège passed they stood to attention and saluted in their pristine white gloves. Many mourners came from the stations that Bradfield had worked at during his career as well as members of the public, some who didn't even know him, yet who wanted to pay their respects. Every aisle and pew inside the church was full and officers stood shoulder to shoulder at the back of the church. Bradfield's coffin was draped in the Metropolitan Police flag and his colleagues, led by DS Gibbs and DS Paul Lawrence, carried the coffin to the altar.

Jane could feel the pit of her stomach twisting as she saw, following behind the coffin, a pretty blonde-haired woman in her late thirties. She was holding the hands of a little boy and girl who walked beside her. Bradfield's widow wore a well-cut black coat and a wide-brimmed black straw hat that hid her face. The little boy had his father's red curly hair and the girl had long blonde plaits. They were both dressed in smart clothes and coats, white socks and black patent-leather shoes.

Jane had felt humiliation when she had been told by Bradfield that she was off the team and should go home, and had been deeply hurt when he had said there was no future in their relationship. She had subsequently felt a huge sense of betrayal when she had discovered, after his death, that he was married with children. Now, standing amongst so many police officers, some of whom she had worked with, all Jane could think of was how foolish she had been. How immature and stupid she had been not to have even considered that he was married. He never wore a wedding ring, so she naively assumed he lived in the section house, and she had never seen a photograph on his desk of his wife or children. She wondered why Kath hadn't told her Bradfield was married. Perhaps in some way she had tried to warn her, or perhaps she just hadn't wanted to jeopardize her position on the team. Either way, Jane harboured no bad feelings for her friend. She had just never thought to ask if he was married, but now she felt used. He had drawn her to him and made love to her, and she had been infatuated, believing at the time they could have had something special together. She had loved and admired him, but it had been a hard lesson. From now on she felt determined to keep a tight hold on her emotions, and never be drawn into another relationship with a serving police officer. The tragedy had not made her want to quit the force, but a change of direction was something she needed if she wanted to move on in her career. She thought about DCS Metcalf's encouraging words and decided she would take him up on his offer of a personal recommendation to become a trainee detective on completion of her probation. After all, he owed her that for her loyalty.

Jane stood upright and faced forwards, holding up the order of service. The choir began to sing 'The Lord's My Shepherd, I Shall Not Want'. She tried hard, but just couldn't get the words out and was unaware that tears were streaming down her cheeks. She made no sound as her heart poured out with sorrow. Midway through the hymn Sergeant Harris, who was standing next to her, pulled out a white folded handkerchief from his pocket, which he quietly and unobtrusively passed to her.

'Thank you,' she said, and wiped her eyes.

Later as they stood in the graveyard and watched Bradfield's coffin being lowered into the ground, the police officers present all saluted. As the vicar read out the words of the Committal, 'Earth to earth, ashes to ashes, dust to dust,' Bradfield's widow and two children wept. The children each threw a white rose onto the coffin and then hugged their mother. Jane shed no more tears, but stared straight ahead and gave no indication of how deeply his death had affected her ... that he'd broken a little piece of her heart.

Want to find out what happened
to WPC Jane Tennison?

Turn the page for an extract
of Lynda La Plante's

PRIME SUSPECT

Available now in paperback and eBook

CHAPTER ONE

Mrs Corrina Salbanna was woken from a deep sleep by the sound of the front door banging in the wind. She squinted at her bedside clock; it was almost two. Swearing in her native Spanish, she threw off the bedclothes and stuffed her plump feet into her slippers.

She shuffled up the steps into the hall and towards the still-open front door, wrapping her dressing-gown around her against the chill. The naked light bulb gave the seedy hallway a yellowish hue that did nothing to enhance the peeling wallpaper and brown, flaking paint. Pursing her lips, Mrs Salbanna slammed the door hard. There was no reason why anyone else in the house should be allowed to sleep if she couldn't.

As she turned again towards her warm bed, she noticed a light beneath Della Mornay's door on the first-floor landing. She put two and two together; it must be that little tart who had left the door open. Della owed three months' rent, and had been warned about bringing men back to her room. Now was the time to catch her red-handed. Moving as fast as she could, Mrs Salbanna returned to the basement and collected the master keys, then panted back up to the first floor.

'Della, I know you're in there, open the door!'

She waited, with her ear pressed to the door. Hearing nothing, she rattled the door-handle. 'Della?'

There was no response. Her face set, Mrs Salbanna inserted the key, unlocked the door and pushed it open.

The large room was as seedy as the rest of the run-down Victorian house, which had been divided into bedsits long before Mrs Salbanna and her husband had taken it over in the sixties, and many of the rooms still had the feel of the hippie years. Only the posters in this room had changed; Jimi Hendrix had given way to more modern rock and movie heroes. The first thing Mrs Salbanna saw was a large photograph of Madonna, lips pouting, which dominated the squalid, clothes-strewn room from above the head of the old-fashioned double bed. A red shawl had been draped over the bedside lamp; in its glow Mrs Salbanna could see that the pillows and red satin eiderdown had been dragged to the far side of the bed, revealing the stained ticking of the mattress.

There was no sign of Della. Shivering, Mrs Salbanna looked about her with distaste. She wouldn't put it past the little bitch to be hiding; she'd been devious enough about not paying her rent. She sniffed: stale body odour and cheap perfume. The smell was stronger when she peered into the mahogany wardrobe, but it contained only dresses and shoes.

The wardrobe door, off its hinges, was propped against the wall. Its full-length, fly-blown mirror was cracked and missing a corner, but reflected enough to show Mrs Salbanna a leg, protruding from beneath the bedclothes on the floor. She spun round.

'You little bitch! I knew you were in here!'

For all her weight, the landlady moved swiftly across the room and crouched down to grip Della's exposed ankle. With her other hand she threw the bedclothes aside. Her mouth opened to scream, but no sound came; she lost her balance and fell, landing on her backside. In a panic she crawled to the door, dragging herself up by the open drawer of a tallboy. Bottles and pots of make-up crashed to the floor as her scream finally surfaced. Mrs Salbanna screamed and screamed ...

By the time Detective Chief Inspector John Shefford arrived the house in Milner Road, Gray's Inn, had been cordoned off. He was the last on the scene; two patrol cars were parked outside the house and uniformed officers were fending off the sightseers. An ambulance stood close by, its doors open, its crew sitting inside, drinking tea. The mortuary van was drawing up and had to swerve out of the way as Shefford's car screeched to a halt just where its driver had intended to park. Shefford's door crashed open as he yanked on the handbrake. He was on the move, delving into his pocket for his ID as he stepped over the cordon. A young PC, recognizing him, ushered him up the steps to the house.

Even at two-thirty on a wintry Sunday morning, word had got round that a murder had been committed. There were lights in many windows; people in dressing-gowns huddled on their front steps. A couple of kids had appeared and were vying with each other to see how close they could get to the police cordon without breaking through it. Five Rastafarians with a ghetto-blaster were laughing together on a nearby wall, calling out remarks and jokes, as if it was a street party.

Shefford, a bear of a man at six foot two, dwarfed those around him. He had been notorious on the rugby field in the late seventies, when he played for England. With his curly hair standing on end, his crumpled shirt and tie hanging loose he didn't look or feel in a fit state to start an investigation. He had been hauled out of the celebration bash at the end of a long and tedious murder case, and he was knackered. Now he was about to lead the investigation of another murder, but this one was different.

Many of the officers in the dark, crowded hallway he had worked with before. He scanned the faces as his eyes grew accustomed to the darkness. He never forgot a face, and he greeted each man he knew by name.

At the foot of the stairs he hesitated a moment, straightening his tie. It wasn't like him to shrink from an unpleasant duty, but he had to force himself to mount each step. He was sweating. Above the confusion of voices a high-pitched wailing could be heard. It seemed to be coming from the direction of the basement.

Hearing Shefford's voice, Detective Sergeant Bill Otley stopped pacing the landing and leaned over the banister. He gestured for his guv'nor to join him in the darkness at the far end of the landing. He kept his voice low and his eye on the men coming and going from the victim's room.

'It's Della Mornay, guv. I got the tip-off from Al Franks.'

He could smell the booze on Shefford's breath. Unwrapping a peppermint, he handed it over. The boss wasn't drunk; he probably had been, but he was straightening out fast. Then Otley shook out a pair of white overalls for each of them. While they struggled to put them on, their dark recess was lit at intervals by the powerful flash of a camera from the bedsit.

As Shefford dragged on a cigarette he became aware of a familiar low, gruff voice that had been droning on all the time he had been in the house. He moved towards the door and listened.

'… She's lying next to the double bed, on the side nearest the window and away from the door. She's half-hidden beneath a red silk eiderdown. The window is open, a chest of drawers in front of it. We have a sheet, a blanket, a copy of the Sunday Times dated December 1990 … Looks like it's been used to wrap something in. She's lying face down, hands tied behind her back. Wearing some kind of skinnyrib top, mini-skirt, no stockings. The right shoe is on the foot, the left one lying nearby …'

'She been raped?' Shefford asked Otley as he fastened his overall.

'I dunno, but it's a mess in there.'

Mrs Salbanna's hysterical screaming and sobbing was getting on Shefford's nerves. He leaned over the banister and had a clear view of DC Dave Jones on the basement stairs trying to calm the landlady. An ambulance attendant tried to help move her, but she turned on him with such a torrent of mingled Spanish and English with violent gestures that he retreated, fearing for his safety.

The pathologist was ready to talk, so Shefford and Otley were given the nod to enter the room. Shefford took a last pull at his cigarette, inhaled deeply and pinched it out, putting the stub in his pocket. Then he eased past the mess of broken bottles of make-up and perfume, careful where he put his size eleven feet, to stand a little distance from the bed. All he could see of Della was her left foot.

The brightly lit room was full of white-overalled men, all going about their business quickly and quietly. Flashlights still popped, but already items were being bagged and tagged for removal. The bulky figure of Felix Norman, the pathologist, crouched over the corpse, carefully slipping plastic bags over Della's hands. He was a rotund man, oddly pear-shaped with most of his weight in his backside, topped off with a shock of thick, grey hair and an unruly grey beard. Rumour had it that his half-moon spectacles had been held together by the same piece of sticking plaster since 1983, when a corpse he was dissecting suddenly reared up and thumped him. But it was just a rumour, started by Norman himself. It was his voice Shefford had heard muttering into a tape recorder.

He looked up and gave Shefford a small wave, but continued dictating. 'Obvious head injuries ... possible penetrating wounds, through her clothes, her neck, upper shoulders ... Lot of blood-staining, blood covering the left side of her head and face. Room's damned cold, about five degrees ...' Norman broke into a coughing fit, but he didn't bother turning the tape off. He bent over the lower end of the corpse, but Shefford could not see what he was doing. Then he glanced at his watch and continued, 'Say two to three degrees when she was found, the lights and everybody tramping around must have warmed the place.' He winked at Shefford, still talking. 'Window half-open, curtains part-drawn, no source of heat ... Door to landing giving a strong draught, front door had been left open ...' He felt the corpse's arms and legs, examined the scalp, then began checking for a weapon or anything lodged in the clothing that might fall when the body was removed, without pausing for breath. 'Complete absence of rigor, no hypostasis visible ...' Again he bent over the body, then sat back, waving a thermometer. He squinted at it. 'Deep rectal temperature ... Can't bloody read it for the life of me ... Ah, time is two thirty-eight am, thirty-five point eight degrees, so assuming she started at thirty-seven that puts it back to ...'

Shefford shifted his weight from foot to foot and swallowed hard. As Norman gently rolled the body over he could see the blood matted in the blonde hair, and he had to turn away. It wasn't the sight of the blood, he had seen enough of that in his time, but how small she seemed, small and broken.

Two white-clad men moved in to examine the carpet where the dead girl had been lying. Norman had another coughing fit and Shefford took the opportunity to ask how long she had been dead.

'Well, my old son, she would have cooled off pretty quickly in here, with that window open an' no heating on ... Any time between midnight, maybe a little later, and ... at a rough guess, twelve-thirty.'

'Was she raped, Felix?' Shefford asked, although he knew Norman wouldn't answer.

Norman just gave Shefford a foul look; he no longer bothered answering questions that presumed he was tele-pathic or had X-ray vision. He looked around the room and called to an assistant, 'Right, body-bag!'

Two men lifted the body into the black plastic bag. Shefford winced and averted his head, shocked at the disfig-uration of her face. He had seen only her profile, which was hardly recognizable as human; her nose and cheek were a mass of clotted blood and the eye was completely gone.

'Not a pretty sight,' said Norman, without emotion.

Shefford nodded, but his voice was muffled as he replied, 'She was, though – pretty. Her name's Della Mornay. Booked her myself when I was on Vice.'

Norman sniffed. 'Yeah, well, let's get her out of here an' down to the mortuary. Quicker I get at her, faster you'll get results.'

Even though he had asked once, Shefford could not stop himself repeating the question, 'Was she raped?'

Norman pulled a face. 'Fuck off, I'll tell you everything

you wanna know after the post-mortem.' He stared around the bedsit while the bag was closed and the body lifted onto a stretcher. 'They'll need a bloody pantechnicon to take this lot down to Forensic. You had breakfast? You'd better grab some before you schlepp over to me. Gimme a couple of hours.'

With a wave, Shefford shouldered his way to the landing. He paused and turned his back to the uniformed PC as he swiftly transferred a small object into Otley's hand. No one had seen him slip it from under the mattress. Otley quickly pocketed the little book.

It was not yet dawn, but the street was just as lively when Shefford left the house. The spectators watched avidly as the stretcher was carried to the waiting mortuary van and the police brought bag after bag of evidence from the house. Mrs Salbanna and Shefford himself had both identified the corpse.

The Scenes of Crime officers, or SOCOs, had started fingerprinting every possible surface, covering most of the room in a film of grey, shining dust. They were none too happy; many of the best spots had been carefully wiped.

After snatching a quick breakfast in the canteen and detailing Otley to make sure the Incident Room was being organized, Shefford was at the mortuary by nine o'clock. DI Frank Burkin and DC Dave Jones joined him there to discuss the day's itinerary. They sat in the anteroom of the main laboratory, all but Jones blatantly disregarding the large NO SMOKING notices.

While they waited, John Shefford used the payphone to call his home. It was his son's birthday the next day and

Otley, the boy's godfather, wanted to know what to buy him. His wife, however, had more on her mind.

'Have you booked the clown for Tommy's party, John?' Sheila asked. 'I gave you the number last week, remember?'

Shefford was about to confess that he had forgotten all about it when he was saved by the bell; Felix Norman's assistant came to fetch him.

'I've got to go, love, they're ready for me. See you later!'

Gowned up, masked and wearing the regulation Wellington boots, Shefford joined Norman.

Two bare, pale feet protruded from the end of the green sheet, a label bearing Della Mornay's name and a number tied to one ankle. Norman started talking before Shefford had even reached the trolley.

'Death, old mate, was around twelve-fifteen – it's a classic, her watch got broken and stopped. The gold winder, by the way, is missing, so they'll have to comb the carpet. The watch face is intact, but the rope that was used to tie her wrists must have twisted the winding pin off the watch. Now, you asked if she was raped; could be. Recent deposits of semen in the vagina and rectum, and in the mouth, extensive bruising to the genital area. I sent the swabs over to Willy at the lab …' he checked his watch, 'five hours ago. Might get a blood type this afternoon. OK, the wounds …'

Norman threw the green sheet over the head to expose the torso, and pointed to the puncture marks. The body had been cleaned, and they showed up clearly.

'Upper right shoulder, right breast, lung punctured here, and here. Another laceration to the throat, sixth deep wound just above the navel. The wounds are neat, made with a small, rounded object, the point narrow, flat and sharp, like a sharpened screwdriver, perhaps. Not all the same depth – one three inches, one six inches, the one in the right breast is even deeper.'

Shefford examined the wounds and listened intently, nodding his head. Felix Norman was one of the best in his field, and Shefford had learned from experience to let him have his say before asking any questions.

Norman continued, 'OK, she also has a deep puncture to her left eye, probably what finished her off. A real mess, wanna see?'

'No, just carry on,' replied Shefford with distaste, running his hands through his hair.

Norman referred to his notes. 'Oh, yeah, this is interesting. Look at her hands. They seem to have been scrubbed, with a wire brush, by the look of them. But there's a nasty little nick here, and there's a smell of chlorine, some kind of household bleach. No doubt I'll find out the exact brand when I've been given the time a man of my calibre likes to have in order to do his job thoroughly! Anyway, it looks as if the scrubbing job on her hands has eliminated any possibility of blood or tissue fragments under the nails. She probably didn't put up much of a struggle, but then, her hands were tied ...'

Shefford avoided looking at the naked torso as much as possible. 'Anything else?'

Norman sniffed. 'Yeah, something strange ...' Laying his clipboard aside, he picked up one of the corpse's arms. 'See, same on both sides? Deep welts and bruising to the upper arms. At this stage I can't say what caused it, but she might have been strung up. I'll have to do some more tests, but it looks like she was put in some kind of clamp. Interesting, huh?'

Shefford nodded. Somewhere at the back of his mind a bell rang, but he couldn't capture the memory ... Norman covered the body again and continued, peering over his glasses, 'Right-handed killer, height difficult to estimate at this stage, especially if she was strung up, but four of the wounds entered the body on an upward slant and two are straight, so I reckon he's around five-ten. But don't quote me until I've ...'

Shefford pulled a face. Norman, for all his bravado, went strictly by the rules and hated being pressed for results before he was one hundred per cent sure.

'Thanks mate. Get back to me as soon as you've got anything. When the report's ready, Bill can collect it personally. And, Felix – I really appreciate it!'

Norman snorted. He had worked fast, but then he and John Shefford were old friends. He watched as Shefford removed his surgical mask and began to untie his gown.

'You got anything, John?'

Shefford shook his head. 'Looks like one of her Johns was into bondage and things got out of hand. See you ...'

At the station, Della Mornay's effects were being sorted and examined. Her handbag had been found, but it contained no keys. They were able to dismiss robbery as a motive as her purse, containing fifteen pounds, was in the bag and a jewel box on her dressing-table, containing a few silver chains and a gold bangle or two, was undisturbed.

In King's Cross, Della Mornay's territory, fifteen of Shefford's men were interviewing every known prostitute and call girl. They were getting little assistance, but the feedback was that Della had not been seen for weeks. There was a suggestion that she might have gone to Leeds to visit a friend dying of Aids, but no name was mentioned.

*

The painstaking task of checking every forensic sample, the tapes of fibres, the fingerprints, was barely begun, and had brought no results so far. The entire area was combed for a murder weapon without success. In that neighbourhood no one ever volunteered information, especially to the police.

Shefford and Otley met up again at Milner Road and spent an hour or so interviewing and looking over the bedsit again, but they discovered nothing new. Mrs Salbanna, recovered from her shock, was already asking when she could let the room.

Shefford was hungry and very tired. He had a few pints and a pork pie in the local, then kipped down in his office while Otley went home to his flat to fetch his guv'nor a clean shirt. Shefford often stayed over at his place and left a few items of clothing there for emergencies.

Although he could have done with putting his head down for a few hours himself, Otley sprayed the shirt with starch and ironed it, paying special attention to the collar. Pleased with his handiwork, he slipped it onto a hanger and sat down for a cup of tea. He had a system for avoiding washing up; he simply used the same cup, plate and cutlery all the time. He ate all his main meals in the station canteen, and had even given up his morning cornflakes because they were a bugger to get off the bowl if you left them overnight.

The silver-framed photographs of his wife, his beloved Ellen, needed a good polish, but he'd have to leave them until his next weekend off. They were the only personal items in the flat that he bothered with. Ellen had been the love of his life, his only love, since he was a teenager. Her death seven years ago, from cancer of the stomach, had left him bereft, and he mourned her now as deeply as the moment she had died. He had watched helplessly as she disintegrated before his eyes. She had become so weak, so skeletal, that he had prayed, anguished and alone, for her to die.

It had been obvious to everyone at work that Skipper Bill Otley had personal problems, but he confided in no one. His solitary drinking and his angry bitterness had caused many arguments, and his boys, as he called them, had at last left him to himself. In the end, John Shefford had taken him aside and demanded to know what was going on, earning his abusive response, 'Mind yer own fuckin' business, my personal life's me own affair.'

Shefford had snapped back angrily that when it affected his work it became the boss's business, and Otley would be out on his ear if he didn't come clean about what was tormenting him. He pushed Otley to the point where he finally cracked.

Once he understood, Shefford had been like a rock. He was at the hospital, waiting outside the ward, when Ellen died. He had organized the funeral, done everything he possibly could to help. He was always there, always available, like the sweet, beloved friend Otley had buried. When Shefford's son was born he asked Otley to be godfather; the bereaved man became part of the family, his presence demanded for lunch on Sundays, for outings and parties. He and Ellen had longed for children, in vain; now his off-duty time was filled with little Tom's laughter and nonsense. So Otley wouldn't just iron his guv'nor's shirt; he would wash it, and his socks for good measure. John Shefford meant more to him than he could ever put into words; he loved the man, admired him, and backed him to the hilt, convinced that he would make Commander one of these days. No one would be more proud of him then than Bill Otley.

With the clean shirt over his arm, Otley whistled on his way back to the station.

At eleven, Detective Chief Inspector Jane Tennison parked her Ford Fiesta and entered Southampton Row police station. It was a crisp, frosty day, and she was wrapped up well against the cold.

She was officially off-duty, but had come in to prepare some final papers for a session in court the next day.

None of the blood samples taken from the bedsitter had yielded a clue to the identity of Della Mornay's killer. Hers was a very common group and the only one found at the scene. But the DNA tests on the semen taken from her body was a different matter.

The new computerized DNA system was still at the experimental stage, but already the results of thousands of tests taken in the past two years had been entered on it. As a matter of routine, Willy Chang's forensic team ran the result from Della Mornay against the existing records and were astonished to find a match; a visual check on the negatives, using a light-box, confirmed it. The man Della Mornay had had sex with shortly before her murder had been convicted of attempted rape and aggravated robbery in 1988.

Willy Chang was jubilant; here was the lever they needed to press the government into releasing funds for a national DNA profiling system. He picked up the phone.

The message caught Shefford on Lambeth Bridge, on his way home for lunch and only a stone's throw from the Home Office labs. He hung up the handset, turned the car around immediately and punched Otley's arm.

'You're not gonna believe this, we got a friggin' suspect! He's got a rare blood group and it's on the ruddy computer!'

For the past three months DCI Tennison had been working on a tedious fraud case involving a tobacconist who was being sued for non-payment of VAT. The man's ferret of an accountant had more tricks up his sleeve than a conjuror, and a long series of medical certificates exempting him from court appearances. But tomorrow, at last, Judge George Philpott would complete his summing-up. Known as the legal equivalent of Cary Grant for his good looks and slow delivery, Philpott had already taken two days; Tennison hoped he would finish quickly for once so she would have time to check her desk before the end of the day.

Not that there would be anything of interest; in all her time on the special Area Major Incident Team, known as AMIT, there had been little but desk work. She had often wondered why she had bothered switching from the Flying Squad, where at least she had been busy. The setup of five DCIs and their teams had appealed to her, and she had believed she would be able to use her skills to the full.

Sitting at her desk, Tennison heard a screech of brakes from the car park. She glanced out of the window in time to see Shefford racing into the building.

'What's DCI Shefford doing in today, Maureen?' she asked her assistant, WPC Havers. 'He's supposed to be on leave.'

'I think he's heading the investigation.'

'What investigation?'

'Prostitute found dead in her room in Milner Road.'

'They got a suspect?' Tennison snapped.

'Not yet, but they're getting all the Vice files on the victim's pals.'

Tennison bristled. 'How did Shefford get it? I was here until after ten last night!'

Maureen shrugged. 'I dunno, guv, I think it was a middle-of-the-night job. Probably hauled him out of the afters session in the pub.'

'But he's only just finished with that shooting in Kilburn – and there were the Iranian diplomats before that.'

Tennison clenched her fists and stormed out. Maureen winced at the banging of the door.

DCI Tennison paced up and down the corridor, trying to talk herself down. Eighteen months she'd been waiting for a decent case, dealing with more paperwork than in her entire time at the rape centre in Reading, and now the boss had gone out of his way to give DCI Shefford the case that should have been hers. She'd known when she applied for the transfer that she would be in for a tough time; had she stayed where she was she'd have been promoted to a desk job by now.

But five years with the Flying Squad had toughened her up. She went back to her room and put a call through to the Chief's office, determined to have it out with him, but he was in a meeting. She tried to work on her statements for the court hearing but her frustration wouldn't let her concentrate.

At midday Tennison was again disturbed by the racing of engines from the car park. Shefford was off again, and in a hell of a hurry. She gave up trying to work and packed her things; it was nearly lunch-time anyway.

Tennison missed the 'heat' as Shefford gathered his team together, his booming voice hurling insults as he fired orders at them. He was moving fast on the unbelievable stroke of luck that had given him his suspect on a plate.

George Arthur Marlow had been sentenced to three years for attempted rape and assault, but had served only eighteen months. He had still been protesting his innocence when he was led away from the dock.

The case had been a long-drawn-out affair as Marlow insisted he was innocent. At first he had denied even knowing the victim, referred to only as 'Miss X', but when faced with the evidence he told the police that he and 'Miss X' had been drinking together in a wine bar. He stated that she had blatantly encouraged his advances, but when it came to the crunch she refused him.

Marlow's blood tests at the time had shown him to have an exceptionally rare blood group; he belonged to a small percentage of AB secreters, of whom there is only one in 2,500 head of population. He had been one of the first to be entered on the new computer, and when a lab assistant working on the Della Mornay case ran his details through the system she hit the jackpot.

The warrant was ready. Shefford, high on adrenalin, called his men together. Already he had dribbled coffee down his clean shirt, and he followed it now with cigarette ash. Otley brushed him down as he bellowed, 'DCI Donald Paxman holds the record in the Met, lads, for bringing in a suspect and charging him within twenty-four hours. Gimme me raincoat ... Fags, who's got me fags?'

He shrugged into his coat with the effortless ability of the permanently crumpled man, lighting a cigarette at the same time and switching it from hand to hand as his big fists thrust down the sleeves. 'We smash that record, lads, and it's drinks all round, so let's go! Go, go!'

Jane Tennison let herself into her small service flat which she had shared for the last three months with her boyfriend, Peter Rawlins. Six feet tall, broad-chested, his sandy hair invariably flecked with paint, he was the first man she had lived with on a permanent basis.

Peter came out of the kitchen when he heard her key in the door and beamed at her. 'OK, we've got Chicken Kiev with brown rice, how does that suit?'

'Suits me fine!'

She dumped her briefcase on the hall table and he gave her a hug, then held her at arm's length and looked into her face. 'Bad morning?'

She nodded and walked into the bedroom, tossing her coat on the bed. He lolled in the doorway. 'Want to talk about it?'

'When I've had a shower.'

They had spent a lot of time talking since they had met; Peter had been in the throes of divorce and Jane had provided a sympathetic ear. Marianne had left him for another man; it had hit him hard because it was not just any other man, but Peter's best friend and partner in his building firm, And she had taken with her the little son he adored, Joey.

Jane and Peter's relationship had begun casually enough; they had been teamed together in the squash club tournament and had since met on several occasions for the odd drink or cup of coffee after a game. Eventually he had asked her to see a film with him, and on that first real date she had listened to the details of his divorce. It was only after several films that he had even made an attempt to kiss her.

Jane had helped Peter to move into a temporary flat while his house was sold, and gradually their relationship had become closer. When he started looking for a permanent place to live she suggested he move in with her for a while. It wasn't very romantic, but as the weeks passed she found herself growing more and more fond of him. He was easy-going, caring and thoughtful. When he told her he loved her and suggested they look for a bigger place together, she agreed. It was a pleasant surprise to her how much she wanted to be with him.

When she had showered, Jane sat at the table in her dressing-gown and Peter presented his Chicken Kiev with a flourish. She was so grateful and happy that she had someone to share her life with that she forgot her problems for a moment.

As he opened a bottle of wine she cocked her head to one side and smiled. 'You know, I'm getting so used to you, I don't know what I'd do if you weren't around. I guess what I'm trying to say in my roundabout way is—'

'Cheers!' he said, lifting his glass.

'Yeah, to you, to me, to us ...'

Marlow seemed dazed by the arrival of the police. He stood in the narrow hallway of his flat, holding a cup of coffee, apparently unable to comprehend what they wanted.

'George Arthur Marlow, I am arresting you on suspicion of murder ...' Otley had to repeat the caution, then remove the cup from Marlow's hand himself to put the handcuffs on him.

Moyra Henson, Marlow's girlfriend, appeared from the kitchen, followed by the smell of roasting lamb.

'What the hell's going on here? Oi, where are you taking him? He hasn't had his dinner ...'

Ignoring her, they led Marlow out to the car as quickly as possible. In his bewilderment, he almost cracked his head on the roof of the patrol car as he was helped inside.

The uniformed officers went in to search the flat, while a WPC took Moyra into the kitchen and told her that Marlow had been arrested on suspicion of the murder of a prostitute. Moyra's eyes widened and she shook her head, disbelieving.

'There's been a terrible mistake, you can't do this to him, it's a mistake ...' She broke away from the WPC and ran to the front door. She shrieked like a banshee when she realized the police were taking out clear plastic bags of clothing at a rate of knots. Marlow's shoes, jackets, shirts, all listed and tagged, were shown to Moyra while she protested shrilly. But she didn't attempt to stop the officers, and they remained for hours, searching and removing items. When they had finished, Moyra was taken to the police station for questioning.

She was no longer irate, but coldly angry. She hated the pigs, hated them. They had already put George inside for a crime she knew he hadn't committed, and now she was sure they were about to frame him for murder. All the whodunnits she watched on video and the moral standpoints of Dallas and EastEnders had taught her her rights, and not to trust the bastards.

Jane lay curled in Peter's arms, telling him about Shefford and his attitude to her; not quite openly antagonistic but near enough. It was pretty much the same with all the men, but Shefford was so macho that he took pleasure in sending her up, albeit behind her back.

It was still a new thing for her to have someone to listen to her problems. She had been in such a foul mood when she had arrived home, making love to him had taken all the tension away. It was good to have Peter, to feel loved and wanted. She told him how the Chief had given her the usual speech about waiting, but she had to make a decision soon. The longer she waited and accepted the cases no one else wanted, the more she knew she would be put upon. If Kernan didn't give her a break she would quit. The men gave her no respect ...

Peter laughed. 'They don't know you, do they?'

She grinned. 'No, I suppose they don't. I'll get a break one day, and by Christ they'll know what's hit them then.'

He bit her ear. 'Get them to play a game of squash with you, they'll soon take notice of that determined little face. First time I played against you I thought: Holy shit, this one's a maniac.'

She laughed her wonderful, deep, throaty laugh. When they made love it no longer mattered that her bosses had overlooked her; only Peter was important. She had said it to him that afternoon, and told him she loved him.

He cuddled her close. 'I'm glad we've got each other, because things are not going too well for me. We may have to stave off looking for a bigger place, the company's in bad shape and I'm having to spend capital until I get back on my feet.'

She murmured that it didn't matter, the place was big enough. She asked him then how it had felt, knowing his wife was having an affair with his best friend, a subject she had always steered clear of.

He sighed, stared up at the ceiling. 'Like my balls had been cut off. I couldn't believe it at first, it must have been going on for years behind my back. Then I felt like a bloody fool, you know, that I hadn't clocked it faster. He was always round the house, but we were partners and I just accepted that he was there to see me. And he was screwing my wife in my own bed!' He punched his palm, hard; it made a satisfying smack. He sighed again. 'I wanted to beat him up, have it out that way, but there was no point. I just walked away from it all. She's got half the money from the house and I bought him out of the company, that's one of the reasons why cash is so tight at the moment. I should have just told him to fuck off, but I'm not like that and there's Joey to consider. I reckoned that if I got nasty about the divorce she'd try to stop me seeing Joey. I love that kid, couldn't bear not to see him.'

Jane stroked his cheek gently. 'Any time you want him to stay he's welcome, you know that, don't you?'

He hugged her. 'Yeah, I do, and I appreciate it. You're the best thing that's happened to me in years. I know things'll work out for you, just be patient.'

She smiled, without mentioning that it was exactly what her Chief's attitude had been. But she had no intention of being patient. Peter didn't really understand how important her work was to her, but he was to find out sooner than either of them anticipated.

George Marlow was quiet and co-operative. His fingerprints were taken and he was led to the cells. He stammered a little when he asked to phone his lawyer, seeming shaken, and gave the number. Although on the point of tears, he went out of his way to be helpful, but he still kept asking why he had been arrested.

Shefford had been on the go all day. Now he was preparing himself to question Marlow. His face was flushed and he was chain-smoking, cracking jokes; it was obvious that the adrenalin was still flowing.

The men on the team were clapping him on the back,

calling him a lucky bastard, what a break! Several were laying bets on the outcome.

DI Burkin suddenly remembered something. 'Hey, it's his kid's birthday tomorrow! While we've all got our hands in our pockets, we gonna chip in an' buy him something? You know Otley, he's so tight-fisted the kid won't even get an ice-cream cornet from him. What d'you say, fifty pence each?' In great humour, they all coughed up.

Before he went down to the interview room, Shefford called his home to tell Sheila, his wife, that he would be late and she shouldn't wait up. He was too keyed up to pay much attention to what she was saying.

'You didn't answer me this morning, John. Have you booked the clown for Tom's party?'

'Yeah, yeah, I'll get it sorted ...' He handed the phone to Bill Otley and whispered, 'Talk to the missus, mate, you're his bloody godfather, after all. I haven't got time ...'

He lit another cigarette and turned to the files as Otley took the phone and promised faithfully that he would dress up as a clown himself if they couldn't get Biffo for the birthday party.

The lads had been wrong about their skipper; Otley had spent more time and money in Hamley's toy shop that weekend than they could credit. The train set had cost an arm and a leg, but he was prepared to dip into his savings. He and Ellen had spent hours planning what they would spend it on when he retired; now his godson would be the one to benefit. It was making the decision that took the time, as well as wandering around enjoying himself in the store.

Otley replaced the receiver and turned to Shefford. 'OK, guv? Need anything else? Marlow's brief's on his way, be about an hour. Arnold Upcher, represented him on his last caper. Tough bastard, but he's fair. Doesn't scream a lot like some of the buggers.'

Shefford winked. 'I want a crack at 'im before Upcher gets here. Nice one for us, eh? What a stroke of fuckin' luck! See if we can't sew up Paxman's record. Get a bottle of fizz over to the Forensic lot, tell 'em I love 'em, and tell Willy to stand by for all the gear from Marlow's place. And, yeah, I'm ready, let's go for the bastard.'

George Marlow was sitting in the cell with his hands in his lap, head bowed. He was wearing a blue striped shirt with the white collar open at the neck; his tie had been taken away from him. His grey flannels were neatly pressed and his jacket hung over the back of his chair. With his Mediterranean looks it was obvious that he would have to shave twice a day, but as yet his chin was clean. He raised his head when a uniformed officer opened the door and asked him politely to accompany him to the interview room.

DCI Shefford had given instructions that Upcher was to be stalled if he arrived early. He wanted a chance to question Marlow without his lawyer present. He drew himself up to his full height, threw his massive shoulders back and strode down the corridor to Room 4C. He noticed the way Marlow actually jumped with shock when he kicked the door open.

With a gesture to Marlow to remain seated, he swung a hard wooden chair around with one hand, placing it exactly opposite the suspect, and sat down.

'George? I am Detective Chief Inspector John Shefford. This is Detective Sergeant Bill Otley, and that's DC Jones over by the door. Before we get involved with your lawyer – I mean, we might not even need him – I just want to ask you a few questions, OK?'

He drew the ashtray towards him, scraping it along the formica of the table until it squealed, then lit a cigarette. 'You smoke, George?'

'No, sir.'

'Good … Right then, George, can you tell us where you were on the night of the thirteenth of January? Take your time.'

Marlow kept his head down. 'January the thirteenth? Saturday? Well, that's easy. I was at home with my wife. We don't usually go out, we get a video and a takeaway … Yeah, I was with my wife.'

'Your wife? You mean Moyra Henson, the girl you're living with? She said she's not your wife, she's your girl-friend. Which is it, George? Come on, son, don't mess us about.'

'Well, she's my common-law wife, we're not actually married.'

Shefford's tongue felt and tasted like an old carpet. He searched his pockets and found a wrinkled piece of Wrigley's chewing gum at the bottom. It must have been there for some time as it had lost its outer wrapper, and the silver paper was covered with fluff and ash from using the pocket as an ashtray. He picked the foil off, examined the grey gum, then popped it in his mouth and chewed furi-ously. Marlow watched his every move, as if transfixed.

Shefford folded the wrapper into a narrow strip, ran his fingernail down it, then tossed it aside and lit a cigarette. 'What were you doing, say around ten o'clock?' he asked casually.

'I'd be at home … Oh, hang on, earlier … I know what I did earlier.'

Shefford inhaled the last of his cigarette and let the smoke drift from his nostrils. 'Well, want to tell me?'

With a rueful smile, Marlow shrugged his shoulders slightly. 'I picked up a girl. She was on the game.'

'You knew the girl, did you?'

Marlow shook his head and glanced at Otley, who was sitting a few feet away taking notes. 'I'd never met her before, but I saw her outside the tube station, Ladbroke Grove. She was, you know, bending down, peering into cars as they went past ... Ladbroke Grove tube station. I pulled up and asked her how much.'

'But you didn't know her?'

'No, I'd never met her before. I asked her first how much, and she said it depends. You know they like to hustle as much as they can out of you ...'

'Oh, yeah? But you been done before, George. You don't like hassles. Della Mornay pisses you off, right? Right?'

Marlow frowned, then looked at Shefford. 'Della Mornay ...?'

Otley checked his watch and wondered how it was all going down in the interview room. It was past seven and Shefford had been at it since four-thirty, now with Arnold Upcher sitting in on the session. Otley strolled down to the basement corridor and peered through the glass panel; he could just see Marlow, sitting with his head in his hands.

'Has he confessed yet? Only it's drinking time!'

The PC on guard raised his eyebrows. 'Been a lot of shouting goin' on in there, and at the last count Shefford had consumed five beakers of coffee.'

'Ah, well, he would – this is pub hours, son!'

Otley turned away and went to the pub to join the

others from Shefford's team. He ordered a round and sat down with his pint, telling them there was no news as yet.

'But he had his head in his hands, looked like the guv'nor's cracked him. Gonna break that bloody record ...'

They set about betting, on how long it would take Shefford to get a confession from Marlow and whether or not he would break Paxman's record. They might not have been so confident if they had been privy to the statement that was being taken from Marlow right then.

PERMISSIONS

SB